LONG BURIED

LONG BURIED Copyright ©2026 Ellery A. Kane

All rights reserved. Except as permitted under the US Copyright Act of 1976, no part of this publication may be reproduced, distributed or transmitted in any form or by any means electronic or mechanical, including photocopying, recording, or any information storage/database system and retrieval system now known or to be invented, without prior permission in writing from the author, except by a reviewer who wishes to quote brief passages in connection with a review written for inclusion in a magazine, newspaper, website, or broadcast.

ISBN: 978-0-578-41389-1

Cover Design: Giovanni Auriemma

Editing: Lauren Finger

Proofreading: Liz Hatherell

Interior Design: Mallory Rock

This book is a work of fiction. The situations in this book are purely fictional, and any resemblance to actual persons, living or dead, events, or locales is entirely coincidental. Long Buried contains adult themes and is recommended for a mature audience.

For my dad

Who taught me to live by the cowboy code

"Guilt? It's this mechanism we use to control people. It's an illusion. It's a kind of social control mechanism—and it's very unhealthy. It does terrible things to our bodies."

—Ted Bundy

CHAPTER ONE

THURSDAY–NOW

THEY say you can't go home again. What they mean is that you shouldn't. *I shouldn't.* I shouldn't be here. I should turn around before it's too late. But I've driven all night on a mission, with a suitcase and a shovel in my trunk, and a world of trouble in my rearview. I can't go back to San Francisco. Not now. Not after what I've done.

I zip past the sign for Sweetbriar, Texas—population 2,675—and make the turn toward the center of town. For twenty years, I've stayed away. Even spending one night here feels dangerous. As if I might not make it out alive. This place is quicksand. And once, it nearly killed me.

But I'm a different person now.

"A different person." My voice croaks over the twang of classic country on STIX radio, the only station that comes in clear this far from civilization.

I take a sip of the watered-down fountain drink I purchased a couple hundred miles ago and start to sing along to distract myself from the voice in my head that tells me I'm not *that* different. Not in the ways that count. Sure, I dropped thirty pounds and outgrew my pizza face. I got highlights and a gym membership and a doctorate degree. A job at Ellington Academy and this little red convertible. But inside, I'm as unchanged as Sweetbriar. A loser through and through. Exhibit A: the last two weeks of my life. A complete shit show.

As I drive down Main Street, I catalog two decades' worth of upgrades. The Wal-Mart added a garden center. There's a Mexican restaurant and a CrossFit gym. They've remodeled the public library and renamed it Finch Memorial in honor of the late Principal Finch. What a hoot. No matter the changes to the outside, I know the beating heart of this place is as dark as it ever was.

The high school has changed too. I've studied it on Google Earth an embarrassing number of times, but still it comes as a shock when I crest the hill and see the brand-new marquee that immortalizes the Sweetbriar Bulldogs as football state champions in 1995 and 1996. The glow from my headlamps illuminates the blocked letters that spell out my doom.

WELCOME, CLASS OF '97!
20TH YEAR REUNION AND
TIME-CAPSULE OPENING CEREMONY
JUNE 2 AT 7 P.M.
FRONT COURTYARD

I park in the spot closest to the flagpole and cut the engine. In the dark, I hear my ragged breathing. I know what I have to do—what I *must* do—but the thought of doing it terrifies me. And the thought of getting caught doing it terrifies me more. Especially after the mess I made at Ellington.

I take a reluctant glance into the sun-visor mirror. Its LED lights reveal the tiny crow's feet under my hazel eyes; the few gray strands poking out around my hairline like uninvited guests. I wear the last two weeks on my haggard face. I can't go on like this.

"Screw it. I've got no choice."

Pep talk complete, I open the door and step into my past. By the time I pop the trunk and secure the shovel and the jug of water I brought to soften the soil, beads of sweat collect beneath my ponytail and roll down my neck. I've forgotten the visceral feel of the Texas heat; like swimming through soup. It's going to be a long night.

Lucky for me, the preparations for tomorrow's ceremony point me toward my target. The banner, the folding chairs... so many of them. My stomach churns in a dreadfully familiar way, and I taste the gas-station hot dog burning at the base of my throat.

Lugging my supplies, I trudge through the manicured grass, leaving the crickets to scatter in my wake. I realize I've forgotten this too: the quiet. In my condo in San Francisco I wear earplugs to bed to drown out the sirens, the traffic, the relentless pounding of the upstairs neighbor's stomping. Here, it's just crickets and mosquitoes. The occasional barking dog.

My foot knocks against something solid, and I stumble forward, nearly tripping over the flat stone nestled in the earth. It may as well be a dead body. I stare at it, frozen, and will myself not to run.

In Honor of Blair Lennox, Class of '97

Well, that's new.

My dad never mentioned it. But then, we never talked about Blair's disappearance. Not before I fled this place like a fugitive, and certainly not after. We didn't talk about much, to be honest. Ever. One perfunctory call every semester I was at Berkeley to chat about the weather or the neighbors or the latest natural disaster. Six months became a year became two became five. And then—

The hoot of an owl stops my heart.

"Focus," I whisper-scream at myself. Already, this plan has disaster written all over it, and I can't afford another one of those right now.

I drop my eyes to the ground. This looks like the spot.

It hits me then I can't afford to be wrong. That otherwise I might be out here digging all night. That I could tear up this whole courtyard and still not find it.

And even if I do, it doesn't change what's already happened. What I've already done.

Breathing through my panic, I upend the water jug beneath Blair's memorial and plunge the end of the shovel through the moist dirt. The clean slice of the blade satisfies me. *I can do this. I will do this.* I feel strong and determined. Capable. I *am* a different person now. *I kickbox. I can deadlift one fifty. My trainer calls me scrappy.*

Another stab of the shovel, and my confidence grows.

People trust me with their children's wellbeing. At the school, they call me Dr. P. I have friends. I've had boyfriends too. A lawyer. An investment banker. I am not a loser anymore.

I dig until I've worked up a steady rhythm and my hands ache with the effort. If I keep this up, I'll be out of here in twenty minutes.

"Hey, what the hell are you doing?" The stern voice comes from the rear courtyard, followed by a searching beam of light meant to illuminate my face.

Like a small animal, my instinct to flee overwhelms me. But I remain as immovable as Blair's stone.

"I said, *what are you doing?*"

He's right behind me. Now, there's no escape. Not from him. Not from any of it.

Reality crashes in. My hands start to shake. I *had* friends—albeit superficial ones who dropped me like a bad habit when the shit hit the fan, a career I loved, a life I built from scraps and tatters a world away from this hellhole. Two weeks and one day ago, I had it all. Until I didn't. Now I have nothing.

I look down at the small hole I dug in the earth, both relieved and surprised at its size. It's possible he won't notice it at all.

"Are you deaf, lady?" With that, a firm hand lands on my shoulder and spins me around.

My mouth drops open. "Duane Dupree?"

He blinks back at me, looking me up and down, and I wither as if I'm eighteen again and ashamed of my very existence. I wait for him to laugh in my face the way he used to do. He had the worst laugh of all of them. A scrape full of scorn and derision.

Instead, he asks, "Do I know you?"

I try to conjure the sort of smart-ass retort he and his crew of meatheads deserved. Something sharp to cut him off at the knees. One of those lines I imagined all those times I pictured his face connecting with my fist at the center of a punching bag. But I can only muster the same mousy squeak he'd expect from me. "It's Juniper Pickett. We went to high school together."

"Junebug?"

He's wearing a police uniform, so I don't dare correct him. I certainly don't dare to tell him where to stick that horrible nickname.

His flashlight follows while his eyes trail the length of me again. Then, he directs the blaring bulb right at my face and guffaws. "No freakin' way."

I hate the way I stand there, silent and cowering behind my hand to shield my face from the light.

After a moment, he lowers the beam and says, "Damn. It really is you. What in God's name are you doin' back here?"

I overcome my temporary blindness and sneak a peek at adult Duane. He's a far cry from the chiseled specimen of a state-championship quarterback who threw a perfect spiral and drew comparisons to Joe Montana and Troy Aikman. He'd earned himself a full ride to UT but blew it all in an instant the summer after graduation when he shot his leg instead of the enormous wild hog he'd been tracking through our pasture for months. With his paunchy stomach straining the buttons of his uniform and his receding hairline, he reminds me of his father.

"Um… the reunion," I say.

He dismisses my answer with a skeptical grunt. "Come to think of it, what are you doing out here in the middle of the night with a…" He appraises me for the third time. Not as a man or my former classmate, but as a cop.

I catch the exact moment he remembers the badge he's wearing. "Put down the shovel."

"Am I in trouble?" I grip the handle tighter. Juniper Pickett doesn't get in trouble. *Didn't* anyway, not until the recent firestorm at Ellington. The very notion of breaking the rules sends my heart snare-drumming.

"Do it now, Junebug. I don't wanna Tase you, but I will." He touches his duty belt in warning.

"Tase me?" When I step back, I nearly stumble into the hole I've dug. My foot rolls, sending a sharp jolt of pain through my ankle, but I keep my mouth shut. I can't have Duane asking any more questions. "Why?"

"For threatenin' an officer of the law, for starters. Failin' to follow orders. Resistin'."

"I didn't threaten you. And I'm not resisting anything."

"Not out loud. But you're holdin' a weapon in my direction. That'll make a man with a badge real nervous." He slips the Taser from his holster and aims it at me. I recognize the cruel glint in his eyes. He's no different than Sweetbriar itself; his insides haven't changed one bit. Same asshole, different package. "You remember how I get trigger happy when I'm nervous."

Panic washes over me until I'm drowning in a memory. Of Duane and his buddy Eric cowboying through my dad's pasture one summer on their four-wheelers, kicking up a cloud of dust and chasing our barn cat, Midnight, up the pecan tree at the edge of the fence line. Of Duane cackling as he pointed and fired his BB gun. Midnight survived the episode unscathed. Me, not so much. I'd thrown a rock that knocked out Duane's taillight, and he'd gone crying to my dad, who forced me to use my allowance to pay for a replacement. *Two wrongs don't make a right, June.*

"I'm givin' ya to the count of three to drop that shovel. Then, I'm gonna have to zap ya, Junebug." He lets out a high-pitched giggle and a burp that makes me wonder what *he's* been doing out here. "One…"

A black pickup truck rumbles down the road toward the high school. Its headlamps spotlight the two of us and the beer bottle I presume Duane left on the picnic table in the courtyard before he made it his mission to harass me.

"Two…"

I raise my hands in surrender, and the shovel topples into the grass.

Duane smirks at it. "Two and a half…"

The truck squeals to a stop in front of the courtyard, lights still blaring. The door flies open. "Are you drinking on duty again, Officer Dupree?"

I know that voice. Twenty years later, and I still can't forget it. I plant my eyes on his cowboy boots to avoid his face. In my periphery, Duane lowers the Taser. I suppose I should feel grateful that I won't endure total humiliation *and* electrocution tonight. But all I can think about now is him. And what's still buried in the ground beneath my feet.

"You're one to talk, Landry. At least I ain't murdered nobody. Least I ain't a cold-blooded killer."

A long, aggrieved sigh. I recognize that too. Once upon a time, teenage Juniper knew the nuances of every Wyatt Landry sound. I could pick his laugh out of a lineup. But he's not laughing tonight.

"Get outta here, Dupree, before I call Sheriff Faulk. I'm not in the mood for your bullshit."

"The sheriff wouldn't take your call if you were on fire. He knows you're the only drunk around here. You're just like your—"

When Wyatt steps closer, Duane shuts his mouth. Because he's still mostly made of hot air. Hot air and spite.

"The sheriff knows I've been sober since I got out. He also knows you're a hack who only got a job on the force because he owed your daddy a favor."

Inwardly, I cheer Wyatt. It's the exact sort of thing I wish I could say. It also makes me feel like a complete doormat who still can't fight her own battles. I muster the courage to ask, "Am I free to go now?"

Duane doesn't answer. As I turn to look at him, he lunges forward to shove Wyatt in the chest. Wyatt casually sidesteps the blow, and Duane stumbles into the shallow hole beside me. His face ruddy with a mixture of shame and anger, he curses at us both.

"It's all makin' sense now." He waves his hands at the ground like a deranged Columbo. "You were out here desecrating Blair's memorial, weren't you? You always were jealous of her. Real jealous."

It's nothing compared to all the other insults Duane hurled at me as a kid. Poison barbs that left scars on my heart. But it stings worse in front of Wyatt. It stings worse *here*, a stone's throw from the elementary school and the playground where I last saw her. Before I can launch a proper protest, Wyatt wraps one calloused hand around my wrist and reaches for the shovel with the other.

"C'mon, Juniper."

He tugs me behind him wordlessly, through the courtyard, and back to my convertible. It's dwarfed by the Ford pickup beside it. I feel the same when I finally lift my eyes to his. As if I'm just a silly kid and he's the grown-up. Now he's in front of me, I try not to stare. He's a man now. With scruffy salt-and-pepper hair and worry lines and stubble that shadows his jaw; a farmer's tan and the ropy muscles that come with hard labor. Is it possible prison made him better looking?

My attempts at online stalking him always came up empty. Wyatt Landry doesn't do social media. Still, years ago, I'd managed to dig up the *Gazette* article about his arrest, which I bookmarked and revisited now and then. Each time his bleary-eyed, bloody-faced mugshot appeared on my screen it felt like pressing a bruise.

"Please tell me this is a rental," he says.

"That's where you want to start? With my car? I haven't seen you in two decades."

"Whose fault is that?"

We both know the answer to his question. Since graduation night, I've been avoiding this place and everyone in it. Mercifully, he doesn't make me say it out loud.

"Anyway, it doesn't seem like that long. Your dad talked about you all the time. He kept tabs on you, ya know? Right up until the end. He still waited for your call every Sunday, even though it never came."

My throat tightens. *Do not cry.* I swallow the lump. I should say something, try to explain, but there's nothing to say that doesn't require a couple hundred more hours of therapy and copious amounts of alcohol.

"Your dad would be mortified if he saw you in this tin can. He would absolutely disown you."

Overcome with too much emotion, a laugh bursts out of me. "He would."

Wyatt kicks the front tire, and I swear the whole car shakes.

"I give these doughnuts twenty-four hours before one of them goes flat. The roads will wreck the suspension too. You should've told them you needed something heavy duty."

"It's not a rental." I glance over my shoulder back to the courtyard, where a red-faced Duane kneels in the grass filling in the hole with his bare hands. I failed at the one thing I set out to do here, the reason I came back. It pains me to think of what will happen now. "I drove it from San Francisco."

Wyatt gapes at me. "You what? That's like fifteen hundred miles…"

"Seventeen fifty, actually."

"Why?"

Another question I wriggle away from. "It's a long story."

"Yeah, I'll bet it's a real humdinger."

I think he's messing with me though I can't say for sure. I used to read him like a book, but he's lived a lifetime since I saw him last. He's written new chapters. Volumes that are entirely beyond my grasp.

Duane trudges down the sidewalk toward us, carrying my water jug in his dirt-caked hands. "You better not show your face tomorrow, Junebug. Nobody wants you here, so you can go right ahead and leave the way you came. You too, Landry." He tucks the jug under his arm. "I'm keeping this for evidence."

"Evidence of what?" Wyatt asks with a huff. "The Texas drought?"

"I'm sure we'll find out soon enough. Won't we, Junebug?" Duane sneers at me as if he knows what I came here to do. As if he knows what I'm hiding.

He doesn't. He couldn't. But it unnerves me anyway, the power he still has over me.

"Don't worry about him." Wyatt watches Duane sway toward the lights of the town square. "He won't remember anything in the morning. In fact, he'll be lucky if he remembers where he parked his patrol car."

"Should we help him find it?"

Wyatt quirks his mouth, lifts his eyebrows, and chuckles. "It's in the other direction."

With Duane disappearing down the sidewalk, I realize we're about to be completely alone. That I'll need to explain myself. If only I knew where to start.

"Here's your shovel." He leans it against the car and turns away from me. "I'll let you get back to it then."

As much as I don't want to answer his questions, I can't stand the thought of him leaving so soon. We haven't even properly spoken. "Aren't you going to ask me what I was doing?"

"Do you want me to?"

I shrug, kick at an invisible rock. "Not particularly."

"That's what I thought."

It irks me the way he makes assumptions as if he knows me—like he *ever* did—even if he is right. "What are *you* doing here? Or did you just happen by at one in the morning?"

"I was taking a drive to clear my head, and I saw your little clown car parked out here in front of the school. It looked out of place, so I figured I'd check it out. It's a good thing I did or you'd be at the mercy of that drunken idiot and his non-lethal weapon."

"Well, I didn't need rescuing. Duane Dupree is nothing compared to some of the kids I work with these days. I'm a psychologist at a private boarding school in the city." I withhold the vital bits, fearing he'd recognize the name of the school. That the story has somehow made it all the way out here to the sticks. I certainly don't tell him I've been placed on unpaid leave, which is just a nice way of saying I've been given the boot.

"A private school, huh? Fancy." Wyatt grins. He's definitely messing with me. "Should I call you doctor?"

"You already knew." It's not fair. Wyatt is a massive unknown to me, and the cavern between us is too wide to cross.

"Your dad may have mentioned it a few thousand times. In fact, I think there might be a leatherbound copy of your dissertation around the house somewhere."

"Ha, ha."

"No, *really*. You'll see."

I try to think of a way to tell him I'm not staying at my dad's house. That I'm not staying at all. Not if I can help it. Then I remember why I came and what I left behind. A job I lost. A condo I can't afford. A life I burned to the ground. I have nothing to go back to.

"I boxed up a couple of rooms. I wasn't sure what you wanted me to do with..." With a pained expression, he waves his hand. "You never returned my calls."

I droop under the weight of it. Guilt, grief. All the years I spent running led me right back to this moment, standing here in front of Sweetbriar High wishing I could be someone else. "I'm sorry. I wanted to. I tried. I just didn't—I couldn't—I—"

He nods as if he understands. But Wyatt isn't a runner. No matter what he's done. He's solid. He's rooted here. The day they set him free from a cell in Huntsville, he caught the first bus right back home. My father told me so. Every day he looks these people in their faces, and he's unmoved by their judgment. It's the ultimate screw-you that I never could pull off. I hate him for it, just a little.

"You're here now," he says.

I suck in a deep, ragged breath and glance up at the courtyard, at the disturbed earth in front of the stone. The whole scene makes me want to climb out of my skin. "I suppose I am."

"I didn't touch your bedroom." He suddenly seems as nervous as me. "It's all set up for you. Your dad kept it the same. Just be sure to check your shoes for scorpions in the morning. Those sneaky critters like to—"

"I know. It hasn't been *that* long."

"The electricity in the front of the house can be a bit spotty. I need to take a look at the wiring. I can do it tomorrow morning if you—"

"I'll be fine. I grew up here, remember? A whole eighteen years."

"Right. Of course you did. Well, if you need anything, you know where to find me."

Wyatt opens his truck door and I remember why I need to leave him be. Why he can't be trusted. He's a convicted killer. A killer who spent ten years behind bars at Huntsville State Penitentiary. A killer with a gun hidden under his driver's seat.

CHAPTER TWO

EVERY Tom, Dick, and Jim Bob in Sweetbriar, Texas owns a gun. But not *that* gun. The antique Smith & Wesson with the wood grip that once belonged to my father.

I tell myself to focus on the road. The meandering strip of dirt and gravel that leads to the fifty acres of land I called home for eighteen years. My high beams cast a wide glow through the tall grass alongside and to the barbed-wire fence beyond. I can't stop playing tonight on repeat. It doesn't help that the lights of Wyatt's beast of a truck are blinding me in my rearview. Or that we're going to the same place. The farm at the dead end of Saw Mill Road.

The closer I get, the slower I go. A part of me wishes for a blown tire, a darting rabbit to cause a skid off into the ditch. Anything to avoid the place I wanted to be rid of forever. I peer into the pitch-black, searching for my father's workshop, but the night swallows everything. It's the first tangible sign of his absence. He spent the evenings of my childhood there, often returning to the house long after I'd fallen asleep. Some nights, I stayed up with my nose pressed to the window and waited for the workshop light to go out, for the soft creak of the door when he returned.

Wyatt flashes his high beams at me. Frowning, I tap the brakes and squint out the driver's side window, trying to make out something—*anything*—familiar in the darkness. By the time I realize where I am, I've nearly missed the turn at the mailbox marked PICKETT. I swing a hard left onto the rutty dirt path that leads to the house. The car bounces and rumbles, jostling me like a pair of sneakers in a washing machine.

Wyatt honks twice and keeps driving toward the road to the caretaker's cottage. It winds into the pasture, alongside the dry creek bed and past the knotted oak tree. The well-worn path narrows at the end then disappears in the buffalo grass that surrounds the two-room cabin where Wyatt lives. Out back there's a shop, a bull pen, and a graveyard marked with river stones, where Dad buried Bert and all the other cow dogs who came before and after him. The spring after my mother died, I painted the door to the cabin myself, a bright blue. Though I've spent the better part of the last two decades trying *not* to remember this place, being here brings it all back.

I put the car in park in front of the main house and cut the engine. With a heavy sigh, I retrieve my cellphone from the passenger seat and force myself to scroll through my missed calls. Four from Headmaster Melhorn at Ellington, three from the *Chronicle*, and a laundry list of unknown numbers. There's also a message from the San Francisco Police Department that I plan to ignore for as long as possible. If I don't listen to it, I can still pretend it didn't happen.

I rest my head against the seat, and all the old ghosts start to flicker at the edges of the darkness. I imagine my father waiting for me on the doorstep, Bert prancing by his side, his tail drumming against my dad's leg. The school bus dropped me off at the corner and I fast-walked the half mile home. While Mom finished up her day at the Sweetbriar Community Bank, Dad would buzz about his latest project and quiz me on math and science over milk and Oreos. The things that could be measured, quantified, verified. By the fifth grade, I could recite the entire periodic table and often did whenever I got nervous, a feat that didn't win me any friends. I start again now, my voice barely a whisper.

"Hydrogen, helium, lithium, beryllium, boron, carbon, nitrogen—"

A cricket lands on the windshield with an emphatic smack, reminding me I'm here. Now. That Dad and Bert are long gone. That I'm officially an orphan. That a detective wants to speak to me about what I've done. The terrible mistakes I've made. It's not the first time.

Like a fugitive fleeing a crime scene, I fling open the car door. I leave my suitcase in the trunk and direct my cellphone flashlight at the entryway; the thin stream of light no match for Middle Of Nowhere Texas. The darkness leaves too much to the imagination, and I scamper up the path to escape the unseen, the unknown. But when I reach the door, dread washes over me, and I can't bring myself to slip the spare key from beneath the mat and open it. I contemplate sleeping right here on the porch in my dad's wooden rocker. Anything to avoid going inside where I'll be trapped with the worst kinds of monsters: my regrets. Like the message from my father that's saved on my phone. The call I ignored a week before he died, the last words he left me spoken to a digital daughter, not the flesh-and-blood one.

Juniper, it's Dad. I need to talk to you. It's important.

The sudden yip of a coyote propels me forward, reminding me I'm a city girl now. I need four solid walls and the kind of predators that walk on two legs not four. Key in hand, I turn the lock and step inside the musty foyer. I aim the beam at the light switch on the wall, relieved that at least one of the old-fashioned wall sconces still works. I navigate around the boxes Wyatt packed for me. He labeled them with a black marker: BOOKS. DISHES. PHOTOS. Another wave hits me. Guilt, this time. I made Wyatt do the dirty work while

I was two states away. He sorted through the refuse of my father's life and plucked out the treasures for me. He even sold the old pickup truck at the tow lot and mailed me the check. Meanwhile, I couldn't be bothered to return his calls.

The kitchen feels particularly lonely. Cabinets, empty. Pantry, bare, except for a box of Ritz crackers and a jar of peanut butter. Not a single one of my father's silly inventions taking up space on the dining table where he could tinker with them. Even his favorite mug—the misshapen one I'd made for him in my high-school art class—has been tossed out or packed away. Only the years-old coffee stain on the counter remains.

I wait for a wave of grief to pull me out to sea, but the tears don't come. Won't. Haven't. Not a single one since the county coroner called six weeks ago to tell me Eugene Pickett had been found dead in the field outside his workshop. The cancer had eaten the vital bits of him before a lethal cocktail of Jim Beam and barbiturates finished the job.

The clock hanging in the kitchen reminds me I should be exhausted. It's one in the morning. That's eleven o'clock in San Francisco. I've been awake for… too long to do basic math. Still, I have to see the workshop for myself before I can sleep.

Dad always forbade me from going inside there alone. *It's too dangerous*, he'd said, which seemed strange coming from the man who rigged homemade explosive devices to scare the crows from my mother's vegetable garden. But I never broke his rule. Well, only that once. I wonder if Wyatt's been inside, and what he's seen there. If that's where he found the gun he decided to claim as his.

Before I lose my nerve, I fish the rusted key off the wall hook by the rotary phone and search the room for a proper flashlight. A reasonable person would wait till morning, but if I go now, under the cover of night, I can pretend it's a dream. I'm not ready to face it in the daytime, when the memories become less squidgy, more solid. With weight that crushes and sharp edges that cut.

When I find the red Eveready in the cabinet beneath the sink—and it works!—I decide it's a sign. My father's tacit approval from beyond. I head out the front door and into the night, where two barbed-wire fences and three acres of land lie between me and the workshop. Originally a hay barn, Dad gutted it and turned it into his mad scientist's haven. I preferred its native form, with square hay bales I could climb to the rafters to visit the family of squirrels that nested there. Once my father got ahold of it, it became his place. An off-limits place. A place where he turned into Doc Pickett, a man I desperately wanted to know but didn't.

I slink through the grass, keeping my head down after I catch a pair of yellow eyes gazing at me in my periphery. It's better to be blind to what's out here. I focus only on my sneakers and hum to myself to drown out the night sounds. Both fences have begun to sag with age and neglect, and I manage to slip through the barbs unscathed. It surprises me how easily it all comes back. How the years seem to fall away. I know which spots to avoid—the burr patch and the massive fire-ant hill I called Red Mountain—and to veer right at the cactus grove.

By the time I reach the workshop it feels as if I've slipped through a wormhole to the past. To thirteen-year-old Juniper exploring the perimeter of the fence line with Bert while my father tended to his secrets. I look at the fancy watch I bought with my first real paycheck from Ellington and remind myself I'm grown up. Thirty-eight-years grown up. I can do what I want, go where I want. Wherever my dad is now, he can't stop me.

I squint up at the large metal door. The moonlight glints off the padlock in a familiar way that sends my heart racing. Once, I'd broken my father's rule. Once, I'd made my way inside. If my plan hadn't been shot to hell back then, I wouldn't be here at all…

The many ifs that follow this thought lead to a dark place, a place I can't allow myself to go. Not tonight. I take a deep breath and fit the key into the lock. With a grunt, I heave the door open, and my father's hidden world takes shape. I imagine him there at the desk, hunched over his Smith Corona typewriter; pencil nub tucked behind his ear, shaggy gray hair covering his collar.

It's how I always imagined him in here. Focused to the point of obsession.

After securing the door behind me with the metal slide bar, I head straight for the bare bulb affixed to the ceiling. One tug of the string chases his ghost back into the shadows. I scan the space from corner to corner, surprised to find the whole place coated with dust. From the long table with its array of test tubes to the peg board where my father hung his safety goggles; to the oak frame of the treasured periodic table he salvaged from a dumpster outside a community college. I wipe the edge of it with my finger and shake my head in disbelief. When did he stop coming in here?

My father's chemicals line the shelves. No longer alphabetized, a few of the bottles are cracked and oozing. I can't believe he let the place fall apart like this. The workshop was his church, and these bottles, his sacred vessels. I scan the rows, thinking perhaps he'd gotten rid of it. But no. It's still here, all these years later. Pentobarbital sodium, a small black skull and crossbones affixed to the bottle. I pick it up, feel the weight of it in my hand. It sends a shiver through me, bone deep. I want to drop it, to run back to the car. To drive away as fast as my so-called doughnuts will allow. Instead, I grip the bottle tighter to stop my hands from shaking and carefully return it to the shelf.

A tangle of paperclips rests on the laminate near the floor-to-ceiling bookshelf, carelessly tossed like debris scattered in a storm. The books, too, seem in subtle disarray. Their spines uneven, as if someone had pulled each one from its place. On the desk, my father's *big idea* notebook lies open; the top page blank and slightly torn. I flip through the last few entries, trying to hide my disappointment. It's all mechanical drawings and chemical formulations. The last one dated 2012, the same year Wyatt was released from prison. No hidden messages. No confessions, apologies, or explanations. I examine the binding more closely. Its frayed edges unnerve me almost as much as the mess. Because I can't help but think the worst: that someone rifled through this place.

Even before Blair disappeared, my father had made his share of enemies. After, the whole town looked at him sideways, as if he had something to hide.

I take another lap around the workshop to search for evidence. Fingerprints in the dust. A scuff mark on the floor. Anything to confirm my suspicions. But the only intruder I find is a field spider as big as my hand that scuttles up its web toward the rafters and away from me, the crazy lady. The kind of crazy that makes a woman drive seventeen hundred and fifty miles with a shovel in her trunk.

Frustrated and exhausted, I migrate toward my dad's chair. The worn leather still holds his shape. I turn and press my nose to it, inhaling the faint scent of him that once brought me comfort. My chest begins to ache. A vicious burn sears my throat. Alone in the tomb of my father's workshop in the dead of night, I can't escape myself. That's the trouble with running away. You can never outrun your own skin. You're stuck in it to the bitter end.

I think of my dad's last moments. How alone he must've felt. How he must've wondered if I still loved him. *He still waited for your call every Sunday, even though it never came.* When the tears finally spring to my eyes, I know better than to try to stop them. I sob until I'm empty. Until there's nothing left but a dull throbbing in my head.

After, I dab my cheeks with my shirtsleeve and open my father's file drawer, hopeful for a box of tissues. Even his old lab coat would do. Instead, I find a stack of folders, disorganized and yellowed with age. My father kept one for each of his research assistants, who were really just high-school volunteers hopeful for a letter of recommendation from the man who created Harvest Gold, the number-one corn fertilizer in North America. Or, more likely, were eager for a peek behind the curtain at nutty Doc Pickett so they could gossip with their friends. Either way, it was a bogus job, and I hated every single one of them for having what I didn't: time alone with my dad in his precious workshop.

I sit up, sniffle. With my tears drained, I feel light. Curious. I lift out the folders and stack them on the desk in front of me. When

I'd seen them last, on the night I wanted to forget, they'd been meticulously arranged in chronological order with Blair's on top. After she went missing, there were no more research assistants for my father. No one set foot in this place but him.

I hunt for the earliest file dated 1991, the year my mother died. It belongs to Diane Brownmiller, a spunky brunette who the kids called Brown Noser. Next to Blair, I hated her the most—because she was the first. The first student my father chose over me, leaving me and Bert to fend for ourselves while he buried himself in his grief. Here. With a veritable stranger.

The folder contains Diane's time logs and a copy of the glowing recommendation letter he wrote for her. The handwritten thank-you card she sent after graduation with a cap-and-gown photo inside. Last I heard, she sells home insurance in downtown Sweetbriar.

I study the photo for a moment before calmly ripping it in two. My brief satisfaction vanishes in an instant when I imagine how my father would react. He could say nothing and everything with a simple look. A subtle downturn of his mouth, a slight narrowing of the eyes. Overcome with guilt, I wait for the universe to drop its axe on my neck. But then I remember why I came back to Sweetbriar. Why I ran away from San Francisco. The axe has already fallen.

I thumb through the rest of the stack, lining up the folders across the desk. I count five in all when there should be six, so I sort the files again, slowly at first, then urgently. Frenzied, I jerk open the file drawer, nearly wrestling it from its hinges. I peer into its depths.

The drawer is empty.

Blair's folder is gone.

CHAPTER THREE

I'M running.

I'm running through the tall grass in the dark.

I'm running through the tall grass in the dark with a shadow man behind me. My fingers gripping the bottle in my hand, as he gains ground.

When I reach Red Mountain my foot snags on a rock and my legs give way. I fall in a heap, whimpering. That's when the fire starts. First, in my feet. Then, my ankles, calves, thighs, stomach. I recoil from the pain, scratching and clawing. Anything to make it stop.

The moonlight makes clear the horror of my situation. Ants move across my skin like a crimson wave. Sensing my helplessness, the shadow man homes in on what he wants and plucks the bottle from my grasp. His face is a dark blur, but I recognize the ring on his finger. My mother gave it to him at the courthouse where they said their vows long before I was born. He never took it off.

"Dad?" My voice sounds small and far away. Not a woman's voice, but a girl's.

I get no answer, and the distance between us turns to an ever-widening chasm. I'm no longer at the farm on Saw Mill Road. I'm smack-dab in the middle of a new nightmare. On my knees in a freshly dug hole, my shovel beside me. I dig with my hands now. Wrists deep, I search until I find it.

I hold it in the glow of the moon and hear myself scream.

I wake up in a panic, wrapped in a blanket on the floor of the workshop. My father's battered briefcase serves as a makeshift pillow. I lie there, paralyzed. My hands clenched at my sides. I dare myself to sit up, to look around, to move. To prove that my father didn't leave me in an ant swarm on Red Mountain. That I'm not holding a human skull in my fist. A skull I unearthed myself.

I slip my hands from beneath the blanket, relieved to find them empty. But the dream fog lingers, poisoning my thoughts until I feel compelled to examine my fingernails for dirt. Satisfied that I haven't exhumed a body, I sit up and expel a breath of relief. I focus on the here and now—the cold floor beneath me, the musty smell of the workshop—talking myself down, the way I've always done with my anxiety-ridden students. It helps a little.

I take my cellphone from my pocket. It's nearly dead, but alive enough to tell me it's only 3:15 a.m. and the Google alert I set up days ago has finally returned a hit. Not just one, but fifty-seven. Fifty-seven mentions of Juniper Pickett.

My stomach flip-flops like a fish out of water. So much for those stupid relaxation exercises—I can't seem to catch a single breath; they're coming too fast.

My name has finally gone public. I hurry to click on the first link: *School psychologist fired amid investigation…*

Nothing happens. Only that ridiculous little wheel spinning and spinning and spinning like a merry-go-round to nowhere. Of course there's no service out here. Still, I hop up and stab at the link again, then fling open the door and wander out into the field, holding up the phone to the sky like a cavewoman summoning an ancient god. I look ridiculous, but I need those magic little bars—just one of them will do. I need to know what I'm dealing with. If it's really as bad as I fear. If it's worse.

I let out a yelp of joy as one, then two, bars flicker to life, and the text of the article appears. I manage to read one and a half sentences before the screen goes black.

"No, no, no!" I clench my teeth and hurl the phone into the darkness. The moment it leaves my hand I'm flooded with regret. I stand there, mouth open, dumbstruck by my stupidity. That's how I know I'm the same Junebug. The same loser who's managed to make a bad situation worse.

Cursing myself, I trudge back inside the workshop and retrieve the flashlight from the desk. I sweep the beam across the pasture as I take one step forward then another. Those two lines I saw play on repeat in my head.

> *Citing reckless disregard for student safety, a representative from Ellington Academy announced the immediate termination of school psychologist, Juniper Pickett, who was in her eighth year at the prestigious preparatory high school. The firing comes in the wake of—*

I could be here all night and never find it. Still, I plod on across the field where my father took his last breaths.

...in the wake of...

I finish that sentence a hundred times, a hundred ways. Each truth more terrible than the last. But none more terrible than living through it. It's been two weeks, but when I close my eyes I'm right back there. In the teachers' lounge, in the middle of a bite of a chicken-salad sandwich.

Another sweep of my flashlight comes up empty, and I pause to take a swat at the mosquito on my arm. I grimace at what's left behind. The legs, no bigger than eyelashes. The bright-red spot of my blood. It smears beneath my fingers, and my stomach turns.

...in the wake of...

I take a few hurried steps toward the fence line, not bothering to look at the ground. An unexpected touch against my leg sends me sky-high and scurrying. I spin around, half expecting to take my last look at the teeth of a rabid coyote.

That's when I see it, spotlighted in the beam. As out of place here as I am.

It's not my cellphone.

It's a folder.

CHAPTER FOUR

A chill runs up my spine, and I look over my shoulder into the inky shadows. There's no one there. No one and nothing. Still, I snatch the folder from the ground and run back to the workshop. I bolt the door behind me and lean against it, breathless and grateful I didn't twist an ankle. I lay the folder on the desk. It's dirty. Its edges, wet with dew. But the name penned on the tab in my father's boxy script is unmistakable.

I open it, then shut it fast, recoiling from Blair's smiling face. She's exactly as I remember: rosy cheeks, sky-blue eyes and teeth like Chiclets. I have to look away from her; from the memory of graduation night. It's like staring into the sun.

With a quick glance, I flip the picture face down, but Blair left her mark there too. Her name in cursive blue ink with a heart above the *i*. I slide it beneath the folder, thinking I should rip it like Diane's. Not in half, but in a hundred tiny pieces I'd toss into the wind or, better yet, burn to ashes.

I can't, though I'm not sure why. I've done much worse. Maybe it's knowing that her parents still live a mile from here. That every July 9th Lydia Lennox pays for a *Happy Birthday, Blair* post in the *Sweetbriar Gazette.* That I saved them all, nineteen and counting, in between the pages of my abnormal psychology textbook.

With the photo safely hidden, I examine the folder's remaining contents. I flip through several pages of Blair's time logs, stopping on the last of them. In the month before graduation, she'd worked in my father's lab every afternoon from 4:30 to at least 7 p.m. In twenty years of trying, I still can't imagine her here in her very own lab coat. She hated science. She cheated her way through chemistry, copying her best friend Jessica's homework. Once, she nearly set the classroom on fire when she hair-sprayed her bangs too close to a lit Bunsen burner.

Yet my father chose *her.* It still boils my blood all these years later.

I turn over the last time sheet, expecting to see a blank white page. Instead, my father's chicken scratch fills the upper right corner of the space. A series of initials and numbers.

PV 15
AD 16
AD 87
PV 2

Instinctively, I search the desk for my cellphone to Google the strange code before I remember chucking it into oblivion. Another stellar decision. Groaning, I close the folder with the photo inside it once more.

With it tucked under my arm, I head back to the house, stumbling across the dark field like a newborn calf. Once the sun comes up, I hope to have better luck tracking down my phone. For now, I retrieve my car keys from the kitchen counter, grateful I shelled out an extra three thousand dollars for the tech package. High speed Wi-Fi, even out here in the boondocks. I remove my laptop from its bag in the back seat and open it on the hood of the trunk. As I wait for the search engine to load, I scan the boundary until I spot the lights from the caretaker's cabin. It's just a single glowing orb in the darkness, but it makes me feel less alone.

I type my name into the search bar. My finger hovers over the enter key, knowing that this one click will summon the dark side.

A new result appears at the top of the list. It's a link to a thread on one of those discussion forum sites. I open it and stare at the post and the smattering of comments beneath it, certain I've got it wrong. That I'm just dog-tired and stressed and hallucinating the words on the screen. But nothing changes each time I reread it, and the match-strike of panic at the center of my chest grows hotter and hotter until it bursts into flame.

This is bad.

This is *really* bad.

This is catastrophic.

I snap the lid shut, shove the computer into its bag, and toss it into the back seat. It lands with a satisfying thwack that makes me wish I'd thrown it harder. I hop in the driver's seat and floor it.

At least this thing can fly. The wheels throw up a cloud of dust and gravel when I make the turn onto the main road. I have a singular focus. Get to the school. Get what I came for. Get the hell out of here. Even if I can't go back to San Francisco, this place is no better. It'll sink me, take me right back to the murky bottom. So, I'll start fresh. Pay Wyatt to box up the rest of the house and the workshop. Donate the entire haul to charity. Sell the farm to the highest bidder. Never, ever look back.

I zip through town, ignoring the speed limit. At four in the morning, only two of Sweetbriar PD's finest will be *on duty*. Which really means catching some z's in the Oak Grove Cemetery at the edge of town, the same way it did back in 1997. Still, I park a block away from the school and carry my shovel. I can't afford any more run-ins with Duane.

When I arrive at the courtyard, I waste no time thinking. I go straight to the same spot and plunge my shovel back into the earth. With the discussion thread on repeat in my brain, I work faster and harder than I did before. I can't stop until I find it. The rest of my life depends on it. I know that now.

Sweat drips down my forehead, burning my eyes. I keep digging.

A blister forms on the palm of my hand. I keep digging.

And when it bursts beneath the friction of the wooden handle, still I keep digging.

I keep digging until there's a noticeable mound of soil near my feet that makes me wonder if I've got the wrong spot altogether. I stop for the length of time it takes to wipe my face in my T-shirt. Then, I keep digging. Because I can't let myself think that tomorrow someone else will unearth my secrets and everyone will see me for what I really am.

A shock judders up my arm the moment I strike a solid object, and I let out a yelp of surprise and relief.

I look down but see nothing. Only the empty grave I've made. I drop to my knees and wriggle my desperate fingers beneath the dirt, searching. Hunkered down there, mucky and frantic as a wild animal, my dream rushes back to me all at once, and with it, a panicked kind of dread. As if I'm too far down the wrong road to turn back.

Haven't I always been since that night twenty years ago? All the running I've done and it turns out I was just a hamster in a wheel, doomed to return to ground zero.

Just then, my hand seizes on something. It feels rough and solid at first, but when I tug it from the earth, it breaks to pieces in my fist.

I open my fingers. A flower button rests in the center of my palm. I recognize it on sight. But it's not the worst of what I'm holding.

I tell myself to drop it. All of it.

To leave it.

To put it back in the ground where it came from.

I never get the chance.

When the Sweetbriar police cruiser zips up the street and flashes its light bars, I stand stock-still, fixed like a deer in the road preparing for impact.

The uniformed officer stalks up the sidewalk. "Don't make any sudden moves, Ms. Pickett."

As if my feet aren't cemented beneath me.

From up the street, I hear Duane's singsong voice. "Told ya she'd come back. Junebug ain't never known when to quit."

I'm not sure what's worse. The fact that I've been outwitted by Duane Dupree; that no matter how different I look on the outside, he sees right past it, knows me still. Or that deep down I understand that the bone in my hand belongs to Blair Lennox. The girl I hated. The girl I wished dead a thousand times. The girl who's been missing since graduation night 1997.

CHAPTER FIVE

AT least I don't recognize this cop. But I do know the surname on his nameplate. *Sitkowski.* He must be Larry's younger brother. The Larry who'd written—*See ya, wouldn't want to be ya*—in my senior yearbook. They share the same stocky build, the same carrot top.

"What the hell is that?" Officer Sitkowski demands.

I hold out my hand to him, a peace offering. "I… I'm not sure." For all the lying I've done lately, I would expect to be better at it. "But I think it's a button."

"Not *that.*" He leaves the button untouched and plucks the whitish gray bone from my palm to examine it. "Shit." He drops it fast, his jaw too. "Hey, Dupree, get on the radio. Call the sheriff. We got a situation here."

A situation. It sounds like something Headmaster Melhorn would say. *Dr. Pickett, please come to the cafeteria. We have a situation.* At a private school like Ellington, most situations boiled down to one cold, hard fact. Kids aren't perfect, and when they try to be, the proverbial shit hits the fan. In my eight-year tenure at Ellington, I'd seen my share of *situations.* Plagiarism, fighting, pregnancy scares. Getting stoned in the bathroom between classes. Self-harm. Self-sabotage. Self-destruction. And then, there was Macy. The Macy situation.

"Ms. Pickett, I'm talking to you." Sitkowski spits the words at me. They land hard as nails.

I force myself to look at him. "I'm sorry. I didn't hear you."

"I asked you a simple question. What are you doing out here?"

A simple question with a complicated answer I'm not ready to give. Certainly not to him and Duane.

"Would you rather do this down at the station?"

"Am I under arrest?"

"Should you be?"

With Duane's voice barking into the radio in the background, I shake my head. "I haven't done anything wrong."

"Well, I'll be the judge of that. You still haven't answered my question." He nudges the bone he dropped with the toe of his boot, then catches me looking. "From what I can tell, at the bare minimum you're defacing public property and trespassing on school grounds."

As he shines his flashlight into the hole I dug, I squeeze my eyes shut. I don't want to see it.

"Sure looks like a bone to me. What do you think, Dupree?"

Duane scampers up the sidewalk, eager to embarrass me. To get even, the way he's always done.

"Yes, siree. That ain't no animal bone neither."

It's unavoidable now. I risk a sidelong glance at the horrible thing rising from the earth. It's long and gray and broken at the end.

"That's an arm, ain't it?" Duane asks, patting his. "What do you call it? The ulner?"

"Ulna," I mutter, queasy at the sound of it. The look of it.

The small piece Sitkowski dropped rests between our feet. I see it now for what it is: a delicate hand bone or a finger. The other four digits lie in the hole in the dirt, perfectly preserved.

"Better cuff her." Duane grabs hold of me as if I might take off running. Gleefully, he adds, "She can't be trusted."

Sitkowski shrugs and removes the cuffs from his duty belt. "Sorry, Junebug. It's protocol in a *situation* like this."

There's that word again. I see Macy's face, sickly pale, the rest of her invisible under a hospital sheet while her stepfather stood watch. Then Blair's face, her mouth contorted in terror that night. That last night, the night of our graduation. Macy. Blair. Macy. Blair. When I blink again, all four Sweetbriar patrol cars line the front of the school, lights flashing. They've called in the whole cavalry.

I thought it couldn't get any worse. Turns out, it can. It does.

I double over and vomit gas-station hot dog on Sitkowski's black boots.

CHAPTER SIX

THE interview room in the Sweetbriar police station looks exactly the way I remember it. Cold, gray, and as small as a closet. The last time I sat in here across from Sheriff Faulk, the ink had barely dried on my high-school diploma. He kept hammering me with the same question—*Juniper, when was the last time you saw Blair?*—and I kept mumbling the same answer until my dad burst into the room and took me home.

Now, it's painfully obvious no one is coming to my rescue, and that Sheriff Faulk still sees me as a liar and probably worse. He's lost most of his hair and packed on a few pounds the last twenty years, but he gives me the same disapproving look from the same beady eyes.

"What brings you back to Sweetbriar, Dr. Pickett?"

I flinch at my title thrown back in my face. He already knows too much about me.

"You are a *doctor*, correct?"

"A PhD doctor, yes." When he lets out a low whistle, I realize I'm already doomed. "And I'm here for the reunion. The time-capsule unveiling."

"Can't say I expected you back for that. Not since you didn't make it for your daddy's burial. But then, I guess the two of you weren't that close anymore, huh?"

I suck down the last sip of the chalky tap water from the paper cup Sitkowski gave me when he stuck me in here two hours ago. "It was complicated," I admit, hoping he'll leave it at that.

"Ain't it always. That's family for ya." He leans back in his seat, rests his hands on his belly, and settles in to the silence.

He's trying to therapize a therapist. He won't get far with that. I once waited a solid forty-five minutes for sophomore Jordan Mayweather to confess he'd stolen the answers to the biology exam. I simply wait out Faulk, and I spot the precise moment he caves—when his nostrils flare in frustration.

"So, you say you came back for the reunion?" he says.

"That's right. Twenty years. I can hardly believe it's been that long. It makes me feel old."

"Hell, you ain't old till you get to the fortieth reunion. That's when you start scanning the obituaries. When that first name pops up that you recognize, it hits you that you're old as dirt. One foot in the grave. You know, your daddy and I were in the same class."

"He mentioned it." I keep the facts to myself. Before Johnny Faulk became Sheriff Faulk, he'd gotten busted for stealing cattle. In Texas, that amounted to the eighth deadly sin, but since he was only sixteen and the son of the most successful rancher in Sweetbriar, he got a slap on the wrist and a sealed juvenile record.

"I was real sorry to hear of his passing. Didn't see him too much around town anymore, especially after he got sick. I suppose he had a complicated relationship with a lot of folks, myself included."

I squirm in my seat, wishing for a place to hide. This is worse than I thought. Not only explaining my failures, but my father's too. I should've expected it.

"I'd really rather not rehash all this, Sheriff. My dad is gone, and what's done is done. I've left all that behind me."

"Have you now?" He raises a skeptical eyebrow. "Officer Dupree tells me he caught you trespassing at the school earlier last night. That you had a water jug and a shovel. He asked you to go home."

"Did he also tell you he was drunk?"

"Then, I hear from Officer Sitkowski that not only did you *not* go home as instructed, but you kept digging. You dug quite a large hole in the courtyard."

"That's not true. I *went* home." It hits me then that I don't actually have one anymore. I certainly can't claim my dad's place. Though it belongs to me now it's more Wyatt's than it is mine. And San Francisco still feels temporary, eight years and three studio apartments later.

"Well, be that as it may, you were the one digging, right, Doc? That doesn't sound like a gal who's left this place behind her. It sounds to me like you were searching for something. Under the cover of darkness, no less. From what I saw in that hole, you have some explaining to do."

I play a mental game of whack-a-mole, trying to unsee it myself. The bones, the button. The *bones.* "What did you see exactly?" I ask.

"Enough to get a big-city forensics team down here. Houston PD should be here in a few hours to assist. They'll get to the bottom of it in no time. So, is there anything you want to tell me?" He waits again, still hoping to outlast me. "You might want to get ahead of this is all I'm saying. You remember how folks around here talk. Gossip spreads fast, and Sweetbriar gossip spreads real fast. Faster than a greased pig."

Of course I remember it all, and that's what he's counting on. He wants me to recall the whispers, the sidelong glances. The outright accusations. The way Sweetbriar cast out my father and me, convinced one or both of us was to blame for Blair's disappearance.

"It looks a lot worse than it is," I say. "I don't know what I dug up, but it's not what I went looking for."

"Alright. Then, what *were* you looking for?"

Sometimes, the only way out is to tell the truth. "The time capsule."

"The time capsule?" He throws back his head and lets out a squawk of laughter that's way too big for these tight quarters.

The woody aroma of his chewing tobacco turns my stomach. That and the bones I still can't unsee.

I force myself into a fake smile, a half-hearted shrug. "Honestly, it was supposed to be a prank. A stupid idea I cooked up last night, when I was loopy from driving. Wyatt thought it would be funny."

"So Landry was in on this too… and he'll vouch for you?"

After he kills me. "Absolutely," I say.

"What exactly were you planning on doing with the time capsule?"

"Dig it up and…" I'm too far in to turn back. "I don't know, hide it somewhere. Or maybe put a few bugs in it."

"Bugs?"

I shrug. "June bugs."

He nods as if he actually believes me. But then he reaches into the front pocket of his shirt and pulls out a plastic baggie. The fact that it's been there all along, that he's been waiting for this reveal, sends a fierce current of hatred through me.

"Sitkowski said you had this in your hand when he came up on you."

I meet Sheriff Faulk's eyes. He wants me to look at it, and I refuse to give him the satisfaction.

"Ain't you gonna take a gander?" he asks with a little shake of the bag.

"I don't know where that came from or who it belongs to. Like I said, my intention was to dig up the time capsule."

"Right. The prank." He lays the bag on the table, pushes it toward me, until I have no choice but to see the yellow flower-shaped button inside. But that's not all. Next to it is a scrap of blue fabric with a few gray fibers clinging to its tattered edges. "I just got off the phone with Lydia Lennox. She confirmed that Blair was wearing a dress like this one on graduation night."

The mention of Lydia hits like a punch to the gut. I imagine her after the phone call, stunned speechless, the way she was in the weeks after Blair went missing. "Are you accusing me of something?"

He doesn't answer right away, lets me think long and hard about it. Then, he swipes the baggie from the table and shoves himself up from his chair. "Not yet. But don't go leavin' town again, 'kay?" At the door, he stops short. "We had to impound your vehicle."

"You *what?* Officer Sitkowski told me I could leave it parked in front of the school. That he'd give me a ride back after… all this." I wave my hand around the room like a crazed wizard, afraid to call it what it is. An interrogation.

"Well, I guess the ole boys must've got their signals crossed because Officer Dupree told me he found it in a red zone. I don't know what you folks do over in California, but here in Sweetbriar we follow the law. You can claim your vehicle at the lot just outside of town."

AFTER robbing me of the last shred of my dignity, Sheriff Faulk directs me to the station's front desk to call for a ride. I trudge toward it, zombie-like, barely flinching when the pony-tailed woman seated behind it squeals at me.

"Oh, my goodness. Is that Juniper Pickett?" She looks vaguely familiar, like everyone else in this godforsaken town. "Damn, girl. You lost weight. I need to know your secret. I barely even recognized you. You must be in town for the time-capsule opening. Am I right?"

My brain tries to form words, polite words, to tell her to shut the hell up. To give me the damn phone. To stop smiling at me.

"Christi Clark," she pronounces herself, pointing to the name badge above her pocket. "Christi Clark, police receptionist. My maiden name was Marshall."

I stare at her blankly. She seems to be blissfully unaware I've been caught digging up a body. But all I can think of are the bones, the blue fabric, and the yellow-flower button. Those essential gray fibers. The remnants of the past I unearthed less than four hours ago.

"The last time I saw your daddy, he mentioned you'd moved to San Francisco. Our little Junebug, a California girl. Who would've thunk it? The farthest I've ever been is Dallas for one of Aubrey's cheer competitions."

She keeps droning on about Dallas and her daughter and the stupid cheer competition while I download a cache of unpleasant memories. Button-nosed Christi Marshall twirled the baton in our marching band in a sparkly leotard and white boots. She and Jessica Carrington trailed behind Blair like stray dogs, waiting for precious scraps of attention. Once, Christi tripped me in the hallway and made a joke about the 5.5 earthquake I'd set off when I fell. As I gathered my books, Blair guffawed and high-fived her, which no doubt cemented it as the best day of Christi's life. And when Blair disappeared on graduation night, Christi all but called me a murderer to my face, confronting me outside the police station days later where she jabbed her finger into my chest and told me she hoped I got what I deserved.

In another universe, I punch Christi in the throat. In this one, I simply glance at my watch—it's just after 8 a.m.—and hope she takes the hint that I'd rather be somewhere else. Anywhere.

"Listen to me, going on about nonsense. Are you here about the vandalism at—"

"My car was towed this morning, and I need to use the phone." I steamroll over her in my effort to flee.

"Oh, you must've been parked in a red zone. The sheriff and his boys are real sticklers about that." She lifts a rotary phone from beneath the counter. "Here ya go. You've gotta dial nine for an outside line." I must make a face, because she adds, "We're still in the dark ages around here."

"That might not be a bad thing," I say. "Because I also need a phone book."

After paging through to the Ls, I dial the number. Of course Wyatt still has a landline. It rings for an impossibly long time, but when he answers my cheeks warm at the sound of his gravelly hello. I am truly pathetic.

"It's June."

"Are you alright?"

I glance at Christi. She takes a measured sip of her coffee and slides a handful of papers from her desk organizer, scrutinizing the top page with the intensity of a surgeon making the first incision. Instantly, I'm suspicious and I cover the receiver with my hand and keep my voice low. Not that it matters. There are no secrets in Sweetbriar.

"I'm alive. I'm in one piece. But I'm at the police station, and my car… isn't."

"Shit, June. What the hell happened? I thought you went to sleep."

Bones, dress, button. Gray fibers.

"Never mind. Tell me later. I suppose you're calling because you need a ride."

"I suppose I do." I catch Christi watching me. No doubt taking notes for her lunchtime gossip sesh. *You'll never believe who's back in town.* "And, Wyatt, can you hurry?"

"Is that Wyatt Landry?" Christi stage whispers, flashing another maniacal smile. "Didn't you have a thing for him, like, since kindergarten?"

I groan and hang up the receiver, intent on fleeing before this morning gets any worse. "I'll wait outside," I say.

"Suit yourself. But it's already hot as blazes out there." She fans herself with her hand. "C'mon, keep a fellow Bulldog company. You can tell me all about California."

Teenaged June would've given a non-vital organ for an invitation like that. I wonder if Christi's forgotten it all. The bullying, the tears, the hell they all put me through. I head for the exit, suddenly desperate for a gulp of fresh air.

"You know, Wyatt is single."

I should keep walking. I know I should. Just push the door open, June. But something holds me there. "Good for him."

"A lot of folks around here think he's damaged goods. Rumor is that he hasn't had any action since he got out of the pen. That's five years ago now. Can you imagine how lonely he must be? Desperate, really."

I blink at her, shellshocked by the sudden realization that she hasn't forgotten any of it. That she's picked up right where she left off twenty years ago.

"Bless your heart, Junebug. You may actually have a chance."

CHAPTER SEVEN

WITHOUT a word, I climb into the passenger side of Wyatt's truck. The police station safely in the rearview, I exhale and sink into the seat.

"My car is at the tow lot."

"Yes, ma'am."

It sounds as if he just rolled his eyes at me, but I can't tell because I'm too embarrassed to face him.

"There's complimentary water in the cupholder and mints in the glove box. Would you like music or do you prefer silence?"

"Ha, ha. I didn't realize a Sweetbriar cowboy knew so much about rideshares." I look at him then. The hard set of his jaw. His standard cowboy hat. The same black Stetson he wore in his competition bull-riding days. The one that earned him the rodeo-circuit nickname JC. *Johnny Cash.* I start to fiddle with the radio, but he stops me with his hand on mine.

"Seatbelt."

My eyes flit back to him. To the flat white scar above his eyebrow where a shard of windshield glass sliced through skin. I don't know how I missed it last night. It matches the exact location of the butterfly stitches and the dried blood in his mugshot. I can't find the other scar along his hairline, the one I'm to blame for. Grim-faced, I buckle up and wait for him to drive.

Though I'd managed to outlast Sheriff Faulk's stony silence, Wyatt's hits differently. It's too heavy, too loaded. It feels like punishment.

"I hope I didn't inconvenience you. I probably could've asked the sheriff for a ride, but I was crawling out of my skin in that place. I just—"

"What the hell is going on, June? I drove by the school. The place is swarming with cops. Big-city cops."

"I messed up." I roll down the window, wishing for the cool morning breeze on my face—cruising with the top down on Embarcadero Way in San Francisco, seagulls overhead, dipping and diving toward the Bay. Instead, I run smack into a wall of Texas humidity. "Can we just go?"

"Not until you tell me the truth."

"About what?"

"About anything." He tugs a folded newspaper article out of his jeans pocket and sets it on the bench seat between us. "About *this*."

Reluctantly, I open it. It's been neatly excised from the paper like the cancerous tumor it is. My throat tightens as I read the headline from ten days ago. Before they called me out by my name.

Was a School Psychologist to Blame?
Ellington Parents Demand Answers.

"Where did you get this?" It's a dumb question. I know exactly *where* it came from. I'd read the same story myself in the *San Francisco*

Chronicle, grateful it omitted my name. But how did Wyatt get his hands on it? "I mean, *how* did you get this?"

"It may come as a surprise to you, but we country folk get the newspaper too."

"Not this one. Unless…" I hang my head. "My dad subscribed to the *Chronicle*, didn't he?"

Wyatt just shrugs, which only makes me more certain and more riddled with guilt.

"It's you, right?" he asks. "The school psychologist in the article?"

"I can't talk about this, Wyatt." I scramble to come up with a reason other than the truth. That I literally *cannot* talk about it. That if—*when*—I have to talk about it, I'll crumble. I will turn to dust. "My attorney advised me—"

"Bullshit." After a hard exhale, he puts the truck in drive and eases onto Main Street. "What *can* you talk about then?"

I don't trust the question. The Wyatt I remember didn't give up that easily. He keeps his eyes on the road, giving nothing away. In the uneasy lull, I can't tell if the storm has blown over or if I'm just standing in the eye of the hurricane.

Past the Sweetbriar Country Store, Wyatt slows down and signals a left turn. In the distance, I spot the chain-link fence of the tow lot. Behind it, my poor convertible waits for me, the windshield dusty and bug-spattered.

I decide to risk it. "Did you know Christi's daughter won a cheer competition in Dallas?"

He groans. "Had to sit through that story, did ya? Good thing you waited outside or you might've been forced to suffer through the pageant story too. Now that's a real gem."

"She hasn't changed that much."

"Most folks don't. Not unless they have to."

I start to argue that it's not *have to*, it's *want to* that makes people change. That's what Dr. P. would say. But what the hell did she know? I'm not so sure anymore.

The gate to the lot slides open, but Wyatt stops short. He doesn't even put the truck in park. "Mr. Trolf will help you from here."

"Tom Trolf? The school janitor?" Then, I see him, stooped outside the booth at the center of the lot with an old hound dog at his side. The dog's tail thumps in the dirt as Mr. Trolf waves to us. "I thought he'd be long dead by now."

"You may not want to lead with that." Wyatt taps his horn and gives the old man a friendly nod. "Be nice to Scout. He likes his ears scratched."

"Noted." I wave back at Mr. Trolf, trying to remember the last time I'd seen him. When he reaches for the can of beer propped on an old barrel, the memory returns with a vicious bite. "I see he's still having beer for breakfast."

"Yeah. Old habits. Turns out they don't die hard. They don't die at all."

I'm not sure if that's an accusation or a confession, so I only mutter my agreement. He's not far off base. Teenaged Juniper needed Wyatt to rescue her too, more than once. Sometimes, he let me down. More often, he didn't.

I open the truck door and hop out. But I can't bring myself to close it. Scout ambles toward me, his tongue lolling from his white muzzle. I smile in spite of myself. In spite of this god-awful morning.

"Wyatt?" When I glance at him, he looks away. I should tell him thank you. Not just for today, but for every day he sat with my father after he got sick and all the days before. The odd jobs, the leaky roof. The fences that needed mending. For every day he did what I wouldn't, couldn't. Didn't.

"I told Sheriff Faulk you were helping me dig up the time capsule. For a prank. If he asks."

"You *what?* Why would you do that?" He shakes his head, more astonished than angry. Which he has every right to be. "Never mind. I rescind the question."

"And there's something else."

Exasperated, he runs his hand through his hair, and I spot it: the inch-long scar he's had since fifth grade. I think of all the time that's passed. How much we've both changed. But that scar is still there. A reminder that some things never do.

"I left my purse at the house. Do you think I could borrow some cash?"

CHAPTER EIGHT

FORTY-FIVE minutes later, I arrive back at the farm at the dead end of Saw Mill Road. Despite my exhaustion, I can't quiet my mind. It spins like the ball in a roulette wheel from one horror to the next. It won't slow down, won't stop. I need to get inside. I need to be alone. As soon as possible.

Yet I don't want to be alone with myself and my run of bad luck. So when Wyatt pulls in the drive behind me, I approach his closed window and ask, "Do you want to come in?"

"I can wait in the truck," he says through the glass. "I don't want to trouble you."

"It's no trouble."

The subtle drop of his chin signals his doubt. "You sure about that?"

I know what I should do. I should walk inside and find my wallet. I should get the man his money and tell him goodbye. I should forget how kind he's been. How he convinced Mr. Trolf to waive the towing and administrative fees for a Bulldog alum. How he spent a solid ten minutes scratching Scout's ears. How he's apparently very single and very desperate, and old habits never die.

I don't do any of the things I should, which only proves how lost I am. Juniper Pickett always does what she should… except when she definitely doesn't. I signal to Wyatt to roll down his window.

With a visible sigh, he relents, resting his arm on the outside of his truck. "If you invite me in, I'm going to ask questions. You don't seem to like my questions."

"It's not the questions I don't like. It's the answers." My sandpaper eyes prick with tears. "I've made a lot of mistakes lately. Big ones."

Wyatt doesn't disagree. Instead, one corner of his mouth lifts. "Remember what your dad used to say about learning from his mistakes?"

"Yeah, that he's made so many he should be a genius by now." I chuckle, already feeling lighter. "Which was funny because he was an actual genius." As soon as I say it, I'm knee deep in a memory, playing store with Eugene Pickett's Mensa card, issued by the Texas Lonestar chapter. My mother had a card too—her Sweetbriar Community Bank badge—that my father kept hidden in a box in the nightstand drawer with the other artifacts he saved. Sometimes, I'd sneak in and open it just to remind myself I hadn't dreamed her. That my mother existed.

After a spurt of laughter, Wyatt's face dims. "You know, I saved that card for you. It's in the box marked—"

"One question," I say, only to shut him up. I don't want to picture that card anywhere but in my dad's wallet in the back pocket of his Wranglers. "You get one."

"One?"

I remember seeing my father's gun secreted beneath his driver's seat. "I get to ask one too."

"Ask away, June. I'm an open book."

He pops the door, and I take a step back. Without so much as a glance over his shoulder, he strides toward the house, and I hurry behind him, feeling scolded. The Book of Wyatt may be open, but it's written in a foreign language. Good luck trying to make any sense of it.

Wyatt uses his key to unlock the door. By the time I catch up with him, he's standing in the kitchen.

"Fine. If you're such an open book, why did you steal my dad's gun? Are you even allowed to have a weapon?"

He frowns at me as if I haven't got the right.

"I saw you with it. It was under your truck's seat." My eyes drop from his to the belt buckle at the center of his waist. It's the same sterling-silver longhorn he wore in high school. A familiar heat creeps up my neck and into my cheeks. I turn away and reach for the crossbody bag I left on the counter, rifling through it so I don't have to look at him.

"You saw me with it, sure enough. But how do you know I stole it? That's a bold accusation."

"It's an antique. A family heirloom. My mom bought it for him the day she agreed to move back to Sweetbriar with him. She told him it would make him—"

"A real cowboy." He finishes my sentence in my father's deep voice. "I heard that story too, a few thousand times."

"Then you know how precious it was to him. He would have wanted me to have it." I sound ridiculous. No better than the spoiled Ellington brats who stretched every fiber of my patience. I have no idea what my father wanted. But that gun, this house, the remnants of his life, it's all I have left.

"Do you want the gun back?" Wyatt asks. "Just say the word. I'm happy to give it to you."

"So you *did* take it."

"Because I'm an ex-con? A criminal? Is that it?"

"Well…" I make a face that I hope says *don't be offended.* It's the same face I deployed countless times at Ellington. Like the first time I met Macy Powell and tried to explain to her stepfather why a girl with mediocre grades and a misdemeanor vandalism charge would never get into an Ivy, no matter how many checks his deep pockets wrote.

The face doesn't work on Wyatt. He seems deeply, flagrantly offended. But worst of all, he says nothing. He just stares at me.

Naturally, I make it worse by laying three hundred dollars in cash on the counter and nudging it toward him. "Here's what I owe you for the tow lot, plus another fifty for your trouble."

He doesn't take the money. He glares at it as if it just spat in his face. "You really are something. You're the one who ran away. The one who stopped returning his calls. You disappeared and it crushed him. Now you have the nerve to accuse me of stealing from him. He gave me the gun for safekeeping a couple months ago. I told him I didn't want it, that I shouldn't have it. But he insisted."

"Safekeeping? Why?"

Wyatt shakes his head. "One question asked and answered. It's my turn now."

"Go ahead then." I try to sound unbothered, but it comes out clipped, sharp. As if I'm ready for a fight.

"What are you doing here? And don't tell me you came back for the goddamned reunion because we both know you'd rather wrestle a kangaroo than set foot on the campus of Sweetbriar High."

"I don't know. I'd say it depends on the size of the kangaroo." When his face doesn't crack, I throw up my hands. "Fine. You're right. I don't want to be here. I wanted to sell the house through a broker, put the stuff in storage, and never think of this place again."

"But?"

"I had to come back to dig up the time capsule. Before the reunion."

"You *had* to? Does it have to do with that article I read?"

My throat closes tight, but I'll be damned if I let Wyatt see me cry. I turn away, and the kitchen sink blurs through my tears. I feel him behind me, closer than before. I hear him breathing at my back.

"Like you said, one question. It's been asked and answered," I whisper.

"Fair enough. But whatever the reason, it's only a matter of time before the cops put it together. Duane isn't smart, but he is persistent."

I don't realize he's left until I hear the door shut. The money sits on the counter, untouched.

After I see his truck kicking up dust outside the kitchen window, I peek out the front to find the Smith and Wesson on the seat of the porch rocker. Frustrated, I snatch it up and head back into the house and straight for my bedroom.

Though Wyatt warned me my dad hadn't changed a thing, it still bowls me over. I walk into my very own time capsule with its pink-polka-dot bedding and Baby-Sitters Club books. The old desktop computer hulks at the center of my desk, like an ancient king, surrounded by the trophies I'd won: Spelling Bee, Science Fair, Valedictorian. The pièce de résistance: my poster of Luke Perry aka *90210*'s Dylan McKay hanging opposite the bed. Even the hairline crack in the door remains.

Immediately, I'm drawn to the only new additions. My leatherbound dissertation—*damn, Wyatt was right*—the title embossed across the front. *Words Can Hurt Me: A Phenomenological Study of Girl-on-Girl Bullying*. Set atop the book, a framed photograph of me in cap and gown at my high-school graduation. My father knew I hated photos of myself—it's the only one in the room—but he'd insisted on taking it, directing me to pose in front of the podium.

I place the gun in the nightstand drawer, then pick up the photo to take a closer look at the girl in it. She's a stranger to me. A stranger I pity. For her forced smile and faraway eyes. For what she had planned. Mostly, for how much she hated being in her own skin, and for no good reason. I look at her now, the girl that I was, and she's not the ogre I remember. She's no different than the girls at Ellington. The ones who throw up in the bathroom, who dab toothpaste on their pimples. Who obsess in the mirror over the bump in their profile and ask Mommy and Daddy for a nose job for their sixteenth birthday.

I shake my head at the girl in the photo, disappointed in her for wasting so much time, and return the frame to the nightstand. As my legs carry me toward the closet, I brush away a tear and slide open the door to survey my sad high-school wardrobe. All oversized Nike T-shirts, baggy jeans, and wind suits to hide myself from the world. A few tragic Laura Ashley dresses, and the white cardigan that once belonged to my mother. She bought it in a thrift shop on Sixth Street in Austin during her senior year at the University of Texas. She called it the button sweater.

It's still here. It smells slightly moldy. I slip it off the hanger and lay it on the bed where I can examine it closer. I run my hand along the elbow and find the small rip in the thin fabric. Only the top button is fastened. The rest of it hangs loose, the white material stretched out and slightly discolored with age.

I last wore the cardigan at the graduation party in the frigid school gymnasium after the ceremony. I remember standing in the corner and nervously fingering the bottom button, wishing the night would go faster. Looking at it now turns my stomach.

I start at the top and close each of the remaining buttons. With each one, I see the disco ball twirling, sending little sparkles of light across the gym floor. There's music playing in the background, but I can't hear it above the voice in my head. The one that's telling me I'm a loser. A weirdo. A hideous, fat, pimple-faced Junebug with no one to love her. That I hate this town and everyone in it, and I'm going to put a stop to it. Tonight.

I take in a quick breath when I reach the last buttonhole. Its yellow-flower button went missing that night and was found today in an unmarked grave. Even worse, a reddish-brown spot stains the fabric above the small slit.

It's finally caught up to me. What I planned. What I did. What I didn't do. I thought I'd put that night behind me, but it turns out it's been following me all along. Stalking me like my own shadow and waiting for the right time to reveal itself.

I ball up the sweater and stuff it in my old JanSport backpack. Then I let myself out the front door and walk toward the row of ash trees at the back of the house. It's a wild place now, where the weeds grow as tall as my waist, tall enough to swallow the remnants of my mother's vegetable garden. When I reach the brush line, I let the memory wash over me. It's better this way. To meet it head-on; the horrible thing that happened here. But I don't linger. If I think too hard, I hear my panicked screams. See my mother's twisted limbs, the unnatural angle of her neck. The underside of the tractor. My father tucked away in his quiet workshop while I tried to make sense of the horror in front of me.

"Oxygen, fluoride, neon, sodium..."

I take another step forward, then another. I keep moving until I spot the outline of the well. Even after Dad built a concrete cover for it, Mom deemed it a disaster waiting to happen. Still, she let me throw a penny down on my birthday. *Make a wish, silly girl,* she'd say. By my thirteenth birthday, Mom was gone, and Dad pronounced it a superstitious ritual that developed centuries ago because the biocidal properties of copper and silver made the water safer to drink. I never went there again.

"Magnesium, aluminum, silicon, phosphorus..."

Now, I beeline straight to the two-foot-high circle of river stone. With a grunt, I strain to push the cover aside. Despite the heat of the day, cool air rises from the dark depths of the well. I lean over and peer in, trying to spot the bottom, the years' worth of pennies I tossed into its belly. But it's only a long, dark tunnel to nowhere.

I wonder what Mom would say now. If she would understand what I'm about to do and why I have no choice but to do it.

Before I drop the backpack, I weight it with a few loose river stones. It makes an eerie splash. I yelp, then laugh at myself. When my noises echo back to me, like distorted reverberations from the past, I shiver. Because I can't tell if it's a giggle or a snarl or a cry or a moan. Or the desperate sound Blair made when she ripped the button from my cardigan.

CHAPTER NINE

FIVE YEARS UNTIL GRADUATION

DAD didn't come home last night.

It's all I can think about on the bus ride to school, even with Duane and Eric pelting my head with spitballs, and on the long trek down the hallway to my locker, and while I find my seat and wait for the homeroom bell to ring. He's worked late before—he always works late—but he's never slept in his workshop.

I checked his bed this morning after Bert nudged me awake. I waded through piles of laundry and stacks of random science books to find it empty. I thought about walking to the workshop to check on him. Pulled my sneakers on and everything. Worry started to creep in. What if I'd lost him too?

But then I spotted him out in the pasture traipsing around Red Mountain holding a beaker like a mad scientist. No doubt testing his ecofriendly ant repellant that only seems to make them bigger and angrier. When I opened the front door to go meet the bus, he stopped and looked at the house. He didn't call out to me. He didn't even wave.

He hates me, and I don't blame him. It's my fault Mom died. I wasn't strong enough or brave enough or fast enough to save her. It's no wonder he can't stand to be around me.

She's been gone for ninety-four days, and he's barely said a word to me about any of it. A few days ago, he sat me down at the kitchen table after school, and I thought, *finally*. Finally, he's going to stop pretending it didn't happen. Instead, he asked, *Do you know a girl named Diane Brownmiller?*

Bonnie Bailey taps me on the shoulder, and I turn around in my seat to face her desk. "Did you hear about the new girl?"

I shake my head, happy to be asked. Happy to be noticed. "No, where's she from?"

Like me, Bonnie gets teased a lot. But she's lucky. She only has headgear. In eleven more months, she'll have teeth like Vanna White, and I'll still be me.

"Dallas," Bonnie says.

"Dallas?" I open my eyes wide and mimic the way the other girls talk. "Dallas? Wow. That's so cool."

To me, I sound like a wannabe, but Bonnie nods enthusiastically. She's a wannabe too.

"Christi said her stepdad used to work for the Dallas Cowboys. They bought the old Crenshaw place. That's near your house, right?"

"Yeah. Right down the road."

"Well, did you meet her yet?" Bonnie leans in like we're sharing a secret.

Pleased with myself, I glance around the classroom to see who's noticed. No one, it turns out, but Wyatt Landry. He nods at me from the back of the class, and my heart flaps around in my chest like it might fly away.

"Not yet." I try to come up with something that will hold Bonnie's interest. "But my dad and I saw them moving in over the weekend. They had a big moving truck from the city."

"You didn't go over to say hi?"

I freeze up under the weight of Bonnie's expectation. I don't say that I actually met the new girl days ago. That I saw her riding her fancy dirt bike up the lane toward the caretaker's cottage and followed her. That I saw her crying in the creek bed. That I think I made a friend. I don't say any of it.

Bonnie murmurs, "Whoa."

Duane gives a low whistle that Mrs. Sherman cuts short with a steely glare. The new girl has made her entrance to first-period homeroom.

"Gosh, she's pretty," Bonnie says. "Her teeth are perfect. I wonder if she had braces."

I spin around from Bonnie to take a gander. I already know she's beautiful. She looks like an actress—even up close. Even sweaty from riding in the heat and bawling her eyes out.

Mrs. Sherman clears her throat. "Class, we have a new student joining us all the way from Dallas. Her stepdad just took over for Doc Murphy at the pharmacy downtown. Young lady, would you like to introduce yourself?"

I would've died on the spot. Literally just dropped dead under the weight of all those eyeballs. But not her. She grows taller, tosses her shiny blonde hair over one shoulder, and flashes a megawatt smile.

"Hi. I'm Blair. Blair Lennox."

"It's so nice to meet you, Blair. Why don't you take the open seat in front of Juniper?"

I shrink into my desk; I wish I could disappear. But the snickers have already begun, and my cheeks burn like I'm under a spotlight. So much for disappearing.

"Hi," I manage to sputter out. My plan to befriend her goes up in smoke. Who was I kidding?

She pretends not to recognize me. I don't fault her for it. She knows a loser when she sees one. "*Juniper?* What a weird name."

In the creek bed, she'd called it old-fashioned. Unique. Sweet.

"Who the heck knows what my parents were thinking," I say to appease her. I'd already told her the whole story. How my dad proposed to my mom under a juniper tree on a camping trip to California. "But I go by June."

"June." I watch her eyes twinkle with mischief. She understands her power. Right now, she's got the whole classroom in the palm of her hand. Except for gray-haired Mrs. Sherman, who can't hear a thing once she's turned to face the chalkboard. "Like a June bug. Those are so gross."

"Eww." Christi makes a face. "Those big brown ones. They're massive."

"If you think the big ones are gross, you should see the grubs," Duane chimes in.

Eric snorts. "We feed those slimy little buggers to my lizard."

Wyatt opens his mouth to save me. I can tell because he gives me a pitying look. I pretend not to notice when he changes his mind. He turns away, probably too worried to watch.

"Shut up, Eric," I say, a little too loudly. Loud enough to reach Mrs. Sherman's ancient ears.

She whips around and points the chalk at me. "Juniper Pickett. We do not use that language in the classroom. Now, apologize to Eric."

I glance at Blair, her face a blank slate. I don't have the heart to hate her. I understand her. She told me too much. *My dad got fired. We had to move here. He did something bad.* She gave me too much power. Now she has to take it back.

I mumble, "Sorry, Eric," with as little gusto as I can manage. Meanwhile, Wyatt's back to giving me his sad eyes.

"Eric, what do we say to June?" Mrs. Sherman prompts like we're toddlers on a playground instead of seventh graders.

"It's okay. I forgive you, June." He mutters something else under his breath that has Duane doubled over in stitches.

Oblivious, Mrs. Sherman returns to writing on the chalkboard, and I sink lower in my seat while Blair slips into the one in front of me. Her hair hangs down past the chair back. It smells like lilacs and makes me regret my chin-length bob. The lady at the Clip and Curl told me it was in style, but it only accentuates my chipmunk cheeks, and by seventh period my ends always flip up not under.

In the sunlight through the window, Blair's hair shimmers. It would be so easy for me to whack it off with my scissors. She wouldn't even realize until the deed had been done, her silky locks lying lifeless on the dirty classroom floor. She'd probably scream. She'd definitely cry. But then, we'd never be friends, and I desperately want a friend like Blair.

I take out my favorite Lois Duncan book and open it to my bookmark. My eyes read the words, but my brain keeps spinning. I can't believe I let her rub Bert's ears. That while she sniffled I walked her bike back down the road and told her it would be okay. That I confided in her about Mom. I'm stupid to think a girl like her would ever want to be my friend.

"Hello, earth to *Junebug*. I asked if I could borrow a pencil."

Blair waves a hand in my face, and I snap back like a rubber band.

"That's not my name," I say.

"I know, *Junebug*."

My face gets hot again. I can't handle another nickname. After I made a blubber glove demonstration for the fifth-grade science fair, Duane called me Shamu for the rest of the year. To be fair, I'd walked right into that one. His eyes lit up the moment I said: *Blubber is a crucial adaptation for whales and can be up to thirty centimeters thick*. It took Wyatt upending a vat of Jell-O on his head in front of the entire school cafeteria to stop him. But then Wyatt got detention and Wyatt's dad got angry, and bad things happened when Mr. Landry went on the warpath. There were always casualties.

I find Wyatt across the room in full concentration on the drawing in front of him. Even with his hair shaggy, I spot the scar with ease. That's what happens when Wyatt comes to my rescue. He gets hurt.

"Here." I shove my favorite pencil at Blair. It's topped with the last of my unicorn erasers, the ones my mom bought me at a craft shop in Houston last summer. "Take it."

Blair lets it drop to the floor and nudges it with the toe of her pristine white Ked, sending it skittering up the aisle. "Oops."

I hurry to retrieve it before it reaches Duane's desk. It stops just short of the no-fly zone and I scoop it up. Pencil in hand, I start back the way I came. Blair smiles at me sweetly—and I almost forgive her—just before she sticks out her foot to send me flying.

Somehow, I end up on my back, staring at the ceiling tiles. Mrs. Sherman rushes over. At least no one's laughing. Yet.

Then, I hear Blair. "Look at her. Poor thing really is a June bug."

The classroom erupts, and I lie there, mortified, until Bonnie and Mrs. Sherman help me to my feet.

CHAPTER TEN

NOW

WITH my old sweater drowned at the bottom of the well, I scarf down three granola bars from my travel stash and retreat to my room. I risk a glance in the mirror—stringy hair, oily face, raccoon eyes—and immediately wish I hadn't. My face reads like a roadmap of the last few weeks; I desperately need a shower and a change of clothes, a swipe of blush and more than a dab of undereye concealer. I need to find my cellphone. I need to find a *lawyer*. Instead, I collapse on the bed and give in to my exhaustion.

I jolt awake, spooked and sweaty. My heart rapid-fires in my chest. It takes me a few breaths to remember where I am and a few more to sit up and swing my legs off the edge of the bed. I don't know what woke me or how long I've been out, but the muted shadow that falls across the room tells me the sun has long vanished from my window. In a panic, I check the alarm clock by the bed before my brain kicks in. The battery, dead. The hands, stuck for who-knows-how-long at 12:10. Disoriented, I stand up and wander into the hall before I remember the watch on my wrist. It's four o'clock in the afternoon, which means I slept for seven hours.

Still in a fog, I find my way to the bathroom sink and splash my face with water. It has the same earthy smell I remember, the same metallic taste. My father never fixed the chip in the mirror where I accidentally banged my curling iron on the first day of seventh grade. When I open the top dresser drawer in my room, I find my favorite purple T-shirt folded as neatly as the day I left Sweetbriar, fleeing to the most faraway place I could conjure: Berkeley, California. It reminded me too much of home to take it with me. I needed to make a clean break. To leave Sweetbriar June in the literal dust.

I try to shake off my déjà vu. Every nook of this house reminds me of who I used to be. Each memory a link in a chain that binds me here forever, no matter how far I run. I see that now.

I tug on my sneakers anyway, needing to be free of this place, and jog in the direction of the workshop. I retrace last night's steps, intent on locating my cellphone. At least I can do that. As I tell my students: slow down, take it one breath at a time, problem by problem. Or in my case, crisis by crisis.

In the afternoon light, the workshop beckons to me the way it did all those years ago. I can almost pretend my dad's inside, *tinkering*. That's what he called it. After his success with Harvest Gold, he sold the patent and kept at it. Always in search of the next big idea, he could never be satisfied. Just before my mom's accident, they argued about exactly that. About how much time he spent working with nothing to show for it. About how he'd burned through half the patent money. About how distant she felt from him. When she shouted it at him—*You'll never be satisfied, Eugene!*—he didn't say a word. He just slipped out the door and retreated to the workshop in tacit agreement, while my mom and I built a pillow fort and ate an entire family-sized bag of peanut M&M's between us. Three weeks later they laid her in the ground at the Oak Grove Cemetery. But that didn't stop him. He pushed harder.

After years of working as a school psychologist, I concluded my dad was built differently. I recognized him in the kids who didn't quite fit in. Who took apart their laptop computers to get a good look at the guts. Who obsessed to the point of distraction. Who punished themselves for every failure. Exacting, distant, fanatical. I understood him better, but I still couldn't forgive him. Even now. Because he left me alone when I needed him the most.

I traipse through the grass for thirty minutes until I finally spot my cell next to a cactus bush. It's warm to the touch, and I hope I haven't cooked it. Then again, maybe I should leave it here to die. Nothing good can come from firing it up and listening to those voicemails. Or reading my termination letter. Still, I can't bring myself to walk away from the digital catalog of my failures. I need to analyze the evidence. Turns out, I am my father's daughter.

Phone in hand, I turn back to the house. As I near Red Mountain, I hear the rev of an engine mocking me at my back. The growl of the four-wheeler sounds like a battle cry, but I shake off my unease. I'm not a kid anymore, and the pecan where Duane treed Midnight died long ago. Midnight too, of course—the only cat in our cow-dog graveyard. Losing her the way I did was the beginning of the end.

The four-wheeler speeds from behind the workshop and heads straight at me. Like a bull aiming at a waving red flag.

"Hey, what're you doing out here?" I yell into the wind. "You're on private property."

The black-helmeted rider crouches lower and accelerates, and my breath quickens. I want to turn and run. But I can't. My body won't do it. It's just like that Wednesday two weeks ago. I sat there like a stone while chaos descended around me.

"Slow down!" I hold up my hands and brace for impact.

A vicious gust of air blows past me, leaving me in a cloud of exhaust. The four-wheeler vanishes over Red Mountain, taking its mysterious rider with it, the sound of the engine getting fainter until it disappears altogether.

Shocked, I stare after it until my nerves stop crackling. Once my legs slowly reawaken, I hurry inside the house and bolt the door behind me.

I have the urge to call Wyatt. To tell him about my brush with death and demand the identity of the maniac behind the handlebars. Living next door, he must know. But I absolutely do not give in. I don't need him coming over here with his questions and his attitude and that stupidly large belt buckle he won bull riding. I channel adolescent Juniper and hole up in my bedroom, where I plug my phone into the wall charger. As I anxiously wait for signs of life, I open a drawer and pull out my 1990s-chic purple T-shirt and a pair of black Umbro shorts. Arrange my hair in a bun with a neon scrunchie. Then, I turn to the mirror and giggle at my handiwork. Until I hear Blair's voice in my head. *Barney the Dinosaur called. He wants his shirt back.*

And *that's* why I left it here.

Thankfully, it takes more than the Texas heat to kill a cellphone. The screen flashes to life, bringing me back to my current crisis. I'm not sure where to look first. At the fire I left burning in San Francisco or the blaze I set last night. Or if I should look at all. My fingers hover over the keypad. Maybe I'll spend the afternoon watching an endless loop of sneezing pandas and cats playing piano.

But I can't bury my head in the sand the way I did with Macy. That's why I'm in this mess. I open the browser and type *Sweetbriar Texas bod—*

What am I thinking? I can't go looking. Not for that. How would I explain it? I wouldn't. Couldn't. I delete each letter one by one. I've already made enough boneheaded mistakes. The proof is in my inbox.

I click on the week-old email from Headmaster Melhorn and open the attachment. It's as dismal as I suspected. Three lines on letterhead. An electronic signature. That's all it takes to end my career.

> After our investigation into the incident on May 17, we determined that, in your capacity as school psychologist, you behaved with reckless disregard for the safety of the institution and in a manner inconsistent with Ellington's Ethical Principles for Staff, a document which you signed at the time of your hiring. As such, we regret to inform you of your termination effective immediately. Please surrender all school property to the Main Campus Business Office by the close of business on June 1.

All school property. That includes my laptop, which I suddenly realize I left baking in the back-seat oven of my car.

With the rumble of the four-wheeler still vibrating my nerves, I hesitate at the door, pressing my ear to it before I open it. I listen the way I had as a kid, convinced any noise I'd heard came from a Freddy Krueger-inspired madman intent on slashing my throat.

I hear nothing, and when I peek out the window I see only empty driveway. Satisfied I won't be hacked to bits, I beeline to the car to retrieve my computer bag. I find it lying on the floorboard of the back seat, the zipper pouch half open. I slide my hand into the bag, relieved to feel the solid outer shell of the laptop. But my relief disappears when I remember the folder, *Blair's folder.* Before I tore out of here like a bat out of hell last night, I tossed it on the seat. I'm certain of it. There's no sign of it now.

I take out the computer, hold the bag upside down, and give it a shake. Five ink pens tumble out, followed by two cough drops and a Band-Aid. A pack of Kleenex and a fidget spinner for my distractible students. All part of the standard school psychologist's emergency kit. I search under the seats, certain the folder slipped beneath them, then crouch low to peer into the crevice between the seats and the console. With each passing second, my worry ratchets up a notch, until I'm tossing out the floor mats and rifling through the glove box.

I don't register the approach of Wyatt's truck until it's too late to hide. As the Ford rumbles up the drive toward me, I face the facts: Blair's folder has disappeared, and I have no choice but to face another round of Wyatt's firing squad of questions. Breathing hard, I collapse against the warm hood of the convertible and wait for him to pull up alongside.

When he rolls down his window, I do a double take at the cowboy in the driver's seat. No more stubble on his jaw, just smooth tan skin disappearing into a light-blue western shirt. Shadowing his eyes, that familiar black Stetson. Though I can't see it from where I'm standing, I'm willing to bet he's still wearing that stupid belt buckle that pronounced him the top bull rider at the 1997 National High School Finals Rodeo.

"Are you okay?" He leans out the window, and I catch a whiff of his piney aftershave.

"I'm fine." I wave him off, knowing I look anything but. Inside and outside, I'm a wreck. A Barney-the-Dinosaur-inspired disaster. "What're you doing back here anyway? I thought you hated me."

"Hate is a strong word. I thought you'd be dressed by now. I came to see if you wanted a ride to the reunion."

I gawk at him as if he's sprouted a pair of wings. To be fair, I haven't stopped gawking since last night. I can't get over him all grown up. He's the same but different, and it makes me nervous.

"Okay, fine," he says. "I came by to apologize *and* to see if you wanted a ride. I was out of line earlier. I shouldn't have accused you of running away, and I should've checked with you about the gun. You're right not to trust me. Why would you? We don't know each other anymore."

I want to argue with him. Though he's not wrong, it stings somehow. I once knew him well, better than anyone. He knew me too, and that also makes me nervous. Because the last time I saw Wyatt, he broke my heart.

"I hate guns," I say. "And I did run away. My dad trusted you. He trusted you with his life. He trusted you more than me."

"That's not true. I was here. He needed someone."

My eyes fill with tears again.

Juniper, it's Dad. I need to talk to you. It's important.

He needed me, and I abandoned him.

I keep talking so I don't cry. "What did you mean about him giving you the gun for safekeeping?"

He quirks his mouth. "Is that your second question?" Ignoring my heavy sigh, he continues, "I'm not saying it's a bad question. I just want to confirm it's the one you're going with."

"Is there another question I should be asking?"

"Honestly, a whole bunch. How about, 'Do you want to come to the class reunion with me, Wyatt?'"

The mere mention of it twists my stomach in knots. "I'm surprised they're still having it at all. I just assumed…"

"Well, the official ceremony was canceled. Unofficially, Christi and Eric are hosting a get-together at the football stadium. We won't have to scale any crime-scene tape, if that's what you're worried about."

"Christi and Eric Clark." It takes me a few breaths to put it all together. "I didn't realize they were married."

"Yep. Married with one award-winning cheerleader. I guess my dad was right. There's a lid for every pot."

"And you're going? To this get-together?"

He grins at me, and it hits the same as it did at eighteen: butterflies in the center of my chest.

"Is that so shocking?" he asks.

"Honestly, a little." I tread carefully, measuring my words. I don't want to insult him again. "Duane tried to pick a fight with you last night. And Christi made it seem like…"

"Like I'm the town pariah?"

I grit my teeth and give him a little shrug. "Maybe I misread it. It's not like I have room to talk."

"No, you read it right. They wouldn't spit on me if I was on fire. It doesn't matter that I served my time. That I haven't touched a drop of liquor since that night. That I think about the wreck every single goddamned day and try to live in such a way to honor the lives I took, Alberto Gomez and his grandson, Carlo. To the folks around here, I'm still that same drunk asshole in the mugshot. My father's son. They have every right to see me that way." By the time he stops, his fingers are tight around the wheel, white-knuckling it. But he doesn't look away from me.

I can tell he's given himself this speech before. Probably a few hundred times. I can relate.

"So why go? Why put yourself through that? You don't have to prove anything to them."

"Oh, I know. But I'll be damned if I'll let them have the satisfaction. It's fun rattling their cages."

I must seem skeptical because he laughs. It's all breath and bitterness.

"Alright," he concedes, "it's more fun with company. What do you say, Juniper Pickett? Do you want to blow their small-town minds?"

There are a million reasons to say no. All the secrets I'm hiding, for one. Like why I came back here. What I'm running from. Then, there's *the body.* Those two words ring in my ears. I want to ask him if he's heard any more about the investigation. If I'll be arrested and if he'll visit me in jail. I want to ask him if he knows the bones belong to Blair, the girl he loved.

Instead, I point to my retro costume. "I can't wear this."

He looks amused. "I thought it was a bold choice. If I'd known you were going with a nineties theme, I would've worn my cargo pants and Doc Martens."

"You never owned Doc Martens." I feel myself smiling without meaning to. "I don't think I ever saw you in anything but Wranglers and cowboy boots."

"Well, then…" He gives himself an approving once-over. "You tell me, Ms. School Psychologist, what do the kids say nowadays? *My fit is fleeky.*"

"Don't ever say that again."

He's still grinning when he asks, "Does that mean you're in, Pickett?"

"I'm in."

CHAPTER ELEVEN

WHILE we're still miles outside of town, the Sweetbriar Football Stadium illuminates the night sky. Friday-night lights. That's Sweetbriar's version of the big city. Back in high school, I spent my Fridays holed up in my bedroom listening to sad love songs and plotting my escape, except for the one time Bonnie dragged me to the homecoming game. It had scarred me for life. For the rest of junior year, nobody let me forget it. Especially not Blair. I wonder if Wyatt remembers. I hope to God he doesn't.

I wring my hands in my lap, grateful I didn't let him talk me into wearing that ridiculous outfit. He waited in the truck, blasting George Strait, while I quickly showered and dressed in clothing that wasn't two decades old. Blue jeans, flowy white tank, sandals. Clothing that implied at least a semblance of normalcy.

"How many of our classmates do you think will show?" My question doesn't sound as casual as I hoped.

"You nervous?"

I shrug as if I can't be bothered, but it's obvious I'm on edge. My foot hasn't stopped tapping against the floorboard, and my thoughts are just as jumpy; popping up in my head and disappearing again.

"I'm sure Duane told everyone about last night. They'll all be talking about it. About me." World weary, I lean back against the seat and sigh. "I guess some things never change."

Wyatt drives in silence, his face darkening with each mile. Something's brewing.

"Who cares what they think?" he finally asks when we're so close to the stadium I can hear the music. The laughter.

"*I* care."

"But why?"

"You obviously don't."

Wyatt turns into the parking lot and chooses a spot on the end with plenty of room for the pickup. As the truck idles, my breath hitches in my chest. I tell myself to anchor to reality. It's not that crowded. Fifteen cars, at most. But my heart starts racing, and fifteen looks like fifty.

"Breathe." Wyatt lays his hand on my bobbing knee, stilling it.

"I am breathing."

"Now you are."

We lock eyes, and no time has passed. We're ten years old, sitting on his kitchen floor, and I'm stitching the gash the monster left on his forehead. The wrong end of a belt buckle will do that. The needle pierces his skin, and he's squeezing my hand. Trying not to make a sound. I'm shushing him. *Don't wake him up.*

Wyatt breaks first, dropping his gaze. He takes his hand away, sets it back on the wheel. "I used to care too, June. Way too much. Then, I stopped. Your dad helped me with that."

"He did?"

"He helped me a lot. I helped him too. We spent a lot of time together." The hitch in his voice breaks me. "Honestly, he was my best friend. My only friend."

I shouldn't be jealous, but I am. Where was my father when I needed help? When I needed a friend. "I didn't realize you'd been assisting in the workshop."

"Oh, I wasn't. You know I'm terrible at science." He chuckles and ignores my confusion. "So anyway, one day, I was going on about how everybody in town just assumes I'm the same person I was back then. A drunk idiot like my dad. And every time I walk into Wal-Mart or Rosarita's or the goddamned library, they're all whispering about me behind my back. You know what Eugene told me? *Nobody's that important, Wyatt. Even Albert Einstein put his pants on one leg at a time.*"

I snort. "That helped?"

"It did. Plus, I started going to therapy. Online. With some lady in Houston. She specializes in treating children of alcoholics. That was his idea too."

I blink at him, trying to process. I can't hide my utter shock. Eugene Pickett didn't do touchy-feely. He didn't do feelings, period. As for my career as a school psychologist, that only made sense to him because it was a practical profession with job security. Mainly because he thought I spent my days getting rich kids into the Ivies, and the world would never run out of rich kids.

"Are you sure we're talking about the same guy?" I say.

A knock on my window startles me. Stock-still, like a wounded wildebeest, I don't dare move.

"Is that Juniper? Oh. My. God. Christi was right. It *is* you."

"Well, we've been spotted." Wyatt raises his eyebrows at me. "There's no hiding now."

"What about running? Is there running?" I laugh, but I'm not really joking. I would gladly run the ten miles back to Saw Mill Road. When I finally turn my head to the window and realize who's waiting for me, panic takes hold again.

"It's Bonnie," I tell Wyatt. As if he can't see her there, waving maniacally. She thinks she still knows me. She has no idea who I am and what I've done. "I can't do this."

"Yes, you can," he says, before he opens the door to the past. To *my* past. To the cauldron of hellfire and brimstone. "Remember, one leg at a time."

CHAPTER TWELVE

FOUR YEARS UNTIL GRADUATION

"PLEASE don't make me go." I pull the covers up to my chin and make a sad puppy-dog face. At the foot of the bed, Bert whines. He's a good boy, helping me sell it. "My stomach hurts."

But my dad isn't buying. "C'mon, June. It'll be fun." He holds up the brochure the school mailed out a month ago with our permission slips. "It's Wave World. The world's best waterpark."

Since he penned his name at the bottom, I'd been praying for a hurricane. A bomb threat. An alien invasion. Anything to get me out of the eighth-grade field trip.

When I roll my eyes, he adds, "You love that place."

I don't have the heart to say I *loved* that place. Past tense. When Mom was still alive and I was just a kid who fit in her lap on the innertube floating down Snake River. I stuffed myself with funnel cake and fell asleep in the back seat on the long car ride home without a care. Now, I despise Wave World, and its stupid *Serious Splash*,

Serious Fun slogan. For me, it's either sit by the kiddie pool alone in my oversized T-shirt, dangling my feet in the water, or risk utter humiliation, parading around in last year's swimsuit that makes me look like a stuffed sausage.

"Seriously, Dad. I feel nauseous." It rolls off my tongue because it's not a lie.

"Juniper." He gives me the serious-dad voice, which I haven't heard in a while. It's actually kind of nice. Like maybe he actually cares. "I don't have time to argue. I'm onto something new. Something big. I need to get back to the workshop. Now, get up and get dressed. Mrs. Schumacher said to have you at the bus by seven thirty."

Another wave of sickness rolls over me as I play out the three-hour bus ride to Wave World. It's a special kind of hell, where everyone sits in pairs—boyfriend, girlfriend, best friend—but me. Ever since first grade, when Duane stuck bubblegum in Bonnie's hair at the Houston zoo, her mother keeps her at home on class-trip days. Which means I'll have to sit next to Mrs. Schumacher, who smells like stale cigarette smoke.

"What if I throw up on the bus? Or in the water? I'd create a biohazard."

Dad sighs and shakes his head. I take it as a sign I'm wearing down his resistance.

"Well, I'm sure the folks at Wave World have seen worse."

"That's not making me feel any better. Who knows what sort of bacteria are floating around out there in *Germ* World?"

"Just steer clear of the kiddie pool. You'll be fine."

Little does he know I'll be posted up there all day, enduring the shrieks and the squeals and the colossal meltdowns. Sidestepping the landmines—the used popsicle sticks, the juice boxes, the soggy diapers—while dodging the barbs of my classmates as they pass by. He has no clue. "I'll bet you wouldn't make *stupid* Diane Brownmiller go on the *stupid* class trip if she didn't feel good."

Now, I've done it. Insulted last year's star research assistant. The girl I referred to in my head as his new daughter.

"You're in the eighth grade now, June. You're not a little girl anymore. You need to stop acting like one." He glowers at me from the doorway, softening only after he hears me sniffle. "I left a few bucks in an envelope on the counter if you want to get a treat. What were those things you and Mom liked so much?"

I forget I'm pretending to be sick. I forget I'm angry. I forget about Wave World too. My whole body tenses the way it always does when he mentions her. The few times he's mentioned her. It's like a shot of ice water down my back. I see her legs, plain as day, sticking out from beneath the overturned tractor. I hear the engine still running. It doesn't seem real, but it is. It *was.*

"You know, they fry them up. Douse them in powdered sugar. If you ask me, it's a heart attack waiting to happen, but the two of you used to—"

"Funnel cake."

"That's right. Get yourself one of those. Or whatever you want."

Suddenly, Wave World beckons to me like an oasis in the desert. I want to be there. I want to be anywhere but here, looking at him, hearing him talk about Mom like it's nothing. Like he does it all the time. Like she might be in the next room making breakfast in her fancy gray suit with her bank badge and American-flag pin on the lapel. I toss off the covers and hop out of bed, already dressed in a T-shirt and jean shorts, my blue swimsuit underneath.

Dad doesn't even notice my obvious lie. "Hurry it up," he says. "Time and tide and buses to Wave World wait for no man."

A rowdy cheer erupts when the massive blue Wave World sign appears out the bus window. Mrs. Schumacher pats me on the arm. "We're almost there, dear."

I nod, tuck my Goosebumps book into my backpack, and prepare for battle. At least she doesn't expect me to be excited, she knows what a loser I am. As she passes out our tickets and rattles off the usual marching orders—*return to the bus by four o'clock, stay with a buddy, don't embarrass Sweetbriar Middle School… that means you, Duane*—I plot my strategy.

The driver opens the door, and it's go time. First student off the bus, first through the turnstiles, exactly as I planned it. I score a table with an umbrella at the outer boundary of the kiddie pool, as far from the main thoroughfare as I can manage. Once the others pass by and into the belly of the park, I'll be in the clear. Out of sight, out of mind, out of the line of fire. I take a seat with my book in hand and prepare to wait out the day. Maybe it won't be so bad after all. Maybe I'll even get a funnel cake.

"What the heck are you doing?" Wyatt appears from behind the mushroom fountain, his chestnut hair already wet. He gives it a shake in my direction.

My eyes dart around the perimeter, searching for the others, but it's just him, shirtless. When did he get so muscly?

"What does it look like? I'm reading." I make a show of dabbing the droplets from the laminated book cover with my beach towel. Anything to avoid looking at his broad shoulders, his bare chest. "And trying to stay dry."

"Yeah, but why?" He flops down in the chair next to me.

My face gets hot. I hope he doesn't notice that it's been happening a lot lately. Like I'm allergic to him, but in a good way. Not that it matters. Bonnie says Blair has a crush on him, and I'm… well… *me.*

"In case you hadn't noticed, June, this is a water park, not a library."

"Wait. This *isn't* a library? These *aren't* bookshelves? You *aren't* a librarian?" I make a face of mock horror.

"Ha, ha. But for real, aren't you going on any rides?"

I know he's only being nice, but I need to get rid of him now. The longer he sits here, the less invisible I become. Me surviving a day at Wave World depends on my invisibility.

"No, it's not my thing. I'll be fine right here. Dry and safely planted on the ground."

"Wanna know a secret?" He leans in. "I hate Wave World."

Before I can ask him why, the devil materializes on the walkway in front of us. She's blonde and tan and straight out of the pages of *Teen* magazine with her red-polka-dot bikini and heart-shaped sunglasses. Flanked by her henchwomen, Blair stops and wiggles her fingers at Wyatt.

"Hey, Landry, wanna do the Devil's Drop with me? Or are you too busy hanging out with your *girlfriend?*" The way she says it implies the obvious: that I'm too disgusting to be anyone's girlfriend and certainly not his.

I glance down at my shapeless body, hidden under my T-shirt. My stomach stretches against my suit. My thighs stick out like ham hocks. And those are the parts I can see. This morning, I spent ten minutes spackling makeup onto my pimpled forehead.

"Wanna go?" he asks me.

I shake my head fast, hoping he'll have mercy on me. That he'll leave me in peace with R. L. Stine. "I told you. I don't like rides."

Blair clears her throat with intention, then scowls at me like I'm a wad of chewed up bubblegum stuck to her shoe. "June bugs don't do water. They don't swim. They don't float. They just sink and drown."

"Well, I'm not going unless June goes. If she agrees, I'm in." It's easy for him to say—he rides bulls for fun. Bulls that weigh over a ton and want to stomp his brains out. For Wyatt, the Devil's Drop might as well be a float down a lazy river. "Whaddya say, June?"

"What are you doing?" I mutter, utterly confused.

"I want you to have fun for a change. Loosen up a little." When he grabs my hand and tugs me up out of the chair, I nearly sprout wings. "One ride," he says. "Then, you can bury your nose in a book for the rest of the day."

I glance at Blair, annoyed with myself for thinking I need her permission. She doesn't even notice. She's too busy ogling Wyatt's pecs.

"Whatever," she says with a flip of her hand. "But I'm warning you, she'll probably break the slide."

"Or get stuck halfway down," Christi adds. "Can you imagine? They'd have to bring in one of those cranes to rescue her."

Jessica and Christi burst into giggles, but Blair doesn't laugh. Her mouth is a straight pink line. I decide right then. I'm going down the Devil's Drop, even if it kills me.

MY bookbag safely tucked in a locker, I trail behind Wyatt and Blair up the six flights of winding stairs to the top of the slide. With each step, my anxiety ratchets up a notch until my head feels light and my vision blurs. Blair clings to Wyatt's arm, shriek-laughing and tossing her ponytail over her shoulder like a maniacal Barbie. I wish he could see through her, but he's too dang nice, and she's too dang sparkly. Meanwhile, every ten seconds, a new rider screeches down the body slide, disappears into the looping tunnel, and lands with a splash in the pool below.

At the top platform, Blair makes a show of reading the safety sign aloud. She turns to me and gives me a once-over—I'm still wearing my T-shirt, of course—then back to the ride attendant. "Better make sure Junebug meets the three-hundred-pound weight limit. Who knows what she's hiding under there."

The attendant frowns, then rolls her eyes. I like her.

"Can me and Wyatt go down together?" Blair asks.

"No. Single riders only."

Blair sticks out her lower lip, but the attendant holds firm, unmoved by her childish display.

"Fine, if you want to be a stick in the mud about it."

"Those are the rules, miss. You're welcome to find another way down if you can't follow them."

As Blair fumes, the attendant winks at me over her head. I *really* like her.

Wyatt glances back at me with a sheepish grin. "You still up for this?"

My body screams *no*, but my head bobs up and down, trying to convince him. I will not let Blair ruin this for me.

"Do you want to go first?" he asks me.

I wait for Blair to pipe up, to push me aside. She always wants to go first, and she always gets what she wants. *That's what happens when you're a daddy's girl*, I'd overheard Jessica tell Christi in the girls' bathroom. *Her stepdad never says no to her. I heard he bought her a real-life pony for her eighth birthday.*

Unexpectedly, Blair sidles up next to me and slings her arm across my shoulders. As much as I want to swat her away like a pesky fly, I'm not immune to the Blair Lennox fairy dust. She smiles and—stupid me—I actually smile back. It's like the last year never happened. The relentless teasing, the snide remarks, the mocking laughter all gone in an instant, eclipsed by her bright light.

Blair waves Wyatt toward the slide. "You go first, Landry. I'll take care of Juniper."

That snaps me out of her orbit and back to earth. The place where I'm me and she's her, and when our paths cross it always ends in my humiliation. Now she's made physical contact and used my given name without insulting me. No doubt she's up to something.

But Wyatt appears oblivious to my silent screams for help. "That okay with you, June?"

What can I say but, "Yeah, sure! See you at the bottom."

"That's the spirit." He holds up his hand for a high five that makes it all worth it. Then, with a signal from the attendant, he whoops and pushes himself down the slide.

"You can't be serious." Blair drops her arm as soon as he disappears into the tunnel. "You actually think he likes you."

"*What?*" My heart starts beating fast, the way it always does when she turns her meanness on me.

"You're forgetting what you told me. Last year in the creek bed. *Remember?* Your little crush. It's obvious, and it's pathetic, Junebug. Don't embarrass yourself. Wyatt's only being nice to you because your dad asked his dad to make him."

Reeling, I step back from her and stumble over my troll feet. An ugly laugh bursts out of her. It enrages me, and that rage gives me courage.

"I remember the creek bed. I remember *everything*," I hiss.

Blair's eyes widen, and I revel in the thrill of shocking her.

"Ladies." The attendant heaves a heavy sigh. "There's a very long line behind you, so let's move it along. Who's next?"

"You're up, Junebug." Blair gives me a small push forward. "Think thin."

I feel her staring at me as I position myself at the start, gripping the sides of the slide as the cool water rushes around my legs. No one knows my mom and I rode the Devil's Drop four times in a row the last summer we came here. That the ride never scared me. But that was before. Before I realized how quickly life can change. How it only takes a few seconds to lose it all.

"Whenever you're ready," the attendant says. "Push off and keep your arms folded across your chest."

"How long will it take to get to the bottom?"

"Less than fifteen seconds. You'll blink, and it's over." Still, she seems to sense my uncertainty. "Don't let her bully you into it. You can always walk down the stairs if you want."

"I'm okay," I tell her, but I don't mean it. Because in fifteen seconds, anything can happen. A tractor can overturn in the garden you planted and crush you beneath its weight. Ribs crack. Lungs collapse. The heart wall ruptures. That's it. Game over. You go to heaven and leave your poor daughter alone.

As I push off, I clasp my arms to my chest, squeeze my eyes shut, and begin: *Hydrogen, helium, lithium, beryllium…*

I'm flying.

Boron, carbon, nitrogen…

The darkness of the tunnel envelops me.

Oxygen, fluorine, neon, sodium—

Suddenly, I squidge to a stop. From outside the tunnel, I hear the methodical *bee boo* sound of an alarm. I try to push myself forward, but the flow of water has stopped. Panic grips me. I am officially in the middle of my worst nightmare.

I'm stuck.

In the tunnel.

On Devil's Drop.

"Hello, miss, are you okay?" The voice of the attendant travels down the tunnel from what sounds like miles away.

"No." I will myself not to cry, but tears thicken in my throat. "The water stopped. I can't move."

"It's alright. The slide has been temporarily disabled because the emergency shut-off button was activated."

"The *what?*"

"There's a button to keep you safe in case of malfunction."

A sob pushes its way up, and I let out a strangled whimper. "*Did it?* Malfunction?"

"Everything is fine. We'll get you moving again in no time." Then, "What's your name, miss?"

"Juniper but everyone calls me… June."

"Okay. Stay calm, June."

Stay calm. It seems easy enough until the stark quiet awakens the thought gremlins. What if the slide collapses the way Blair predicted? What if I plummet to the concrete below? What if they *do* have to bring in a crane to get me out of this thing? Of all the what-ifs, there's one that makes my stomach ache. What if Blair was right about Wyatt? What if he's only pretending to be my friend?

As I stare up at the ceiling of the tunnel and contemplate my fate, it hits me like a brick to the face. I saw the red emergency button on the landing near the slide. Blair must've seen it too, the perfect weapon within arm's reach. She pushed it. She did this to me. She trapped me here.

I hate her. *Magnesium, aluminum, silicon…*

I hate her so much. *Phosphorus, sulfur, chlorine…*

A siren interrupts my third recitation of the periodic table.

"June, are you doing alright down there?"

I imagine my classmates congregating at the pool below, pointing and laughing. Knowing Blair, she raced down the stairs to tell everyone the news. I am not alright. I'm mortified. Humiliated. Scared out of my mind. Cold too. Though the tunnel feels warm from the sun, my wet T-shirt clings to my body, and my arms are freckled with goosebumps.

"I guess so," I hear myself say.

"Good. You're doing great."

But I'm not doing anything unless *not* having a complete nervous breakdown counts.

"The fire department has arrived. Along with our team, they'll be assessing the ride for any safety issues."

"How long will that take?"

"We're not sure yet. I'll let you know as soon as I find out."

I take a big, shaky breath.

"In the meantime, someone is here to keep you company."

"Wyatt?" I ask without thinking. In the silence that follows, I'm grateful no one can see me. Of course it's not him. He zipped down the slide and splashed into the pool like a normal person. A very handsome normal person.

"It's Blair, silly. Your friend."

I must have hit my head or passed out from shock. Maybe I *am* having a nervous breakdown.

"I told them how anxious you get sometimes. They made everybody else evacuate the slide, but they let me stay for emotional support…"

Blair keeps talking, but I can't hear her. My brain short-circuited after the word *friend.*

"June? Are you there?" Blair uses her sugary-sweet voice. It's so convincing.

"I'm here. Where else would I be?"

"Good news! The fire department gave the all-clear. I'll meet you down at the bottom with Wyatt."

I barely have time to process the news before the attendant warns me to brace for the incoming stream of water. It jets down the slide, carrying me with it. In seconds, it spits me out into the pool.

I hold my breath when I go under. When my head breaks the surface, I wait for the jeers, the cruel jokes, the spiteful snickers. More self-conscious than ever, I keep my body hidden beneath the water. The fire truck pulls away as a new line forms on the stairs to Devil's Drop.

Blair swims over to me with Jessica and Christi dog-paddling behind her.

"Are you okay?" she asks. "I heard some bratty kid hit the emergency button because his mom told him he was too short for the slide."

I stare at her, my mouth slightly hung open. I nod.

"What a little jerk." Jessica rolls her eyes. "I hope he doesn't grow an inch until he's thirty."

The three girls float away from me, giggling, as Wyatt drops in from the side of the pool. I can hardly look at him.

"I'm sorry I made you go on that stupid slide," he says. "I told you I hate Wave World. Nothing good happens here."

Still curious, I'm too mad now to ask him why. I don't even have a good reason to be angry at him. I just am. "It's fine. I'm fine. You don't have to make me feel better."

"It sure was nice of Blair to wait up there with you." He seems shy all of a sudden. "She's pretty cute, huh?"

"Uh… yeah. I guess so."

On cue, Blair executes the perfect underwater handstand, her painted toes pointed to the sky. When she emerges from the water, she gives a bow, and her audience applauds. They've moved right past me, all of them. I'm a speed bump, practically invisible.

"Jessica said she likes me." Wyatt wiggles his eyebrows, but I can tell he's serious. His cheeks are bright red. "What do you think I should do?"

I let myself sink to the bottom of the pool like a cannon ball, blowing bubbles until Wyatt gives up and swims away. I bob in the water for a while. Waiting for anyone, even Mrs. Schumacher, to notice me. My fingers and toes turn pruney.

By the time the bus pulls into the Sweetbriar Middle School parking lot, the whispers make their way to the front. To Debbie and Tara's seat, the one right behind a snoring Mrs. Schumacher.

Debbie says, "I heard Wyatt asked Blair to go steady."

Tara replies, "I heard that Blair said yes."

CHAPTER THIRTEEN

NOW

THE moment I open the truck door, Bonnie squeals and launches herself at me like a missile intended for maximum impact. The last time I saw her she wrote in my yearbook with a flower pen and dashed off to take photos with her new best friend, Jennifer Riley. After they met on the tennis team freshman year, I'd become old news. Truth be told, I always suspected she was waiting to trade me in for someone better. Prettier, skinnier, normal-er. Someone who wasn't nicknamed after a scarab beetle.

She releases me, then takes me by the shoulders and gives me a firm shake. "I can't believe it's really you. You look fantastic! What have you been up to?"

I give her a once-over, searching for signs of the girl she once was. But her frizzy brown hair looks sleek and shiny in a high ponytail, and she's traded rompers and Laura Ashley dresses for a pair of skinny jeans.

"Uh, I…" Getting fired. Digging up a grave. Deflecting the sheriff's inquisition.

"Come on." She drags me away by the hand before I can answer. "We have all night to catch up."

I glance over my shoulder at Wyatt. With a wide grin, he mimes putting on a pants leg.

Walking side by side with Bonnie is a comfort. Like pulling on an old favorite sweater to find that it fits you just the same.

"Do you live in Sweetbriar?" I ask her.

"Heck no." But then she laughs. "Adamsville. I made it a whole fifteen miles away. Not like you, Miss San Fran, living it up in the big city."

I shrug. Apparently, the news of my demise travels more slowly than anticipated.

"You actually did it, June. You got out of here. I always knew you would."

As we approach the stadium, the sound of Bryan Adams crooning from a boom box mingles with the chatter. His raspy tenor singing "Everything I Do" takes me back to where I don't want to go. To graduation night. To what happened after.

"Alright, spill it." Bonnie stops short of the gate and leans in to whisper, "What have you heard?"

Naturally, I feign ignorance.

"About the body?" she asks. "Do you think it's really her?"

I know which *her* she means. And I know that it is. *Her.* "I suppose it might be."

"Damn." Bonnie shakes her head, looking more affected than I would've imagined. To her, Blair is probably just a hazy memory. To me, she's in technicolor. "I always thought she was still alive. That she ran away and changed her name and was living a glamorous life in New York City or Paris or… heck, maybe even Tuscaloosa. All these years, and I never imagined her gone. *Dead* gone."

"Some people are like that," I say. "They seem charmed. Invincible. Like nothing bad could ever happen to them. But bad things do happen. To everyone. No one's immune. Not even Blair Lennox."

Bonnie looks at me a little too long. I wonder if I've said the wrong thing. If I've given too much away. She keeps quiet while we walk through the chain-link gate toward the field. On the home-team sideline a small crowd mills around a few picnic tables. I recognize Duane and Christi. Wyatt, of course. The others are familiar strangers. Caricatures of people I used to know. People I forgot on purpose.

Bonnie must sense it. My urge to run. She stops before we get too close and asks, "Have you kept in touch with anyone?" As if she and Wyatt weren't among the only signatures in my yearbook.

I shake my head. "Not really. My dad told me bits here and there, but…"

"What about Wyatt? He and your dad got pretty close after—"

"I'd rather hear about you." I don't want to talk about my father—not here, not now, not with her. "Does Jennifer still live close by?"

"She passed away last year from breast cancer. We weren't really in touch anymore, but her daughter went to sleep-away camp with Bella."

"And Bella is…"

Bonnie beams. "My youngest."

In a blink, I'm face to face with a family photo on a phone screen. One of those portraits of carefully orchestrated spontaneity. Bella suspended mid-air, swinging gleefully, between her proud parents.

"This is Bryce, my husband," she tells me. Flanking them, two boys. Miniature versions of Bryce, clad in the same shade of blue with the same mischievous grin. "And these are my sons, Brett and Baxter."

As Bonnie scrolls through her gallery of domesticity, it shocks me how inadequate I feel, how alien. How far behind. It turns out nothing's changed at all. Bonnie has built an entire B-themed family, and I'm completely and utterly alone. A jobless, childless, husbandless orphan.

"We have two Frenchies, Basil and Bandit."

I can't even keep a plant alive.

"Oh, and we just renovated our kitchen. Paid an arm and a leg for a granite countertop, but it's stunning, isn't it?"

I can't remember the last time I cooked a meal for anyone other than myself. My poor laminate countertop mostly serves as a makeshift desk.

"This is from Brett's kinder graduation... and here's Bella at her first soccer game... and..." Bonnie pauses on another stunning family photo taken at the beach. One of the boys sits atop his father's shoulders. "Okay, I'll stop now. I'm being such a momzilla."

"Not at all. You have a beautiful family." I recognize the twinge of sadness in my voice. All these years later, I'm still an outsider. It's the reason I'm here. The reason none of my boyfriends lasted beyond six months. The reason I made all the wrong decisions with Macy.

I can't bear the pity in Bonnie's eyes, so I stride ahead and she follows. The stadium looks smaller than I remember. Fifteen rows of bleachers on each side of the field. A small press box and a scoreboard, proclaiming the Sweetbriar state championships.

"I'm surprised they never upgraded the football field." I drag two folding chairs to the twenty-yard line, a safe distance from the rest of the crowd.

"Oh, they did." Bonnie chuckles. "This is the practice field now. The new stadium is on the other side of town. You know, the funny thing is they built it the year after we graduated, and they haven't had a winning season since."

"Sounds like karma to me." I gaze out toward the end zone, remembering Blair with a homecoming mum the size of her head pinned to her cheer uniform. One of the ribbons read LANDRY in silver letters. I wanted to rip it off and choke her with it.

"Bulldogs for life!" Eric shouts from behind the barbecue grill. He and Duane and another former meathead named Travis bark in unison, as they clink bottles of Shiner Bock.

Bonnie groans, but it's more amusement than intimidation. To her, they pose no threat. They never have. To me, their revelry feels predatory. Every sound they make raises my neck hair.

"Remember Coach Mac?" She leans in to point out the older man who just arrived. As he slaps Travis on the back, it's impossible to ignore the flex of his oversized biceps. His boulder shoulders protruding from either side of a Sweetbriar Bulldogs tank top. "AKA Big Mac."

I giggle at the silly nickname we had for him back then. Before every home game he'd rile up the sidelines by downing three cheese burgers from the local Dairy Queen. It was the closest thing our little town had to McDonald's, and Coach Mac was our Tom Landry.

"Toby McLean? He's still coaching?"

"Not anymore. He works at the new CrossFit gym. But I'm pretty sure he's still a regular on the bodybuilding circuit."

"Clearly." I quirk my eyebrows. "He looks like the kind of guy who lifts heavy machinery for fun. But good for him. He must be over fifty by now."

"C'mon, Coach Mac, it's tradition!" Duane hoists a burger over his head, chanting, "Big Mac! Big Mac! Big Mac!" until Coach McLean throws up his hands and surrenders.

"Fine. Just one for old time's sake. I'm vegan now."

Bonnie and I watch the burger disappear into Coach McLean's mouth in four large bites. Naturally, Duane and his crew erupt into cheers as if the man's just cured cancer or won an Olympic medal. I look around for Jessica, Duane's better half. They'd exchanged their vows at the Baptist church one month after graduation. That same summer, Dad had found Duane in the pasture with a self-inflicted, bullet-shattered femur that effectively ended his dream of NFL stardom. To hear my father tell it, Duane never did get that hog, which gave me infinitely more satisfaction than earning my doctorate degree. I find Jessica in her happy place at the center of an adoring crowd, showing off her new designer handbag with its recognizable chocolate-brown color and LV logo. Either it's a fake or Duane sold a kidney, because I'm fairly certain Sweetbriar's finest do not earn Louis Vuitton salaries.

Bonnie gives me a nudge. "Do you remember all the rumors about the football team?"

"Rumors?" I play dumb.

Wyatt saves me when he motions me over to the picnic tables. Two plates in hand, he straddles the bench and pats the seat next to him.

"Looks like you've been summoned," Bonnie says. "What's going on with you two anyway?"

"Nothing. He's just being friendly."

"Mm-hmm." She gives me a sly smile. "So you don't still have a crush on him then?"

"On Wyatt? No, of course not. That was a long time ago. A lot happened. He spent ten years in prison, Bonnie. He's an ex-con."

"A dangerously handsome ex-con."

I laugh her off and make a hasty getaway. Though I have to admit, she's not wrong. Objectively speaking. By the time I reach the table, Wyatt isn't alone, and he doesn't look happy about it. He's got a plastic fork in a death grip in one hand, and a bottle of water in the other. He jabs at his plate, angrily spearing an innocent potato.

"Holy shit. Christi was right." Eric gapes at me as if I've descended to the field on a light beam. "I was just telling Wyatt how surprised I was to see him here. But you, man oh man, that's a real shocker. I honestly can't remember the last time I saw you."

I remember it precisely. He had a full head of hair then and less paunch around the middle, but I still see the same cruel boy who raised the barrel of his BB gun at sweet Midnight and threw tater tots at my head in the lunchroom. Who made up a song about how I was as ugly as a June bug. "Yeah, it's been a while since graduation night."

"That long ago, huh? Time sure does fly. Can you believe we were supposed to be digging up that time capsule about now? Poor Blair. May she finally rest in peace."

When Christi sidles up beside him—with her big blonde hair and tiny shorts—he forgets all about our murdered classmate and his wishes for her eternal salvation. Teeth bared, he preens like a peacock. Christi wiggles her fingers at me as her eyes pinball between me and Wyatt. In my head, I hear her mocking me. *You may actually have a chance.*

"She's a school counselor now, honey."

"*Psychologist*," Wyatt interjects. "At a private school in San Francisco."

"Well, I'll be damned. Good for you, Junebug."

Christi elbows him, correcting him under her breath, but her smirk gives her away.

"Oh, sorry, June," Eric says. "My bad. I'm glad to hear you're doing so well out in California."

"*So* well," Christi repeats. "I'm surprised you decided to come back at all. And what a shame your visit got off to such a tragic start. I can't imagine what a shock it must've been for you to… you know… find Blair like you did." She plows on, barely stopping to breathe. "I'm just glad her parents don't have to wonder anymore. For years, me and Jess took Lydia out to eat on Blair's birthday just to get her out of the house. We became her honorary daughters, I suppose, trying to fill the hole Blair left. But who could ever live up to such a…" Christi sniffles. "Oh, here I go again, carrying on. I don't intend to make you feel any guiltier than you obviously already do. I mean, you look like you've been through it."

"I…" Twenty years, and I'm still tongue-tied, hostage to a mean girl. It's worse that Wyatt has to see it. That he's staring at me like that.

"If you ask me," he says, "June looks beautiful."

Christi's eyes bug, and she shuts her mouth for one glorious second before she flits back to the group of women gathered near the bleachers. They close ranks around her, giggling and casting pointed glances in my direction. Duane swoops in, drunk and unruly. He dips Jessica and plants a wet kiss on her mouth before she pushes him off with a disgusted grunt. Undeterred, he laughs and claps the grill tongs at the rest of them. They shriek and scatter like crows. It's high school all over again.

"He's hammered," Wyatt says. "As usual."

"You would know," Eric mutters under his breath. "Hey, June, did Christi tell you about our daughter, Aubrey? She'll be a senior next year, and she's hellbent on the University of Texas. We were hoping you could take a look at her application, review her essays. Maybe write one of those letters of recommendation when the time comes. Christi wants me to get your email."

"Sure. Whatever you need. You know, UT's Dean of Students graduated from Ellington Academy back in the day, so I could even put in a good word for her. Not that she needs it, of course. I'm sure she's a shoo-in." Wyatt frowns at me while I paste on my best fake smile and add, "Happy to help an old friend."

"Wow. *Really?*"

Eric passes me his cellphone, and I type my email into the contact he created for me: JUNEBUG SCHOOL COUNSELOR. He doesn't know it won't work anymore. That they cut off my access days ago. That I'm officially disgraced. When he extends his hand, I take it and channel my rage through my fingers, squeezing hard.

"That's so—ouch! That's quite a grip you've got there."

Wyatt snickers. "Your burger's getting cold, June."

"I'll leave you two alone to catch up." Eric backpedals away from us, pointing at Wyatt. "I'm sure Landry has a lot of tall tales to tell. Did you know he used to work in the death chamber down in Huntsville?"

Eric leaving with my useless email address might be the best part of the reunion so far. I celebrate with a bite of a lukewarm burger and a heavily mayonnaised potato. A sip of soda from an ice-cold can. "I haven't had a Dr. Pepper in years."

"It used to be your favorite." Wyatt fixates on his plate, long-faced. "Hey, what he said about the death chamber… it's—"

"He's an idiot."

Wyatt's laugh takes me by surprise. It's half boy, half man, and it makes me feel free even here in this place with these people who don't know me anymore. Who never knew me. Who only thought they did.

"Thanks for forcing me to come tonight. It hasn't been awful."

"Well, if I knew you'd set the bar that low..." Wyatt motions to the center of the field, where a few of our classmates slow dance on a small portable stage. "Can you still two-step?"

Seventeen-year-old Juniper dies a little when the music changes from a Faith Hill ballad to a well-worn Los Del Rio tune. "No, but I can Macarena."

Wyatt laughs again, and I follow him to the dance floor.

THE next hour passes in a blur. I dance and smile and reminisce. Tommy Hansen—voted teacher's pet—works as a loan officer at the Sweetbriar Community Bank. Tara Paulsen teaches kindergarten. Turns out that Christi and Eric aren't the only odd couple. Nerdy David Minkowitz married hippie Luna Zamora. I hear about all the ups and downs that life can take in twenty years. Breakups, breakthroughs, Botox, and babies. I tell my spiel—school psychologist, San Francisco, happily single—the way I practiced it in my head, and no one doubts me. And when Wyatt spins me around to "Mr. Vain," I start to believe the last two weeks never happened. Even the black cloud of Blair's disappearance seems to dissipate, leaving the class of 1997 momentarily free of its lingering gloom.

"Hear ye, hear ye..."

I stumble to a stop on the dance floor. Again the hair prickles on the back of my neck. Like a rabbit hiding in the grass, I freeze. But it's too late. Duane has me in his sights. Eyes locked on target, he takes a swig from his—*fourth, fifth, sixth?*—beer bottle. Then he wobbles up the steps to the first row of bleachers and leans over the railing. He tips back his head, raises his arms, and clears his throat. "Class of

19... 19... 1997... I have a very, very, *very* important announcement to make."

My stomach flip-flops at the sight of him. At the way his words roll, thick and slimy, off his tongue. At the way twenty-something heads turn toward his voice. But mostly, at the way he's still staring at me, glassy-eyed.

"Let's hear it, Dupree!" Travis yells from the stage, riling him up.

"Please don't encourage him," Jessica says before she hides her face.

Duane points his finger into the crowd. It weaves as if he's tracking a moving target and lands squarely on an open table six feet away from the stage. "Juniper Pickett." He steps up to the second row, sways, and nearly falls over. Then, he finds me again. "Junebug."

"Get down before you kill yourself." That's Wyatt talking.

But Duane doesn't listen. He climbs to the third row, toddling to the center of the bleachers. He still thinks he's the king of this place. It would be sad—pathetic, really—if he didn't scare me.

"Kill myself, huh? Real funny, isn't it, Junebug?" He chuckles at Wyatt. "You should ask *her* about that."

"Seriously, Duane." Bonnie appears beside me and puts a protective hand on my shoulder. "Leave her alone. You're being an asshole."

Red-faced, Jessica lets out a guttural cry of frustration, then flees to the bathrooms with her fancy purse on her arm and Christi at her heels.

"We dug up the time capsule, Junebug. We opened your letter." With surprising dexterity for a drunken fool, Duane slips his cellphone from his back pocket and holds it up toward the crowd.

The one-hundred-yard world I currently live in feels as small as a shoebox. As claustrophobic as a coffin.

"I took a picture of it. Whaddya say I read it? For old times' sake."

I shake my head. Can't stop shaking it.

"Or maybe you'd like to tell us what else you dug up last night. *Who* you dug up."

Time slows, but my heart races. It's drumming at a frenetic pace, the way it did that dreadful Wednesday afternoon two weeks ago at Ellington when Mrs. Mendoza staggered into the teachers' lounge during fourth period, slurring her words, and collapsed to the floor in a heap. I ran down the hall toward the nurse's office, passing three sick students doubled over at their lockers and another passed out on the steps. The scene unfolded just like this one. A bad horror movie, with me as the star.

An awkward silence falls over the stadium. There's only Trisha Yearwood and the sound of my desperate breathing. I shake off Bonnie's hand and bolt from the stage, fleeing for the exit. I don't look, but I hear him anyway. His accusation strikes me like a bullet in my back. Two bullets. Kill shots.

"You murdered Blair, Junebug. And you murdered her baby."

CHAPTER FOURTEEN

LIKE a runaway train, I tear through the parking lot toward Wyatt's truck. Of course, it's locked. Cursing, I veer off in the direction of the road. I hate Duane. I hate Sweetbriar. I hate myself. When I reach the pavement, I drop into the ditch and keep running. The tall grass folds under the weight of my frantic strides.

I start at the beginning with hydrogen, hoping I can drown out Duane's voice and the sound of my ugly crying. *You murdered Blair, Junebug. And you murdered her baby.*

"Helium, lithium, beryllium!" I shout as I run.

Her baby?

"Boron, carbon, nitrogen!" Between sobs, I struggle to catch my breath. Stars flicker at the edges of my vision.

I murdered a baby?

"I didn't murder anyone!" Lightheaded, I stop and put my hands on my knees. A few breaths later, I open my eyes, but the world keeps spinning round and round and round. Like a tire. Like a tire on a truck. Like a tire on Wyatt's truck.

He pulls up alongside me and yells out the open passenger window, "Get in."

"No." I wipe at my face, wet with tears and sweat and snot, and force myself to move. I hate Wyatt too.

"June." He honks the horn at me. "Get in the goddamn truck."

I keep my head down, tromping on legs of lead. "I'll walk."

"Ten miles? In the ditch? In the middle of a panic attack? C'mon, don't be stubborn. It'll be dark soon."

He's right. In another life, I would've stopped to enjoy the twilight. The orangey-blues of the sunset. The rising moon. The expanse of sky I never could see in San Francisco. My dad told me it was the dry air that made the colors so bright. But my mom called it Texas magic. Now, the beauty of it mocks me. I'm a stranger here. An impostor.

"What does it matter to you anyway? You only feel sorry for me." Sickeningly familiar, his pity dredges up a memory. "Just like you did that day at Wave World."

Wyatt hits the brakes, and the truck jolts to a stop next to me. "*What?* What are you talking about?"

Of course he wouldn't remember. "Never mind. Just go. Leave me alone." I shoo him away without looking up or slowing down. I will not surrender. I would sooner die out here on Farm to Market Road 57. "I said *go*."

"Yeah, I heard you. But there's no way in hell I'm leaving you. The way I see it, you've got two choices. You can either ride in the truck or I'll be driving behind you all the way home. Either way, you're not getting rid of me."

"You sure about that?" I cast a withering glance at him while I stalk through the ditch. "Remember, I *am* a murderer."

"Yeah. So am I."

AFTER ten long minutes, Wyatt honks at me again. Two insistent taps before he rolls down the passenger window. "Looks like a storm brewing in the west. You're gonna get wet, June."

As if I'm not already soaked with sweat. "Don't care."

"Suit yourself."

When the first raindrop hits my face, it's a relief. A cool kiss of mercy. I almost smile. Within seconds, that single drop turns into a torrential downpour. Thunder rumbles low in the distance.

Another blow of the horn, and Wyatt yells out, "What about getting fried by lightning? Do you care about that?"

Mud cakes the bottom of my sandals, making every step effortful. My soaked jeans stick to my body like a second skin. The sky illuminates for a heartbeat, and I see Mr. Cotter's red barn up ahead. Nine more miles till home.

Dejected and chilled to the bone, I emerge from the ditch and shrug my shoulders at the silhouette in the window. Wyatt idles the truck. The wiper blades make a shushing sound of despair. As I open the door, I say nothing. I have no intention of speaking. Not now. Possibly never again. Speaking is so overrated.

Wyatt passes me a blanket from the back seat, and I wrap it around my shivering body. He cranks the heat and drives slowly, the rain battering the windshield and washing across the two-lane roadway. He smartly doesn't breathe a word about Duane or Blair or the stupid reunion he dragged me to. I almost wish he would so I could maintain my indignance. I need fuel for my fire.

"Power's out," he announces when we make the turn onto Saw Mill Road.

Sure enough, the lights I left on in the entryway have gone dark. I can't even see the front door. The thought of spending the night alone in a thunderstorm in the pitch-black with the ghosts of the past terrifies me.

"It's fine. I have a flashlight. I'll light some candles. It'll be cozy."

"Damn, June. You sure are as stubborn as your daddy."

I huff at him.

"Let me come in with you, at least. Get you situated. It's raining cats and dogs."

"I don't need any help." The thunder rolls in the distance; another lightning strike illuminates the sky. "You've done enough for one night."

"You can admit you had fun. You said you did."

"Until I didn't. I shouldn't have gone. Now the whole town thinks I murdered Blair and buried her body in front of the school before I absconded to San Francisco."

"We don't even know for sure that it's Blair."

"Wyatt..." I let the rest of it go unspoken. Because he loved her. Because he must blame himself like I do.

The rain pounds on the roof of the truck like a stampede of wild cattle. Duane's voice breaks through, unwanted. I can't get rid of it. *You murdered Blair, Junebug. And you murdered her baby.*

"*Was* she pregnant?" I don't mean to say it out loud, but it's too much to hold inside. As soon as the words slip out, I lose it. At least Wyatt can't see me in the dark. The shake of my shoulders, the tremble of my lip. That's what I tell myself. But I feel his eyes on me, and I wonder if he can read the question blaring in my head. *Are you the father?*

"All I know is that I stopped trusting Duane in the first grade after he ate my favorite blue crayon and blamed it on me. He's full of shit, June."

I sniffle quietly. "And if he isn't?"

"Then that's even worse. He shouldn't be saying any of that to anyone. It's an ongoing investigation, and he's an officer of the law, as much as it pains me to admit."

An ongoing investigation. Who knew I'd find myself in the middle of two of those at the same time?

It hits me then that I'm still sitting in Wyatt's truck. That I'm soaking wet and exhausted. That I don't want to go inside. That I'm afraid of what Wyatt knows about me. And terrified of what he doesn't. "Do you think he read my time-capsule letter out loud after we left?"

Wyatt scoffs. "I think he passed out after we left. And if he didn't, Jessica knocked him upside the head a few times." After another furious roar of thunder, he turns to me. I can see my haggard reflection in the rain-streaked window behind him. "I have a generator at the cottage. Your dad would take me out behind the barn if I left you here by yourself."

"Fine. But you have to tell me about the death chamber."

"If you tell me what happened at Wave World."

I nod, but only because I'm freezing and it's pouring and the thought of a warm house is impossible to resist. "You really don't remember?" I ask, as the truck rumbles up the dirt road alongside the creek. Muddy water roils down the usually dry bed.

"I didn't say that."

HALFWAY between Wyatt's truck and the door to the cottage, I stop short, and my sandals slip in the mud. The rain breaks through the sopping-wet newspaper Wyatt gave me to cover my head, and I let out a frazzled groan. But I can't will myself forward with a pair of yellow eyes watching me from the porch.

"Is that a raccoon?" I shout, suddenly grateful Ellington required a rabies shot for staff and students last year after an incoming freshman was bitten by a coyote on the soccer field.

Wyatt runs past, pulling me along behind him. "C'mon, it's just Willie."

"Willie?"

We arrive on the porch, both of us breathless. A damp orange tomcat immediately addresses Wyatt with a mew of disdain.

"Willie Nelson. The last of your dad's old barn cats. He enjoys mice, sunbathing, and freedom. Rain, not so much. I usually let him wait out the storms in the house."

"He seems upset." Which isn't untrue, but it's me who's most unnerved. After the loss of Midnight my father had long insisted, *No more pets for me. I need to focus on my work.* It hurts to know how much he changed without telling me. But then, so did I.

"Nothing a can of tuna and a warm fire won't fix. Right, Willie?"

Willie regards me with skepticism while Wyatt turns the key in the lock and opens the door. I reach down to offer a gentle rub, but the cat scoots away from me and bolts inside as if he's seen a ghost.

CHAPTER FIFTEEN

THREE YEARS UNTIL GRADUATION

I close my biology textbook and return my study guide to its proper place in my notebook. Confident I'll ace the final tomorrow—I can draw a double helix in my sleep—I flop back on my pillow and stare at Luke Perry. It's so much better than looking at the empty foot of my bed where Bert used to curl up and snore during homework time.

"Only three more days, Luke." Three more days and thirty-six more school bells till summer. "Do you think I'll survive?"

Naturally, Luke doesn't answer. He responds the way he always does, with his flirty eyes and bad-boy smirk. Sometimes, I pretend he's my boyfriend. Dad didn't even notice when I hung the poster last month. I expected him to object. That he'd furrow his brow and say, *Really, June? Aren't you a little young for that show?* Then, I'd roll my eyes and tell him, *I'm in the ninth grade, Dad. Besides, everybody watches it.*

But that argument only happened in my head. Instead, Dad sulked after his newest fertilizer formulation killed his test crop of corn, which meant he then barely slept, hardly ate, and spent almost every waking hour in his workshop. Which is where he's been since the bus dropped me and Wyatt off at the corner two hours ago.

"Sorry about Bert," Wyatt had said as the bus pulled away, leaving us in a cloud of dust and gravel. "He was a good dog. He had a long life."

I didn't trust myself not to cry, so I only nodded. I'd found Bert under the huckleberry tree last weekend. He hadn't come when I'd called him. With Dad MIA, I'd struggled to carry the limp body back to the house myself, thinking about how my father had left me alone again. Like after Mom's accident, when I'd stupidly tried to save her. As if I could lift the two-ton tractor off her, and she'd be fine again.

"I picked out a real nice river stone for his grave, if you want to come see it later."

"Isn't your girlfriend coming over?" I never called her by her name. I couldn't bear it.

He shrugged. It's a sore spot between us. One that's best avoided. "My dad even let me use the chisel to put his name on it. We can take it out there together."

My heart swelled, picturing him hammering out Bert's name. But then I thought of Blair and the way she always hung on to Wyatt at school and the way he let her do it. "I have to study for our bio test first. I might not have time."

"You know the highest grade you can get is an A-plus, right? There's no plus-plus-plus. You're making the rest of us look bad. Besides, you're already Mr. Weasel's favorite student."

"It's Mr. *Feavel.*" I grin. "And I know."

NOW, in my bedroom, I turn back to my poster of Luke. "What do you think? You won't be jealous, will you? It's not like that. He doesn't see me that way, and he never will."

Still, I fiddle with my bangs. Dab concealer on the huge pimple on my chin. Turn to the side and suck in my stomach. Stand on tiptoe to make my legs longer. It's no use. I'm a hopeless case, and it's so unfair. Mom was crowned Miss Sweetbriar 1973. She had flawless skin and an hourglass figure. That's the sad story of genotype versus phenotype, as Mr. Feavel would say.

"This is as good as it gets, Luke." I blow him an ironic kiss before I slip out the door.

It's a five-minute bicycle ride along the road to the caretaker's cottage, but I make it in three, cutting through the field on an old cattle trail. Straight away, I notice the empty driveway, which can only mean one thing: Wyatt's dad, drunk at the Roundup Saloon. Then I spot Blair's blue dirt bike in the grass, and the urge to kick it overwhelms me. I should turn back before I do something stupid. Before Mr. Landry comes home, all wound up. But the glow from the front window draws me in like a moth to a flame. Ever picked at a scab? Pressed a bruise to make it hurt? That's what this is.

I leave my bicycle in the yard and approach the house with the care of a burglar. I crouch and peer up into the open window. A *Three's Company* rerun plays on the television. Blair sits cross-legged on the sofa with Wyatt's head on her lap and her fingers buried in his hair. They both laugh at the same time.

Watching them together reminds me of how naïve I am. How weird. How lonely. Touching a boy like that—touching *Wyatt*—doesn't seem like something I could do in real life. I think I might spontaneously combust upon contact. I wouldn't know what to say or how to act or where to put my hands. Blair moves expertly, without a hint of unease. But what hurts the most is that she's there at all. That he's invited her into the space he always kept hidden from everyone except me. He's embarrassed of his dad and their house, and the way it reeks of alcohol and stale Marlboros. Still, he's let her in. He must really love her.

Blair leans down, and I lean closer too, examining the scene the way my father studies corn cells under a microscope. When she kisses him, my lips tingle. And when Wyatt suddenly sits up and grabs her, pulling her onto his lap, I stop breathing entirely. I watch for a moment longer, transfixed. I can practically feel Wyatt's Wranglers against my thighs. But that will never be me.

Blair turns her body slightly, glancing purposefully at the window, a secret smile playing on her mouth. She sees me. She. Sees. Me.

I push away from the ledge, scrabbling in the dirt, and run toward the back of the house. I can't get away fast enough. I take cover in the shed, where I find the carved river stone on Mr. Landry's workbench.

RIP BERT, THE BEST DOG

1984–1994

I trace my hand across the letters, the smooth rock. It's easy to tell Wyatt did it himself—the cuts are inconsistent, the lines shaky. But it's the best thing I've ever seen—and the worst. Because it means Wyatt loves me too, but not the way I love him. I sit down on a bale of hay with the stone in my lap and weep.

"Where's that good for nothin' boy?" Mr. Landry stumbles in the doorway, pickled drunk. I can smell him from here. "He was supposed to be at the bull pen an hour ago to practice."

A few years back, when Wyatt got good at riding bucking bulls, Dad helped Mr. Landry build the bull pen and the practice barrel that sat outside the fence. An old gas drum, atop a rusted coil spring, mounted to a tire rim that Wyatt called Bodacious after the top-rated bull at the National Finals Rodeo.

"He's not here." I wish I could make myself invisible.

"I can surely see that, young lady. Are you sayin' I'm blind? Or stupid?"

When Mr. Landry gets drunk, Wyatt gets hurt. It's a truth I've accepted over and over again since Wyatt's older brother drowned in a boating accident and his mom took off and left them high and dry.

A truth I stitched up with a sewing needle and cleaned with a wet rag. A truth Wyatt kept tucked away like a poison pill in his pocket.

"Well, what do you have to say for yourself?" Mr. Landry towers over me, his mustached face shadowed by his gray cowboy hat.

"Nothing, Mr. Landry. I was just leaving." The stone feels warm against my chest. Warm and heavy. If it came to it, could I swing it? Could I use it as a weapon? How bad would it hurt him? I can't even bear to watch Dad kill a spider.

"Not till you tell me where I can find my son."

I bolt for the door, stone in tow, but I only make it a few steps. Mr. Landry closes his hand around my arm and squeezes. I can't look away from his knuckles. They're bruised, bloodied, evidence of the monster inside him.

His grip tightens. "Don't make me have to hurt ya."

"He's in the house," I squeak like a mouse in a trap.

"And what about that fancy dirt bike out front? That yours?"

I want to lie. I really do. "No, sir."

"That's what I thought. He's with that little Lennox girl, ain't he? Hell, at this rate he's gonna get her knocked up before she turns fifteen." He notices me then. Like he's really seeing me for the first time, and I wish he hadn't. "He don't appreciate a woman's body, does he? Them curves. *Volumptuous.*"

I do not correct him. With a grunt, I pull my arm free and run toward the cow-dog graveyard. I drop Bert's stone by the mound of fresh dirt and keep running.

I look over my shoulder once to see Mr. Landry stalking out of the shed the way he came, hollering for Wyatt. I'm ashamed to admit I hope he finds him.

CHAPTER SIXTEEN

NOW

BEHIND the blue door, the caretaker's cabin looks nothing like I remember. I hesitate in the foyer, dripping rainwater on the hardwood and trying to reconcile Mr. Landry's wood-paneled man-cave with the cozy space in front of me. The dingy green sofa and cigarette-burned recliner no longer live here. I hope they died as terrible a death as Mr. Landry himself. *Cirrhosis*, my father told me on the phone, two years after graduation. Neither of us could be bothered to pretend we were surprised or sorrowful. *Wyatt's taking it hard*, he'd said. *It's tough to lose somebody you're hellbent on tryin' to hate.* You should call him. Of course, I didn't.

Until I interned at a public middle school in the Tenderloin, I never understood why my dad kept paying Chet Landry long after he stopped tending to the test corn my dad planted, instead spending his days drinking and blaming Wyatt for his brother dying and his mother leaving. But my dad kept paying. Let them live in the cottage.

Then I learned to begin each counseling session with the most basic of Maslow's needs: *Did you eat breakfast today?* After that internship, I understood my father better. If he'd kicked out Chet, where would Wyatt have gone?

Wyatt appears with two fluffy bath towels while Willie lingers a few steps behind him, still understandably wary of me. When Wyatt passes me a towel, I gape at his swollen red knuckles, which I hadn't noticed in the dark cab of the truck.

"What happened to your hand?"

"Nothing."

"It doesn't look like nothing."

He shrugs, intent on deterring me with denial and avoidance. Clearly, he's forgotten my chosen profession. But I let him think he's won. For now.

"I like what you've done with the place." I run the towel through my wet hair. "I hardly recognized it without that green sofa."

"Yeah, that was a real statement piece. Nothing says *drunk loser* quite like pea-green velour. I'll tell ya, carting that thing to the burn pile with your dad was a whole new level of satisfaction." His smile flattens. "And closure."

There's so much I want to say. Too much. But I can't decide where to start, so I follow Wyatt into the living room without speaking. He heads down the short hallway to the bedroom he once shared with his dad, and I trail behind. No more empty vodka bottles on the floor, no more piles of dirty laundry or paper-cup spittoons I used to dodge like booby traps. Just a bed—Wyatt's bed—oak-framed and draped with a rustic blue quilt and his mother's rocking chair posted up in the corner. The one item his father hadn't carted off to the dump the day she left.

Willie ducks beneath the bed.

"I think he's scared of me," I say.

"Nah. He doesn't like most people. The Dupree twins give him a hard time, chasing him around on the four-wheeler. The apple doesn't fall far, apparently."

"Duane and Jessica procreated? That explains why I nearly got run over in the pasture this afternoon. Someone flew past me driving like a bat out of hell."

"That sounds about right. Just between us, I sneak over their fence at least once a month and let the air out of the tires. They're not as bad as Duane though. In small doses."

"Do the demon twins ever steal things?" I ask, thinking of Blair's missing folder.

"Last year Caleb stole a beer from your dad's fridge, but he learned his lesson real quick. I went full Chet Landry with him on the barrel that day, and he barfed a couple times. I promised not to tell his mother. But Cody takes after Jessica. He knows better… *than to get caught.*" He chuckles, then gives me a quizzical look. "Why do you ask?"

But I'm too stuck in the past to answer. "The barrel? You still ride?"

"Hell, no. I tried once after I got out of the pen. Broke my wrist and crushed my ego. It turns out I don't like pain anymore. Now, I coach." Wyatt grins at me. "Your dad helped me build a practice ring a year or so after I came home. He engineered the best barrel I've ever seen. He even fronted me some money to run an ad in the paper. I told him nobody would trust me with their kids. He said, *They will if you win one.* And, damn, if he wasn't right. I coached a kid from Adamsville, and he took first in the—"

He stops abruptly and springs into action, rummaging through his chest of drawers. "You're freezing," he says, as I rub the goosebumps on my arms. "Let's get you some clothes to change into. I'll toss your wet ones in the dryer and get a fire going. Then, we need to have a talk."

"I thought we were talking."

"A serious talk."

My stomach drops at the thought of all the topics I definitely don't want to talk about, but I play it off with a smile. "About Wave World, you mean?"

He answers me with a stern look. "You really are a lot like your father. Stubborn. Avoidant. The two of you like a pair of ostriches with your heads in the sand. Do you know how many times I told him to get on a plane? Go to San Francisco. He'd say, *She's an adult. It's up to her. She doesn't want to see me.* After he got sick, I even bought him a ticket. He got a refund and donated the money to the Sweetbriar High science club."

"That tracks." I take the clothing from him and hold it tight to my chest to soften the blow. But it stings anyway. Regret, bitterness, longing. Losing my father hasn't been easy, but neither was loving him. "I wish I'd known. He wasn't good at talking with me. Not about the stuff that mattered."

"Hmm. Sounds vaguely familiar."

"Alright, alright." I flutter my hand to usher him out of the bedroom. "Point made. Talk, good. Ostrich, bad. That goes for you too, you know." I rub my hand over my knuckles. "Don't think I forgot about *this*."

"Didn't think you would. But really, it's no big—"

My incredulous expression stops him. At Ellington I called it the *dog ate your homework look*, and it's ninety-nine-percent effective at yielding a full confession.

The one percent being Wyatt, of course.

After he ducks out of the doorway, I hurry to remove my wet clothes. Still shivering, I tug on his threadbare sweatshirt, athletic shorts, and a pair of wool socks, and rub my hair with the towel until it stops dripping. But I can't leave yet, not even with Willie silently judging me from his perfect loaf position. Because I'm in Wyatt Landry's bedroom, his private sanctum, and teenaged June would kill me if I didn't snoop a little.

The bookshelf in the corner draws me in right away. I pluck the 1997 Sweetbriar Bulldog yearbook from its position beneath a stack of *Texas Farm & Ranch* magazines. My yearbook had exactly five inscriptions. Though I tossed it down the garbage chute days after I arrived at UC Berkeley, I know the names by heart. Bonnie, Wyatt,

Larry, Duane, and Blair. I shudder at the memory of the words Blair wrote on the inside back cover, just hours before she disappeared.

I saw you. I know what you did.

My heartbeat quickens the same way it did back then. Guilt squeezes my chest in its inextricable vice. Desperate for a distraction, I flip open Wyatt's yearbook. It's plastered with ink and silly platitudes.

Stay cool, man!
2 good 2 be 4gotten.
Remember me when you're famous, cowboy!
Keep ridin' them bulls!

I find my block of handwriting on the back page between Darcy and Shelly, two cheerleaders who urged Wyatt—*Don't have too much fun without us!* Someone had struck a red line through my signature and written LOSER. I cringe at what I wrote. At my immaturity, my jealousy. The thinly veiled rage he must've sensed between the lines.

I hope you have an amazing life with Blair... you deserve it!

It hurts to remember that girl, how depressed she'd been. The worst of it is knowing I haven't left her far behind. Twenty years later, I'm still sidestepping that same dark hole.

When I flip the page, eager to end my secondhand humiliation, I find Blair's inscription. An entire paragraph fawning over Wyatt and their future together so that everyone who came after would be subjected to her BL + WL 4ever nonsense.

"You okay in there?"

Wyatt's voice startles me. I drop the yearbook on my foot, yelping as Willie darts under the bed.

"Fine. Totally fine." Cursing the stupid book and its stabby spine, I return it to the shelf as quickly as I can and hurry to the door. Wyatt's right there, waiting for me, in a new pair of Wranglers and a white T-shirt. "Just stubbed my toe on your bed post."

He nods skeptically. I limp along behind him to prove my point, hobbling to the closest spot on the sofa and flopping down with a dramatic sigh. While he stokes the fire and settles into the leather armchair, I sneak a look at him, surprised to find he's worse off than I am. Pale as a ghost. Eyes, red-rimmed.

"It sounds like it stopped raining," I offer, gesturing at the curtained window.

"Yeah. The creek's gonna be up tomorrow. I think we got at least two inches in that downpour. That'll sure help with the drought." Texas weather, the most reliable form of small talk in Sweetbriar, and the best way to avoid real conversation. But true to his word, Wyatt sits up straight, clears his throat. Serious talk incoming in three, two, one—

"When you were in the bedroom…" His voice trails off as he holds out his cellphone.

I don't want to take it. I'd rather stay an ostrich. But I spot the name Lydia Lennox, and my curiosity wins out. Blair's mother posted on Facebook one hour ago, asking for prayers for her sweet daughter—*she's my precious angel now*—and her family. *Jim and I are devastated.* And then, there was this:

> To my cherished grandchild, whose life ended before it began, you would've been our greatest treasure.

Stunned, I scroll to the comments. It's no less punishing than reading the note Macy left in her locker, implicating me. The principal showed it to me the day after, laying it on his mahogany desk like a crime-scene photo. This hits the same. It's a gut punch that sucks the air right out of me.

"Did you read what they're saying? Everyone knows what happened last night."

"That's what you're worried about?" Wyatt can't hide his disgust. "She's dead, June. And she—"

My heart falls at the crack in his voice. I've been so busy running away I never saw it through his eyes. How it surely destroyed him when she disappeared. How he became a suspect like my father. Like me. No wonder he'd followed in Chet Landry's footsteps and drowned himself in a bottle.

"I'm sorry. You're right. I know you… loved her." Somehow I still hate admitting it out loud, which only speaks to the depths of my pitifulness. My selfishness. "And she was obviously head over heels in love with you."

His laugh doesn't make a sound. He looks past me into the orange flames flickering at the center of the fireplace. It's a thousand-yard stare. Even after Willie wanders in from the bedroom and curls on his lap. Even when the log settles and sparks, and I startle, he just sits there. Here but not here. A million miles away.

"Let's be honest. Our relationship was a total disaster. We broke up so many times. Got back together. It was complicated. You remember that, right?"

"First loves always are."

"Blair… wasn't…"

I hold my breath and wait for him to say more. But whatever she wasn't, he keeps it to himself, and I'm tired of this dance. The one where neither of us says what we really feel or asks what we really want to know. We've picked up right where we left off on graduation night—with him behind the wall he's built around himself—and I'm reminded of all the reasons I cannot trust him. Not then, not now.

"Did you know she was pregnant?" I blurt out.

He whips his head at me, finally back in the present. "Of course not. I had no idea."

Now I'm the one avoiding his eyes—so he won't see how absolutely convinced I am that he's a liar.

"It's not mine, June. If that's what you're thinking."

I curl into the corner of the sofa, my thoughts spinning out like a blown tire. "How can you be sure? Unless… did the cops talk to you back then? Do you know how far along she was? They talked to you, didn't they? What did they—"

"Because we never had sex."

"You never had…" I blink at him, dazed by his revelation. "I don't understand. You dated for what… five years? Every time I saw you together, she was all over you."

Wyatt shrugs. "Well, believe me, it wasn't my choice. Not with my raging hormones."

I try to make sense of it, but it's no use. The entire story I told myself—about him, about her, about the two of them together—unravels in an instant, and a single, awful question beats against my brain, demanding release.

"If you're not the father, who is?"

"I have no idea. You know we weren't in a good place when she disappeared. She was hot and cold, and I was clueless as to what she wanted. She skipped prom, for God's sake. That should've been the biggest clue. Now, I can guess what she was hiding. But at the time, the sheriff thought I was the one being evasive. They hounded me for months after you left. They searched the cottage, interviewed me for eight hours straight. They even made me take a polygraph. And the whole town just assumed I…"

"I didn't realize. That must've been awful." No wonder he and my father had gotten close over the years. They'd wrestled the same demons, been hunted by the same wolves. "I told them you were at the party the whole night. That we left together. I can't believe they thought you would've hurt her."

"That was one of their theories. I suspect the sheriff liked my dad for it better. They'd been wanting to see him behind prison bars for years. Hell, so had I. They were probably hoping he'd killed her and I'd helped him dispose of the body. Get rid of two Landrys with one stone, so to speak."

A flash flood of memories rushes in, and I hold tight to the arm of the sofa to keep my head above water. I can't get swept away. But there's Chet, teeth bared and raging at Wyatt with a bullwhip when he caught us fishing at the creek after dark. There's Chet, hurling beer bottles at the wall on a random Saturday night. There's Chet, with his tentacle-grip on my teenage arm, leering at me as if I was a grown woman.

"I know what you're thinking," Wyatt says. "I agree. He could've done it. He was mean enough. Hateful. Downright evil, when it comes to it. And he despised Blair. He didn't want me to have anything he couldn't."

In truth, it's only half of what I'm thinking. Because there are men who explode like Chet, and there are men who implode like my father. Men who meet all of life's tragedies with their fists raised, and men who don't meet them at all. Instead hiding out in a workshop working on a pipe dream.

"There was talk about my dad too."

All that time Blair spent alone with my father. Naturally, after she went missing, people talked. By people, I mean everyone *but* my dad. He never so much as breathed Blair's name to me, though I know he spoke to a big-city lawyer at least once. The day before I took off for California, I listened to a message on the answering machine from Ned Smithers of Smithers and Sons.

When Wyatt doesn't speak, I blurt out, "Did my dad say anything to you about her?"

"Damn, June. You honestly believed those bullshit rumors? That was all made up by the sheriff. With Jim Lennox breathing down his neck and no evidence to tie me or Dad to Blair's disappearance, he was desperate for a suspect. Who better than the cowboy scientist who never fit in?"

Wyatt's not wrong. My father made an easy scapegoat.

"Is that why you ran?" he asks. "The ink was barely dry on our diplomas, and you just up and left."

"I had to. I hated this place. I couldn't stand to be tethered here one second longer. The moment I left, I felt free." What I don't say is that the farther I got from Sweetbriar, the more lost I felt, like a stray balloon caught by the wind. I told my roommate at Berkeley I'd grown up in Idaho—it seemed so bland that no one would question me. Headmaster Melhorn and the rest of Ellington Academy believed I'd been raised in Walnut Creek, just outside of San Francisco. None of my ex-boyfriends lasted long enough to learn the truth. The only time I spoke about my hometown was with Macy, and only because she'd found out for herself through a modicum of online sleuthing no one else had ever bothered with. *A girl went missing from your hometown?* she'd asked. *Did you know her?*

"You weren't the only one who felt trapped here. Your dad always said it was his fault you left, and I blamed myself. I thought you hated me after what went down on graduation night. I know I blew it. Just like homecoming and, yeah, that day at Wave World. I swear, when they shut that place down for safety-code violations, I sucked down a whole bottle of champagne."

I widen my eyes at him.

"Don't worry. It was years ago. Before… you know… rock bottom." He gazes at his injured hand in his lap, wincing as he flexes his fingers. "And *this*… I… I shouldn't have—"

Willie's ears prick, and he bolts back to the bedroom. The urgent scrape of his claws against the hardwood unnerves me, and for good reason. Seconds later, a fist beats at the door. A relentless pounding that doesn't let up.

"What did you do to my daughter, you sorry bastard?"

It takes a lot to scare Wyatt. Not the bulls he rode with names like Stomper and Red Devil. Not Principal Finch or his paddle. Not even the hungry pack of coyotes he'd once chased away from Bert. Of course, Chet Landry always had his son's number, but Wyatt kept it hidden as best he could. *My dad likes it when I'm scared*, he told me once. *That's why I ride. I want to show him that I ain't scared of nothin'.*

The Wyatt I once knew only feared two people, and one lies in Oak Grove Cemetery. Just bones, teeth, and spite by now.

"Is that…?" I whisper.

"Dammit, Landry, don't make me break this door down!"

Wyatt flinches, then takes a breath and nods. "Jim Lennox. Blair's stepdad."

CHAPTER SEVENTEEN

THE first time I met Blair's stepdad, he waved me and my dad over to the drug counter in Main Street Pharmacy to introduce himself. *Call me Dr. Jim*, he'd said, pointing to his gold pharmacist name tag. *You look to be about the same age as my stepdaughter, Blair.* It made sense they weren't biologically related. Short, round, and unassuming, he looked nothing like her. He shook my hand and smiled at me, and I wondered if Blair had lied about the bad thing he'd done. That was before I knew the world was full of wolves in sheep's clothing.

Jim bangs on the door once more and forcefully twists the knob. "I'm not leaving."

I wait for Wyatt to respond. To say something. Do something. With his jaw clenched and his hands tensed on his knees, he looks prepared to ride the meanest bucking bull in the county. Like a loaded spring ready for fight or flight.

"C'mon, Jim," a woman's voice pleads. "Just let the police handle it. Let's go home."

"A lot of good they did all these years. They should've just left his sorry ass up in Huntsville where he belonged."

When Lydia whimpers again, Wyatt leaps up from the armchair and yanks the door open so fast I don't have time to run or hide.

Dr. Jim doesn't miss a beat, and he doesn't back down. Though he's a head shorter, he stabs his finger into Wyatt's chest. "It's about damn time you came out and faced me like a man. You always were a coward and a drunk like your father."

"I came out to tell you that I'm sorry to hear about Blair and to ask you to leave. Look at your wife," Wyatt says as Lydia tugs at Jim's arm. "You're upsetting her."

"I'm fine," Lydia says, suddenly emboldened. "I certainly don't need your help."

Not to be outdone, Jim puffs up his chest. "Don't you dare lecture me on how to take care of my family. You're lucky I'm standing here asking questions. If I had my way, you'd be answering to the barrel of a shotgun."

"Either way, I don't have any answers. I don't know what happened to Blair. I wish I did. Now, I'd like you both to—"

"So it was immaculate conception then, was it?" Jim stops the door with his boot. "Her friends told us she snuck out to meet you all the time. We found the condoms in her room. Apparently, you were too boneheaded to figure out how to use them." With that, he brushes past Wyatt and through the open doorway into the living room.

Grief hardened all Jim's soft edges and whittled him down to sinew and bone. Behind his spectacles his eyes look sunken and tired, even when he narrows them at me. The fly in his ointment.

"Aren't you that Pickett girl?"

"Juniper," I say with a skittish wave.

"What the hell are you doing here?" he asks me, voice sharp as a whip. "I thought you lived in *Cali-forn-ya* with all the movie stars. You know, lifestyles of the rich and famous. Wannabes, I call 'em."

"I came for the reunion, and I… uh… my power went out in the storm."

"Oh. Your power went out." He scoffs. "That explains why you were out in front of the school digging up our daughter's remains. For all we know, you and Wyatt were in on it together. You were always following him around like a little lovesick puppy."

Suddenly, Lydia appears from behind him, and I suck in a breath. All these years, I'd pictured her the same. Blair would forever be seventeen, and Lydia would always be the big-haired blonde bombshell from the big city. But her luxurious curls have thinned and grayed. Her once dewy skin is now mottled with sunspots.

"Did you hurt my baby?" she asks. I can't tell if it's meant for Wyatt or me until she adds, "She was nothing but nice to you. She thought it was so sad you didn't have any friends. *Poor Junebug*, she'd tell me. *She doesn't even try to fit in with the rest of us.* If you did something to her, if you helped him cover it up, you better say it now. You owe her that much."

I stand up on shaky legs and lock eyes with her, the former President of the PTA and the Junior League. I wish I could take back all that time I spent pitying her. I wish I could burn those birthday newspaper clippings and throw the ashes in her smug face.

"Your daughter hated me. She made my life a living hell."

Wyatt shakes his head at me. "June, don't."

"They're here for the truth, and the truth is that Blair was not a perfect angel. Far from it. She was an insufferable snot. I didn't kill her, but I—"

"June!"

"I *wanted* to."

Lydia slaps my face, but I barely feel it on my hot cheeks. Twenty-six years of pent-up rage will heat you like a furnace. I wish I could say I feel better now. But really, I'm just a simmering shell.

"I hope you burn in hell, the both of you." She stalks away from me, leaving Jim behind in the uneasy silence. He follows quickly after her.

After the door shuts, they linger on the porch. Stunned, Wyatt and I stand there and listen.

"They know," Lydia says. "They know what happened to her. That's why they're in there together, conspiring. You heard the sheriff. The preliminary results on that bottle they found... where do you think something like that came from?"

Panicked, I fling open the door before Wyatt can stop me. "What bottle? What are you talking about?"

"As if you don't already know," Lydia hisses back.

She's right. I *do* know. It's the 50-milliliter bottle I pilfered from my father's workshop the night before graduation, leaving only one on the shelf. The bottle with the skull and crossbones.

Jim guides his wife away from me, and I'm not sure which one of us he's protecting. At the bottom of the steps, he turns to look back at me. To cast one more stone.

"Blair was poisoned with pentobarbital."

CHAPTER EIGHTEEN

TWO YEARS UNTIL GRADUATION

I eat lunch in stall number five in the girls' restroom near the teachers' lounge. It's the biggest stall on the end, so I can spread out. There's plenty of space for my *elephant legs,* as Blair calls them. It has a brand-new privacy door that nearly reaches the ceramic tile, courtesy of mortal enemies Doris Wilson and Tammy Jensen. In February, they got into it in here—a major girl fight—and when Doris smashed Tammy's saxophone case against the door, the door bent down the middle and fell off the hinges.

Doris and Tammy got suspended for a week, but I considered the whole episode a win. There's no longer any reason to venture into the lunchroom and dodge enemy fire. The taunts and jeers—*Hey, June bugs don't eat French fries! Oh, wait, Junebug eats everything.* The errant tater tot flung at the back of my head. The worst part, the seven empty chairs surrounding me. Bonnie sat with Jennifer and the rest of the tennis team now. Sometimes, Freddie Figeroa joined me, but I loathed those days. He smelled like sweaty gym socks, and Duane always called it out—*Junebug and Freddie sittin' in a tree, k-i-s-s-i-n-g...*

Compared to that hell, stall five may as well be a corner booth at the Olive Garden in Houston, the only restaurant I'd ever visited outside of Sweetbriar. Before Mom died, we ate lunch there every August during our annual school-clothes shopping trip.

Today, I lay my backpack on the floor and take a seat at my makeshift table. I plate my PB and J on my chemistry notebook alongside a box of raisins and open my well-worn copy of *The Westing Game.* It's all going to plan until I hear the main door swing open.

No one uses this bathroom at lunchtime. It's too far from the cafeteria and too close to the teachers' inner sanctum. Careful not to make a sound, I peer through the thin seam in the door and see Christi leaning over the sink, reapplying her lipstick in the grimy mirror.

"*Gawd.* Can you believe she broke up with Wyatt again? I don't know how he puts up with her. She can be such a bitch."

Nodding her agreement, Jessica rifles through the side pocket of her bookbag and retrieves a pack of Virginia Slims. She keeps one cigarette for herself and passes the other to Christi, lighting them both with a Zippo she produces from her bra. "She thinks she's all that and a bag of chips."

Christi takes a puff from the cigarette and disguises her cough with a laugh. "Yeah, and just because she grew up in Dallas. Big whoop."

"I know. If I hear her talking about the stupid Cowboys one more time, I'm going to strangle her with the strap of her Dooney & Bourke." Jessica pauses to take another drag.

I hold my breath. My eyes start to water from the smoke.

"You know what I heard..."

"What did you hear?" Christi asks greedily.

"You can't tell a soul."

"I promise I won't."

"Pinkie swear?" Jessica holds out her finger, and I watch them take the formal oath. The moment it's done, Jessica spills it. Like she's been waiting for the right time to sell out her so-called best friend. "Okay, so you know how Blair is always talking about how her stepdad worked for the Cowboys as their… what do you call it?"

"Sports pharmacist," Christi answers. "Is that even a thing?"

"Exactly." I can practically hear Jessica's eye roll as she flicks the ash from her cigarette into the sink. *Gross.* "And they supposedly moved out here because he wanted to get away from the big city and live a simple life with us country bumpkins. Well, according to my brother, that's a total lie."

Christi gapes at Jessica in the mirror. I'm equally shocked. Not by the revelation that Blair kept secrets—I'd known that since our first meeting in the creek bed—but by the glee on Jessica's face as she prepares to betray her. The eagerness in her voice. The complete lack of remorse. Is it possible she's worse than Blair?

"So this guy in Patrick's fraternity at Baylor had a cousin who worked for the team, and he told Patrick that Dr. Jim got fired for stealing a playbook and selling it to the Redskins. Plus, he was already on thin ice for sleeping with a bunch of women in the front office, including Blair's mom. She did PR for the team."

"That is crazy. Blair told me her mom met him at a Junior League charity benefit."

"Not true. Unless it was a fundraiser for wayward blonde bimbos. She was pregnant with Blair at the time but didn't even know who the dad was. Apparently, Dr. Jim has a type."

I shake my head in disbelief and tune them out as the topic turns to Jason Morton, the cute senior pitcher who pitched a shutout at the game on Friday. Jessica and Christi know almost everything Blair spilled to me that first day except the final straw that sent Jim packing. He'd been caught stealing team merchandise, including an autographed football that had been intended for a charity auction. If you asked me, Dr. Jim's type was crisp and green.

The door swings open again, and Christi cuts off mid-cackle.

"You started without me?" Blair demands, waving an indignant hand at their cigarettes. "Did you even check the stalls first? There might be a rat, if you know what I mean."

"Give it a rest," Jessica says. "There's no one in here."

"You two are such novices." Blair kicks open the first stall, and I shudder. Then the second and the third. "Junebug eats lunch in here on the daily."

Christi and Jessica exchange a look that matches my panic. But there's nowhere to go, nowhere to hide. I only have one option. I stuff the contents of my lunch table into my backpack and scramble to my feet. I flush the toilet.

"I know you're in there."

I can see Blair's blue eye through the crack. It's different today. Puffy and tinged with red, like she's been crying.

I push open the door, and she jumps back. The other girls hurry to douse their cigarettes.

I try to sound brave. "What gave it away, Sherlock? The flushing toilet?"

"Whatever."

I frown at Blair's lame comeback. She's obviously not herself today. But Jessica wastes no time picking up the slack. She crowds me into the corner.

"Were you listening in on our conversation, Junebug?"

"I may have overheard a few tidbits. I really can't remember." I shrug, then glance over her shoulder in Blair's direction. "It might come to me later though."

Jessica's eyes widen in a way that makes whatever happens next totally worth it. "Well, if you say anything, we're going to tell everyone we saw you making out with Fat Freddie behind the bleachers."

Blair and Christi laugh.

"Fine." I push Jessica out of my way. "Then I'll tell Principal Finch I caught all three of you in here smoking. It would be a real shame if you and Blair missed out on cheerleading tryouts next week because you were both suspended."

"You wouldn't dare lie about me," Blair says. "I didn't even take one puff."

At the exit, I pause. I should leave while I'm ahead, but I can't. In this war, I've had too few victories. "Unfortunately for you, I have a loose relationship with the truth. But, apparently, I'm not the only one. Isn't that right, Blair?"

I relish the utter silence I leave in my wake.

BY sixth-period American history, the whole high school buzzes with the news of the umpteenth Wyatt–Blair breakup. I swear, they may as well call Sweetbriar High *The Days of Our Lives.* Wyatt looks thoroughly pissed, and Blair keeps sniffling and asking for a hall pass. Every time she leaves, a cascade of whispers ripples down each row. The going theory: Blair didn't show up for Wyatt's bull ride in the Mesquite Championship after promising her stepdad would drive her. Seems like a lame reason to split, but I can't say I'm not thrilled at the news. Not that it means anything. Wyatt barely acknowledges me at school these days, and I avoid him to save him the trouble of ignoring me. But when we see each other at the cottage, it's like we're different people. Our real selves.

Mr. Genova writes a question on the board for our last Thursday pop quiz. I flip to a clean sheet of notebook paper and start to write my name in the top corner. When the intercom buzzes, my hand jumps and my cursive *k* looks more like an *h.*

"Juniper Pickett, will you please report to the principal's office?"

My mother's accident comes rushing back. It's been years, and still my stomach drops to my knees. If something happened to my dad, where would I go?

Of course, Duane pipes up first. "Sounds like Junebug's gonna get squashed by Mr. Finch."

"Duane, please keep your thoughts to yourself." Mr. Genova shoots a warning look in his direction.

But as I gather my belongings, the rest of the class forms a chorus of *oohs.* Except for Blair, who simply wiggles her fingers at me in an ominous wave goodbye.

MRS. Morley ushers me into Principal Finch's office with its single window overlooking the courtyard. When he unfolds himself from behind the desk and shuts the blinds, my chest starts to hurt.

"Please sit down." He gestures to the single wooden chair facing him. It reminds me of the Quiet Chair, where Duane spent most of first grade.

"Is my dad okay?" I blurt out.

Mr. Finch's face scrunches in confusion, and his glasses migrate down his nose. He pushes them back up before he says, "*Your father?* He's fine."

"Oh. Am I..." I can't even bring myself to say it. I've never been in trouble before. "Did I do something wrong?"

Mr. Finch opens his bottom drawer and retrieves a carton of Virginia Slims. He sets them on the desk with a scowl. "Well," he says, "what do you have to say for yourself, young lady?"

My thoughts start spinning. While he drums his fingers expectantly on the desk, I try to focus on my breathing with the usual run-through of the first twenty periodic elements. "I don't know what you're talking about, Mr. Finch. Those aren't mine."

"We found them in your locker, June. Three of the other students saw you smoking in the girls' restroom during lunch."

"That's not true. I don't smoke." The panic in my voice makes me sound uncertain.

"Are you calling me a liar?"

"No! Of course not!" *Oh God.* I've just shouted at the principal. "I'm sorry for raising my voice. But I can explain everything. Earlier today, I saw Christi and Jessica smoking those in—"

Mr. Finch holds up his hand like a stop sign, and I swallow the rest of my protest. Because it's no use. Like everyone else, he's blinded by Blair's perfection. Plus, he and Jim Lennox are golfing buddies. "June, blaming others is a sign of immaturity. Now, I already spoke with your father, and he gave his permission for the standard consequences in a situation like this."

The walls start to close in around me. Mr. Finch fades in and out. I see the coatrack. Mr. Finch's framed college diploma. His name plate. His wiry little mustache. It's all spinning and spinning. I grip tight to the chair and hope it stops.

"You have two choices, June. You can either accept a one-week suspension and miss your final exams, or agree to the paddle."

Suddenly, that's all I see. The paddle hangs behind his desk. I stare at it, wondering about the small lettering at the bottom that's too small to read from here.

"The paddle? My dad agreed to that?"

Mr. Finch nods like it's the most normal thing. Like I'm the one being unreasonable. "He's concerned about you. He says you don't have many friends. He doesn't want you to go off track. And neither do I."

My anger is a chemical reaction. Like baking soda and vinegar. Right now, this volcano is about to blow. Already, I'm crying tears of outrage. "How would my dad know anything about my life? He's barely around."

"Well, he knows enough to be worried about you, and I am too. This isn't like you. You're one of our best students." He pauses just long enough for me to think he might change his mind. "But I can't make any exceptions. I have to treat all my students the same. So, what will it be?"

I bury my head in my hands.

"Juniper?"

"I can't miss my exams."

Mr. Finch pushes a box of tissues at me and hoists himself up. While I blow my nose, he reaches for the paddle. Up close, I can read it now. The small letters spell out: The Educator.

"Three licks on the backside then. Bend over the desk. I'll be quick about it."

Each strike stings worse than the last. It's not the wooden paddle—Mr. Finch keeps his word—it's the shame.

I close my eyes and picture Blair and her little *screw you* wave. In my head, I say it over and over. I wish I could scream it, but that would only make this worse. *I want her dead.*

CHAPTER NINETEEN

SATURDAY—NOW

I wake up in Wyatt's bed. After the emotional rollercoaster of the Lennox family visit, he insisted on taking the couch, and I'd been too exhausted to argue. But I'm not alone. Around 4 a.m., Willie staked his claim to the other half of the blanket. His furry body curls alongside me. I scratch behind his ear, and he starts to purr in his sleep.

Part of me wishes the morning had never come. I know what's waiting for me on the other side of that door. Wyatt and the questions I still haven't answered. The San Francisco detective I've been dodging. The Sweetbriar police too. My classmates. Blair's family. My father's ghost. It's reminiscent of our College Prep Day at Ellington, when a long line of desperate and entitled parents assembled outside my office to give me the third degree.

The smell of eggs and bacon lures me from the room. Willie follows.

"Mornin'," Wyatt says from behind the small cookstove. "I guess you won Willie over."

I shuffle awkwardly in Wyatt's socks. What do you say to a man who suspects you poisoned his ex-girlfriend? He'd all but said so last night after Blair's parents left in a storm of fury. "It stopped raining."

"Sure did. Power's back on too." He passes me a plate and a glass of orange juice, and I glance at his hand. Last night's redness has turned to a dark-purple bruise. "I can drive you back home after breakfast. I've got a kid coming at noon to use the practice barrel. And I might pick up an afternoon shift at the feed mill. They hired me back part-time when I got out. Helps pay the bills."

I eat my eggs in solitude and pretend he doesn't want to get rid of me. That it doesn't hurt. I suppose I should be grateful for the almost-silent treatment, but now that he's not talking, I find myself wishing he would.

"Have you heard anything more about…?" I'm such a coward. I can't even say her name.

Wyatt grimaces.

"Never mind."

He puts his plate in the sink and comes to sit beside me on the sofa. He volleys his cellphone nervously from one hand to the other. Not surprisingly, it's of the old-school flip variety. "Duane posted in the Sweetbriar Reunion group chat this morning."

"Oh, God."

"Do you want to—"

I grab the phone from him before he finishes the question and stare in horror at the snippet Duane had screenshotted and attached from a true-crime blog.

> Killer News *has confirmed that Dr. Juniper Pickett, fondly known by her students as Dr. P, is suspected of aiding and abetting sixteen-year-old Macy Powell in her poison plot that nearly claimed the life of five Ellington students, one faculty member,*

and one alumni sponsor. Authorities believe the victims unknowingly ingested a toxic substance during a club meeting. No charges have been filed as of yet, and San Francisco police remain tight-lipped on the evidence against Pickett. All victims are expected to make a full recovery.

Duane had captioned his text: *History repeating*. Which meant he wasn't lying about reading my letter.

I want to cry. I feel sick to my stomach. Instead, I turn to Wyatt. "You have a flip phone."

"I just figured how to use the fancy remote for my TV, so I'm not sure I'm ready for the big leagues yet."

"But you're in the group chat?"

"A necessity. It stops them from spreading gossip about me. At least to my face." He laughs a little. "Want me to add you?"

"Very funny." I hand him back his cellphone and immediately spring to my feet, pacing to the window so I can avoid his eyes. "It's not what it sounds like."

"Hey, you don't owe me an explanation. I served ten years in prison for vehicular manslaughter. I wore the same damn white uniform and ate the same slop as the next man. And, yeah, Eric wasn't lying. I even worked on death row. The last two years of my term I took a job as the chaplain's clerk. He spent a lot of time down there, ministering to the condemned. Anyway, people are complicated, June. They make mistakes."

I squint into the sunshine beaming through the window. It's impossibly bright. Almost as if yesterday's storm never happened. But I can spot the tracks in the mud from Dr. Jim's ancient red BMW. I can't believe he's still driving that old thing, but it's further proof time has stood still for the Lennoxes. For them, it would always be May 30, 1997. A part of me got stuck there too.

I glance over my shoulder to find Wyatt looking right back at me. I think of all those years I spent running. Of the sweater I tossed to the bottom of the well. The warning signs I'd ignored with Macy.

"I've made mistakes, but I'm not a murderer."

Even as I say it, it sounds like a lie.

FIFTEEN minutes later, Wyatt ushers me and Willie out the door with my stack of dry clothing in a plastic bag from Hometown Grocery. He tried to convince me to let him drive me back, but I insisted on walking the familiar path between our houses. I need to clear my head. Because I need a clear head to do damage control. He was only pretending to be nice. He wants to be rid of me. I could tell by the way he completely ignored my claim of innocence. The way he washed our dishes and wiped the counter at lightning speed.

After Wyatt bids me farewell, Willie leaves me too and flops down in a sunspot, too carefree to be bothered with my problems. I walk alongside the creek toward Saw Mill Road. Yesterday's storm filled the dry bed with mucky water, but it won't last long. By tonight it will subside, and a week from now the creek will be dry again. It's a running joke every Texan knows: Wait long enough and the weather will change. If only my troubles would disappear like that. Right now, I'm getting swept along, barely keeping my head above the floodwater and searching for a branch to cling to.

By the time I reach the house, I know what I have to do. I retrieve the workshop key and head into the pasture, still carrying Wyatt's shopping bag. I move as quickly as I can, dodging mud puddles. I'm in the literal middle of nowhere, but I can't shake the sense of eyes on my back. The certainty I'm being watched.

A quick turn of the key, and I slide open the door. Within seconds, I find what I came for and drop it in with yesterday's clothing. As I turn to go, I take a second look at the wall. At my father's prized possession: his framed periodic table. The light from the half-open doorway hits the space between the wall and the frame, exposing a strange jut in the profile. It makes me wonder enough to shut and bolt the door behind me, to rush back to the wall and hoist the whole thing off its hooks.

It's a bit like wrangling a big fish; I'm breathing hard, and I nearly fall backward before I manage to set down the frame and lean it against my father's desk. There, taped to the backing, I find the pages that were torn from my father's notebook. As I slide a careful finger beneath the tape, a strange sound pricks my ears from outside. My heart skips when I recognize the clang of the padlock. Fear pulses through me, but I simply stand there, listening, while the intruder jostles the handle; my limbs as lifeless as one of my father's glass beakers. Head, as empty too.

I'm terrible in a crisis, useless. That's obvious. Since the first time Duane and his cronies shoved me into my locker, I've been more freeze than flight or fight. The last few weeks only confirmed it. Helpless, I hold my breath and wait for the door to open.

It takes an embarrassingly long time for my brain to remember that I bolted the door from the inside. No one's getting in here. The realization fills me with relief.

But then, I hear the rev of an engine mocking me.

I tuck my father's notes inside the plastic bag and tiptoe to the door to press my ear against it. That steady growl unnerves me, especially after yesterday. I feel cornered in here, like a mouse hiding from Midnight in the wood stack. The walls close in around me. My heartbeat sounds impossibly loud. It throbs beneath my jaw, feeling as if it is intent on bursting my carotid. Years have passed since my last real panic attack, though last night at the reunion I'd come close. I'm a doctor now, for God's sake. But none of that matters. I might as well be fourteen, hunted in the hallways of Sweetbriar High with Duane aiming rubber bands at my backside.

I drop to my knees and peer through the space beneath the door frame where, years ago, the rainwater eroded a slender peephole my father never bothered to fix. As a kid, I snuck glimpses of him through it from the outside, but never lingered long enough to get caught. Back then, I felt like a spy intent on uncovering my father's secrets. Now, I just feel crazy, lying on my stomach and squinting into the morning sunlight with my heart still pounding in my ears.

I catch a glimpse of a familiar four-wheeler as it speeds away from the shop and disappears over Red Mountain. I should feel better—my breathing slows—but I can't shake this awful dread. It clings to me like a heavy coat. My thoughts race as I pace the workshop floor.

The reckless rider.

Blair's stolen folder.

The last voicemail my father left me before he dropped dead in the pasture.

The gun he gave to Wyatt for safekeeping.

Terrible questions start to drum in my head, one *what if* after the other. *What if he didn't take his own life? What if he was murdered? What if they come for me?*

A strange crackling fills the workshop. I lower my head again to the peephole, expecting to find a mangy coyote in the grass gnawing on a rabbit carcass. Instead, I inhale a mouthful of smoke.

I press my hand to the door and yelp. It's hot to the touch.

Wrapping my hand in my shirt, I unlatch the bolt and give it a push. The door doesn't budge. I kick it hard. So hard it judders my bones. Once, twice. But the door only rattles. I'm trapped.

Full-on panic sets in, as my father's workshop starts to burn around me.

CHAPTER TWENTY

AS the flames breach the doorway, I choke on the thick, black smoke. Coughing into my shirt, I clutch the plastic bag to my chest and head for the back of the workshop to find the extinguisher. Surely, my father had one, though I can't recall seeing it the night before last.

The fire moves with me, as fast as a snake. It slithers up the walls and around the perimeter, striking every surface in its path. It devours my father's desk, his briefcase, the chair I slept in. Explodes the bottles and beakers on the shelf one by one. The heat pushes me farther and farther back. It's unbearable. And it's coming for me. I have to get out of here and fast.

Crouching down, I squint into the haze and spot the red-bracket wall mount for the fire extinguisher. It's empty. Nothing left to do except fight my way out. I take yesterday's shirt from the plastic bag and wrap it around my mouth and nose as a makeshift mask. Toss the rest of the clothing on the floor and stuff the bag and what's left in it into my waistband. Then I grab the heaviest object within reach—my dad's Olympus microscope. Hoping the leaky pipes rotted the cedar exterior of the building, I pound it against the drywall.

Again!

My eyes tear. My legs weaken. But I yelp with relief when the drywall gives way to the spongy wood beneath it.

Again!

I can't stop coughing. Still, I manage to knock out a small hole big enough for my fist. I can see the blue of the sky. Can taste the mercy of the fresh air. I *am* scrappy!

I raise the microscope and wallop it again and again. Each time, I suck in another mouthful of smoke; the heat moves closer; and I grow weaker. Soon I can barely muster the strength to lift the thing.

With one last effort, I collapse onto the floor. I close my eyes and travel back to age eighteen. To graduation night. In my hand I hold a vial of liquid pentobarbital. I want to disappear. I want to make them pay. Blair, especially. In another life, no one stopped me. In another life, I'm already dead. Long gone and far away from here.

A crash brings me back to my body, and suddenly I'm floating. The smoke becomes blue sky. The hard hot floor becomes warm grass. Wyatt crouches over me, looking worried.

"June! Are you okay?"

"Been better." I turn my head to see the workshop engulfed in flames and throwing sparks at the grass, dangerously close to Wyatt's truck.

"The fire department is on the way. I'll do what I can with the extinguisher from my truck. But it doesn't look good." He runs off before I can stop him.

It's no use. By the time the fire truck arrives from downtown Sweetbriar, there won't be much left. Just the concrete foundation and the charred remains of my father's legacy. There was a time when I would've been glad to see it go. The place that stole him from me. Now, it only feels like more unfinished business. Like losing him all over again.

At least I have the notes he hid. I touch my waistband for confirmation.

As Wyatt tries to hold back the blaze, I lie there, exhausted and confused, my lungs still burning. I can't make sense of it, but I know this: Dad was onto something, and he paid for it with his life. It's undeniable now.

Wyatt pauses at the entrance to the nearly decimated workshop. He kicks at an object on the ground. After spraying it with the fire retardant, he leans down to take a closer look. Then his eyes land back on me.

"What is it?" I try to yell, but the words only scrape against my raw throat.

He walks toward me, and I repeat the question. It's nearly drowned out by the sirens of the arriving fire truck, but I can tell from the concern on Wyatt's face that he heard me. That he doesn't want to answer.

"The door was locked."

"Yeah, I bolted it from the inside. I didn't want to be—"

"No, June. The door was *locked*." He waits for the realization to hit me. "From the outside. They closed the shackle on the padlock. Whoever set that fire didn't want you to survive it."

MY clothes smell like smoke. My mouth tastes like ash. My eyes still burn, even after the paramedic—also known as my former classmate Sadie Piper—flushes them with water. But Sheriff Faulk doesn't care about my brush with a fiery death. He still thinks I'm guilty of something.

"What the hell happened out here?" he asks as he approaches the back of the ambulance.

Figures he would turn up with his too-tight Wranglers and his judgmental sneer.

With a nod from Sadie, I lower the oxygen mask from my face to speak. "Somebody tried to kill me."

"Oh, really. How do you know that?"

Sadie snorts in disbelief.

As Suspect Number One, I can't afford such luxuries. "Well, I was in the workshop when the fire started, and I heard a four-wheeler outside. Then the whole place caught fire, and I nearly died. If it wasn't for Wyatt, I would have. He found the padlock still attached to the door with the shackle closed. What more evidence do you need?"

"It seems mighty convenient that you're the only one who saw this mystery arsonist. Next thing you'll be telling me he dropped down from a spaceship in the sky."

"I didn't *see* anyone. But a four-wheeler can't drive itself. Are you saying I set the workshop on fire?"

"You tell me." Of course, he doesn't let me tell him anything. "Maybe you wanted to destroy evidence. Like the *pentowhatzit* your dad kept up in there. Isn't that what you used to poison sweet Blair?" It's obviously a rhetorical question. "Before you whacked her in the back of the head."

I'm grateful for the Mylar blanket Sadie wrapped around me. It's the perfect cover for the bag still hidden in my clothing. If only I could duck beneath it and disappear myself. "I have no idea what you're talking about."

Undeterred by my denial, he adds, "Or maybe you decided to finally end it all. The way you intended to twenty years ago. Just like you laid out in your letter."

I should keep my mouth shut, especially with Sadie eavesdropping and my lungs burning as if I swallowed a handful of hot coals. Smoke inhalation, be damned. "So I managed to padlock myself inside the workshop. Is that what you're saying?"

"What I'm saying, young lady, is that I know all about you and what you've been up to lately. We get the news down here too, you know. From what I hear, you managed to get yourself in a mighty big shitstorm out there in California. So you ran back here and brought trouble along with you." He shakes his head as if he's disgusted by the sight of me. The nerve of a city slicker like me to bring trouble to Mayberry. "I already know you lied to me. It might be that you couldn't handle the heat. You wanted out of the kitchen, so to speak."

"Take a few more deep breaths, June." Sadie guides the mask back to my mouth.

I can't tell if she's on my side or just doing her job. Either way, I appreciate the interruption. It's as necessary as the oxygen.

While I focus on my breathing, I survey the damage to the workshop—it's a total loss, but thanks to the heavy rain last night, the grass didn't catch fire—and to myself—still here with only a small burn on my hand and smoke in my lungs. I have Wyatt to thank for that and so much more. He refused medical treatment to help the crew battle the fire and directed them to the point of origin at the front door.

When he wanders up, face covered in soot, I feel grateful for that too. I need a buffer between myself and the sheriff.

"You alright?" Wyatt cuts his eyes in Sheriff Faulk's direction.

I only nod, hoping the sheriff will lose interest in me and focus on identifying an actual suspect.

"So, Mr. Landry, how did you end up out here?"

Inwardly, I sigh. My hopes dashed by the sheriff's accusatory tone.

"I was out in the practice pen getting ready for a lesson. When I saw the smoke, I drove through the gate and came right over. I figured June might be in trouble."

"You managed to get out here that quick, huh?"

"It's a damn good thing I did. And that I had a hatchet in my tool box. Otherwise, we'd be having a different conversation."

The sheriff grunts and spits into the dirt in a convincing display of complete apathy. Or as my dad would say, *He doesn't give a hill of beans about you, June.*

"I assume you must've gotten a looky-loo at that four-wheeler, seeing as how you got here so fast."

Wyatt shakes his head. "Whoever it was probably cut across the main road and through the Peterson farm."

"That's a no, then." Somehow, Sheriff Faulk manages to make me look like a liar even when I'm not talking.

"There's a good chance this fire is related to the vandalism," Wyatt says. "It's probably the same culprit."

"*Vandalism?*" I rasp into the mask. It takes me a moment to remember the last time I'd heard that word. At the police station, Christi had mentioned vandalism, but I'd been too overwhelmed to pay attention.

"Doubtful," Sheriff Faulk replies. "That was a childish prank. Arson is serious business. We still need to confirm whether this fire was deliberately set and whether it started from the inside or the outside."

He gives a hard rap on the ambulance that makes me jump to my feet. I pull off the mask and return it to Sadie. I can't sit here any longer dodging his metaphorical punches. Keeping myself cocooned in the blanket, I retreat to the safety of Wyatt's side.

"It was a little more than a childish prank," Wyatt says. To me, he adds, "Your dad's workshop was vandalized a week before he died. Someone spraypainted the outside wall and broke Foghorn's neck. Left the poor guy strung up by the feet in front of the shop door. Your dad was scared. He thought—"

"Foghorn?"

"Your dad's rooster. After Mrs. Peterson died last year, her daughter couldn't find a home for him, so your dad offered. Mainly, he just fought with Willie Nelson and crowed at off-hours."

I stare blankly, trying to adjust my image of Eugene Pickett yet again. I didn't know him at all. Not anymore. "But why would someone do that?"

"Your dad thought he was being watched. He wouldn't say much about why or by who. Apparently, he tried to tell the cops, but nobody took him seriously." Wyatt looks to Sheriff Faulk.

He answers by hocking up another glob of spit and launching it into the grass.

"I didn't see any spray paint," I mutter, mostly to myself. This must be why Dad called me. He needed me, and I didn't answer.

"I power-washed it off for him. Then, a few days later, he was gone. Caleb Dupree found him in the pasture."

Guilt sinks in another hook. It's the double-barbed kind that keeps a poor fish like me wriggling. Still, I can't stop myself from asking, "What did they paint?"

Wyatt doesn't want to tell me. It's written all over his face. He exhales. "*Die*, in all capital letters, above a drawing of a big face with an X over the mouth."

My heart breaks at the thought of my dad, already so close to death, reading that all by himself. But with the sadness also comes anger that I promptly let fly in the sheriff's direction. "You ignored that? It doesn't sound childish. It sounds like a threat."

"We *were* looking into it, but there wasn't much to go on. We have no reason to believe it was connected to your father's death. He was a very sick man. He knew his time was coming, and he didn't want to suffer. Frankly, I can't say I would've done it any different."

"I certainly hope you won't stop looking into it. Especially now this has happened. I could've died today. My father's already dead. You can't tell me that's a coincidence."

"This ain't the big city, Ms. Pickett. We have limited resources. But, rest assured, crime don't sit well with the residents of Sweetbriar. No matter what the perps might look like or how many fancy letters they may have after their names. In fact, you're lucky I don't arrest your neighbor here for assaulting one of my officers last night. Mrs. Dupree had to drive her numskull husband to the emergency dentist in Adamsville this morning. Seems he misplaced a tooth at the reunion courtesy of Mr. Landry here."

I stare blankly, my smoke-filled brain reeling, while Wyatt launches a protest that involves the words *drunken rant* and *police misconduct.*

By the time I come to my senses, Sheriff Faulk announces, "I don't have time to deal with these juvenile antics. I'm a professional lawman with serious crimes to investigate. Now, if you'll excuse me." He tips his cowboy hat and saunters away like the villain in an old western.

Heaving a sigh, Wyatt shakes his head in frustration and follows him. I watch for a moment as Wyatt points emphatically to the shackled lock on the ground. The sheriff appears unmoved.

"That man thinks he's Clint Eastwood," Sadie says as she shuts the ambulance door and prepares to leave. "Somebody should tell him he's more Keystone Cops than Dirty Harry."

My laugh turns into a wheezing cough that makes Sadie frown with worry.

"If that keeps up, you should see a doctor. They may need to prescribe an inhaler or a steroid to reduce the inflammation in your lungs."

I nod and offer my thanks. "I didn't see *you* at the reunion," I say, picturing eighteen-year-old Sadie accepting the senior award for Most Artistic. Like me, she spent high school navigating the front lines of the fringes. Unlike me, she found a place to fit in there, a bunker to hide from enemy fire.

"Every day in this town reminds me of high school. I don't need to relive it. But I do wish I'd been there to see Duane get a dose of his own medicine. I heard he went down like a sack of potatoes." Her smile disappears quickly. "You know, I was on call the day they found your father out here. They dispatched an ambulance. My partner and I responded."

"You saw him?" My heart starts pounding wildly. "Could you tell what happened to him?"

Sadie takes a furtive glance around us, then lowers her voice to a near-whisper. "There's no doubt he ingested poison. We ran a tox screen. But I noticed something else. Something suspicious. It could've been nothing, but…"

I lean in, imploring her.

"There was a large knot on the back of his head. A goose egg. Like he'd bumped it or taken a hit. I noted it in my report."

"Does the sheriff know?"

"Of course. He knows everything that goes on around here." Sadie grimaces. "But that's not even the worst of it."

I brace myself, wondering how much more I can take.

"I checked the logs later. Someone altered my report, June. The part about his head injury, it was deleted. Like it never happened."

IT'S only me and Wyatt now. Me and Wyatt and the brutal midday sun baking the charred remnants of my father's workshop. I know I can't stay here all day. I have to keep moving, keep breathing, keep living. I have to open this plastic bag and read my father's notes. I have to face the truth about what happened to him and to Blair and to Macy. To me. But a part of me wants to stay stuck in this field forever. I'm not sure I have the strength to do what needs doing. Worst of all, I feel just as alone as I did when I fled this place twenty years ago.

Wyatt touches my arm, and I flinch. "I'm sorry, June. I know this is a lot. You must be—"

"How did you know I was out here?" As far as questions go, it's not a knife. It's more of a poison dart. Stealthy and subtle.

"What do you mean?"

"You told the sheriff you thought I might be in trouble. But how did you know I was inside the workshop?"

He screws up his face. I can't tell if he's dumb as a turkey or clever as a fox.

"Were you watching me?"

He grabs for the bag, still stuffed beneath my—well, *his*—shirt. But I jump back.

"Should I be?" he asks. "You came here for something and in a big hurry. What are you hiding under there?"

"Nothing." I want to trust Wyatt. He quite literally saved my life. Apparently, he punched Duane in the face… *for me.* I want to tell him about the notes and the pentobarbital and the whole truth about the way my life went to hell in San Francisco. But I can't get past all the times he let me down.

I walk off in the direction of Red Mountain, toward the house, and I don't look back.

CHAPTER TWENTY-ONE

ONE AND A HALF YEARS UNTIL GRADUATION

WHEN the three o'clock bell rings, the best part of my day begins. Blair hurries off with her lemmings in tow to catch the last rays of September sunshine at the city pool before it closes for the fall. Even Duane and Eric can't be bothered to torment me. Not since Duane managed to become a licensed driver last month. Eric hangs out the passenger side of Duane's muddy Jeep and hoots at the girls as they speed out of the parking lot.

I wait outside near the marquee in the courtyard that proclaims tonight Homecoming 1995 for the Sweetbriar Bulldogs. I smooth my hair, dab the oil from my nose and forehead with a tissue from my backpack, and reapply my cherry ChapStick. When Wyatt bursts through the front doors, a zip of excitement shoots through me. I quickly tamp it down.

"Ready?" he asks with a spirited jiggle of his truck keys.

Like it's an actual question. Like I don't count down the entire day waiting for this moment.

"Will you let me drive?" I grab for the keys.

But he holds them just out of my reach. "Not unless you want your dad to kill me. You just got your learner's permit and, no offense, the last time you drove my life flashed before my eyes."

Defeated, I climb into the passenger seat in surrender. This is one argument I will never win. All because I veered off the road and narrowly missed a fence post. In my defense, Wyatt was to blame. He'd accidentally grazed my arm reaching for his soda can in the console, and I lost all my faculties.

"I told you. There was a squirrel."

"Right. The invisible squirrel. It sounds like a superhero name. *It's a bird. It's a plane. It's the Invisible Squirrel.*"

When he chuckles, it's like a warm sweater wrapped around me, and I can pretend it's just the two of us now and forever. Unfortunately, forever lasts only as long as it takes to make the drive from Sweetbriar High to home. The way Wyatt drives that's less than twenty minutes, even in the beater truck he rescued from the scrapyard with his rodeo money.

"So, are you going to the homecoming game?" he asks.

I cut my eyes at him, trying to convey the absolute ridiculousness of that question. "Bonnie asked me if I wanted to go but..." I shrug. I don't want to admit to Wyatt—or to myself—that I'm Bonnie's second-choice friend. Probably even third or fourth. She would never have offered if Jennifer wasn't home sick with the flu, and Sara and Dominique, the other two in their tennis foursome, weren't in Dallas for a Mathletes competition.

"But?" Wyatt prompts.

"But I'd rather have a root canal."

"Honestly, me too," he says. "I need to get a couple of practice rides in before the State Fair rodeo next week. But Blair will kill me if I don't show."

"Yeah, she will. You'd be deader than dead." Last I heard, Blair had dumped Wyatt again in the never-ending rerun episode of Sweetbriar Days of Our Lives. "Can you imagine how mad she'd be if you stood her—"

"Shit." Wyatt curses and slams the brakes. "Sorry. I totally forgot. Do you mind if we stop at Mrs. Avery's flower shop real quick? I've got to pick up Blair's homecoming mum."

"Sure." I try very hard not to roll my eyes at the stupidest tradition this side of the Rio Grande and a waste of a perfectly good fake chrysanthemum. "So, you and Blair are back together then?"

"Hell if I know. It changes by the day. She can't make up her mind lately."

I go through the whole *if you can't say something nice* conversation with myself a few times, as Wyatt takes the right turn on Main Street and parks the truck in front of the flower shop. A white mum with all the trimmings hangs in the display window. Blue and white ribbons stream from the center, and the silver football garland shimmers in the sunlight. It pains me to admit that it's pretty and that I almost wish I had someone to buy it for me.

"I'll be right back."

Wyatt leaves me inside the truck with all my unrequited desires. I crank up the radio and stare after him like a sad puppy.

When he emerges from the shop with Blair's homecoming mum, I can't keep a straight face. The fake white flower must be the biggest one Mrs. Avery ever designed. It's adorned with blue and silver pom-poms, a plastic football, and a huge white ribbon down the center that reads "HEAD CHEERLEADER."

Wyatt opens the driver's side door and passes me the monstrosity. I lay it on my lap and comb through the sea of garland and gaudy ribbons. One catches my eye.

"I thought Blair hated bull riding." I touch the blue fabric with the large gold-embossed bull and "LANDRY" spelled out beneath it.

"She does." He smirks. "I asked Mrs. Avery to add the bull. Blair doesn't know about it."

I gape at him, certain he hasn't considered the potentially fatal consequences of his decision.

"I figure, I'm paying for the damn thing, right? It's not cheap. I had to pick up an extra weekend shift at the feed mill to afford it. And she hasn't been to a single rodeo. Meanwhile, I go to every football game to watch her cheer. A little bull on a stupid mum is the least she could do."

"It's kind of big though." I sneak a glance at him, trying not to laugh. "And it's gold."

"Do you think she'll hate it?"

"Do you *want* her to hate it?"

He doesn't say anything at first. Just backs up and starts driving out of town, where the road gets so narrow only one vehicle can fit. I stay still, careful not to break the spell. Wyatt never talks to me about Blair.

"No. Maybe. I don't know. Sometimes I get the feeling she... have *you* heard anything?"

"*Me?* About Blair?" I don't tell Wyatt that I still spend most lunch hours in the girls' bathroom hopeful for a crumb of gossip. Blair never lets down her guard, not since Cigarette-gate, but Jessica and Christi don't bother to check the stalls before they dish about their favorite topic: Blair, and how mean and snotty she can be. Of course those sentiments come as no surprise. But, sometimes, they drop a bomb. Sometimes, I think they want me to hear them.

"Yeah. Are there any rumors? You know, about her and other guys."

It's painful to watch his discomfort. I want to put him out of his misery, but then again, what I have to say would only make it worse. And the last thing I want is to make Wyatt's life worse. He already lives with an ogre, who left another black-and-blue mark on his face last weekend after he was disqualified from the Amarillo Junior Rodeo for taking too long in the chute.

"Not that I've heard. Why don't you just ask her?" Not that she'd tell him the truth. Whatever the truth may be. *I heard she did it with the Adamsville quarterback after the game under the bleachers,* Jessica told Christi, in between laments in the mirror about her small boobs.

"I did ask her," Wyatt says. "But she didn't take it too well. Imagine the Tasmanian Devil in a cheer uniform."

I *can* imagine it. Mainly because I've spied on them enough to know the exact shade of red Blair's cheeks turn when Wyatt ticks her off. I've watched her stomp her feet. I've heard her snarl. Once, I witnessed her pounding her fists on Wyatt's chest after he told her he couldn't afford to buy her diamond studs for her birthday.

Wyatt lets out a long-suffering sigh. "Who am I kidding? She'll hate the ribbon. She'll probably strangle me with it."

"Well, I like it." As soon as the words leave my mouth, my face gets hot. I turn to look out the window to hide my blush, afraid it will give me away. For the first time ever, I wish for the turn onto Saw Mill Road, but we're still at least a mile away.

"I thought you hated homecoming and mums and all the stupid girlie stuff."

"I do. Sort of." It's hard to explain to a boy, much less to Wyatt, the difference between actually hating something and only pretending to hate it because you want it so bad. "But that mum in the window wasn't so terrible."

"I'm confused," he says as if I just asked him to prove the Pythagorean Theorem.

"Typical," I say.

He snorts.

Five minutes later, Wyatt lets me out by the mailbox. I carefully set Blair's mum on the seat and wish him luck.

"Hey, June?"

I look back over my shoulder to see him hanging out the driver's side window.

"Should I take it off? The rodeo ribbon?"

In my dream world, I say, *Only if you give it to me,* and he throws the truck in park and saunters over and kisses me like we're Frisco and

Felicia on *General Hospital.* But in this world, the painfully real one, the best I can do is, "No. Not if you have an ounce of self-respect."

OPENING the mailbox ranks as my second favorite part of the school day, which only confirms what a loser I am. But there's a little magic in unlatching the lid and peering inside at the stack of possibilities. Some days it's bills or junk mail. On good days, I find my glossy copy of *YM* magazine or the *Sweetbriar Gazette.* Once, I spotted a spider the size of my palm perched atop the electric bill. Usually though, there's absolutely nothing inside, only an empty cavern of disappointment. Still, here's me clinging to the gambler's fallacy that surely today—*this time*—the mailbox will contain a lifechanging delivery.

Hot from the sun, the metal latch burns my fingers. When I pull open the lid, excitement zips through me. A large brown envelope fills up half the mailbox. Before I hold it in my hand, I already know it's special. Unusual. Mysterious, even. With no address or stamps on the front, I wonder how it got there. I slide it out to examine it. It's well-worn and thick with handwritten pencil markings on the back.

SB 11

Intrigued, I peek inside to find a stack of cash.

"Juniper!"

Startled, I drop the envelope into the dirt. "Coming, Dad!" I call back.

Still buzzing from the shock of seeing my father in the doorway, I rush to collect the envelope, to dust it off. I can't remember the last time he met me after school. That he wasn't in his workshop doing God knows what with Stacy Pearsall, this year's research assistant. But then I recall Stacy left school early this morning after she sprained her ankle in PE, which explains it.

I trudge up to the house, stopping to say hi to Midnight. She stays close to the house now, sleeps even more than usual, and avoids all humans but me. Dad says she's a grumpy old lady, but she still purrs when I scratch her chin.

"Who's that from?" my dad asks, eyeing the envelope.

He holds open the door for me like this isn't *The Twilight Zone.* I half expect a glass of milk and a plate of Oreos to be waiting for me on the counter. For him to launch into his favorite game. *Six*, he'd say and point to me, expectantly. *Carbon!* I'd shout back. And off we'd go until I missed one.

"June, the envelope, who's it from?"

"Don't know," I say as I gawk at the kitchen table. The surprise of the envelope—the crisp bills wrapped in a rubber band—pales in comparison to the homecoming mum resting there.

My father lingers in the doorway with the envelope. His brow furrows when he opens it. "You didn't look inside?"

"I… It wasn't addressed to me, so…" I can barely focus. The mum looks as pretty as the one in the window. But why is it here? "What's in it?" I ask him.

"Just a bunch of coupons Mrs. Peterson clipped for us." He tosses it in the junk drawer and points to the table. "So, do you like it? Is it too much?"

"Yes. I mean, yes, I like it. It's *not* too much. It's perfect."

"I thought maybe you'd want to wear it to homecoming tonight."

I swallow a lump.

"I know it's unexpected. Maybe it's corny. But I drove by Mrs. Avery's shop this morning, and I saw it hanging in the window. It looked like something your mother would've—"

Overcome, I launch myself at my dad, nearly bowling him over. He squeezes me, and I have to bite the inside of my cheek not to cry. Sometimes, it hits like a Mack truck, what you've been missing.

"You'll wear it then?"

I nod with my face smushed against his chest. "Can I call Bonnie to pick me up?"

"Sure. Unless you want me to drive you."

"Don't push it, Dad."

We both laugh, and the moment feels so perfect I almost forget he lied to me about the envelope.

THE first half of the football game I find myself having fun. Mainly because my three biggest bullies can't bother me. Duane plays quarterback and Eric, wide receiver. When the biggest big guy on Adamsville's defense flattens Duane beneath him, causing him to fumble, I let out a squeal of pure glee that gets me some dirty looks, but I don't care. I wish I could watch it again on slow-motion replay. Predictably, Blair hogs the spotlight with her pom-poms and her toe touches and the massive mum Wyatt bought her clinging for life to her cheer vest. After saying a surprised hello to me, Wyatt posts up on the front row of the bleachers, his eyes glued to Blair. My eyes, glued to him. And everyone else's eyes glued to the field, where the Sweetbriar Bulldogs seem poised to end their five-year drought against the Adamsville Cougars. Since Coach Mac took over last spring, the team looks bigger, stronger, and faster—so much so that the *Sweetbriar Gazette* proclaimed the state title as ours to lose.

At halftime, I leave Bonnie to watch the marching band and twirlers and head to the concession stand for nachos and a Dr. Pepper. From behind me, I hear Wyatt's raised voice. When I turn to look, I see him arguing with Blair under the bleachers, his fists clenched at his sides. Her swingy ponytail trails down her back to the top of her short cheer skirt.

"Fine. Get rid of it then," Wyatt says.

"It doesn't go with the rest of my outfit. I'm a cheerleader, not a cowgirl."

"You can't hardly even see it. And June said she liked it."

Immediately, I skirt out of the line and crouch behind the dumpster near the concession stand, where I can listen in. My heart pounds.

"Well, congratulations, Wyatt. The biggest loser in our class is obsessed with you. She's a total stalker. She probably calls her pillow by your name." Blair mimes holding something, presumably my pillow. I'm glad I can't see her snooty face when she mocks me. "Oh, Wyatt. I want you to be my first, but be careful, I might crush you with my thunder thighs."

"You're ridiculous. You know what, her homecoming mum is better than yours. And you know what else, Blair? I bought it for her."

Flummoxed, I lean against the cold metal of the dumpster. I don't dare move. Should I be flattered or furious?

"You, *what?* Have you lost your mind?"

"Maybe I have. But at least June appreciates me." I peek out at them to see Wyatt hanging his head. "I'm not stupid. I've heard the rumors about you… and other guys."

"What are you trying to say? That just because I don't want to wear your dumb rodeo ribbon, I'm cheating on you? Do you want to break up?" Blair's sudden sobbing draws the attention of a few fans standing at the fence. Their concerned glances only fuel her. "Are you saying you don't love me anymore?"

"C'mon, Blair. That's not what I'm saying."

Suddenly, the dumpster lid opens. Mr. Humphrey, the President of the Bulldog Boosters, deposits two large bags of trash from the concession stand. I try to catch the metal flap as it descends, but I'm too late. The clang draws everyone's attention.

Wyatt gapes at me, as Blair spins around. She torpedoes toward me like a small blonde missile. Her blue eyes black with rage.

"Do you honestly think you have a chance with *my* boyfriend?"

No. My mouth forms the word, but no sound comes out.

"Good." Knowing we have an audience, she keeps her voice at a low growl. "Because you don't. You're nothing. You're less than nothing. Go crawl in a hole and die." She rips the mum from my shirt and tosses it in the dumpster. Then she cues the waterworks again. Tears freely flowing, she runs toward the bathrooms, and I'm left behind to be stared at by a crowd of judgmental faces.

Wyatt emerges from beneath the bleachers. His eyes meet mine. I'm back in my dream world, where he professes his undying love for me and we leave the game together holding hands, and I don't even care that he used me to hurt Blair. But that doesn't happen. Far from it.

Instead, he says, "I'm sorry," and chases after her.

GO *crawl in a hole and die.* I can't get Blair's hateful voice out of my head, even with Mr. Trolf rambling on about the weather and the football team and which teachers leave the biggest messes for him to clean up.

I had to get out of there. I couldn't wait for Bonnie. I couldn't face her anyway. So I'd fled to the parking lot where I found the school janitor sitting in his truck singing along to the radio and begged him for a ride home. My dad would kill me if he knew. He thinks Mr. Trolf drinks too much since his wife died. Secretly, a part of me didn't care if we crashed. If Mr. Trolf dead-ended his cargo van into a tree, it would put us both out of our misery.

But Mr. Trolf takes every turn carefully, slowing down to point out this farm and that one. To show me the house where his wife grew up and the tank where he and his best friend went fishing thirty years ago. Meanwhile, Blair's words seep into my veins, as poisonous as venom, until I believe I said them to myself. *Go crawl in a hole and die.*

"You can let me out here," I tell Mr. Trolf as soon as we reach the turnoff for Saw Mill Road. "I'll walk the rest of the way."

"Ya sure? It's no trouble."

"No, really, it's fine. I don't want to wake my father."

"Seems like he's awake." Mr. Trolf points down the road to the house. "See there, he's got a visitor."

As impossible as it seems, I spot Dr. Jim's unmistakable red BMW parked in our driveway. My wheels start spinning. Did Blair tell her dad about our argument?

"You alright?" Mr. Trolf asks. "You look a little green."

I nod and hurry to open the passenger door before I upchuck all over Mr. Trolf's bucket seat. "Thanks again for the ride."

"Take care, okay. Don't let those kids get to ya."

I had presumed the day couldn't get any worse. But even the school janitor knows I'm a loser. After he drives away into the darkness, I wonder what would happen if I stood in the middle of Farm to Market Road 57 and waited. Surely, by morning, I'd be flattened beneath the wheel of a pickup truck. Only Midnight would miss me.

Go crawl in a hole and die.

Just then, a car speeds by the turnoff, and the whoosh blows back my hair. I shake off the thought of death by automobile and force myself to walk home. With every step I play out the conversation, imagining all the ways Blair could have managed to make things my fault. But I come up empty. I didn't even speak.

Before I reach the door, it opens, and Midnight bolts out, her fur raised. She vanishes into the barn. Dr. Jim storms out behind her and shakes his fist at my father's shadow in the entry.

"I have a Doctor of Pharmacy degree. How dare you question my code of ethics? I won't forget this, Eugene!"

"Neither will I."

I keep quiet, as Dr. Jim revs up his sports car and tears down the driveway, narrowly missing a tree. Dust flies up in the moonlight.

"Dad?" I croak.

"Over here." He waits for me on the porch. "I wasn't expecting you back so early. And where's your…?" The way he holds his hand over his heart makes my chest ache.

I glance down at the small tear in my shirt. "It's a long story." That's the best I can do without breaking down. I want to tell him how Wyatt lied. How Blair attacked me. How I tried to fish the mum from the dumpster before Jessica and the rest of the cheer squad spotted me, pointing and laughing from the sidelines. "What did Dr. Jim want? He sounded upset."

My father mulls over his answer. "Apparently, a package was left for him in our box. I had a few questions for him before I returned it."

I'm not brave enough to ask anything more.

Hours later, after I've poured my heart out to Luke Perry and I'm certain Dad's asleep, I slink back to the kitchen and open the junk drawer. I search it as quietly as I can, then every other drawer in the kitchen. The mysterious envelope full of cash is gone.

CHAPTER TWENTY-TWO

NOW

BEFORE I dare retrieve the Hometown Grocery bag from beneath my shirt, I gulp down a glass of water and retreat to the bedroom and lock the door behind me. An accidental glimpse in the mirror horrifies me. Hair askew. Clothing dirty. Soot all over my face and arms. But I don't have time for a shower. Not now. Not with the entire town of Sweetbriar, Sheriff Faulk included, closing in on me, and that SFPD detective leaving another urgent message pleading for my return to San Francisco to answer for what I've done. And it's only noon. I wipe my face on the inside of my shirt. That's the best I can do for the moment.

The plastic bag sticks to my sweaty skin. I toss it on the bed as if it could hurt me. Which isn't so far from the truth. Carefully, I lay out the contents. The bottle of pentobarbital and the torn pages from my father's notebook that he'd hidden behind the periodic table.

I start there, trying to make sense of what I know now. That the cancer didn't kill my father—a monster did. The same monster who vandalized his workshop, murdered his rooster, and set the place on fire. But why?

A scan of the notes perplexes me. One page contains a hastily scrawled address in Adamsville beneath the double-underlined words *Post.* Another, a series of numbers and initials like the ones on Blair's missing folder, the folder I'd found in the pasture where my father died. More ADs and PVs. I try to picture it—Dad, running for his life with the folder in hand. Maybe he tossed it along the way or dropped it before the monster overtook him, cracked him on the head, and forced the poison into him.

I shudder at the thought of his desperate last moments and flip through the notes once more, certain I've missed something. This can't be it.

It's what's *not* there that crushes me. No *Dear June.* No deathbed musings. Nothing that sounds like him at all.

At least the address gives me a place to start. I type it into the search bar on my phone and study the results, enlarging an image of a single family home on the outskirts of Adamsville. After a few clicks, I determine the names of the most recent owners: Gina and Thomas Moseley.

An urgent knock at the front door interrupts my search. I peer out the window to see Wyatt's truck parked at the edge of the drive. Of course he would come back here, determined as a hound dog to sniff out my secrets, which I promptly stuff back in the bag and hide under the far pillow. He knocks again, as if to dare me to pretend I'm not here.

"Fine," I mutter to Luke Perry. "He'll have it his way."

When I fling open the door, I forget how disheveled I look. I forget a lot of things at that moment. Because Wyatt isn't alone, and I would be less surprised to see a unicorn standing beside him.

"Friend of yours?" he asks, pushing the girl forward. "I found her rummaging around in the shed. She says she knows you."

The last time I saw her the nurse had just administered activated charcoal, and I'd fled from the hospital like a coward. Like a *guilty* coward. Nearly three weeks had passed since then, and she looks different. Older, thinner. With her purple bob faded to black, an oversized The 1975 T-shirt hanging off one bony shoulder, and a ratty backpack off the other.

"What are you doing here?" I finally ask.

There's no denying her smart-ass smirk. "Isn't it obvious? I'm doing exactly what you're doing, Dr. P."

"Which is?"

She gives Wyatt a pointed glance, shrugs. "Hiding out."

Denial won't work with her. The girl scored off the charts on the IQ test I administered, even though she'd flunked out of two private schools before Ellington and was barely staying afloat there. "How did you get here? And when?" I ask.

"Bus, car, yesterday. I get we're in the middle of Nowheresville, USA, but it's not like we're on the moon."

"A car?" I scan the empty dirt road for signs of an unfamiliar vehicle. "Like an Uber? A taxi? They can track that, you know. Not that I'm saying you should avoid being tracked. You shouldn't even be here at all. I mean—"

"Relax. I hitchhiked."

"Oh, great. That's a comfort. I'm sure your stepdad will be thrilled." The moment I told Apex Cellular CEO Hugh Lockwood that his stepdaughter wasn't the problem, he had it in for me. Apparently, he wasn't paying the $25,000 yearly tuition for a touchy-feely hack like me to tell him how to parent his kid. He was paying for me to get her into a goddamned Ivy. His exact words.

"Ditched my phone too," she boasts. "I'm a *murderino.* That's a—"

I suppress a groan. "So you're criminally sophisticated now? You may want to keep that to yourself."

Wyatt clears his throat. He looks smug as he holds out his hand to her. "Wyatt Landry. And you must be Macy."

CHAPTER TWENTY-THREE

MACY lets herself in, drifting first to the kitchen. I watch her with caution, like one of Wyatt's practice bulls, certain she's dangerous, but not sure if she's inclined to merely buck me off or stomp on my head.

"You got anything to eat, Dr. P? I'm starving."

While I try not to panic, she opens the box of Ritz crackers from the pantry. She stuffs two into her mouth before promptly spitting them into the sink. Frowning at the box, she announces, "Expired in 2013. I was *like twelve* the last time these were edible. I hope I don't get food poisoning."

A part of me wants to laugh at her, this girl who voluntarily ingested pentobarbital. But then, she spins around, arms outstretched with that wicked little grin, and I wonder what she wants from me. Another part of me, a substantial part, fears her. I've told her too much.

"So this is where you grew up. This is the infamous Sweetbriar."

"Well, technically, I'd call this the *outskirts* of Sweetbriar. But yes, I was raised in this house."

"By your dad, Eugene, after your mother died," she says, before she hops up on the counter like a child and turns to Wyatt. "And this is Wyatt Landry, the hot cowboy. The one who—"

"Can I talk to you, Macy? *Alone.*"

She giggles at my mortification, but follows me into my bedroom, where she stares dumbfounded at my posters. I may as well have covered the walls in Egyptian hieroglyphics.

"Wow," she says. "This place is like a museum. Isn't that Fred from that show *Riverdale?*"

"Otherwise known as Dylan McKay… from *90210*? C'mon, *90210*." All I get is a blank stare that snaps me back to the harsh reality of all this. "Never mind. We have to call your parents. You cannot be here right now."

"I can't go back. Please." With a dramatic groan, she flops on the bed.

For the first time, I notice the dark bruise in the crook of her elbow from the IV. It's hard to be mad at her. But I am. Mad and nervous, wishing I'd hidden the grocery bag anywhere else.

"You have to go back, Macy. I'm worried about you. What happened was…" I hesitate. I don't want to trigger her. Her sixteen-year-old brain can't grasp the enormity of what she's done.

Briefly, she covers her face with her hands. When she lifts them, her eyes are teary. "I know it was messed up, okay. I had no idea what would happen. I just couldn't take it anymore. I didn't mean for them all to get so sick."

"I understand. You know I do. But you can't outrun this."

"If I go back, they'll throw me in jail. Not *baby* jail. Real jail."

"We don't know that for sure." Though I can't imagine any other outcome. No amount of money or clout can undo seven counts of attempted murder. Five of the eight students in the Harvard Bound program, along with their faculty sponsor Mrs. Mendoza, and

Ellington-Harvard alum Devin Delacourt, ingested a nearly lethal cocktail of pentobarbital and soda. So had Macy.

"Oh, yes we do. Mom begged Hugh to hire some big-shot lawyer to get me out on supervised release. *He* said they want to try me as an adult. That they'll convince the judge I can't be rehabilitated in juvie. That I could get a *life* sentence. You know how I am. Now picture me being locked down in a fortress of mean girls. I won't last a month. Plus, the attorney said it's in my best interest to spill everything, which means Hugh will have a coronary, and Mom will be on her own again. So the moment I saw an opening, I cut off my ankle bracelet, tossed my cell down the garbage chute, and bailed."

I sit down on the edge of the bed alongside her and try to remind myself of my training. I'm supposed to specialize in kids like her. Troubled kids with hearts full of secrets. Kids who don't fit in. Kids like I was. But in the six months since I'd started counseling Macy at her parents' request, she'd refused to tell me why she hated herself and her classmates, even after I'd taken a stupid risk and disclosed way too much about myself and my experiences at school. In our last session, I'd given her an ultimatum: *Tell me what's going on with you or I'll have to involve your parents.* The next day she'd blown up both our lives. Turns out I'd all but given her the instruction manual.

That's why I don't ask what she means about spilling everything. I can't afford any more bombs. Instead, I play it safe, stick to the less incendiary topics. "How did you know I was here?"

"I didn't. But I remembered what you told me about Sweetbriar. How this place is as far from civilization as it gets without going off-grid. I mean, a girl needs electricity and running water. And, let's be honest, I can't live without pizza or *Real Housewives*."

"Heaven forbid."

She sits up, excited by my jokey tone. "So you'll let me stay?"

"Macy, I'm already in huge trouble. The note you left made them think I conspired with you."

"But I told them you had nothing to do with it. That you were only trying to help me and didn't know what I was planning."

She's right, though I doubt the cops will be persuaded so easily. For her stepdad and his fancy attorney, I make the perfect scapegoat. Still, I nod to reassure her. "I'm in the middle of another mess right now. You being here will only make it worse."

Macy takes my cellphone from the dresser. "Can I borrow this?"

After I unlock the screen, she jabs at it a few times until she finds what she's looking for, and holds up the screen. A headline reads: Body Unearthed After Twenty-Year Search for Missing Texas Teen.

"You mean this mess, right? The dead girl. The one who hated you. I saw it in the local newspaper in Wyatt's trash bin."

I don't answer, but my horrified face gives me away. It's made the paper. Of course it has.

"Whatever it is, I can help," she says. "I specialize in messes."

"Macy…"

She starts to cry, softly at first, then harder. So hard her shoulders shake. Twenty-four sessions give or take, and it's the first time I've seen the girl drop her guard.

A soft knock at the door pulls me away. Wyatt says, "Is everything okay in there?"

I look at Macy huddled on my bed, her knees curled to her chest. A far cry from the spitfire who once lectured Headmaster Melhorn about the impact of plastic straws and punched her worst bully in the face. I don't recognize this girl at all.

But I can't let Wyatt know how *not okay* I am, so I mutter, "Yes." Then I turn back to Macy. "Twenty-four hours," I tell her. "Then I have to let the authorities know where you are. That you're safe. We both have to face this, and we can do it together." I sound calm and convincing. The sort of person who can meet any challenge. Inside, it's another story. The thought of facing the wreckage of my life makes me queasy. So, I leave Macy in the bedroom to compose herself and close the door behind me before she can ask too many questions. Before the cracks show in my carefully collected façade.

When I direct Wyatt to the kitchen, he replies with a stern raise of his eyebrows.

"I need a favor," I tell him. "Could you not mention this... *her*... to anyone right now?"

"Do you really think that's a good idea, June?" It's obvious he thinks it's a terrible one, possibly my worst yet. "Her face is all over the news. They're saying she's unstable, unpredictable. That she could be a danger to herself or others."

I hate that he's right. But even more, I hate that I failed Macy. That I couldn't stop her the way I stopped myself. "Well then, it's lucky I'm a school psychologist. I've been working with her for months. She trusts me."

"Not to be a total jerk, but that didn't do much good, did it? I know I don't have room to talk, but..." His voice softens.

I imagine he's thinking about that night he got loaded at the Roundup Saloon—the *Sweetbriar Gazette* article had him at three times the legal limit—crossed the center line as he drove home, and ran head-on into the Gomezes' Honda, scrunching it like an accordion.

"But?" I prompt.

"But you're only delaying the inevitable and risking a lot in the process. What if you're wrong about her? What if she hurts someone else?"

"I know. And you're not a jerk for saying it. I've replayed this whole thing with her a thousand times. Right after it happened, it's all I could think about. Replaying every session. Rereading every note in her school file. What did I do wrong? What did I miss? I just have this hunch there's something she's not telling me. I can't send her back there without knowing."

"I get it. It's tough when someone you care about keeps you in the dark." His mouth quirks.

"Uh, yeah, it is, Mike Tyson." I glance at his bruised hand. "Why didn't you tell me you punched Duane?"

"Because I'm not proud of it. I let him get under my skin, and I did something stupid. I stooped to his level. To my dad's level. I acted like the knucklehead I used to be. And with my past, I can't afford to make those kinds of mistakes." He shakes his head at himself, then takes a breath. "But between you and me, I should've knocked him on his ass years ago for how he treated you. So, I can't say I regret it. It was long overdue."

Never has a justification of violence so warmed my heart.

"And, hey, I'm sure you know what you're doing with Macy. I won't say anything about…"

As he nods his head in the direction of my closed door, Macy bursts out from behind it holding the Hometown Grocery bag. "What's this? I found it under the pillow."

CHAPTER TWENTY-FOUR

I snatch the bag from her hand so quickly the contents tumble to the floor. My father's handwritten notes land at her feet. The bottle of pentobarbital shatters, leaving a small puddle of liquid and caked sediment in the jagged-edged bottom. Macy stoops down to examine a piece of the broken glass. The piece with the skull and crossbones.

"Be careful, Macy." I try to ignore the heat of Wyatt's stare, but it's too much. "It's not what you think," I tell him.

"You keep saying that."

Macy busies herself collecting the sheets of paper and studying them. "Were these your dad's?"

I return to ignoring Wyatt. "How'd you know?"

"Because it looks like a secret code, and I remember you saying he was a mad-scientist type." She reads some of the initials and numbers aloud. "So, what does it mean?"

"I'm not sure. I found them taped behind a framed periodic table in his workshop. I looked up the address. It's a house in a neighboring town." I shouldn't say more. Wyatt even gives me a warning glance. But I can't help it. Now I know it, I have to say it out loud. "I think my dad was onto something. And it got him killed."

Macy gasps. "I thought you said he was sick with cancer," she says.

"He was, but it turns out he had a bump on his head when they found his body. A bad one."

Wyatt looks frozen, as if he's under a spell. I search his eyes and get nothing in return.

"They covered it up and made it sound like he killed himself. Right before he died, his workshop was vandalized. Someone threatened him. And today—"

"June. Stop." Finally, he speaks.

But now I just wish he hadn't. "Stop what?"

"You really want to do this here?" He cuts his eyes at Macy. "Now?"

I shrug, practically daring him. Macy's eyes pinball between us a few times before she slinks into the living room with my father's notes, leaving the broken bottle of pentobarbital to remind me of all my worst mistakes. I nudge the jagged pieces with my foot.

"Fine. Have it your way, then," he says. "The day before he died, your dad was helping me with a bull-riding lesson. He stumbled and smacked his head on the gate. That's the most likely explanation for how he got the bump."

"Maybe. But you can't be certain of that. And what about the vandalism? You told the sheriff that was suspicious."

"I told the sheriff I strongly suspect the vandalism and the fire are connected. I'd bet money that one of the Dupree twins had a hand in both… probably Caleb. He's had some troubles lately. But there's not some massive cover-up going on here, June. I told your dad the same thing. Maybe it was the cancer or his age—I don't know—but he became paranoid in the last few months. That's why I encouraged him to let me take the gun for safekeeping. I didn't want him to hurt himself or anyone else."

I want to tell Wyatt I don't believe him. That he's lying. That he should leave my house and never come back. But the words I want to say disappear. Because I can't argue with him. How can I? He was here when I wasn't. I don't have a leg to stand on.

Swallowing the lump in my throat, I bend down to collect the remnants of the bottle. Wyatt joins me there, but I don't look up. I only see his knees next to mine.

"You miss him." Carefully, he places a broken shard in the plastic bag. "I get it. It's too late now to make up for the time you lost. But poking around and making accusations won't bring him back, and it certainly won't win you any friends in the sheriff's office. Believe me, I know. With Sheriff Faulk breathing down your neck about Blair, you don't need any more enemies."

"I'm well aware of that." I grab the last piece of the bottle too fast, nicking my index finger. I suppose I deserve it and worse. "Why do you care what happens to me anyway? You think I murdered Blair."

Wyatt looks worried by the thin line of blood on my finger, but wisely keeps his hands to himself. "I never said that."

"You didn't have to."

His sigh could move a mountain. "I know you lied about that night. I know you saw her after we..."

"We all saw her. She made sure of that. In that short blue dress." It's a petty thing for me to say, a jealous thing, but it spews out anyway.

"Fine. You disappeared from the gym. You argued with her. You fought. I ran away like a coward when I saw the two of you going at it." He waits for me to deny it, but I simply stare at him. I feel my mouth go slack, tongue dead. No one saw me. No one. Especially not Wyatt.

"Hey, check this out."

Macy appears in the doorway holding my cellphone, and I come back to life. I've never been more grateful for an interruption.

"I found some info on the family who lives in that house. The address your dad wrote down. Their son Chase died last year in a car accident. Look."

> *Sixteen-year-old Adamsville football star Chase Moseley perished in a single car accident early this Saturday morning. Sources close to the teen say he was acting strangely at a party and started a fight with a teammate before driving off at an excessive rate of speed. A short time later, Chase lost control of his vehicle and struck a utility pole. The electric vehicle caught fire, causing his death. Due to the condition of Chase's remains, authorities were unable to perform an autopsy to rule out alcohol and drugs as a factor in the crash.*

"There's a Facebook post from his mom too," she says, tapping at the screen until it appears. Gina Moseley had authored the post in mid-February.

> Friends, we need your help. Two months ago, our son Chase died. In the weeks leading up to his death, he wasn't himself. He was angry, moody, and withdrawn. The school hasn't been able to give us any answers. We believe there's more to this story and that this strange envelope might be a clue. We found it in his backpack after his death.

Macy gasps when I snatch the phone from her hand, but I have to see it up close. After Wyatt's little speech, I'm doubting my instincts. I enlarge the photo with my fingers, and it's my turn to draw in a breath. I recognize the envelope, or rather the markings on it. *AD 5.* It looks just like the one I found in the mailbox on Saw Mill Road all those years ago.

CHAPTER TWENTY-FIVE

ONE YEAR UNTIL GRADUATION

AS I search for a seat in the crowded gymnasium, I curse my dad—he still won't let me take the truck to school and today the bus driver hit a pothole on Farm to Market Road 57 and blew a tire, forcing us to wait for a backup. It's a cascading catastrophe, like the great East Japan earthquake we studied in physical science. The earthquake caused the tsunami that caused the nuclear accident that caused me to have no choice but to sit next to Freddie Figeroa.

Seconds after I take my seat, Duane starts in. *Junebug and Freddie sittin' in a tree, k-i-s-s-i-n-g*... You would think he'd come up with something new by now, but no matter how big his muscles get, his brain remains pea-sized.

"Don't forget your ballot." Freddie offers me a slip of paper from the stack at the end of the bench seat.

Reluctantly, I accept it, rolling my eyes at the typed print at the top. Vote For Your 1996–1997 Varsity Bulldog Cheer Squad: Circle Five Names Only.

Coach Mac approaches the microphone, and the neanderthals erupt, led by Neanderthals-In-Chief Duane and Eric. "Big Mac! Big Mac! Big Mac!" At least, the coach's arrival has interrupted Duane before he gets to the part with me and a baby carriage.

"Alright, alright. Quiet down before you make me eat a cheeseburger or three at 8:15 in the morning."

That brings another raucous cheer. Since Sweetbriar High hired Toby McLean three seasons ago as the head football coach, he's been a crowd favorite. For starters, he's the youngest teacher at the school and the best looking. But let's be real about what matters most around here: Coach Mac can win big games and banners. Like the 1995 state-championship pennant hanging from the rafters.

"We are here for one reason and one reason only. To select your next varsity Bulldog cheer squad and head cheerleader." He waits for the applause to die before he revs them up again with a wave of his hands. "As you know, Sweetbriar High has the best cheerleaders in the great state of Texas. Award-winning in their own right, this spring they took home the NCA Championship in the Small High School Division."

On cue, the fifteen candidates parade out of the locker room. With their requisite white T-shirts, blue shorts, and matching blue bows, they resemble a small cheer army. Each girl wears their competition number pinned to their chest. They assemble in front of the panel of professional judges seated at the scorers' table. I recognize one of the judges as Blair's mother, who apparently cheered for the Cowboys for three seasons before taking that PR job. Anywhere else, it would be unfair, unethical for her to be on that panel, but in Sweetbriar it's just another Thursday.

As the audience quiets, Coach Mac continues. "After each candidate performs a cheer of her choosing, you will circle five names—and five names *only*—on your ballot. Your votes will be tallied in conjunction with the scores of the professional judges. The top-scoring eight girls will be named in the 1997 varsity squad, and the young lady with the most popular votes will be your head cheerleader."

Next to me, Freddie lets out an embarrassing whoop. I pity him. He still tries to fit in. I abandoned all hope years ago.

"First up, candidate number one, Blair Lennox."

Blair steps forward, while the other girls take their seats in the front row. I scan the bleachers for Wyatt, but come up empty, which marks his third day absent and makes me even more certain that Chet Landry beat the hell out of him again. When I tried to check on him after school yesterday, his dad told me he fell off the practice barrel and, in his words, *took a nasty lick upside the head. He better hold on tighter if he wants to go pro.*

While my stomach churns with worry, Blair pastes on her perfect smile and squeezes her arms tightly at her sides. "Ready? O-kay!"

"Gosh, she's so good, ain't she?" Freddie whispers to me like we're best buddies.

I nod at him. I know next to nothing about cheerleading, but I do know that when Blair yells, "Give me a B!" even I want to shout "B" right back at her.

When she reaches the end of the cheer, I ready myself for her grand finale. She always outdoes herself with some fancy trick that gets everybody all riled up, and I'm ashamed to admit that each time—every tryout and pep rally—I say a little prayer that she'll faceplant.

She puffs out a breath before taking off down the middle of the court.

"It's gonna be a flip," Freddie whispers, in awe.

As Blair executes a perfect roundoff cartwheel and starts her back handspring, Wyatt appears in the door with the blackest black eye I've ever seen. I catch the moment Blair spots him there and loses her focus. She throws herself backward, but lands short, with a bone-crunching thwack against the hardwood. She screams a terrible scream—it's the only sound in the pin-drop gymnasium—then crumples into a ball, holding her ankle.

"My baby!" Mrs. Lennox practically vaults over the scorers' table.

Coach Mac runs too. The two of them huddle over Blair while the rest of us pretend not to watch. If she had been anyone else, I would've felt awful. But she's Blair, and I can't stop the refrain in my head, that evil voice insisting she deserved it. That her suffering is well-earned.

With the help of her mother and Jessica, Blair struggles to stand. Tears track down her face, as she hops on one leg. Coach Mac scoops her up and heads toward the corner of the gym where I'm sitting. He carefully deposits Blair on the bottom bleacher and kneels beside her to examine her injury.

"It'll be fine," he tells her. "I'll talk to the judges. You'll get a do-over."

Of course she will. A girl like Blair gets every mulligan she asks for.

"But I won't make head cheerleader. Not after that disaster. I looked like a total amateur. Nobody will vote for a screwup."

"Listen to me." Freddie and I both lean forward as if he's talking to us. "You are the returning captain of this squad. Stop doubting yourself."

Blair nods and sniffles and waves off her mother. The show must go on.

Zombie-like, Mrs. Lennox returns to the scorers' table and prepares to judge candidate two, Alyssa Mann. When Blair notices, she starts crying again. Alyssa plays basketball, and she jumps higher and yells louder than Blair. Never once has she called me Junebug to my face. Immediately, I circle her name and turn to find Wyatt. He must be crushed. But he's already gone from the doorway and jogging across the court.

An irate Coach Mac steamrolls toward him, heading him off before he reaches Blair.

Freddie and I exchange a worried look. "Poor Wyatt," he says. "Coach looks like he swallowed a bumble bee."

I would laugh but it's true.

"You idiot! What were you thinking barging in during her routine like that? She could've broken her neck!"

Wyatt gawks at him, dumbstruck, but he doesn't protest. He only hangs his head like he had it coming. "I—I didn't know… I didn't know the tryouts had already started."

Blair hiccups a sob that seems intended to make Wyatt feel worse. Her breathing gets faster and more frantic until I start to panic myself. *Hydrogen, helium, lithium…*

"Let me talk to her," Wyatt says. "I can calm her down."

"You've done enough, young man. I'll handle it from here." Coach Mac retrieves Blair, hoisting her in his arms like a beautiful sack of potatoes.

As he heads toward the locker rooms with his precious cargo in tow, I stupidly envy her. I want to be the dainty sort of girl men carry. The leading lady. Dylan McKay's Brenda Walsh. Not the hyperventilating freak show that I am.

When I hear Principal Finch bark, "Juniper!" I snap to attention.

"Get down here and help Coach McLean with Blair."

"Yes, sir." My heart still pounding, I scamper onto the court and follow them. I can't imagine what help I could possibly be in this situation, but at least it gets me out of watching these stupid tryouts. And there's the added benefit of Coach Mac's movie-star good looks. I'm not immune to blue eyes and biceps.

"Are you alright?" I ask Blair.

She must really be down and out because she only manages a half-hearted scowl at me over the coach's beefy shoulder.

I revel in my momentary upper hand. "Does your ankle hurt?"

"What does it look like, genius?"

Now, that's more like it.

Satisfied I've won by default, I try to be useful to Coach McLean by opening the door to the team rooms. I don't belong here in the bowels of the gymnasium, not even with the coach beside me. I can't do a push-up to save my life, and it's a toss-up whether I or Freddie get picked last for dodgeball.

I keep my head down as we pass the recently renovated weight room—the remodel courtesy of the Booster Club—and approach the new training room. Since Coach Mac arrived and started winning, the boosters can't seem to stop throwing money at Sweetbriar Athletics. Meanwhile, it's been decades since the last upgrades to the science lab and the library.

"We'll get your ankle fixed right up," Coach Mac tells Blair.

She smiles up at him while yours truly, ever the dutiful servant, opens yet another door. I have an impulse to let it go, to watch it close on Blair's injured leg. To make her smile disappear again.

"You're Eugene Pickett's daughter." Suddenly his eyes settle on me. As if he read my mind. As if he knows what a no-good, awful person I am, taking delight in Blair's misery. "He's the one who invented that Harvest Gold stuff, right?"

That takes me by surprise. No one ever asks about Harvest Gold anymore. Not in Sweetbriar, where everybody already knows your business, sometimes before you do.

"That's right. He sold the patent before I was old enough to walk."

I dare to glance in Blair's direction as Coach Mac sets her on the training table and retrieves the athletic tape. But she's fussing over her reflection in the oversized mirror, dabbing at the mascara streaks on her face.

"What's your dad working on these days?" Coach Mac carefully removes Blair's shoe and sock, ignoring her wince of pain.

My eyes widen at the size of her foot, the puffiness. The reddish hue of a new bruise.

"I can't say much. He's really secretive about his work." Truthfully, I don't *know* much, but it hurts to admit that out loud.

"Chet Landry said he's been experimenting with livestock. That he's cooking up a super-cow concoction to produce the leanest beef cattle in the country."

Blair and I both startle at the mention of Wyatt's father. For a brief moment her confusion matches mine before she steers the focus back to her favorite topic of conversation. Herself.

"Oh my God. I have the ankle of an ogre. It looks deformed. Is it broken?"

"It's probably just a bad sprain, but I'll tell your mother to take you down to the ER in Adamsville and have it examined."

"Can't you just tape it up and give me a shot or something? I can still finish my tryout. We have the group cheer at the end with the pyramid. I have to be there or—"

When he grabs her knee and gives it a pat, she stops mid-sentence. To be fair, if the coach touched my knee, I'd probably die right there on the spot.

She lets out a frustrated groan. "My life is over. I may as well just die right here."

Coach Mac shakes his head at her, then turns away to retrieve the athletic tape from the supply cabinet. I reach for the scissors, anticipating his needs.

"May as well," I mumble, offering her the scissors. She glares at me. "Too messy?" I ask.

"Ha, ha. Junebug's a comedian." With the coach still distracted, she adds, "My ankle hurts worse just looking at you. Why are you even still here?"

It's a good question, but I don't answer it. I like her better this way. Wounded, vulnerable. It makes me brave. I shrug at her, daring her to tell me to leave.

Coach Mac interrupts our stalemate. "Hey, Blair, weren't you thinking of applying for Dr. Pickett's research assistantship?"

Blair mirrors my wide-eyed expression. "Uh, not really. I suck at science. You know that."

"I hear he writes one heck of a recommendation letter. It might help you get into UK." The coach takes the scissors from me with a firm nod.

"He means the University of Kentucky," she informs me, as if I didn't know. As if she didn't affix a giant Wildcat to the center of her "My Future" collage in art class. "They won the UCA Division I-A championships last year. Which means I have no chance of making the team unless I get *head cheerleader*. Which means I have to finish my tryout. C'mon, Toby."

Just then, a figure passes by the door, a familiar face visible through the small window. Overloaded, my brain fritzes. Too many thoughts at once. Too many questions. What if Blair applies for the research assistantship? What if she gets it? Did she just call the coach by his first name? Is that her stepdad pacing in the hallway?

While I chase my mental rabbits, Blair remains singularly focused.

"Did someone call my stepdad? That's just great. He's already got a stick up his butt about me and Wyatt."

But then Dr. Jim keeps walking and disappears down the hall.

"What's he doing here?" she asks.

Coach Mac says nothing. He affixes the tape to Blair's foot, round and round and round, and snips it off at the end.

Blair takes a shaky breath. "Seriously, Toby, why is he here?"

I try to make sense of this strange trip that began with Wyatt's black eye and a failed back handspring and ended with me here, more confused than Duane in trigonometry.

Through the awkward silence, I backpedal toward the door. "Unless you still need me, I'll just..."

Neither seems to notice my slow departure. Grateful, I turn to go.

"Juniper, wait." Coach Mac's hand drops onto my shoulder. His massive state championship ring looms in my periphery. He guides me into the hallway, shutting Blair out.

I blink up at his cool blue eyes and winning smile, wondering what he could possibly want with little old me. Maybe he'll thank me for being so helpful today. Maybe he'll ask me to be the team manager next year. Maybe he'll let me call him Toby too.

"Tell your father my offer still stands. He knows where to find me."

Completely clueless, I can only murmur an okay. I walk back in the direction we came, feeling the weight of his gaze on my back.

I spend the rest of the school day anxiously awaiting the final bell. I don't even raise my hand in physics when Mr. Markel asks for volunteers to assist with his eddy-current tube-magnet demonstration. I can't stop replaying my exchange with Coach McLean and lamenting at how little I know my own father. It's pathetic how I lit up when Coach called my name. How I actually thought he wanted to thank me. Instead, I left feeling even more alone. More invisible.

Blair never returned to class after her injury. Neither did Wyatt. But I saw a note passed between Alyssa, Jessica, and Christi that made it seem like Blair would be allowed to redo her routine for the judges at her mother's request. Because *life ain't fair, June*, as my dad would say. *A fair is a place where they judge pigs.*

Then during my lunchtime eavesdropping, I overheard Bonnie tell Jennifer that Wyatt had shown up at the Adamsville ER with a bouquet of roses, only to be sent packing by Dr. Jim himself. It sounded like a stupid rumor to me, but it still made my stomach ache.

As soon as the bus lets me off at the corner, I book it to the caretaker's cottage. I have to ask Wyatt for myself. To *see* him for myself. As much as his black eye worried me, it worried me more that he'd left home. That he'd come to school of all places, where the teachers weren't supposed to look the other way. If Mr. Landry found out, he would blow a gasket.

I practically skid to a stop when I spot the truck in the driveway. Wyatt's dad doesn't leave the Roundup until he's good and pickled. That's after six o'clock on most days. It takes a special occasion to lure him home early, and by special, I mean a burr in his saddle that the liquor can't fix.

The smart thing to do would be to turn around and beeline it back home. But then, I hear them out back in the bull pen. Raised voices and angry snorts.

"Go on if you think you're tough. Get up there. Show me what a big man you are."

"Dad, please. Just stop."

"You think you're hot shit runnin' around with that little tart. Tellin' everybody our goddamned business. You don't like the way I run this house, is that right? But you ain't got the balls to say it to my face, do ya? Nah, you're a coward just like your mother."

I can't leave Wyatt alone with that monster. Preparing myself for the worst, I slink into the shed and arm myself with a wrench from the tool rack. I tiptoe toward the noise with my makeshift weapon, taking cover behind a rusty feed trough.

An angry black bull paces the perimeter of the pen, stamping its hooves in the dirt and butting its head against the gate. When the bull passes him, Mr. Landry jolts its hindquarters with the cattle prod. Wyatt once told me that bucking bulls were born angry, bred to be violent. I see it now for myself. That red-eyed, fire-breathing bull wants to stomp somebody's head.

"What are you waitin' for, cowboy?" Mr. Landry turns the prod on his son. He must've got the head-stomping gene too. "Ya need a little motivation?"

Stone-faced, Wyatt jumps up on the gate and prepares to mount the savage beast. This isn't how it's done. I don't know much about bull riding, but I do know that. There's no flank strap to hold on to. Wyatt isn't even wearing his cowboy boots.

Mr. Landry's excited whoop sends my stomach to my knees. I emerge from behind the trough, intent on stopping Wyatt's death ride. But footsteps behind me freeze my mouth shut. I grip tight to the wrench.

"What in the devil is going on here?" my father asks. "That's *my* bull, Chet. Are you stealing cattle now?"

I notice, then, the small EP branded on the bull's hindquarter. A few months ago, my dad bought thirty head of cattle from a foreclosed ranch in Dallas as part of a new project. Another of the secret inventions he hoped would save the world, or at least his small-town piece of it.

Mr. Landry sobers up fast. He lowers the cattle prod and tries to hide it behind a fence post. "Nah. Just borrowin' him to teach Wyatt here a lesson. This boy ain't showed me a lick of respect."

My father walks past me without a word. Heat wafts from him. "That bull is not for riding."

"Why not?"

"You know damn well why."

They stand chest to chest, neither giving an inch, but slowly Mr. Landry backs down. He lowers his gaze, hunches his shoulders. It's a sight to behold. Chet Landry, folding like a lawn chair in my father's presence.

"I expect him back in my pasture in twenty minutes. Let's go, Juniper."

I sneak a glance at Wyatt and his black eye. I can't read him at all until I spot his hands on the gate, white-knuckled. Dad tries to put his arm around me, but I shake him off and stand firm. His strength makes me gutsier than I am. Gutsy enough to stick up for my friend.

"I'm not leaving Wyatt here alone. Did you see his face?"

"It's alright, June. Just go with your dad. I'll be—"

For a drunk, Mr. Landry moves quick. Before I can react, he's in my face with his bloodshot eyes and his sour breath. I drop the wrench into the dirt as the memory rushes back. His hand around my arm. *Volumptuous.*

"Now, young lady, this here is a family matter. You skedaddle."

"Hey, leave her alone." Wyatt springs off the gate and steps in between us.

I gawk at him, equally terrified and awed.

"Now you wanna be a man?" Mr. Landry squares up, his fists raised and ready. Eyes darkened with rage, no different than that bull stamping in the pen. "C'mon, let's go."

"Think about what you're doing. That's your son, Chet. He's not the one you're angry with." My dad talks softly to him, slow and measured. The way he used to coax Bert out from under the bed after a thunderstorm.

It works for about a half second before he redirects the poison inside him.

"Oh, get off your high horse, Pickett. It ain't like you're winnin' father of the year. June here probably forgot what your ugly mug looks like. You spend so much time in that workshop of yours, playing with those little school gals. Hell, I can't blame you. I'd want a piece of that—"

It happens faster than a lightning strike. Dad lays him out with one punch, then doubles over, cradling his hand.

"Shit. That hurt." That's all he says before he stalks off into the pasture in the direction of home.

Stunned, Wyatt and I stand there like fence posts. I tell myself not to cry, but I can't help it. When he turns to me, I crumple against him, and the whole day comes loose onto his shoulder.

"I'm sorry," I say after I come to my senses.

But Wyatt doesn't let go. He strokes my back, then my hair. I don't dare move. I wonder if I'm dreaming. If he's dreaming. Then, he stops, just like that, and laughs like we're buddies. Which we are. Friends. Only friends. *Barely* friends. Of course.

"What were you gonna do with that?" he asks, pointing to the wrench at my feet.

I feel silly. Stupid. "I dunno. Smack your dad upside the head, I guess. I can't believe *my* dad hauled off and punched him. Do you think he's okay?"

We both look at Chet, still prone in the dirt. His beer belly poking out from under his shirt. His right eye already swollen shut.

"He hasn't been okay since 1985."

"What happened today?"

"I couldn't miss her tryout, you know. So, I snuck out. I… I wasn't thinking. I'm so dumb. I shouldn't have come in late. I just—"

Something ugly flares inside me. I hate Blair for making him like this. I hate him for wanting her. "Did you go to the ER?"

He nods. "That went over like a ton of bricks. Her dad told me to get lost."

"Why?"

"'Cause he blames me for—"

"No. *Why did you go?* She's not a good person, Wyatt."

He shrugs. "I love her, I guess."

"*You guess?* Does she love you? Does she even like you?"

"Why are you asking me that, June?" His eyes search mine.

"Because I—"

Mr. Landry snorts, sits up. Spits blood into the dirt. "A girl like that, I'll tell you what she loves. She loves slummin' it. She loves pissin' off Mommy and Daddy. Just bidin' her time till somebody worse comes along to piss 'em off even more. She loves jerkin' your chain. But she sure as shit don't love you."

Wyatt swallows hard. Then, he leaves me. I hear his truck peel out. Mr. Landry curses under his breath, but makes no move to get up. The bull watches us from the pen, its thick-muscled flank still trembling. Its breathing, labored.

"Why do you have to be so mean to Wyatt? All he ever tries to do is please you."

"Ain't mean. Just honest."

Arguing with Mr. Landry is like wrestling a pig. There's no clean way to win. I pick up the wrench and head back toward the shed.

"You know my boy is a lot like your daddy. Skittish as a wild horse."

I refuse to hear whatever he's about to say. But he calls after me, insistent.

"You keep chasing that horse, June, and he'll never stop running."

I find my dad in the kitchen icing his hand with a bag of frozen pizza rolls. I want nothing to do with him, but then I hear his voice in my head. His words to Chet Landry. *He's not the one you're angry with.* I hate that they apply to me too.

"I'm sorry you had to see that, Juniper. I let my emotions get the better of me. A real man doesn't need to use his fists to win an argument." He sets the makeshift ice pack on the table, revealing his plum-sized knuckles, and flexes his hand. "Is Wyatt okay?"

"What do you think, Dad? You saw his face." I sigh. "Isn't there something we can do?"

"We are doing something."

He doesn't elaborate. But I know what he'll say if I ask. He's said it before. *I gave Chet Landry a job when no one else would. I gave him a roof over his head. I tried to get him help once too, and he chased me off with a shotgun.*

"Something more?"

"I'll talk to Mr. Landry tomorrow. We both have to remember that he's hurting too. He lost his son… his wife."

When my dad's voice trembles, I can't bear it. I pour a glass of water from the tap and set it on the table for him, a peace offering.

"Do you know Coach McLean?" I ask.

He takes a long drink, then wipes his mouth on his shirtsleeve. "Doesn't everybody?"

"Uh, what I mean is, do you know him personally? Are you friends?" It's a ridiculous question. My dad doesn't have friends. Hasn't since my mom died. I'm not sure he knows how. All his friends were hers.

"I can't say I've ever had a real conversation with the man, but I don't imagine we'd have much in common. Why do you ask?"

"He told me to pass along a message to you. Something about how his offer still stands." I watch his face, but as usual, he remains stoic. "He mentioned your project with the livestock."

Beneath the table, his foot taps like a metronome. "It's nothing you need to trouble yourself with." Abruptly, he shoves up from the table and turns his back to me, fiddling in the cabinet. A baking sheet tumbles from the top shelf. "Whaddya say we cook these pizza rolls up for supper?"

"So was that bull out there part of your experiment?"

Dad ignores my question. It's his super power. He opens the bag of frozen rolls instead. I can't remember the last time he baked anything. I frown as he fumbles with the oven dial.

"Dad? The bull?"

"I didn't realize you were that interested in my work. You can always apply for the research assistant position. It's open to all high-school seniors."

I bite the inside of my cheek to keep from screaming at him. I want to chuck a pizza roll at his head. To tell him that he would never pick me, no matter that I'm the most qualified.

"You have to preheat the oven first." Begrudgingly, I sidle up beside him. After reading the instructions on the bag, I adjust the dial and take a seat at the table to wait in silence.

A knock startles us both. "Probably old Chet come to say sorry," Dad says.

I make a skeptical face. Chet doesn't apologize. Sure enough, it's Wyatt at the door, looking more hangdog than usual. I tell my heart to settle down, to stop hoping. But he came back sooner than I thought, and he came here of all places. His eyes flick up to mine and back down again.

"Uh, Mr. Pickett, my dad asked me to come over. He wanted me to tell you something."

"Alright, son. What is it?"

"That bull of yours dropped dead in the pen."

CHAPTER TWENTY-SIX

NOW

"PROMISE me you'll stay in the truck and keep this on your head." I tap the brim of the Astros baseball cap Wyatt retrieved from his closet while I begged him to drive us. Now, it rests atop Macy's sleek black bob.

She flashes her best doe-eyed smile at me. "Relax, Dr. P. We're not even there yet." There being the outskirts of Adamsville. The home of Gina and Thomas Moseley.

"I'm serious, Macy."

"Okay, okay. I promise. But I still don't get it. It's not like these randos will ever recognize me. I'm not Ted Bundy."

Wyatt's gaze meets mine in the rearview. He looks worried; a reasonable response to driving around with two wanted suspects. At least I'm in the back seat with Macy where I can keep my voice low and dodge his judgmental side-eye. That he agreed to help me at all, despite his skepticism, came as a welcome shock. I'd showered in five minutes flat, afraid he'd change his mind.

"Your face is all over the national news since you ran away," I say to Macy. "People are looking for you. The cops. Your stepdad." I'm not sure who scares me more. When I told Hugh that Macy seemed depressed, that she might need medication, he'd stormed out of my office, slamming the door so hard my framed diploma had crashed to the floor. No daughter of his—step or biological—would be taking the easy way out, as he'd put it. *She'll pull herself up by her bootstraps the way I did.*

"Whatever." Macy slumps in her seat, the same way she'd done in so many of our sessions. Hugh's expectations came with a tangible weight. "Now his reputation is on the line, all of a sudden he cares about me. I don't buy it."

"Sometimes parents get mixed up too. Your stepdad means well. He just doesn't know how to…"

"*Not* be a barbarian? Remember how he threatened to send me to some military school in Arizona after I missed curfew?"

I sigh with the realization this is one argument I won't win.

"We're almost there," Wyatt announces as we approach Adamsville, population 5,103. "The big city."

Macy snorts. But twenty years ago a trip to Adamsville felt like an adventure—with its Whataburger and Payless and Mr. Gatti's Pizza. The year my mom died, we'd drive there every Friday afternoon to the Blockbuster. Taking the empty VHS case up to the counter felt exciting. Like the start of a weekend adventure.

The massive sign alongside the blacktop welcomes us to Cougar territory.

"I didn't realize they'd won the last five state championships," I say, reading the bright-white print. "Is that why Toby McLean retired?"

"Retired? More like strongly encouraged to find other employment. But that's what happens when you get caught in a compromising position with a—" Wyatt glances back at Macy and stops short.

I wait for her to say something, but she doesn't seem to notice. Instead, she points to my cellphone. Only two more miles, according to the maps app. My stomach churns with nervous energy.

"Turn right on County Road 40," Macy tells Wyatt, reading the directions over my shoulder. "It's on the left."

At the end of a dirt driveway, the Moseleys' two-story farmhouse awaits us. It could use a fresh coat of white paint and a mow. Grass has overtaken a helmet-shaped football sign decorated with Chase's name and jersey number 5. The way it's half-toppled in the weeds reminds me of an old gravestone. Alongside the house, I find more reminders of the boy who once lived here. A ten-speed bike with a rusty frame. An old tire hanging from a rack to form a makeshift target. A deflated football. The clues lead to a small shed at the back of the property with a hand-painted sign that tells me to KEEP OUT and another that reads GO COUGARS. Dandelion and thistle choke the dirt path that I imagine was once worn out by Chase's sneakers.

Wyatt parks his truck beneath a sprawling oak tree, but it's unbearably hot, even in the shade. The moment I exit the back seat, sweat starts to bead beneath my hair.

"I'll leave it running," he tells Macy. "But you better be here when we get back. And don't you dare think about changing the radio station."

"Scout's honor." Right hand raised, she drawls, "It's STIX classic country all the way, cowboy."

With a tip of his black Stetson, Wyatt shuts her inside. Halfway to the door, he says, "For the record, this is a bad idea. You shouldn't go poking around in snake holes."

I would like to remind him that he made it clear the only danger here exists in my mind. That I'm as paranoid as my father. But I owe him. Even if he does think I'm one card short of a full deck. "You can wait in the truck if you want. Macy would love nothing more than to grill you about the Sweetbriar dating scene. She can probably set you up on Tinder. Have a date lined up before I get back."

Wyatt makes a face. As if she's no different than any other teenage girl when we both know the truth. "I'll take my chances with the snakes."

Flies buzz around the screen door on the porch, the lucky few making their way through a small tear in the corner into the air-conditioned hallway. I peer through it too, searching for signs of life. Finally, the blistering heat forces me to act. I knock three times on the wooden frame. From inside, I hear the scrape of a chair and slow, plodding footsteps. When the door opens, I second guess myself. Because this woman can't be Facebook Gina Moseley with her spunky smile and perfectly posed profile picture. Her girlish frame, dwarfed beneath Tom's brawny arm. This woman is a husk, a skeleton in a nightgown at two in the afternoon. Skin and bones and drooping eyes. Scarecrow hair. She's halfway living, halfway dead.

It seems to require all her effort to push the wooden front door shut and close us out. "We're not interested," she calls from the other side as an afterthought.

"I'm not selling anything," I call back. "I need to talk to you about Chase." I wave off the flies that drone around my head and knock again.

Wyatt gently taps my shoulder. "Maybe we should go."

But I can't leave. Not after discovering my dad's notes. Not with his last voicemail haunting me. I have to do this for him. I have to see it through.

"Please, it's important. I saw your Facebook post. I recognize—"

A man appears from around the side of the house. Sweat drips down his face into the yellowed neck of his T-shirt. In his right hand, he grips a hammer. Like his wife, the real-life version of Thomas Moseley scares me a little.

"Who the hell are you?"

I try to look friendly, innocent. Not like the sort of person who's been questioned by the police. Who's been implicated in crimes. Plural.

"Juniper Pickett," I say. "I was just telling your wife that I recognize the envelope she posted online. In the photo." His frown deepens. "She asked the community for help."

He comes closer until I can see the sadness in his eyes. "She's not well."

"But the envelope—"

"I'm sorry. You need to leave." Now, he's on the porch with us. Him and the hammer. "This kind of thing only makes it worse. It takes her weeks to recover."

Gina flings the door open, wide-eyed, suddenly much more alive than dead. "Pickett? Are you related to Eugene?"

"Go back inside." Thomas tries to corral his wife, but she pushes past him, as sneaky and stubborn as a cat.

Of course, I don't help matters either. "That's my father. Did you know him?"

"He came here a few months ago. He said he thought he knew what happened to Chase, but he couldn't prove it. He told me he'd come back, that he'd tell me everything, but he never—"

"You tell him to stay away from us." Thomas puts himself between Gina and me. As if I'm the one wielding a hammer.

I forgot how quickly things can unravel. How a lunchroom quarrel can go from spat to battle royale in ten seconds flat.

"After your father showed up here talking nonsense, my wife nearly got herself arrested down at the school. Her doctor said the stress of his visit brought on another break with reality. She's delusional."

"I'm not delusional, Tom. Coach Hardwick knows more than he's saying. That envelope is real, and so was the boatload of cash inside it. Eugene believed me." Gina turns her focus back on me, her voice growing increasingly frantic. "Your dad told me he got one too, a long time ago. Is he here with you? I need to talk to him!" Desperate, Gina reaches for me. As if I can take her to my father. As if he had the answers. As if the answers could ever bring her peace.

Wyatt jerks me out of the way, and she stumbles forward into her husband, scraping her knee against the hard dirt. She's so frail, so delicate, I wait for her to shatter like bone china. But, somehow, she manages to stay on her slippered feet. Only her gritted teeth reveal the depth of her anguish.

"I'm so sorry." I try to sound comforting while keeping my distance. Being a school psychologist, I'd learned firsthand how violent grief can become. The bigger the grief, the bigger the explosion. Like the time freshman Jeremiah Porter cold-cocked the senior who'd driven his older sister straight into a tree. "Eugene passed away. I'm sure he wanted to come back to see you. He would have."

"Oh my God. He was right. They *were* after him." Gina crumples again. As Thomas tries to hold her up, the hammer clatters to the ground. "They got to him. They killed him."

"*Who?*" I sound equally unhinged.

"Did they follow you here?" Eyes darting, she grabs for the hammer. With a primal yell, she wields it at an unseen foe. "Where are they?" she demands.

I can't tell whose side she's on. Only that it's not mine or Wyatt's or her husband's.

"There!" She swipes at the air again, nearly losing her balance.

"There's no one here." Thomas tries to hold it together, but his voice trembles. "Give me the hammer."

Instead, she runs off with it into the grass, stopping when she reaches the football sign. She swings it mercilessly at the wooden helmet, and it breaks on the first blow.

Before Thomas chases after her, he levels me with a hard truth. "I warned you this would happen. Get off my property. *Now.*"

Wyatt tugs at my arm. "We should go."

I follow his lead. Keep my head down and my steps quick. I should've listened to him from the start. I thought I'd gotten past this years ago—my bad decisions. Irrational, foolish. Downright dangerous. But the last few weeks have told otherwise.

"You're one of them!" Gina shouts.

I don't look back.

Wyatt reaches the truck first. He turns to me, his face ghost white. "Where is Macy?"

I fixate on the empty back seat, frozen, until Wyatt points behind me. At Macy in a full sprint from the KEEP OUT shed. At Gina on her heels, teeth bared and hammer ready. Macy runs straight through the broken #5 yard sign, flattening it.

"Get in!" Wyatt yells to me as he runs to the driver's side and starts the engine.

I open the door and fling myself inside. My heart throbs in my throat.

Seconds later, Macy bounds in after me. Thwarted, Gina wails and thwacks the hammer against the window. The glass cracks. It's the last sound I hear before Wyatt floors it.

CHAPTER TWENTY-SEVEN

AFTER we blow by the Adamsville city-limits sign, Wyatt pulls off in the ditch. He hasn't breathed a word, hasn't so much as glanced in the rearview, but the back of his neck gives him away. It's bright red. As if he's radiating heat.

"You're paying for that window."

Huddled next to me in the back seat, Macy looks younger than her sixteen years and light years away from the tough little smarty pants who showed up on my doorstep.

Teary-eyed, she hugs her knees to her chest. "I know you're mad."

Wyatt harrumphs.

"Okay, *really* mad. You have every right to be. But I—"

"I had one rule."

"I didn't change the radio station."

"Fine. I had two rules, but only one that mattered." He smacks the steering wheel, and Macy and I both jump. "Dammit. I don't even know you and I'm already sticking my neck out here. And I'm not the guy who can afford to stick his neck out."

"This is my fault," I say. "All of it. I'm the one who asked you to come."

"I—" Macy tries again.

"Believe me, I'm not happy with you either," Wyatt says to me. "That woman nearly took us all out."

I make a face at him, hoping he can't see it. "She had a hammer not an assault rifle."

"I—"

"Are you saying your skull is harder than that window?" He points at the split glass on the back passenger side. "Because it looks like a cracked egg."

Macy interrupts my withering sigh. "Stop arguing!" she shouts. "I found something in the shed. It was taped up under the weight bench." She reaches into the waistband of her leggings and removes an unmarked prescription bottle. After unscrewing the cap, she fingers a green-and-white pill, showing it to us. "It's Prozac, Ellington Academy's favorite happy pill."

Wyatt looks unimpressed. "Okay. So Chase was depressed. It's hardly a smoking gun."

"But why was he hiding it?" Macy asks. "From that Facebook post, it sounded like his mom and dad knew he was down in the dumps. Why is there no prescription label?"

I examine the bottle more closely. The top of the cap features the familiar red, white, and blue Main Street Pharmacy logo.

"Did you see anything else in the shed?" I ask. "Anything that would explain that strange envelope? Gina said it had a lot of cash inside, just like the one that was in our mailbox."

"Seriously? You're encouraging her?"

"Well, it's a little too late to stop her, right?" I pat Macy's knee and she manages a smile. "We're all okay. We're all in one piece. No harm, no foul."

"Oh no," Macy mutters, peeking out the back window at the flashing red and blue lights.

Cursing under his breath, Wyatt slams the gear into park. "You were saying?"

A uniformed officer emerges from the Adamsville Police Department cruiser and saunters up to Wyatt's open window.

"Howdy, folks. I'm Officer Mason." He leans in and gives me and Macy a friendly nod.

As I nudge the pill bottle under my thigh, I force myself to breathe.

"Ya'll havin' car trouble?"

"Nah, we just took an afternoon drive and got turned around," Wyatt says, a little too casually. "Is this the way back to Sweetbriar?"

The officer nods, smiles, but it doesn't reach his eyes. "You live out there?"

"Yes, I do. Born and raised."

"Well, that explains it then. 'Cause you look mighty familiar."

I can only imagine the dark web spinning in Wyatt's brain. The bad movie that plays on repeat. The way my father told it, the crash had happened halfway between Sweetbriar and Adamsville. Alberto Gomez and his eight-year-old grandson, Carlo, were headed back to Sweetbriar from Houston, where they'd attended Carlo's first Astros game. Having worn out his welcome at the Roundup, Wyatt was headed to a late-night bar in Adamsville. If Alberto had taken one more minute navigating post-game traffic; if he'd agreed to stop for a burger and fries; if Wyatt had been a little less drunk and a lot less stupid… You could *if* your way to oblivion, and it wouldn't change the cold, hard facts. Two body bags and one bloodied mugshot on the front page of the *Gazette.*

"You sure I don't know you from somewhere?"

Wyatt takes a few slow breaths. He must be weighing his options. "They used to call you Peelin' Pete."

"I'll be damned. They sure did!" Incredulous, Officer Mason slaps his leg. "Hell, that was a lifetime ago."

"Twenty years, give or take."

It dawns on him slowly; a cloud passing over the sun. "You're Wyatt Landry, ain't ya? Shoulda recognized that black Stetson. Ole JC. You were the only junior rider who managed to go eight seconds on Fu Manchu. Man, I was jealous."

Wyatt's laugh sounds forced.

"You still on parole?"

"No, sir." Wyatt must know the score now. That he's on the losing end of it. "I completed supervised release about two years ago. No violations."

Beside me, Macy's eyes widen. I nudge her hand with my pinkie, hoping she can play it cool.

"Impressive." But Peelin' Pete makes it sound more like a wad of gum stuck to his boot. "In case you were wonderin', I already knew all that, Landry. I knew from the moment I pulled up. I was only testin' to see if the pen made an honest man out of ya."

Watching Wyatt bow his head to another jackleg small-town cop depletes the last of my patience. "Are we free to go, Officer?"

Wyatt issues a warning glance at the rearview, and the cop ignores me altogether. Typical. Cops around here only notice me when they shouldn't.

"You weren't out at the Moseley place, were ya?"

"Moseley?" Wyatt repeats. He's as bad a liar as I am.

"Gina and Thomas. You might've heard about their boy, Chase. Got himself in a real bad fight with a utility pole. He had one of them fancy electric cars. Burned right up. A damn shame. He played football with my son, David. He was a helluva quarterback, a Division One prospect too. His poor mother got the worst of it. She can't accept that he's gone. You know how that goes. Blaming everybody for her kid's mistakes."

"That *is* a shame. I hadn't heard of him. But then, I don't pay much attention to football since Sweetbriar stopped winning."

"Man, I tell ya. How the tide has turned. The Bulldogs score about as often as I do, if you catch my drift."

He leans in and wiggles his eyebrows at me—*now, I get noticed*—and I wish I could disappear. Beside me, Macy grimaces.

"Anyhoo…" If Wyatt's hoping his frenemy forgot the question, he's out of luck. I can tell by the lilt in Officer Mason's voice. By his eager grin. "Were ya out at the Moseleys? 'Cause we got a call about a black truck speeding off their property."

"It wasn't *this* black truck."

"Fair enough. I figure you're bound to know better than to be on the wrong side of the law these days. Especially with that body that turned up at Sweetbriar High. And pregnant too. Damn, man, didn't you used to date her?"

Wyatt stares straight ahead. I picture him at eighteen, fending off the questions, the insults, the whispers, the side-eyes. It's almost too much to bear, the way I left him to the wolves.

"I heard they called in them big-city cops for this one. Buddy of mine says that gal got knocked in the head. That's what killed her. But they also found some blood on her dress that ain't her type."

I know the dress he means. It lives in my nightmares. A Bulldog-blue mini-dress that swiveled every guy's head at the graduation party. Before the ceremony, I overheard Jessica tell Christi she thought it came from the local dollar store's sales rack, which I suspected was true. They also thought Blair had put on a few pounds. But to me, that dressed looked like a million bucks. When I close my eyes, I can still see it. The way the blood turned it brown.

Officer Mason lets out a low whistle. "Ain't that polyester somethin'? It'll outlive us all."

CHAPTER TWENTY-EIGHT

SEVEN MONTHS UNTIL GRADUATION

MRS. Dalton stands at the chalkboard waiting for the first-period bell to ring. As the latecomers file in, she adjusts her pointy black witch's hat and presses play on her spooky mix tape. I can't help but tap my foot to Michael Jackson's "Thriller" no matter how much I hate Halloween. Before Mom died, we spent Halloween night huddled under a blanket, gorging on candy and watching *Something Wicked This Way Comes.* Now, it's just another annual reminder of what's missing. Of what will never be again.

"You didn't want to dress up this year?" Mrs. Dalton sets a pumpkin-shaped cupcake on the corner of my desk.

Why did she have to say anything? Her question hangs over me like a spotlight even after I shake my head.

"You know Principal Finch awards a prize for the best costume, right?"

I shrug, wanting to get rid of her and fast. Oblivious, Mrs. Dalton moves on to deposit her Halloween wishes to the rest of the row while I steel myself for the onslaught of meanness headed my way.

First, Duane in his Superman cape. "Junebug don't need a costume. She can't get any scarier."

Then, Jessica, his Lois Lane. The diabolical duo have been inseparable since Duane's six-touchdown performance against Adamsville two weeks ago. Since the *Sweetbriar Gazette* called him the next Joe Montana. "Actually, she can get a whole lot scarier. Picture Junebug… *naked.* Now that would scare the bejesus out of anybody."

"Except Fat Freddie." Duane cackles. "He likes 'em plus-sized. More cushion for the pushin', huh, Freddie?"

Poor Freddie in his Stay Puft Marshmallow Man costume. To be fair, he walked right into that one.

"Shut up, Duane," Wyatt mutters.

I keep my eyes on the desk, no matter how much I want to look at him in the outfit Blair picked out to match hers. It would only make my situation worse. In my periphery, I see the stuffed parrot we found at the dollar store and sewed onto the shoulder of his shirt.

"Okay, Captain Hook," Duane deadpans. "Why don't you go walk a plank."

"Gentlemen, settle down." Mrs. Dalton casts a cutting glance. With her green makeup and glued-on nose wart, she looks practically menacing. "Before I turn you both into toads."

I go far away, back to Mom and me and Jim Nightshade. *By the pricking of my thumbs, something wicked this way comes.* But a chorus of raucous laughter zaps me back into the god-awful present. To Blair, strutting down the aisle, smirking.

"I thought she was supposed to be Tinkerbell," Jessica whispers to Christi.

"Me too. Guess she changed her mind." They both wrinkle their noses at Blair's hideous disguise. Brown turtleneck, brown pants. Everything brown. Even the paint on her face.

"What is *that?*" Jessica asks, grabbing on to one of Blair's eight pantyhose legs. "It's grotesque."

Wyatt looks as panicked as I am. He stares at Blair, open-mouthed, as she takes a twirl around the room. She stops beside my desk and waits until I gaze up at her.

"Isn't it obvious?" She bobs her head, wiggling the forelegs attached to her headband. "I'm a June bug. See the resemblance."

Of course, the entire class erupts into laughter with everybody pointing and staring at me. That's how it feels anyway. Like I'm on display at the freak show alongside the Bearded Lady and the Lion-Faced Man. Surrounded by her adoring crowd, Blair preens, while beneath my shame, a dark heat rises. Hotter and higher until I can't help myself.

"June bugs only have six legs, dummy," I mutter under my breath.

"What did you say?" Blair demands. Then, louder, loud enough to draw Mrs. Dalton's ear. "Did you call me a dummy?"

Mrs. Dalton frowns at me. "Juniper, we don't use that kind of language with our friends."

Suddenly, I'm on my feet, standing without permission, nose to nose with Blair. She looks ridiculous with those big googly bug eyes affixed to her forehead. But I'm not laughing.

"Good. It's perfect then, because Blair is definitely not my friend."

Everyone ceases to exist but her and me and the cupcake on my desk.

Blair reads my mind. "You wouldn't dare."

I want to. I want to so bad. I want to smear it all over her face until she cries. Until she can't breathe. Until she begs for mercy. I reach for it, hold it like a baseball ready to throw. The smell of the sugary icing wafts into my flaring nostrils.

"June, don't." Wyatt's voice bursts the bubble.

I drop the cupcake and run.

THE day only gets worse. Mrs. Dalton assigns me lunch duty for my outburst, so I'm relegated to wiping down tables and cleaning up trash while Blair wiggles her fingers at me from the popular table. At lunchtime, Principal Finch awards her second place in the costume contest—"Blair Lennox, as the mutant eight-legged June bug"—despite her entire premise being factually incorrect. Sadie Piper takes first prize, a twenty-dollar gift certificate to Dairy Queen, with her portrayal of a framed *Mona Lisa.* And I take five tater tots to the head before I manage to duck into the supply closet to wait for the bell.

When it finally rings, I wait another five minutes for the lunchroom to clear. Which only gives me five minutes to make it to fourth-period government at the far end of the quad. I hurry to my locker and fling open the metal door. Hundreds of dead June bugs tumble out at me and onto the freshly polished hallway floor. I jump back with a shriek, crunching a few carcasses underfoot. A note taped inside reads:

UR BETR OFF DED.

I recognize Blair's handwriting.

I hear a snicker behind me. Duane stands there, gloating, in his tight blue onesie and red cape. Ignoring him takes real effort, but it's well worth it. Duane withers without attention. Withholding it, that's his Kryptonite. I take out the textbook I came for and calmly shut my locker.

"Looks like you found your family, Junebug. Big, brown, and ugly. You look just like 'em."

I walk right past him, and I plan to keep going. To not give him a second glance. But then he shoves me, hard, and I fly forward, landing on my knees. My textbook slides down the hallway like a hockey puck and lands against Wyatt's boot.

"Leave her alone, Dupree."

"Who's gonna make me?" Given the size of Duane and his muscles, it's a reasonable question. These days, he's more Incredible Hulk than Superman.

"I am." Wyatt takes a running start, launching himself at Duane's chiseled midsection.

Duane stumbles backward into a row of lockers. Briefly stunned, he blinks a few times. His eyes growing as dark as a comic-book villain's. He lets out a guttural roar before he rushes Wyatt.

I hear my small voice cry out in protest as he drops Wyatt with a single punch from his hammer fist. But he doesn't stop with one. Or two. Or ten. And suddenly Wyatt looks like an old rag doll fished out of the trash. Limbs, loose. Face, blood-battered.

"Stop!" I yell, grabbing at Duane's forearm.

But I am a June bug after all, small and powerless. He flings me off and pummels Wyatt once more for good measure.

When it's done, Duane stands over him, exhausted. That's how Principal Finch finds him. With sweat dripping from his face. Blood, from his shaking hands. Wyatt, contorted on the floor, unmoving.

"June, go get the nurse." Principal Finch points to the small room at the end of the hall.

My head bobs up and down, but I can't move. I can't even recite the elements. Can't remember what comes after hydrogen.

"June, go!"

My legs carry me to the door before I remember that Nurse Maureen eats her lunch off campus at the Shady Glen Nursing Home, where her father lives. Still, I try the knob anyway, surprised to find it open, to hear voices on the other side.

"This is all I could find. He watches me like a hawk."

After a brief silence comes the rustle of papers. "This ain't shit." Then, "Figure it out, Blair. I need you."

"I'm trying my best, Toby."

I crack the door wide enough to peer inside the dark room. To spot the folder on the floor, papers askew. Blair hurries to collect them while Coach Mac stands over her.

When Blair finally rises to standing, the coach rests his hand on her shoulder. "Well, try harder," he says. "And change out of that ridiculous costume. What are you supposed to be anyway?"

Blair's eyes briefly lock with mine. It's the first time I've seen her terrified, and it thrills me and scares me all at once. She sidesteps him and heads toward the door, giving me away.

"Juniper." His wooden face, his flat tone. It all sends me back into a panic. "I didn't hear you come in."

I stammer, desperately trying to find my center again. "Wyatt… uh, he's… Duane went crazy on him. And I thought—"

Whatever I thought disappears like a rabbit in a hat. Because Blair brushes past me and a single page drops from her hand. It flutters down to land on my sneaker.

"Give me that," she says, snatching it back.

But not before I see the handwriting scrawled across the page. I would recognize my father's chicken scratch anywhere.

I stay up late, gorging myself on old Halloween candy, and wait for Dad to return from the workshop. Luke doesn't mind that I lick the chocolate from my fingers, as I tell him the whole awful story that ends with Wyatt propped against the lockers in a pool of his own blood, one eye swollen shut. He begged Principal Finch not to call his father. As usual, Blair got off scot-free with Principal Finch for my locker, pinning everything on Duane. The only upside was that Duane had been suspended for a week. Five whole days that I wouldn't have to look at his stupid, smug face.

By the time the front door finally opens, the moon hangs like a pale lantern over the farm and I can barely keep my eyes open. I find my father in the kitchen under a cloud of frustration, washing dirt from his hands and tending to a blister.

"What happened?" I ask.

He grunts, mutters under his breath. "Lost another one. Went straight through the back fence. Probably eating Mrs. Peterson's hay as we speak."

I know better than to press for any details. The topic of the livestock experiment has been off limits since that bull died in the riding ring last spring. Since then, my dad had paid Mr. Landry extra to dig a large pit in the corner of the pasture. The death pit. That's what I call it now, three carcasses later.

Dad dries his hands on a dishtowel and opens the refrigerator. "What're you doing up so late?"

"Uh, well... I need to talk to you about Blair."

He stares at the mostly empty shelves before he secures a plate of last night's leftover mac and cheese, and pops it in the microwave. Finally, my question seems to reach him. "You mean Blair Lennox?"

For better or worse, there's only one Blair in Sweetbriar. "Yes, Dad. Blair Lennox. Your research assistant."

"What about her?"

The microwave begins its one-minute countdown.

"I saw her at school today with some of your notes."

"Well, that's not so unusual. I gave her a list of readings. A few books and journals to request from the library."

"It didn't look like that, Dad. I know you have a thing about the lab being a sacred space. Nothing goes in or out without your permission, and—"

"She's very interested in my work. Curious, observant. A real scientific mind."

I want to tell him about the Bunsen burner. About the cheating. About the time she confused Einstein's theory of relativity with the law of gravity. About the note she left in my locker and how sometimes I think it's true. But I can't break his heart. No matter how many times he's broken mine.

"Can you trust her though? Do you think she's a good person?"

The microwave dings, and I lose him to day-old boxed macaroni. As he blows on a heaping spoonful, the telephone rings from the wall behind me.

"Who's calling so late?" he wonders aloud, with no intention of answering the phone or my question.

"Pickett residence," I say into the receiver.

"Put Eugene on the phone," a familiar voice demands. "One of his godforsaken science experiments got loose again. It flattened my fence and ate all my begonias. When I tried to shoo it away, the damn thing chased me. I barely escaped with my life."

"I'm sorry, Mrs. Peterson. He's been looking for that cow. I'll get him on the phone right away."

With his mouth full, my dad waves me off. Already, he's reaching for his jacket and his Smith & Wesson revolver. In a garbled voice, he says, "Tell her to stay inside. I'm on my way."

THAT night, I dream about June bugs. Thousands of them in my room. Crawling on my face. Clogging my throat with their hard shells and scratchy legs. When I scream, they spew out of me in a thick brown swarm, and I awake with sweaty sheets and a sloshing stomach.

"Too much chocolate," I whisper to Luke and his bedroom eyes. I turn onto one side, then the other. But I can't shake the seasickness. So I lie on my back and recite the periodic table until I'm back on solid ground.

"June."

I duck under the covers, frozen, and question my grip on reality. Is Luke Perry talking back to me? Is this a chocolate-induced hallucination? Is it possible to overdose on fun-sized Snickers? I quickly peek out from beneath the blanket and spot movement at the window.

"Juniper Irene Pickett."

But it's not Luke's voice I hear. Honestly, that would be less shocking than Wyatt Landry kneeling in the grass outside my bedroom and using every one of my names.

Now that the question of my sanity appears settled, I flat out panic. Because this isn't *90210*. And I'm no Brenda Walsh. I'm me. *Junebug*. In a ratty pair of plaid pajamas with zit cream on my face and half my hair smushed flat from lying on my side.

"What are you doing out there?" I ask through the closed window.

He giggles at me. That's the first sign.

"Are you drinking?"

"Course not." The half-empty wine bottle dangling from his hand tells another story. He drops it in the grass. "That's not mine." He frowns at it so convincingly I almost believe him. Then he puts his swollen face right up to the glass and fogs it with his breath. Writes JUNE and a smiley face in the condensation.

It hurts to look at him. The goose egg on his forehead. His swollen eye and split lip. The dried blood staining his T-shirt.

I slide the window up a few inches so I can scold him properly. But I lose my nerve when he drops his head onto the outer window sill, giving me an unobstructed view of the devastation Hurricane Duane left behind.

"C'mon, June. Pretty please. I can't go home. My dad will kick my ass."

"For being drunk?"

"Hell, no. He'd probably give me a medal for that." This time, his laugh is joyless. "For getting whipped by Duane Dupree. My dad thinks he's a pansy."

"Has he seen Duane lately? Even his muscles have muscles."

"Yeah, well, to my old man he'll always be the kid who cried in the chute at the 1992 Junior Rodeo. That was the last time Duane got near a bucking bull, and that one was a baby." Wyatt struggles to his feet, swaying right then left. Steadying himself, he hooks his thumbs in his belt loops and drops his voice an octave. "'Are you tellin' me you let that little mama's boy get the best of ya? I didn't raise no sissy.' That's how it'll start. Then he'll push me around till he's good and lathered up and wait for me to smart off. After that, all bets are off. You know, one day he's gonna kill me."

I wish I could tell him he's wrong. That he's crazy. But I have no doubt that Chet Landry could kill his own flesh and blood without blinking.

"Nobody will care, June. Nobody but you."

"That's not true. What about Blair?" Just the sound of her name and I'm queasy again.

Wyatt scoffs and kicks at the wine bottle with the Boone's Farm Strawberry Hill label. "Blair doesn't give a rat's ass about me. But you do." He returns to my window with a look so earnest I can hardly breathe. "That's why I'm here. At *your* window. Not Blair's."

Now I know he's drunk, and I don't hate it as much as I should.

"Your dad's still out at the shop. See." He points off into the pasture at the yellow glow. "He won't know if I sleep over. I'll be gone by the morning. I swear."

I pretend I haven't already decided. That I haven't wished for this on a thousand stars. Luke and I both know I would never turn Wyatt away. Not if he was on fire or contagious or projectile vomiting.

"Fine."

With a giggle-burp, he tumbles in through the open window like a puppy, bowling me over. I feign an attempt to push him off me.

Time slows even as my heartbeat races. For a moment, I think I actually might be Brenda Walsh. Wyatt's warm breath on my face smells like strawberries. His lips part. My whole body throbs beneath him.

A single gunshot fires in the distance. It slams a door between us.

"Shit." Wyatt sits back against my bed, leaving me cold and more alone than ever. "Guess your dad had to put down another one. What's he giving those cows anyway?"

CHAPTER TWENTY-NINE

NOW

"SO, what now?"

Macy flops back onto my bed, while I watch Wyatt's truck through the window, kicking up dust on Saw Mill Road. He didn't say much on the drive back, but then neither did I. Macy filled the silence by recounting her adventure in the KEEP OUT shed, and I tried to focus on anything but Officer Mason's mention of Blair's cracked skull; the bloodstain on her blue dress. When Wyatt parked in the driveway, long enough to let us out, he uttered two words: *Be careful.* Around here, that seems easier said than done.

"Now *nothing.* Not for you. You almost got us in a serious mess back there. It's one thing to get *me* in trouble, but Wyatt doesn't deserve that. He's worked too hard to earn his way back." I take another frustrated glance at my father's notes before stuffing them in my dresser drawer under a pile of scrunchies and slap bracelets.

"I was just trying to help." Macy sits up, suddenly eager, and starts leafing through a stack of old *YM* magazines she found in my bookcase. "What's the deal with you two anyway?"

I pretend not to have a clue. The way Macy always did in the sessions where I pried. Asked too many questions, assumed too much. She would hide from me like a turtle, pulling her hoodie over her head and cinching it tight.

"Did you ever… you know…" She purses her lips and makes a kissy sound. "Ride a cowboy?"

My withering sigh makes her laugh, and I join in, grateful that it eases the knot under my ribs a little.

"Was he really on parole? You never mentioned that before."

I shrug at her. Because there's a lot I didn't mention and too much I did.

"I guess I don't see him that way. To me, he's just Wyatt Landry. The boy I grew up with. *My friend.*" It sticks in my throat like a barb. Because I haven't been a friend to him. Not then or in the years that came after. If I'd done what I meant to do, Wyatt would be dead with the rest of them.

When Macy clears her throat, I realize I've been staring off at Luke Perry again.

"Besides, when it happened I was already gone from Sweetbriar in every way. I'd finished college and started grad school. I hardly ever thought about this place." Never mind that it lived in me all that time as vital as an organ.

"But you thought about him." I can't deny it, even if my silence only serves as confirmation. "If he went to prison, can you be sure he didn't…" She doesn't finish the rest. Doesn't need to.

"I'm sure." I take a seat on the edge of the bed. "Let's talk about you for a minute."

"Let's not." She slumps onto the mattress and screams into my pillow. Still hiding her face, she says, "Why don't you just suffocate me with this thing? I'll enjoy it more."

The shrink in me can't fight my niggling worry. The ugly memory of Macy in that hospital bed keeps pushing its way through.

"This is serious, Macy. I'm concerned about you. Are you thinking of hurting yourself again?"

"Not as long as I don't have to go back there."

Which may as well be a yes. Because Macy and I both know she can't run forever. Neither can I.

I take my phone from my pocket and head to the *San Francisco Chronicle* website. Thankfully, I have to scroll down to find the latest Ellington Academy headline—past protests and corruption, robbery and sexual assault. The conveyor belt of tragedy advances, inching our tiny cataclysm toward obscurity.

Authorities Still Searching for Female Juvenile Involved in Alleged School Poisoning

"I don't want to see it." Still, she peers out from beneath the pillow.

"They interviewed your stepdad. Aren't you curious?"

She holds up an issue of *YM* with a Blair lookalike on the cover. "Kind of like I'm curious about *How to Read his Body Lingo.* I can't believe you bought into this garbage. What does *YM* stand for anyway?"

"Young and modern." I wait for it. The unrivaled brutality of the teenage comeback. The obvious deflection disguised as caustic humor.

"More like: *Yikes, misogyny.*"

I take my own shot—the unaffected persistence of the school psychologist—and show her the article on the screen, the quote from Hugh Lockwood.

"See that. He says, 'You're not in trouble, Macy. We want to help you. We love you. Please come home.'"

That warrants a finger in the mouth, fake gagging.

"It looks like they spoke with Devin as well. The Harvard guy. He says he doesn't blame—"

With unexpected fury, she snatches the phone from my hand. Her eyes tear up as she reads aloud. "'She's obviously a troubled girl with emotional issues. She needs a mental-health facility not a prison.' Well, screw him. I'd rather have emotional issues than..."

"Than what?"

"Nothing. Never mind."

Just then, the phone rings in her hand; its annoying little jingle too light-hearted for our weighty conversation.

"It's SFPD," Macy says. "Should I tell them to f-off too?"

I watch her stab the screen—*decline call*—embarrassed to admit how afraid I am of the voice on the other end. The detective I've been dodging. I don't know what to say, so I say nothing at all.

She tosses the phone on the bed, and we both look at it until it buzzes, alerting me to a new voicemail. I have to listen to it. Eventually. But I'm not ready to face another unfixable problem. Like the button and the blood stain and the gray fibers. My dead classmate. The burned-out shell of my father's workshop.

"I'm hungry," Macy announces.

That's a problem I can fix.

"I need to run an errand in town. I'll bring something back with me."

"Cool. No meat though. Friends not food, remember." She fluffs up the extra pillow behind her and settles in with a *YM*. "I'll be here learning *How to Spot Him, Snag Him, and Keep Him Forever.* Riveting."

I take the magazine right out of her hand. "You're not staying here by yourself. Not after that stunt you pulled. You need a babysitter."

"Rude." But she doesn't protest.

I only hope I can convince Wyatt.

FIFTEEN minutes later, I leave Macy at the caretaker's cottage with Wyatt, promising to return with pizza for dinner and a few other essentials. Black eyeliner and Peach Snapple, according to Macy. What Wyatt doesn't know won't hurt him, and what he doesn't know concerns my intentions for that unmarked prescription bottle.

Main Street Pharmacy holds the coveted corner spot on the town square, next to the Yellow Rose Theater, the single-screen cinema where the cool kids made out on Friday nights. In other words, not me. I hate that place as much as Wave World. Possibly more.

Over the last twenty years, the pharmacy expanded, taking over Albert's Shoe Repair to add a new home-and-garden section filled with Texas flags, armadillo planters, and longhorn wall decor. But I still know the fastest way to the back counter runs through aisle seven, the incontinence supplies.

I hang back until ten minutes to closing, surveilling the one-woman crew behind the counter. There's no sign of Dr. Jim, of course. But I want to know who I'm dealing with, preferably someone I don't *know* at all. A tall order in Sweetbriar.

After the last customer shuffles out with his walker and medication in a white paper bag, I make my approach. Instantly, I regret it. Because I recognize the last name embroidered in red on her white Main Street button-down.

Missy Cook graduated two years after me. Back then, her parents managed the Dairy Queen and gave out free Blizzards on her birthday. Now, it looks like she'd sooner drop dead than eat an ice cream. Her sinewy biceps stretch her shirtsleeves. As she straightens the *Congratulations, graduates* sign on the counter, a vein pops from her forearm.

I mutter a greeting.

"Oh, wow," she says, gaping at me. "It's really you. I thought folks around here were just telling stories."

"Hi, Missy." I force myself to muster an ounce of enthusiasm in the face of yet another person who knew me way back when. Who can't wait to drag me back down into the sinkhole of the past. "You look great."

With a broad grin, she flexes one arm. "A bunch of us train with Toby—you remember Coach Mac?—over at the CrossFit gym. When I started, the only lifting I did was fork to mouth. Now, I can do thirty wall balls in a minute. You should come check it out."

I can't tell if she means it or if she's only being Sweetbriar nice: the sugary-sweet coating on a poison apple.

"You look like you can crank out a few pushups," she says. "We could use another woman on our CrossFit competition team."

I make a noise that implies I might consider it. The workout I can handle. But the idea of my former classmates watching me turns my stomach. To them, I'll always be Junebug.

"I'm not sure how much longer I'll be here." Even to me it sounds like wishful thinking when I'm a lab test away from being arrested for Blair's murder. I suppose it would be fitting that I'd be trapped here. In the one place I wanted to escape. "I only came for the reunion."

Beneath her nod, I sense her knowing. No doubt she's seen the group chat. "How can I help you, June?"

"Can you tell me anything about this bottle?" I take it from my pocket and reluctantly slide it across the counter when she holds out her hand.

"It's one of ours, obviously. But there's no prescription label." She screws off the cap and peeks inside. "Looks like Prozac. Where did this come from?"

I flash to Gina Moseley, hammer raised in fury, and my heartbeat picks up steam. "I'd rather not say."

Missy raises her eyebrows. In a small town, *not saying* isn't an option.

"Would the pharmacy ever knowingly distribute medication in an unmarked bottle?" I ask.

"Not unless we wanted to lose our state and federal licenses. Maybe you should talk to the store manager. I'm not sure I like where this is—"

"What about Dr. Jim?" I blurt it out before I can think better of it.

The scowl darkening Missy's face tells me I've crossed the line. "Are you seriously asking me if Dr. Jim has ever broken the law? This is Sweetbriar not San Francisco. And Dr. Jim is no drug dealer. That poor man lost his daughter, and here you are accusing him of… of *what* exactly?"

"I'm not accusing anyone of anything. Just asking questions." When you cross one line, you may as well blow through another. "But you remember the rumors, don't you? About the football team?"

When she replies with a clueless shrug, I finally say it out loud. It's only taken me twenty years. "You know, them being juiced up? *Steroids?*"

"As I recall, those rumors were started by your father. Now, if you don't mind, I need to empty the register. It's closing time." She simmers at a low boil until I turn to go. "On second thought, don't come by the gym. You've changed, June."

"And thank God for that." I take the bottle and stuff it back into my pocket, but I can hardly focus. *Started by my father?*

As I wander back down aisle seven, a young man in a sweaty Adamsville Cougars T-shirt brushes past me on his way to the counter. He bumps me with his shoulder and nearly knocks me over. At least it snaps me out of my daze.

"I need to see Dr. Jim. Now." Two massive cougar paws slap the counter, punctuating his demand.

"Dr. Jim isn't here."

He huffs. "When will he be back?"

"I don't know. He's on leave due to a family emergency." A description that seems insufficient for the unearthed body of his missing pregnant stepdaughter.

"What?"

Missy shrinks back, but I don't feel bad for her. It's probably the most interesting shift she's ever worked at Main Street Pharmacy.

"We have another pharmacist filling in from League City. She'll be here first thing tomorrow when we open."

With a grunt of frustration, the boy sweeps his hand wide and sends the graduation sign flying. Missy yelps, as I swallow a gasp. Oblivious to my presence, the boy stalks down aisle seven, swiping at the row of adult diapers. They avalanche onto the polished concrete, but it doesn't slow him down. I run after him. Out the automatic sliding doors and into muggy Texas twilight.

"Hey, wait up."

He approaches a black Jeep and gives the back tire one, then two impressive kicks. Finally, he sputters out, leaning against the tailgate and breathing heavy.

"Are you okay?" I ask him.

Apparently, teenage boys don't differ across geographies. He gives me the same shrug, the same blank stare I'd come to expect at Ellington.

"You play for Adamsville." *Duh,* his face says. "Did you know Chase Moseley?"

"What's it to you?"

I pull out my cellphone, my fingers fumbling across the screen. Finally, I manage to find it. Gina's Facebook post. The photo of the envelope. "Do you recognize this?"

"Is she bothering you, DJ?" The voice comes from behind me. But it's unmistakable. I can still hear her cackling at Blair's jokes. Whispering *Junebug* every time I sharpened my pencil. "Leave him alone. You're picking on a kid."

"Picking on him?" When I turn to face Jessica, she's not alone. I wonder if I'm hallucinating. The two boys flanking her both look exactly like the eighth-grade version of Duane: awkward, pimple-faced and slouching in front of the Duprees' flashy red Hummer. So, apparently Duane sold more than just a kidney. "I'm just talking to him."

DJ bails out, and I don't blame him. Caught between two thirtysomethings still hung up in their high-school drama, he hops into his Jeep and rides off into the Texas sunset, taking his rage on the road. As he leaves, I spot the paint on his back window proclaiming him a rising senior, Cougars #87.

"Shouldn't you be in a jail cell already?" Jessica asks. Caleb and Cody twitter in response like dueling Bart Simpsons. "Everyone knows what you did to Blair. What you were planning. That poor girl died for the rest of us. All because of your jealousy. To think, she and Wyatt were gonna have a baby."

"Is that what you believe?" My anger has weight. It's heavy as a brick thrown through a window, and I hold on to it to keep from spiraling. I hate how close to the truth she's come.

"That's what I know. The evidence proves it."

"What evidence?"

"I really can't share any more. It's official police business. Of course, I have special privileges being the wife of a sworn officer." She points her perfect nose into the air, and I wait for her to spill it. Because I recall there's one thing Jessica can't do and that's shut her mouth. "The dead can speak, Junebug. And sometimes they have a lot to say."

Her words send me right back to the school flagpole, caught in the act with Blair's bones in my hand. I'm certain if she could speak, she would have told me to get my filthy Junebug claws off of her. All eight of them.

"C'mon, boys. We're going to be late for dinner with your father."

Caleb frowns. "With Dad? I thought you were pissed at him after he got his tooth knocked out by that bank robber and—"

Jessica's icy glare freezes her son's lips shut while I hold in a laugh. *Bank robber?*

"Yeah, Mom," Cody chimes in. "You said Dad looked like a hobo when he decided to get the cheap clip-on tooth and not the implant. And then Dad said we couldn't afford—"

"Hush. Both of you. It's called a removable partial denture, and it'll do just fine until we can get an appointment with a cosmetic dentist in Houston."

Chuckling to myself, I watch the twins traipse behind her across the street toward Mary's Diner, jostling each other until she casts another scathing glance over her shoulder. She holds the door for them, then lets it close behind them. My mirth fizzes out at the sight of her.

"Hey, Junebug. Better get a lawyer."

I sit in the dark in my little clown car and doom scroll through my life. First the articles. Then the emails. I reread the dismissal from

Headmaster Melhorn and reluctantly open a new message from Hugh Lockwood—marked urgent—who apparently will sue me for everything I'm worth if I assisted Macy on her deep dive into juvenile delinquency, etcetera, etcetera. He's called me too. A few times. With each voicemail, he sounds less and less like a worried stepfather and more like a homicidal drill sergeant.

I look up lawyers in Sweetbriar. There are two in the area, and I know them both. Calling either of them feels like admitting to something, and I'm not ready for that. One of the men, Geoffrey Berstein, managed my father's will. He read me the brief document on the telephone, his nasally voice pronouncing me the proud owner of all the things I'd never wanted. With one exception. The caretaker's cottage and the surrounding ten acres would go to Wyatt free and clear.

I save the worst for last. It takes all the courage I can muster to press play on the voicemail from SFPD.

"Hello, Dr. Pickett. This is Detective Tristan Voss of the San Francisco Police Department. I need to speak to you urgently about your student, Macy Powell. Macy cut off her ankle bracelet a few days ago, and her family suspects you may have assisted her in fleeing house arrest. As Macy's counselor, I'm sure you're aware of her serious mental-health issues and your professional obligation to report any danger to self or others. Macy's behavior before absconding leads me to believe she is unstable and dangerous. She broke into a house, set a small fire, and stole a vehicle, which she abandoned outside of Los Angeles. Please contact me immediately."

Three rounds through the periodic table, and my head stops spinning. Two more, and I stop breathing like a fish out of water. But I'm halfway back to Saw Mill Road by the time I realize I forgot the damn pizza.

CHAPTER THIRTY

THREE MONTHS UNTIL GRADUATION

JUST *get through this week.* That's what I tell myself every morning but especially *this* morning, Valentine's Day. I side-knot my favorite purple T-shirt and tug on my Levis. Curl my bangs and spray them to high heaven. Try to do my makeup like the *YM* article about Neve Campbell's *natural look*. Then, I pose for Luke while pretending he's Wyatt. Since he and Blair broke up again, I don't feel full-on delusional. More like hopefully deranged. It doesn't help that I replay the almost-kiss every night while I listen to Travis Tritt's "Drift Off to Dream" on repeat. I doubt Wyatt ever thinks of it, if he remembers it at all.

The worst part of today—Sweetbriar Sweethearts—starts at lunchtime, when the cheerleaders set up a table outside the cafeteria and sell red roses. In sixth period, they go from class to class handing them out. Technically, it's a fundraiser for the American Heart Association, which I can't be mad about. But, practically speaking, it's a public declaration of my status in Loserville. Never have I ever received a rose. Not even from Fat Freddie. Last year, Mrs. Morley gave Blair a paper grocery bag to carry her haul, including twelve from Wyatt.

With my stomach in knots, I forego my usual Pop-Tart breakfast. Still, my insides loop the loop when the phone rings.

"Hello."

"Hey, June. It's Wyatt."

I stop breathing.

"Sorry to call so early, but I can't give you a ride to school today."

"Oh, okay." That's what happens when I try.

"I think I might just skip altogether. It's gonna be weird with Blair and the whole Sweethearts thing."

"Is that today? I totally forgot."

"Yeah. Pretend I got you one, okay?"

Deranged June files that away for further examination. "You sound… off. Is everything alright?"

"How do you always know?" He heaves a sigh into the phone that makes me shiver. Like he's right here next to me. "Dad got pissed last night, and he went full Exorcist in the living room. I can't leave him like this."

"Do you need help?"

"No. Do not come over here." He lets out another breath. "I mean, I don't want you to see him like this. He'd hold it against you." Then, he adds, "I'll see you later though."

Before I can process that—*Where? When?*—I'm listening to the steady beep of the dial tone.

With a quick glance at the clock, I lug my backpack over my shoulder. I can still make the bus if I hurry. I don't want to disturb Dad again. Since the death pit claimed its fourth victim, he's been more on edge than ever.

I fling open the door, nearly landing on my butt when my foot slips on something smooth and red. It's an envelope with my name printed on it in block letters. Naturally, I tear it open as if my life depends on it, reading it while I run to the bus stopped at the corner.

June,

It's so weird to write this down but I can't say it out loud. I've tried. I like you a lot. Not in a friend way either. If you feel like I do, meet me at the Yellow Rose tomorrow night at 7.

Wyatt

The day passes in a euphoric blur. The whole universe shifts to my side, my team. Team Juniper. Blair barfs in the middle of second period and disappears into Nurse Maureen's office for the rest of the day, which means her bajillion roses go unclaimed to wither and die, and five whole classes pass by without the sound of her stupid voice. In sixth-period honors English, Mrs. Kendall reads my *Romeo and Juliet* essay aloud and no one calls me Junebug.

"Insightful work, June," she says after the bell rings. She hands me my paper titled: "'Star Crossed Lovers': The Role of Fate in Shakespeare's World." The bright-red A beams like a smiling face at the top. "You really knocked it out of the park on this one. Any college would be lucky to have you next year."

When I get home, my hermit father actually emerges from his workshop and presents me with a Valentine's heart-shaped box of candy and a silly teddy bear. He doesn't protest at my request to be chauffeured to the movie theater and forks over twenty bucks for treats.

Before we leave, I change into the flowy red blouse Bonnie convinced me to buy two years ago, when I still counted her as a friend. It's never been worn. With a last look in the mirror, I say goodbye to Luke and ask him to blink twice if I'm dreaming. He just stares back at me with his broody eyes.

"Drop me off here," I tell my dad when we reach the entrance to the town square. "I'll walk the rest of the way."

"Are you sure? It's cold out. I can take you to the front."

"Dad. *Here.*" He doesn't argue. "Don't worry about picking me up. Wyatt will give me a ride home."

"Oh, okay then. Tell him I said hello."

As soon as I open the truck door, I get queasy. Nervous and worried and filled with doubt. It's freezing, even after I tug on my mom's button sweater, and the lighting beneath the marquee feels too harsh. I flee to the dimly lit corner by the shoe store, where I duck into the shadows every time someone—not Wyatt—passes by. Time drags slowly but also too fast, marching toward seven o'clock with the inevitable cadence of a funeral procession.

Finally, I see Wyatt's truck round the corner, and my heart leaps in my chest. But it's all wrong. He doesn't stop, and he's not alone. His father rides shotgun, looking surprisingly sober and fully recovered from his demonic episode. As he drives down Main Street in the direction of home, my heart plummets back to earth. Crash and burn.

I stumble out from the darkness into the glare like it's my first day on this awful planet and step squarely into the path of Blair and her minions. Duane and Jessica joined at the hip. Christi trailing behind with a tall spiky-haired boy in an Adamsville letterman jacket.

Jessica stops short when she spots me. "Oh my God, Blair. She actually showed."

A laugh bursts out of Blair that's as aggressive as a sucker punch. "Junebug, honey. Did you actually think Wyatt sent you a Valentine? You got dressed up too. How utterly pathetic."

"Damn, Blair. That's cold." Even Duane pities me.

"Cold as ice," Christi agrees. "But also, kind of hilarious."

I march up to Blair and force myself to look at her. Her face shimmers so beautifully in the light it makes my chest ache with envy. "Why do you hate me?"

She blows out a dismissive *pfft*. "I don't hate you. I don't think of you at all. You're nobody to me, and you're nobody to Wyatt."

It's not true about Wyatt. But it feels true. The barb of it hooks into the softest place in my heart. It hurts like a real wound, and a wounded animal always lashes out. "Wyatt almost kissed me."

Hysterical laughter sputters from Blair and her crew. "*I'm so sure*," she says. "Were you on drugs at the time? Were there also rainbows and pink bunnies?"

"If you don't believe me, ask him yourself."

"I don't need to ask him. I already know he feels sorry for you. You're like an annoying kid sister he wishes had never been born. A total embarrassment. You should do him a favor and just go die, Junebug."

I don't know when I started crying, but my cheeks feel hot and wet. I try to say something, anything. Only a feeble gulp comes out.

"Don't all bugs die after a month or something? You should do that."

I take off running, grateful I wore my Keds, and don't stop until I reach the Country Store three blocks down at the edge of town. I buy a bag of peanut M&Ms and take the change to the pay phone outside, planning to call my dad. But when I pick up the receiver, the clerk knocks on the window.

"It's broken, hon."

So I sit on the concrete step and wait for a while with Blair's nastiness in my head. It's strange how her voice becomes mine. How her hate clings to me like a second skin. Finally, I spot a familiar blue Cadillac at the pump.

"Of course, dear," Mrs. Peterson says when I ask her for a ride. She's more dressed up than I've ever seen her. A cream sweater and slacks and pointy shoes. Not her usual rubber boots and farm jeans. "It would be my pleasure."

"I don't want to bother my dad. He's been so busy lately with…" I wave my hand in the air to imply our shared knowledge of the nature of his busyness. But I'm certain Mrs. Peterson knows loads more than I do.

"Well, he ought to be more worried about you than his science projects." When I don't reply, she pats my knee softly. "How was your Valentine's, dear? You look very pretty in your red blouse."

"Thanks, but it could've been better." Understatement of the century.

She drives for a while in silence. Cranks up the heat so it's nice and toasty. "I know the feeling," she says, almost to herself. "My Ralph lives at Shady Glen now. He doesn't remember my name or what day it is, but he's convinced we know each other somehow. Which I suppose is all that matters."

"I'm sorry."

"Forty years of marriage, and that's what you get. That's your prize. Ain't life grand." With a sad shrug, she continues. "I suppose I'm lucky though. Your father, he never got over Annette, did he?"

It's been so long since anyone spoke my mother's first name aloud that it stuns me. At the funeral, of course. *Have mercy on your servant, Annette Pickett, and make her worthy to share the joys of paradise.* And before that, my father running across the yard, wild-eyed, as the paramedics carted my mother's body away. *Annette!*

"He doesn't talk about her much."

"Exactly."

WHEN Mrs. Peterson drops me off, Midnight greets me at the door with a croaky meow. We head straight for my room to examine the Valentine once more. How could I have been so stupid? I study the black ink under the lamp light, marveling at the skill of Blair's forgery. She even got the J right with the big loop at the bottom that reminds me of a lasso. Disgusted, I slip the card into the February issue of *YM* and toss it in the drawer. I return the red blouse to the closet, shaking my head at the tag hanging from the back. At least Blair missed that faux pas.

With Midnight tucked at my feet, I try to sleep. But it's useless. I keep replaying tonight. What I should've said. What I should've done. What a loser I am. Wyatt *would* be better off without me. He wouldn't be expected to come to my rescue. Wouldn't have that bump on his nose from Duane's pummeling last year. Or that scar on his hairline. He and Blair can ride off into the sunset.

My father would be better off without me too. He could hole up in the workshop all day and night without a kid to weigh him down. A kid to remind him of what he lost. I used to believe running away to college would solve everything—that's why I applied early decision to Berkeley—but now I know that no place, not even California, will ever be far enough. Because it's not this place I need to escape. It's my very self.

Once I think it, it can't be unthought. It takes on a life of its own and grows like a poisonous weed, and I let it lead me where it wants to go.

I slide the large envelope from under my mattress, where I'd hidden it on Monday when it arrived.

Congratulations, June! You have been admitted for the fall semester of 1997 to the College of Letters and Science… Welcome to the family and Go Bears!

I'd planned to show it to my dad over the weekend, maybe when he slept in on Sunday morning. But now, what's the point? He can save his money and use it on a brand-new microscope.

Resigned, I stuff the whole packet into the trash beneath my snack wrappers and soda cans. Then, I open *The Complete Works of Shakespeare* textbook to reread the final scenes of *Romeo and Juliet.*

"Put this in any liquid thing you will and drink it off; and, if you had the strength of twenty men, it would dispatch you straight."

It sounds so romantic, so effortless. To simply leave this hole-in-the-road town forever. To sit on a cloud over Paris or Hawaii or the Great Pyramids and watch the world go by. It wouldn't hurt. It would be like falling asleep.

I close my eyes and imagine it, my soul floating above my body, and I realize the best part. If I die—*when I die*—my mother will greet me.

CHAPTER THIRTY-ONE

NOW

IT'S no Mr. Gatti's, but the deep dish from Luigi's Pies on Main Street fills my car with the delicious aroma of mozzarella and mushroom, and for half a mile I forget about Pharmacy Tech Missy and the pill bottle and Jessica's veiled threats. But then, I spot the flashing lights in my rearview. Here we go again.

My convertible rumbles over the bumpy gravel shoulder as I pull to a stop, and I say a silent prayer for my doughnut tires. Officer Sitkowski emerges from the patrol car and stalks toward my window, glowering like I spit in his coffee.

"Follow me to the station, Ms. Pickett." He barely glances inside. A lucky break since I set the pill bottle in the cup holder. "The sheriff would like a word."

AT the station, Sheriff Faulk wastes no time with pleasantries. He doesn't bother to sit down or remove his cowboy hat. Just hands me a cotton swab and says, "We need your DNA, Dr. Pickett."

"What if I say no?"

"We have a warrant."

Though it's the answer I expected, it still sends me into panic mode. With no choice, I swab the inside of my cheek like a common criminal. At least I don't have to contend with the real detectives from the Houston PD… yet.

After bagging my sample, he asks, "Anything you want to tell me?"

Through the static of fear, I weigh my options—which aren't really options at all. No matter what I do now, I'm caught. The best lawyer in the world can't change the past. What's done cannot be undone.

"I heard you found blood on Blair's dress. It belongs to me."

His non-reaction gives him away. He's holding his breath, awaiting a full confession. "Okay," he says.

"Blair and I had a fight that night. A physical fight. She got some of my blood on her, and I got some of hers on me." *And it felt good*, but I don't say that. Or how I'd been waiting for so long to watch her suffer.

"So that's why you had that scratch?"

As if it happened yesterday, I remember the photos they snapped in this very room. My face. My hands. The jagged mark on my arm. The story I spun out of sheer panic.

"Not a tree branch, then?"

I nod, knowing that was the least of the lies I told.

"What was the fight about?" He looks at the chair as if he might sit down, but decides against it. Probably afraid to spook me.

"What wasn't it about. It's no secret Blair and I hated each other. She made my life a living hell starting on the day she moved to Sweetbriar." My legs shake beneath me when I stand, but I hold firm. "Before I say any more, I'd like to consult with an attorney."

"Fair enough. Consult away." But he blocks the door, glaring at me from beneath his brim like a real John Wayne. "I reckon you had plenty motive to want her gone. Tell me, June, are you sorry she's dead? Are you sorry that Lydia Lennox had to bury her only child?"

I want to say yes. That for a while Lydia was all I thought about. That I'd even sneaked over to their house the day I left for Berkeley, watching her through the window as she sat zombie-like on the sofa. That her face haunted me for years. I want to tell him that guilt follows me like my shadow. But I know better than to pull the trigger on a loaded gun.

AFTER finding a note from Wyatt on the front door of my father's house—*We went to my place for sustenance*—I drive the rest of the way to the caretaker's cottage, my headlights guiding me down the bumpy road in the pitch-black.

Wyatt opens the door before I knock and takes the greasy Luigi's box from my hand.

"Don't ask," I tell him, as soon as he gives me the look—part exasperation, part worry. "Where's Macy?"

"Asleep in my room."

"Want a slice of cold pizza?"

"I thought you'd never ask." Already he's rifling through the cupboards for plates and utensils.

"You need a fork to eat pizza?" I ask, smiling for the first time in hours. "You're less redneck than I remember."

His laugh soothes me until he says, "Hey, June. Where did you get this?" In a sneak attack, he slides a *YM* magazine across the counter toward me. Tucked inside the pages like a bookmark, a bright-red card.

"What is that?" I ask, feigning ignorance. As if I don't remember every single word he *didn't* write. "Is that from my bedroom?"

He walks over, plucks out the card, and hands it to me, his cheeks a vibrant red. "You tell me. Macy had it."

"Of course she did." I open it, trace the handwriting with my finger. It breaks my heart all over again. "It's from Blair. Valentine's Day senior year, she left it on my doorstep. I thought you wrote it."

Plate in hand, he sits down on the sofa with a weary sigh. "Let me guess. You went to the Yellow Rose, and I didn't show. Is that why you didn't come with your dad to see me ride in Fort Worth that weekend?"

I nod, remembering how guilty I felt sending my dad alone. Especially when Wyatt got disqualified for using his free hand, knowing that would warrant another beating from his very own monster.

"Even worse," I say, "*you* didn't show, but Blair did." I shrug and drop onto the seat next to him. The card, a burning-hot coal in my hand. "Pathetic, I know."

He reaches for my arm, then changes his mind.

Twenty years later, the rejection still stings. "It's okay. You don't have to make me feel better. I'm over it. It was a lifetime ago. It was just Blair being Blair, and me being stupid for believing it."

"I couldn't say it out loud, June. I tried."

I frown at him. "Yeah, that's what it says."

"I know. I wrote that part." He stares straight ahead, unreadable, and my heart starts flapping like a bird caught between my ribs. "I like you a lot. Not in a friend way either."

"You... You *what?*"

He takes the card from me and opens it. Points to the first line. "I wrote that part too. Real smooth talker, huh? But I chickened out and tossed it, probably in the trash in my room. Blair must've found it and added the rest."

"That sounds like her alright." Meanwhile, I rethink my entire existence.

"So you actually went to the Yellow Rose looking for me?" he asks again.

As if admitting it the first time wasn't humiliating enough, I reply with a slow blink that gets a chuckle from him. But there's a softness in his eyes that makes me say, "Honestly, back then, I would've gone to Mars if you asked me."

"Same."

He sounds sad, and I think I know why. We were young together and now we're not. We're different people in different worlds, and so much has happened. Seven thousand days' worth.

"I didn't always show it. I let you down too many times."

"Name one." I cut my eyes at him, eager to lighten his mood.

In unison, we both say, "Wave World," and laugh.

But it's graduation night I'm thinking of. I sit back and stare up at the ceiling, replaying it all. Tracing it back to Valentine's 1997 and marveling at Wyatt's revelations. The day everything changed for the worse. The first in a long line of dominoes that made me believe the world would be better off without me in it.

"Pizza?" he asks, reminding me of the cold slice on my plate.

I can't remember when I last ate, but I'm not hungry.

"Don't you want to try Luigi's pie? It's the most authentic Italian this side of the Rio Grande. It's not every day you see a menu with the words *add ranch dressing for a dollar* next to every item."

"You know, you lied to me that day," I say, before I take a bite. "You called me that morning. You told me you had to miss school because your dad was on a bender. But I saw you later. You and your dad drove by the town square. He looked perfectly sober."

Wyatt settles in, thinking for a while. Then, he smacks the sofa. "Oh, yeah. You're right. That's another memory I repressed. This one is gonna sound crazy."

"Well, that is my specialty."

"Alright." He turns to face me. "Picture this. It's Valentine's morning. Eugene calls my dad and offers him money to break into Dr. Jim's house. Naturally, Father of the Year recruits me to do it, since I can run faster if I get caught. The trouble is that neither of us really knows what we're looking for. Your dad only mentioned *research.* So I swipe the spare key from the flower pot and let myself in. I snoop around a bit. Find nothing."

"Okay."

"But Eugene isn't satisfied. He asks dad to break into the pharmacy. Says it's a matter of life and death. When you saw us that night, that's where we were headed."

"*What?* Did you find anything?"

"I never went in. Dad started getting the shakes and wandered off to the Roundup, and I fell asleep in the truck."

"It reminds me of something I haven't thought of in years. Something equally weird." I tell Wyatt the story of Blair and Coach Mac in Nurse Maureen's office, and my father's notes spilled on the floor. About the way he dismissed my concerns and sang Blair's praises.

"Well, he must've seen something that changed his mind about the Lennox family. Either you got him thinking or those were the first signs of his paranoia."

"But he never mentioned it to you? You said you two got close."

"Whatever it was, he kept it to himself. We didn't talk much about the past. I got the feeling it was a sore subject for him like it was for me. He was always talking about mindfulness. About living in the present."

I shake my head. Eugene Pickett didn't do mindful. His brain always had one too many tabs open. "I don't know what to say. Obviously, he evolved."

"Don't be so sure about that." Wyatt gives me a wry smile. "It's a good way to avoid guilt. Trust me, I know."

WITH Luigi's slice and our conversation roiling in my stomach, I leave Wyatt on the sofa and crack the door to check on Macy. Still wearing her The 1975 T-shirt and leggings, she's half-tucked beneath a blanket with Willie Nelson curled between her legs. I try to reconcile this Macy with the other one. The girl who used me to hurt people. The girl who lied. Who did something bad and ran away. I suppose when it's said and done, she's not so different than me after all.

As I stand there, watching her, a terrifying realization grips me. Not that I'm like Macy. But that I'm like Blair. Certainly no better than and possibly worse.

When Macy opens her eyes, I have the sudden thought that she was never sleeping. That she can read my mind right down to its rotten core.

"Did you bring pizza?" she asks.

I nod. "No Snapple though. That's blasphemy around these parts. Here, we drink sweet tea. Southern style. Lots of ice."

Macy rolls her eyes at me and laughs. "Texas really is its own country."

"And don't you forget it." I sit on the edge of the bed. "So, what did you two do while I was gone?"

"Played with his catnip mouse. Lost it under the sofa. Tickled his belly, which apparently is off limits." Macy grins at my annoyance and scritches Willie's head. "*Oh*, you mean me and *Wyatt?* We mainly talked about you."

I choke on a laugh. Play it off. I want to hear every detail, but I can't stop thinking about those voicemails from Detective Voss and Macy's stepfather. "Really? Is that how he ended up with my *YM* magazine?"

Ignoring me, she continues. "You know, how smart you were growing up. How you came to his rescue every time his dad went off the rails. How you could recite the whole periodic table from—"

"Did you set a fire, Macy?"

"Who told you that?"

"You didn't answer my question."

Willie scowls at her—*how dare you?*—when she sits up abruptly. "I might have."

"You either did or you didn't."

"Fine. I did. *Happy?*"

"No, I'm not happy. This just keeps getting worse. You keep making it worse. Do you understand that?" Instantly, I regret it. I sound exactly like her stepfather, doling out blame. But I can't stop myself. I wonder if I've messed up again, if I should've called the detective the moment she showed up here. "What did you burn?"

She lets out a little breath. "A painting."

"A painting. Whose painting?"

"Devin's." The staccato back and forth reminds me of our first sessions at Ellington. One-word answers until she trusted me. One step forward and two steps back. I'd been wrong to assume we'd made progress.

"Devin Delacourt?" I ask. "The Harvard guy?"

She bites her bottom lip. Nods.

"Where was it, this painting?"

"In his house." When my mouth drops, she adds, "I put it out before it did any real damage. Honestly, I did him a favor."

"Oh. Fantastic. I'm sure Devin will be so grateful. Was it his car you stole?"

She shrugs.

"What was the subject? Of the artwork, I mean?"

"I don't know. Some hideous abstract shit he painted himself." Each word is a nail, hard and final. "He's lucky that's all I did."

Shaking my head, I stand up and walk toward the door, suddenly anxious to be free from her. But when I turn back to find her with her face buried in Willie's fur and her thin shoulders shaking, I'm sucked right back into the vortex of Macy Powell.

"I can't help you unless you tell me what's really going on, Macy. I feel like I don't know you at all."

Tearful, she reaches into her pocket and pulls out a torn piece of notebook paper. As she carefully unfolds it, I recognize my adolescent handwriting and the date at the top. *May 22, 1997.* I'd rewritten it so many times I could recite the words by heart.

"I could say the same, Junebug."

Dear Class of 1997,

Mrs. Kendall said to write this letter to our future selves. The selves we'll be in 2017, when we all meet back here at Sweetbriar High for our twentieth high-school reunion.

My chest tightens like a vice until I can hardly utter a word of protest. I grab for the page, desperate, but she holds it just out of my reach. Sensing my outright lunacy, Willie bolts for the door.

The past descends like a meteor sent to destroy me. Dead on impact.

CHAPTER THIRTY-TWO

TWO MONTHS UNTIL GRADUATION

AT the beginning of sixth period, Mrs. Kendall greets us from the blackboard with an eager smile. "Alright, seniors, it's time to vote for your class gift. Remember, whatever you choose will be the legacy you leave behind for the students of Sweetbriar High."

She steps aside to reveal the numbered choices neatly printed in white chalk and chosen by our esteemed class president, Eric Clark. Frankly, I'm surprised a four-wheeler with a Bulldog vanity plate didn't make the list. As she explains each of the options, Eric editorializes in pink-chalk parenthesis.

An oak tree planted in honor of the Class of 1997 *boring*

A new Bulldog mascot costume "The old one smells like feet and corn chips"—Dawn Yancy, current mascot

A time capsule of mementos and letters to be unearthed at the twenty-year class reunion and compiled into a memory book cool idea, Mrs. K

Even without Eric's endorsement, it's obvious how the vote will swing. Since Mrs. Kendall told us about her childhood visit to Seward, Nebraska to get a glimpse of the world's largest time capsule, it's all anybody can talk about. How awesome it will be when our amazing future selves return to Sweetbriar to unearth it. When we're all doctors or lawyers or famous celebrities living in New York or Hollywood or Paris, France with our adorable 2.5 children.

That's what they all believe awaits them, like that paper fortune teller game. *You'll marry Duane and live in Dallas and drive a Ferrari and work as a pediatrician and have five kids.* Little do they know.

"Please write your choice on the slip of paper on your desk. Eric and I will tally the votes from all the senior English classes during seventh period."

"C'mon, losers." Eric waves his hands up and down, trying to rile up support. Too bad most of his meathead crew didn't make the cut for honors English. "Who needs more trees?"

His ridiculous display prompts a brief, "No more trees!" chant from the back of the room that Mrs. Kendall quickly extinguishes.

I circle number one, pressing the pen so hard I nearly rip the paper. Because I don't want to put high school in a time capsule. Not a single second of it. I want to shove it down the throat of an incinerator and watch it burn to ash.

As we pass our papers to the front of the room, I try not to look at the votes. But I start to feel queasy on a sea of threes. *Trees not threes*, I want to shout. A whimper escapes my throat, and I fight back tears. What is wrong with me?

"June, are you alright?" Mrs. Kendall asks when I hand her the stack from my row. "You look a little pale."

I hold it together long enough to mutter, "I don't feel so good."

"Take a pass. Go to Nurse Maureen's office."

The moment I open the classroom door, I feel better. A weight lifts from my chest. My feet return to solid ground. I can't go back to sixth period. Not today. So I slip into the library instead. With an innocent smile at the librarian, Mr. Jinks, I head to my happy place in the science section and open Primo Levi's *The Periodic Table.* I quickly realize it's misfiled, because it's not really about the elements at all. But I keep reading until I hear the muffled sound of crying from behind the encyclopedia shelf.

I peer through the space left by the book in my hand, and jump back, startled. Because Blair Lennox doesn't do libraries. Even weirder, she's got an actual book in her lap that she's snotting all over. Seeing her here, sitting cross-legged on the floor, reminds me of the time Mrs. Peterson and her husband invested in emus, and Mom and I laughed every time we saw them running along the fenceline with their long legs and tiny heads, completely out of place in Middle Of Nowhere Texas.

"What's wrong with you?" I demand through my peephole.

She looks up, sees me, and cries harder. "Leave me alone."

"I would if I could. But the library should be a quiet place, and you're not being very quiet."

"Whatever. Stop trying to be a bitch, Junebug. You're not very good at it."

"So, let me guess." I join her on the other side of the shelf, intending to try harder. "You broke up with Wyatt again, and now you're playing the victim. *Boo hoo.*"

That strikes a nerve. Probably because it's true. I heard Christi and Jessica gossiping in the bathroom about the latest episode in the Blair–Wyatt saga. In Jessica's words: *Blair said Wyatt is smothering her. He's totally obsessed with her, like stalker level. She needs her space.*

"You should be happy we broke up." She lifts her teary eyes, a devilish glint beneath the wet sheen. "Oh, wait. You don't have a chance with him anyway. Never mind."

Ignoring her, I continue to give my best effort at bitchiness. "Or did you royally screw up with my dad when you stole those notes from him? Let's face it. You'll never get into UK without that recommendation letter. Your grades suck."

"I didn't steal anything, and he already wrote me a glowing letter. You're just jealous because he likes me better than you. He wishes he had a daughter like me instead of an ugly Junebug."

Damn, she's good. "A letter can be rescinded, you know. If new information comes to light."

"Like what?"

With a put-on shrug, I pretend to know more than I do. Which is exactly nothing. "Like whatever scheme you and Coach Mac have cooked up. Folks are bound to find out eventually. You'd be smart to fess up now. Put the stinky fish on the table before the whole school can smell it."

Finally, I hit pay dirt. Indignant, Blair jumps to her feet and squares up to me. But something's off, and I can't tell if she wants to fight me or hug me. To run away or collapse in a heap. I wait, completely at her mercy. As usual.

When she extends her hand, I flinch. She doesn't even tease me. Instead, she holds out her book, urging me to take it.

"*The Bluest Eye?*" I ask, thoroughly confused. The only time I ever witnessed Blair reading a classic, she'd been cramming the CliffsNotes.

"It's really sad," she says with a gulp.

I drop my eyes to the Nobel Prize distinction on the cover. The downhearted little girl in a brown hat. I remember crying too, when I read the last few pages.

"I know."

But Blair has already bolted.

AFTER dinner, I ignore my homework. I lie on my bed and study *The Bluest Eye.* Inside the cover, I penned my name beneath Blair's on the library checkout card, and Mr. Jinks stamped it due on April 14.

I almost asked Wyatt about Blair on the drive back to Saw Mill Road. But I couldn't bring myself to utter her name to him. Especially after he told me he voted for the tree too and only because I told him I hated the idea of a time capsule. For a brief moment, I almost felt hopeful again, happy even, but then I remembered Wave World and homecoming and the Yellow Rose and how much of a loser I am.

What does Blair know about sadness? About loneliness? About loss? She can't possibly relate to the work of a literary genius like Toni Morrison. Luke seems unconvinced. He judges me silently from across the room.

"What do you want from me?" I ask him.

Of course, there's no answer. He's made of paper. This is what it's come to. This is my life. Talking to a poster and waiting for a reply.

As I start to doze off, the front door opens, and I hear a voice alongside my father's. A quick check of the time on my bedside alarm—9:15 p.m.—reveals it's much too early for him to close up shop for the night. A worm of worry wriggles in my stomach.

"Can I get you something to drink?" A current of tension thrums in my father's voice and urges me out of bed.

I creep to the door.

"No, thank you, Eugene. This ain't a social call." I recognize the throaty twang of Sheriff Faulk.

"Well, I figured as much, seeing as you came in uniform. How can I help you, Johnny?" I smirk at my dad's subtle dig. Sheriff Faulk doesn't like to be reminded of his nickname. John Faulk became a sworn officer of the law. Johnny made a name for himself breaking it.

"We've been getting some complaints down at the station about your research project."

"Complaints from who? *Mrs. Peterson?*" My father laughs alone.

"I ain't at liberty to say. But some folks around here don't like how you're treating your livestock. You and me, we grew up different. Take 'em out back, put one between the eyes. Don't let 'em suffer. But you know how these young people can be with their newfangled ideas. Pretty soon we'll all be eatin' tofu."

My heart sinks. I warned my dad about the death pit in October after that night with Wyatt. Pleaded with him to stop the whole project. But he couldn't. Wouldn't. *It's my next big idea, June. It's going to set us up for life. But I've got to work out the kinks first.* Now, those kinks had come back to haunt him.

"What are you saying, Sheriff? Stop dancing around it and spit it out."

"I had lunch with the county attorney this week. The way he sees it, you got two choices: Either stop this nonsense altogether or use a more civilized form of echinacea."

My father snorts. "I think you mean euthanasia."

"That's what I said, Eugene. *Youth-in-Asia.*" Each syllable a warning to my father to not dare make fun of him again. "I'm sure the vet down in Adamsville can recommend something..." Sheriff Faulk yammers on and on, taking a victory lap after he's won the battle. It's hard to beat a gun and a badge.

But my mind wanders back to the library. To Blair. To the ugly words I said to her. She's behind this, somehow. I just know it. She chose her stinky fish. She put it on the table. Turns out it looks a lot like my father.

CHAPTER THIRTY-THREE

NOW

I try again to pry the letter from Macy's death grip, and a small corner of notebook paper tears off in my hand. "That wasn't meant for you to read," I hiss.

"Well, you probably shouldn't have left it stuck inside a *YM* magazine. I thought it was a love letter to Wyatt not a—"

"Don't say it." I may not be the worst school psychologist in history, but I'm quickly climbing the ranks. I can't bear to hear my own facts spoken out loud. How did I ever think I could help anyone?

Poor Willie Nelson agrees. He scratches at the bedroom door, insisting on his release. But I don't get up to open it because Wyatt will hear, and when Macy makes a move in that direction, I stop her.

"Now I get why you're freaking out about me. You told me you had thoughts, plans. *Ideation*," she says, parroting my grown-up word. "You didn't tell me you actually went through with it."

"I didn't."

Macy oozes skepticism at my half-truth, and she's not wrong to doubt me. If I'm being honest, I *tried.* I really tried. She stabs her finger on the last part of the letter as proof. Then, she starts reading it again. Her voice, impossibly loud. Loud enough for Wyatt to hear. At least, that's the horror I imagine.

> *Before graduation, we'll gather around the flagpole—all seventy-three of us—and watch Principal Finch fling the first shovel of dirt over the time capsule. We'll each get a turn.*

"Macy, please stop."

But she doesn't, and I give up trying. It's pure torture, and I deserve it.

> *If only I could skip a step and climb in beside it. Lie there, cold and gray and lifeless. But I can't. Not yet. Because you all were right about me, but also wrong. I'm not the meek, helpless girl who goes gently into that good night. I want to rage. I want the last word. I want you all to pay. Twenty years from now, you will all still remember me. If you survive tonight*

"*If?*" Finally, mercifully, she lays the letter on the bed and looks at me expectantly, demanding an explanation. "Does Wyatt know about this?" she asks.

"No. No one does." But even as I say it, I realize how wrong I am. The cops unearthed the time capsule. Duane said it himself. Sheriff Faulk too. If they read it, then most of Sweetbriar knows, Wyatt included. "At least no one knew before a few days ago. Now, I'm not sure." My throat starts to close up. Face gets hot. Eyes teary.

"Did you kill Blair?" Macy whispers. "Wyatt told me she had pentobarbital in her bones. And that she was pregnant. I mean, I sort of kept asking until he gave it up."

I focus on Wyatt's bookshelf and let my panic run its course. *Hydrogen, helium, lithium, beryllium, boron, carbon, nitrogen…*

"Are you okay, Dr. P? Should we do some breathing exercises?"

I take the letter, fold it up and stuff it in my pocket. "Did you find any others?"

"There's more?"

"I wrote a lot of them. Different versions. An angry version. A sad version. A poor-me version. I thought I threw them all out, but I must've missed this one."

"I won't tell Wyatt if you… *you know.*" With a grimace, she runs her finger across her neck. "People like that should get what's coming to them. Sometimes street justice is the only justice."

I frown at her. There's a familiar pain in her voice. "Are we still talking about me and Blair? Or is this about you?"

Macy's half-hearted shrug seems like a small window of opportunity.

"If I tell you everything about me and Blair, the whole story, you have to do the same. You have to explain to me what happened at Ellington. And with Devin and his painting. And why. Because it's not making sense."

For a second, I have her. Maybe I'm actually a better school psychologist than I thought. Until she stands up and puts her sneakers on. Until she marches over to the door and flings it open. Willie zips out with judgmental speed.

"If that's the deal then I don't want to know."

I hurry behind her, afraid she'll blurt it all out to Wyatt.

But she only mutters, "I'm going for a walk. Don't try to stop me."

"It's dark," I say. "Don't go far. And for God's sake, don't let anyone see you."

She doesn't turn around, but I feel the eye roll. "I'll be sure to avoid the fence line. Those cows can be real busybodies."

Willie trots after her. Worried, I watch for a moment out the kitchen window, but Macy doesn't go beyond the glow of the porch light. She takes a seat on the exposed root of an oak tree and runs her hand along Willie's back.

"What was that about?" Wyatt asks.

I leave the window and drop onto the sofa, exhausted by my life. My choices. Myself. This marathon day that's never-ending—even now with the clock approaching ten. "She won't tell me what really happened. How can I help her if she doesn't trust me?"

"Good question."

I get nervous when Wyatt sits across from me in the armchair. He reminds me of Sheriff Faulk about to give me the third degree.

"You don't really trust me either," he says.

"Of course I do."

"C'mon, June. Let's be real. You never told me why you were out there digging the other night. You've been avoiding the question."

Briefly, I contemplate running. Right out the door and away from here. But what good has that ever done me? "You saw it, didn't you? Duane posted my letter to that stupid group chat."

A derisive puff of air. That's what I get in response. Then, "Duane may be dumb as a box of rocks, but Jessica would never let him do something that boneheaded. So, no. Duane didn't post your letter. I'd already seen it."

"*What?* How?"

"Your dad found it way back then, a few days after you left. He even called some big-shot lawyer from Dallas about it. After I got out of the pen and we got close, he asked me to look at it. To tell him what I thought. You know, given my experiences in prison."

"Your experiences?" I stare at him blankly, flooded with shock. Anger. Betrayal. "And that made you an expert in what exactly?"

He absorbs the blow and says nothing.

"Tell me. What is it that you think my dad suspected me of?"

"I don't know what *he* suspected, but…" His mouth becomes a hard line that speaks without words.

What it conveys, I'm not ready to hear. Not even now, twenty years later. "No," I tell him. "I don't want to have this conversation."

"It seems like we're having it." Leaning his elbows on his knees, he drops his head in his hands. With a sigh, he looks up at me, and his brown eyes pin me there. I may as well be Velcroed to my seat. "It's going to come out sooner or later. Like I told you, the police aren't going away. If they talked to you again tonight, it sounds like they have evidence."

"Why can't you just say it? You think I murdered Blair."

One shoulder lifts, drops again. "I saw you two fighting. I told you that. You hated her. When I read the letter, it all made sense."

I suppose I can't blame him, but I do. Him and my father. Especially my father. "If that's what you thought of me, why didn't you go to the police?"

"I had my reasons."

"Which are?" It's his turn to suffer on the hot seat.

"Well, your father asked me not to say anything about the letter, for one. He wanted to protect you."

"Was that the only reason?"

"I was still on parole. My reputation was shit. After the accident, everybody concluded it was a given that I'd hurt Blair too. I figured the cops would blow off whatever I had to say as me trying to pin the blame on someone else. I wanted to fly under the radar."

"I see. Self-preservation. I get it." But I absolutely don't get it. My chest radiates heat. I could breathe fire right now.

"There was another reason too. It had to do with… my feelings. My feelings for you. You were my first love, June."

"That's not fair. You don't get to say that now when I'm furious. When it's too late."

"It's not too late."

I watch, like a bystander in my own life, as he approaches the sofa with his arms outstretched. I can't not put my hands in his. It's a physical impossibility. He pulls me against his chest, and I feel his heart racing against me.

"Just tell me, June," he whispers against my hair. "Tell me, and I can help you. I've been there. You're not a bad person. We'll figure it out together."

I didn't know Wyatt could break my heart again. Until he did. I push him away from me. "I already did tell you. You're just too self-righteous to hear me. If you cared so much back then, why did you..." I can't say it. I just shake my head at him.

He looks wounded, then angry. Then, just plain sad. "When I read that letter, I cried. But after a while, all I could think about was how you addressed the whole class when you wrote: *If you survive tonight.* How you signed it: *Bottoms Up.* Now Blair's been found... well, you were going to poison us all, weren't you? And that included me too?"

It's the question that's haunted me. That comes to me in the middle of the night when I can't sleep. That has no real answer. If Blair hadn't interfered, what would I have done?

"I don't know," I tell him honestly. Before he can react, I grab my keys and walk out the door. "Come on, Macy. Go get your backpack. We're leaving."

"Why?" But she sounds more curious than annoyed.

"We're going back to my dad's place."

She gives Willie a farewell scratch behind the ears. Then she retrieves her backpack from the entryway and climbs into the passenger seat. For once, she doesn't ask any questions, and for that I'm grateful.

CHAPTER THIRTY-FOUR

"I didn't really mean it," Macy says once I back out of Wyatt's driveway. "About you killing Blair. I know you'd never do something like that. You're not a terrible person like I am."

"Macy, you're not—" I start to tell her that she's not terrible, but experience tells me it doesn't really matter what I think. "You know, I have done bad things. Things there was no excuse for. There was no *excuse*, but there was a reason." I glance over in time to see her take it in, file it away to mull over later. That's enough for me for now.

"It's so peaceful and quiet here. Is it weird that I like it?" She gazes up out the passenger window at the starry sky. They don't make skies like that in San Francisco. "I know you hated it."

"Honestly, I didn't hate Sweetbriar. I hated *myself* in Sweetbriar." The truth of it aches right down to my bones. "After my mom died, I was so lonely. I blamed my dad, but he was lonely too. We were just two ships drifting on our own private oceans."

"I get that. That's how I feel about San Francisco. After my mom and dad got divorced, and Mom met Hugh, and Dad took that job in New York, I felt like everybody was starting over, and I got left behind. And Hugh never had kids of his own, so it's like I'm his last chance. He wants me to be this perfect little angel who acts so grateful that he's running my entire life like one of his corporations. I can't talk to my mom either, since she'll just take his side."

I nod, hoping she'll fill my silence.

"At least you had Wyatt. I left all my real friends behind in Chicago."

"It helps to have a friend," I say. "Even if it's just one."

She flashes me a devious grin. "He said he'd teach me how to ride a bull. That it's really not that hard. You just close your eyes and hold on."

I roll my eyes and snort, but it makes me sad to think how much of life is like that. Holding on with everything you've got. For Wyatt. For me. For Macy too.

"Did you two have a fight?"

When I make the turn for home, I think of him. Five hundred yards and a fence between us. How close we've always been and how far apart. "More like a long overdue conversation." I stop the car in the drive and shut the engine. Fear cuts through my melancholy, sharp and cold as a blade.

"Did you leave a light on?" I ask Macy.

We both frown at the soft glow coming through the front window.

"I don't remember."

Then, in a flash, a dark figure bounds out of the house, climbs over the porch railing, and disappears into the night.

"Wait here." I push open the door and follow, stumbling blindly through the grass. I fumble with my phone, but there's no time to deploy the flashlight, and the light from the screen does little to illuminate the pitch-black.

I listen for the sound of footfalls. Snapped twigs. Ragged breathing like my own. But I hear nothing. Only the panicked chirps of the crickets beneath my feet.

When I reach the row of ash trees, the weeds devour me, clinging to my legs like desperate fingers until I stand still. Heart racing, I hold up my phone and search the darkness. The shadows pulse with life—sinister life—until I turn my light on them, exposing them as ordinary tree trunks. A fence post. An old tire from the tractor that killed my mother, which my dad never bothered to get rid of. The well.

Swallowing a lump of unease, I turn my back to it all. With each step, I feel it behind me. An unnamed something that wants to claim me. That wants to drag me back to the past. I don't dare turn.

As I round the corner, finally, I see Macy huddled in the passenger seat with the interior lights on. She looks terrified.

I crack open the door. "Did you see anything?"

"I don't think so." She rubs her hands over her visible goosebumps. "But I changed my mind. Give me the bright lights of the big city. Like Vegas-level bright."

"Let's get inside."

She makes a face at me. "Are you sure you wanna go in there? Shouldn't we call the police or something?"

I play it out, imagining Officer Sitkowski pulling up in the yard to mock me. Or worse, Duane Dupree. If they spotted Macy, recognized her, it would be game over for both of us.

"Whoever it was ran away. They're not coming back tonight."

She stares at the half-open front door that looks straight out of a horror movie. The lock jimmied open. The boxes Wyatt carefully packed lie overturned and pushed aside. Two of them—marked *Eugene Bedroom*—have been gutted. The tape cut. The insides strewn across the hardwood floor.

"You go first," she says.

I nudge the door the rest of the way, and Macy follows.

She picks up a small item at her feet. "Wow. Your dad was a genius." I barely hear her until she holds it out to me and says, "A literal card-carrying genius."

"Yeah, he was brilliant." The well-worn Mensa card feels warm in my palm. As if my father just took it from his wallet.

"What do you think they were after?" She stacks some of the papers and books that have been cast aside, including one of his favorites, Out of My Later Years by Albert Einstein.

"The question is, did they find it?"

As I sort through the mess, Macy drifts off toward my bedroom. She flicks on the light and peers inside. Her wide-eyed gasp tells me the intruder left an unforgettable mark.

"Oh my God. *Psycho.*"

I hurry to the doorway, expecting to find it in shambles. But there's only my graduation photo, ripped from the frame, and stuck to the wall right beneath Luke Perry. Nailed there with my scissors straight through the heart.

Macy and I exchange the same stunned look before I say, "We're sleeping in the car tonight."

CHAPTER THIRTY-FIVE

SIX WEEKS UNTIL GRADUATION

I still spend the lunch hour in the bathroom. It's the best time to make plans. Like *when* I'll end it all and *where.*

After my father visited the vet in Adamsville, he returned with a bottle of pentobarbital sodium that became my *how.* One library visit told me all I need to know. It's a sedative, a barbiturate that causes death by respiratory arrest in high doses. It works fast too. Dad proved that himself when he injected the latest casualty and enlisted Mr. Landry to help him roll the carcass to the pit. It's not as romantic as Romeo and Juliet's apothecary, but I figure it'll take me out quicker than a thousand-plus pound bovine.

The bathroom gossip forms the soundtrack to my plans. Mostly, it's in one ear and out the other. Nonsensical fluff that means nothing to me now.

Did ya hear that Duane got a full ride to UT? Coach Mac says he could start as a freshman and then go pro. We'll be millionaires by his twentieth birthday. I knew Jessica was full of it because Wyatt told me so. NFL requirements dictated that she would have to tough it out for three years with a college boyfriend.

Blair didn't get in to UK. She has to go to [insert noise of disgust] community college. That one checked out. Blair had been sulking for weeks now. Meaner than ever, she wore the same T-shirt every day: the baggy Bulldogs one she'd stolen from Wyatt. Christi and Jessica had iced her out. And in the shocker of the century, she skipped prom. *It's so not fair. You can't win Prom Queen when you're not even at prom.* On that, I agreed with Jessica, mainly since Wyatt had been voted Prom King, immortalizing them in coupledom. Not that I'd been there to see his coronation. I'd spent prom night with Luke, a well-worn Judy Blume, and a batch of comfort brownies.

Did you write your letter for the time capsule yet? Mrs. Kendall said I could put my pom-poms in and a letter with all my favorite things about Duane. Like the way he does that thing with his tongue when he kisses me. Gross, Christi said, on behalf of girls everywhere.

Today, Jessica bursts into the bathroom alone, muttering under her breath. She kicks the rubber trashcan a few times with her pink Keds and paces like a tiger in the small, dank space. Seconds later, Blair enters. They don't bother checking the stalls anymore. I'm nobody to them, as Blair aptly put it, and nobodies don't have ears or eyes or hearts. Nobodies are ghosts. Nobodies can peep through the slim opening in the stall door without being noticed.

"I'm sorry, Jess. I know you don't want to hear it, but he's scary. I'm worried about you. That stuff he's using, it's making him…"

Jessica stops cold. "A goddamn professional athlete. That's what it's making him. What do you know about it anyway, huh?"

Blair's shoulders slump in defeat. But her, "I know enough," sounds like a threat; like a loaded gun—and I'm grateful not to be on the other end of it for once.

"So do I. So you really should shut up and butt out."

"*Or what?*"

"You know *what.*"

They glare at each other the way Midnight used to stare at Mrs. Peterson's calico Precious before every one of their fur-flying fights. It's honestly terrifying.

Finally, Blair speaks. "I don't know what it is you think you know, but you don't scare me. I still remember how you told me you wet the bed at a slumber party in the third grade. And that time you practiced French kissing on your old American Girl doll. And—"

"At least I'm not going to community college. At least I'm not—"

I'll never know what else Blair is and Jessica isn't, because the door swings open again, and Mrs. Kendall bursts in.

"Girls, I can hear you yelling in the hallway. What is going on in here?"

Neither says a word.

"Well, this isn't how best friends act, especially the month before graduation. You two are going to miss each other, and you need to start acting like it. Now, is there anything you need to tell me?"

Blair and Jessica utter a synchronized, "No, Mrs. Kendall," before she ushers them into the hallway. She then waits for an impossibly long time.

"June? I know you're in here."

I wait too, but she doesn't go away. Like a frightened turtle, I poke my head out of the stall. She's too nice to mention my eavesdropping.

"Mr. Iverson told me you haven't put your name on the Future Board yet." My heart sinks at the thought of poor Mr. Iverson, our ancient school counselor, poring over his pride and joy. A huge whiteboard outside his office where seniors announce their college acceptances. "What are you waiting on?"

"Umm…" I certainly can't tell her the truth. That I have no future. That when the rest of the class of '97 departs Sweetbriar for the rest of their lives, mine will be mercifully over. "I forgot."

"Are you sure there's not more to it than that?"

I shake my head, but my eyes tear up and give me away.

She makes a face at me, the pitying kind. "Mr. Iverson spoke to your father this morning. He wasn't aware you were accepted to

UC Berkeley. You've nearly missed the deadline to mail in your first semester's tuition."

"I'll write it on the board today," I tell her. "I promise."

"I already did it for you. Come look."

Sheepishly, I follow her out of the girls' bathroom. With the lunch period nearing its end, the hallway bursts with life. Laughter and high fives and last-minute homework. The whispers start as we make our way toward Mr. Iverson's office, then the giggles and the pointing. A familiar panic grips me even as Mrs. Kendall soldiers on oblivious, or pretending to be.

The color leaves her face when she sees it. She tries to steer me away, but it's too late. "Who did this?"

No one fesses up, of course. But they all laugh. They're all guilty. Hurrying to the board, Mrs. Kendall scrubs it with her shirtsleeve, but it's written in permanent marker.

Next to my name, it reads: *Junebug University. Go Die in a Bug Zapper!*

"Oh, June. I'm so sorry. I had no idea." She scowls at the crowd gathered in the hallway, and they slowly disperse.

"It's okay, Mrs. Kendall. It's not your fault." I can't handle any more sympathy, so I flee in the opposite direction. Out the west exit of the school and toward the agricultural and mechanical buildings at the edge of campus. I hide in the welding shop for the next two and a half hours. Mr. Panetti doesn't care, as long as I don't drill a hole in my leg or anybody else's. That's what he told me.

Five minutes before the final bell rings I wave to Mr. Panetti and leave the shop to wait at Wyatt's truck. On my birthday, Dad finally gave in and told me I could use the truck, if I wanted. He even offered to buy me a used car in Adamsville. But I declined for reasons I kept to myself. Namely, I'm too selfish to give up the happiest twenty minutes of my day. Still can't. Not yet. Even though I only bring Wyatt down, somehow he manages to tolerate me.

"Hey," he says. Like it's any other day. Though I suppose it is, and that's the worst of it.

I grumble back at him, slinging my backpack onto the bench seat. Still, I breathe easier in this world where it's just the two of us on Farm to Market Road 57.

"What's with you?" he finally asks.

"Don't pretend like you didn't see it."

Wyatt heaves a weary sigh. "I saw it."

"Okay, then you shouldn't have to ask. You should know."

He drives on for a bit, gripping the wheel tighter with each mile. Then, he whips his head toward me. "Why do you care about what those losers think? You're so much better than they are."

"Yeah, right. Says Mr. Prom King. Don't even try to make me feel better."

"I'm not. I'm just statin' facts here. Come September, you've got a one-way ticket to California. I'm the one stuck here with my crazy dad, trying to make a go of it on the rodeo circuit. He says I've got one year to make it to the PBR or it's off to HCC with Blair."

"You'll make it. You're the best bull rider I know."

"I'm the only bull rider you know. So you better give me the HCC pep talk too."

"Well, then, Wyatt, community college isn't so bad. Houston is a big place. Besides, I'm sure you'll be back together with Blair by then." My jealousy slips out in a derisive snort. "The saga continues."

He shakes his head, disgusted. With himself or with me. It's hard to tell. "By the end of next month, none of this high-school drama will matter anyway."

I stare off and picture life unfolding without me. My father trudging to and from his workshop. Midnight rolling in a sunspot. Wyatt and Blair, walking hand in hand on a tree-lined campus. "That we can agree on."

By the time we reach Saw Mill Road, I feel Wyatt's eyes on me. As if he wants to say something but can't work up the nerve. It's only a matter of time before he tells me to scram. To get lost. He's too nice for his own good.

"Is that Blair's bike in your front yard?" Wyatt stops the truck at the mailbox, leaving me with another thought to ponder before I hop out.

"That's weird." I squint through the trees at Blair's blue dirt bike laid on the grass. "She usually leaves it out by the workshop."

"I thought the research thing was over anyway," he says.

I tell him goodbye and tromp off toward the house with dread weighting every step. I turn the doorknob slowly, quietly, for no reason other than the pit in my stomach.

I hear the crying first. Then my dad's voice, soothing. "It's okay. It'll be okay."

When I step into the hallway, I see them at the kitchen table, and my whole body goes cold, then hot. Because he looks like *her* father, not mine, with his arm around her shoulder. I can't remember when he last comforted me. Even at Mom's funeral, he'd been distant, sitting as stoic as a soldier in the pew next to me.

Then, my father sees me. We lock eyes, and he motions me away with a flutter of his hand. Like I'm the intruder here.

That is the moment I decide. It's not just my life that will end on graduation night. Later, I write it, rage-scrawling the first draft of my time-capsule letter.

I want the last word. I want you all to pay. Twenty years from now, you will all still remember me. If you survive tonight.

CHAPTER THIRTY-SIX

SUNDAY—NOW

I wake up at dawn in the driver's seat with a crick in my neck and a pounding headache. Macy softly snores in the back seat. Too proud to call Wyatt and too paranoid to call the cops, we hadn't left the front yard. But I'd hardly slept. I couldn't shake the thought that the intruder would return to find what they'd come for—or worse to finish me off. To put a sharp point through the flesh-and-blood June. Every hoot and howl jarred me awake, eyes wide and searching for an elusive figure in the darkness.

I leave Macy to sleep and return to the house to find the box marked TOOLS/SUPPLIES. The first order of business is securing the front door with a padlock and hasp until I can get to the hardware store to buy a replacement knob and a doorbell camera. Of course, I can't do a thing about the windows. One large rock would make quick work of them. Come to think of it, the hasp and padlock too.

As I cross the porch in a cloud of defeat, I spot a curious piece of mesh fabric snagged on a nail on the weathered railing. I recognize the color as Bulldog blue. The intruder must have gotten caught on the nail when he made his daring escape. I hope it took a chunk of flesh with it.

I tuck the fabric into my pocket for safekeeping and push the door open gingerly, half expecting a masked villain to jump out at me. But it's only me and the mess left behind. Receipts and newspaper clippings and yellowed copies of *Scientific American*—the refuse of my father's life. A man I hardly understood then and even less now. I wonder if it was the notes they were after. The ones he'd left hidden in the workshop behind the periodic table. The strange code I still hadn't deciphered. Come to think of it…

I leave the clutter behind and hurry into the bedroom, my heart scampering just as fast. I fling open the dresser drawer and breathe sweet relief. The scrunchie/slap bracelet pile remains undisturbed, my father's secret notes still intact. Immediately, I put them in my pocket alongside the mysterious fabric.

Then, another fear grips me, as jarring as a hand to the back of my neck. Even before I walk to the nightstand, I know it in my bones. I slide the drawer open to find it empty. My father's Smith & Wesson, gone.

I sit on the bed at ground zero, where nothing makes sense, and stare at Luke Perry like old times. Until I look up to see a face in the doorway and scream.

Macy screams back.

"What are you doing?" I yell at her.

"*Me?* What are *you* doing? You left me in the car with a psycho on the loose." She drops her backpack on the floor and throws up her hands. "I thought you'd legit been murdered with that pair of craft scissors."

I laugh half-heartedly then shiver. "I didn't think I'd be gone long, but then… well, it turns out Psycho stole my dad's gun out of the nightstand."

"Holy shit. Uh, sorry for cursing, but…"

"It's alright. It's definitely a *holy shit* situation."

Macy plops down beside me and laments. "What are we gonna do?"

"*We?*"

She shrugs. "It helps to have a friend, right?"

My words come back to bite me. But I can't argue. It *does* help. I won't tell her that she's a student, a client—not a friend. That I'm a professional. We're too far past that now. I left *professional* flaming on the side of the road long ago.

"I know I'm just a kid, but I'm here, and I want to do something good. I need to do something good."

I nod at her, and I mean it. I understand her in ways she may never know.

"Remember how overwhelmed I was my first week at Ellington? Hugh had forced me to enroll in like seventeen AP classes plus that stupid Harvard Bound program, and he wanted me to volunteer at the homeless shelter in the Mission so I could look *well-rounded* and *non-elitist.* You told me to write it all down. All my worries, all my problems. Just keep writing until one of three things happens."

I take it from there. "A solution emerges, you feel better, or your hand gets tired."

"Exactly, and I should've listened to you. I should've kept writing." Macy rummages through her backpack and produces a pen and journal I recognize from the stack in my office. Maroon with a gold-embossed fox on the cover, she picked it out herself, though I'd never seen her write in it. The pages are still crisp and blank, but a few are missing. Their torn edges left behind. I have a sickening feeling at least one of those missing pages ended up in Macy's locker. Otherwise known as the suicide note she'd addressed to me. Three brutal lines I'd memorized.

I can't do it anymore. The only way out is to do exactly what you planned in Sweetbriar. Tell Hugh and Mom I'm sorry for disappointing them.

After my thoughts settle, I realize she's right. I draw a circle in the middle of the page and label it: Blair. For better or worse, she's always been at the center of the universe. I make a line that I call Dad and one for Coach Mac and Dr. Jim. Jessica and Christi. Duane and Eric. Wyatt and his father Chet too. Some lines lead nowhere. Others connect. I talk as I go, narrating the past as best I can remember it. The mystery envelope in the mailbox claimed by Dr. Jim. Coach Mac's interest in my father's research and the stolen notes. The rumors about Duane and the rest of the football team. Finally, Blair's unraveling, which coincided with my own.

Only one of us made it out alive.

"Do you still have your dad's notes?" Macy asks when I finish.

I fish them out of my pocket, relieved she didn't ask about graduation night. That part I keep to myself. Telling it would be impossible. As impossible as dredging up the blood-stained sweater from the well.

She studies his writing, reads aloud, "AD… PV… and the envelope you found in high school had an SB, right?"

"Yeah, SB 11. Chase Moseley's envelope had AD 5."

"Five," Macy repeats. "Five, like the number on the sign I trampled. And AD for Adamsville?"

Instantly, the pieces click into place like the impossible equilibrium experiment my dad showed me as a kid. But I have to be certain. Thank God for the Internet, even if it also preserves all my disasters. With a few clicks and a long scroll, I find it.

"Look." I enlarge the horizontal photo on my phone with my fingers until I spot him. "That's Duane in his football uniform, circa 1997." The caption reads: *Sweetbriar Standout Wins Class 3A Player of the Year.*

Macy's mouth falls open. "Number eleven from Sweetbriar."

"SB 11," we say in unison.

"What about the PV?" Macy asks.

"It must be Pleasant Valley High in the neighboring county." I close the journal and hop up. "I think we need to talk to Coach Mac."

"We?" she echoes.

With a shrug, I say, "You can come. But only if you stay in the car and don't get us arrested. And bring that baseball cap."

"You won't even know I'm there."

AFTER securing the door with a prayer and a padlock, we take our show on the road. Destination: the Texas Strong CrossFit gym, where Coach McLean teaches his "Sweaty and Steady" 9:45 a.m. class every Sunday, Monday, Wednesday, and Friday.

Macy reads from their Facebook page as we drive. "*Come get sweaty with Coach Mac.* Eww. The guy seems like a walking sexual harassment complaint. But he got a ton of comments… well, mostly flame emojis."

"Did I tell you there's not much to do around here?" My nervous twitter matches hers.

I circle the Texas Strong parking lot, looking for an open space. Apparently, most of Sweetbriar lifts heavy objects with Coach Mac on Sunday mornings after the 8 a.m. church service, because the only available spot sits at the edge of the lot.

"It's only 9:10," Macy says. "Do you think Mac Daddy's here yet?"

We both see it at the same time. A massive silver pickup truck with chrome everything and a white rear-window-decal that reads "Big Mac." Like its owner, the truck takes up space. Two spaces, to be exact.

Macy guffaws. "I guess that's a yes."

Minutes after I put the car in park, Toby McLean bursts through the front door of the gym to greet a young blonde woman in spandex.

"Is that his girlfriend or his daughter?" Macy asks.

The resounding answer comes when Coach McLean bends down and picks up the girl with one arm beneath her long, tan legs. Suspended on his massive forearm, she kisses him.

Macy groans in disgust. "And he was your high-school football coach? The one you were talking about with Wyatt who got caught in a compromising position?" She widens her eyes at me to punctuate her point.

"I didn't think you heard all that."

After spinning the girl around, Coach McLean returns her to her feet and slaps her on the butt as she walks inside. When she laughs, she looks so young.

"Don't take this the wrong way, Dr. P, but for a school counselor, you can be a little..."

I grimace at her. "Dense? Slow?"

"I was gonna go with clueless, but yeah. Those work too." She slips the journal from her backpack and opens it. "Look at your murder-gram."

"Are we calling it that?" But I look. At what's been right in front of me all along since the morning Blair sprained her ankle during cheer tryouts. Since catching them alone in the nurse's office. Since Blair cried over *The Bluest Eye.* "Blair and Coach Mac."

Macy gives a sage nod while the world as I knew it crashes around me, and Blair's sharp claws and bared teeth fall away to reveal a soft underbelly, a vulnerability I never saw.

"Oh my God. *Her baby.* You don't think..." I can't finish that sentence, but Macy's face gives her thoughts away. "Wait here."

My blood boiling, I stalk toward the front door of the large metal building. I blow past the front desk and the two bright smiling faces behind it. I must look slightly unhinged because neither comes after me into the sea of sneakers, Lycra, and chitchat.

Coach McLean stands at the front, commanding the crowd like a politician. I try to hold it together, but when he strikes a pose in the mirror, flexing his massive bicep at his giggling girlfriend, I can't stop myself.

I shout above the booming music, "I need to talk to you!"

He flashes a wolfish grin. Up close, he shows his age—the deep wrinkles in his leathery face—and his attempts to fight Father

Time—bleached white teeth and unnaturally dark-brown hair. "Hi, little lady."

I blink at him.

"Toby McLean, pleased to meet you."

"We've already met." I ignore his outstretched hand until he drops it at his side. "Juniper Pickett. Class of '97. Eugene Pickett's daughter."

"Whoa. No way. They used to call you Junebug." He drops his eyes to take me in. "Whaddya know, you got hot."

In the mirror behind him, I witness my face contort with unbridled disgust and imagine myself landing a solid jab-cross to his chiseled jaw.

He merely shrugs. "I skipped the sexual harassment training." He chuckles. "So sue me. It's a compliment."

"Oh, well in that case…" My sarcasm flies right over his gelled head.

"You here for Sweaty and Steady? Just grab a mat, a jump rope, and a spot in the front, if you can find one. I'd warm up with a few double unders and a—"

"I'm not here for the class. I need to talk to you about…" *Blair* is on the tip of my tongue, but I hold back, afraid I'll scare him off. Instead, I lower my voice and whisper, "Steroids."

His eyes bug out. "Steroids? This body is *au naturale.*"

The women in the front row inch closer, curious. Their ears perk at his outburst, and at me, the outsider in jeans and a T-shirt who apparently dared to challenge the purity of Big Mac's composition.

"It's not about you."

He frowns in confusion.

"Duane Dupree," I say. "Years ago, someone mistakenly left an envelope of cash in my dad's mailbox with Duane's football number on it. Dr. Jim came and—"

"Outside." The veins in his neck strain as he jerks his head toward the door. I follow him into the parking lot. He waves nervously at the arriving CrossFitters. As they disappear inside, his face darkens.

"You've got a lot of nerve showing up here asking me questions. From what I heard, you're suspect numero uno in a murder investigation."

I won't let him derail me with the truth. "I'm right, then. Duane was on steroids."

"Hell, I don't have the slightest idea. If he was, nobody clued me in."

"What about Blair? Did she know about your scheme? About your little secret code? SB 11?"

I watch his face. Wait for the sign that will tell me what I already suspect. That Blair knew everything. That he fathered her child and had as good a reason to want her dead as I did.

"Blair..." It comes out rusty. As if it's a name he hasn't said in a while, and for good reason. "Honestly, I thought she ran away. Figured she'd turn up in Sweetbriar for the twentieth reunion in her cheer skirt or somethin'. She was so excited about that damn time capsule. But I've heard all the talk. All the suspects. If you ask me, she spent a lot of time with your daddy, even after he wrote her that letter she wanted."

A memory drops like a curtain across my eyes. Dad consoling Blair at the kitchen table as she sobbed. *He knew.* He must have.

"I still miss her every day," Toby offers. "She was a special girl."

The sight of his young, blonde girlfriend beckoning to him from the door squashes my growing bud of sympathy.

"C'mon, Toby. Folks are getting restless."

He nods and waves her inside without his usual fanfare.

"Does your girlfriend know she looks exactly like Blair?"

I leave him there, speechless, and beeline it to the car, where I find Macy slumped down in the seat with the baseball cap pulled tight to her face.

"Did someone see you?" I ask, already panicked.

"I don't think so, but the cops cruised through here twice." She keeps quiet while I back out of the lot and turn onto the road for home. "If they find me here, what will happen to you?"

"*To me?*" I hear Detective Voss's stern voice in my head, calling Macy unstable and dangerous. What did that say about me, the one who'd been assigned to help her? "I'll have a lot of explaining to do."

Her mouth twists. It's getting harder for her to hold back.

"It would help if I knew *how* to explain."

When she reaches for the radio dial, I stop her.

"You know, you never asked what Coach McLean said."

"Didn't need to. I know the type. Deny, deny, deny. Am I right?"

With a quick jerk of the wheel, I pull a Wyatt, veering onto the grassy shoulder. I put the car in park and turn toward her. She looks terrified, and I am too. Terrified of scaring her off. Of saying the wrong thing. Of not knowing where to start.

"Why did you set Devin's painting on fire? I thought you liked him. Hugh said he was impressed by your—"

"My *independent spirit?*" Her laugh sounds more like a cry. "Yeah, he used that line on my mom too. I *did* like him. At first."

"Okay." I don't dare to breathe. Her sudden show of trust is too delicate to risk.

"I'll show you the painting," she says. "Give me your phone."

With a few clicks, she arrives at her destination. She holds it out to me, tears already streaming down her cheeks. "He didn't even bother to take down the post. That's how arrogant he is."

I recognize the article in the online magazine *Modern San Francisco.* Hugh had emailed it to me a few months ago, bragging about Devin Delacourt, the up-and-coming artist mentor in the Harvard Bound group who had taken Macy under his uber-talented wing. To hear him tell it, the guy was the next Jackson Pollock. I'm certain I rolled my eyes as I skimmed and deleted it. I doubt I'd given the featured painting a second glance. But now, I can't look away. Devin poses in front of the piece titled *Muse* with his hands hidden in the pockets of his chinos. It's a female form painted in bold primary colors and draped seductively, legs and mouth open. The hair—angular, purple, short—a dead giveaway.

I glance at Macy, horrified.

She nods. "Whatever you're thinking, you're right."

"Does anyone else know?"

"No, and I don't want them to. They'll find a way to blame me... especially Hugh. Technically, it *is* my fault. I flirted with him at the first Harvard Bound meeting, mainly because I thought it would piss Hugh off. When he asked me to pose for a painting, I agreed. When he kissed me, I kissed him back."

"Macy, this is not your fault. He's... what... *thirty?*"

"Twenty-nine. But he said I'm an old soul. Mature for my age."

"Seriously? You are *sixteen.* And no offense, you're *not* that mature."

"I know. Sixteen and stupid. I told him I wasn't sure about what we were doing and that I wanted to slow down. That's when he showed me the finished painting hanging on the wall of his living room. He broke down and told me he hadn't done anything that good in years and I was his muse and he would either get me into Harvard or get Hugh off my back. He just needed one favor."

"One favor." Two words straight from the depths of hell.

"He wanted pictures. Of me. For inspiration, he said. So, I took some."

She stares off for a moment, and we watch a rusted-out pickup rumble by on the highway. That old feeling returns, the urge to run. I wish I was in that truck, disappearing over the horizon.

"But he kept asking for more."

I drop my head in disgust. In anger. With Devin, of course, but with myself too for not asking the right questions. For not seeing the obvious with Macy. With Blair.

"I finally worked up the courage to tell him no, and it was like flipping a switch. He threatened to tell Hugh that I'd pursued him and offered him the pictures in exchange for his help. Then, that article came out, and the rest of Harvard Bound got wind of it. They knew it was me in the painting, and they all thought I was just sleeping my way to Harvard." With a scornful laugh, she adds, "Which would take a lot of sex with my grades."

I can't even crack a smile. "You must've been so overwhelmed. I thought I was helping, but I completely missed the boat."

"You *were* helping. You are still." She sneaks a glance at me. "Do you hate me?"

"Of course not. You could've come to me, but I understand why you didn't, and I certainly don't hate you. I remember when a problem feels so big that it overshadows your whole life. It's like a massive eclipse that makes everything cold and dark and lonely. Before you know it, you end up doing something you regret. Something you can't take back."

Now, we're both sniffling. It's strange and terrible how history repeats itself.

"I'm just glad you told me now. We'll figure it out together, okay?"

She nods and points up ahead to the last string of shops, the final blip of civilization on the Farm to Market Road. "Is that a Dairy Queen?"

"It is. How do you feel about ice cream for breakfast?"

A Reese's Peanut Butter Cup Blizzard fixes everything. Well, most things. *Some* things. At least, we both stop crying, and I manage to drive us back to the house without getting arrested. We also make a successful pitstop at Smith's Hardware, where I duck behind the wall of fasteners to avoid Christi and her mini-me daughter.

When I make the turn onto Saw Mill Road, a familiar unease greets me like an old friend. Even though the hasp remains firmly in place across the door, padlock secured, it's only a matter of time before my past catches up to me. I hear it now at my heels, its breath hot on my neck.

"You should call Wyatt," Macy says. "Ask him to hook up the doorbell camera."

"I'm perfectly capable of doing it myself."

"Duh."

I shake my head at her, amazed she can still find the humor in this mess. "Let's look through the rest of my dad's boxes first. The ones that were torn open. I think Blair might've told him she was pregnant. Maybe he left proof."

We sit side by side and tackle the first and then the second box. I sift through every page, search beneath every book jacket. Amid the dust, I find a few treasures—like a photo of my mom and me, all smiles on an innertube on Snake River, my cheeks and shoulders pinked from the sun. But it's her that I can't turn away from. I look exactly like her now. A carbon copy. Aching, I lay it beside me and continue the search.

"What is Harvest Gold?" Macy asks. She hands me a bound copy of my father's patent application, yellowed with age.

"The life's work of Eugene Pickett. The only reason we could afford this place. My dad sold that patent for five million dollars."

Macy stares, wide-eyed, at the inch-thick stack of paper. "This thing?"

"Well, the chemical formula inside it anyway. Companies pay big bucks to grow corn with drought and disease tolerance. Apparently, Harvest Gold was the best they'd ever seen."

She flips through the pages in astonishment. "So your dad really *was* a mad scientist?"

"He's the one who taught me to recite the periodic table." I see him then, in a dusty corner of my mind, laughing with my mother in the garden, his face smeared with dirt. "But he had other sides too. Sides he lost after my mom died."

I sit back among my father's possessions and sigh. "It's like we're chasing a ghost. Maybe I need to accept there's nothing here to find. It burned up in the fire. Or our mystery psycho ran off with it. Whatever *it* is."

But Macy keeps digging until she reaches the bottom of the third and final box marked *Eugene Bedroom*. She giggles, as she passes me a framed photo, one I'd never seen. One I don't remember him or my mother taking. *Halloween, 1986* is written on it in my father's scrawl, and it brings me back to tears. Little June in a lab coat and goggles with her crazy Doc Brown wig.

"You said you found those notes in your dad's workshop hidden behind the periodic table, right?" Macy brightens as she hops to her feet. "I have an idea."

I follow her into the bedroom, where she stands eye to eye with Luke Perry.

"It makes sense, doesn't it? It's the last place anybody would look."

I shrug, not wanting to get my hopes up again, but she's not wrong. That poster hasn't moved since the day I hung it there.

"My dad hated it," I tell her. "He never said it out loud, but every time he came in here he gave Luke a nasty look. I'm surprised he didn't burn it the day I left."

"But he didn't," Macy says eagerly. "He never took it down."

"You look. I don't want to be disappointed again."

Without hesitation, she steps forward and puts her fingers on the top corner of the poster. "I'll be gentle, Luke." With the care of an archaeologist unearthing the bone of a T. rex, she removes the thumbtack, pulling one side free and then the other.

I can't bear to look, so I focus on Macy's back. The T-shirt of mine she borrowed.

"Juniper," she says.

"Yes?"

"*Juniper.* That's what it says. *Look.*" She lowers the poster and points at the large envelope taped to the wall. "It's for you."

CHAPTER THIRTY-SEVEN

ONE WEEK UNTIL GRADUATION

I stand in the mirror in the Bulldog-blue graduation gown I picked up from the library after handing Mr. Jinks a check from my father. The standard gown only cost thirty-five dollars, but my father insisted on the valedictorian sash, which brought the total to a whopping fifty bucks. It's a sad sight: me in a polyester sack. Especially when I consider what it means. That it'll be the image my father's left with when I'm gone.

A soft knock on the door jolts me. It may as well be a battering ram.

"Juniper?"

I tear off the gown and toss it onto the bed. I don't want my dad to see me in it. To lie to me about how pretty I look or how proud he feels. Ever since Mr. Iverson called him about my acceptance to Berkeley, he's been putting on a real show. But he still hasn't asked why I didn't tell him in the first place. Typical Eugene with his head buried in the sand.

I open the door to find my father in his work boots. His hands, dirty. Face, dripping sweat. I glance down at my bare feet and plaid pajama shorts. It's a strange juxtaposition, him and me.

"It's midnight," he says.

I frown at him, confused at first, and turn toward the clock on my nightstand where the numbers flash 9:33. I start to protest. "It's only…" But then, I realize. "Midnight?"

"Poor old gal lived a good life. I found her lying in the onion planter in the garden."

"Mom's garden?" I don't know why that makes me angry. So angry I can barely breathe. "What were you doing there?"

My question confuses us both. But Dad doesn't set foot in the garden. Not since that day six years ago that cracked our lives right down the middle, leaving a monumental divide neither of us can cross.

"Cats have a sense about these things, you know. They go off on their own when it's time."

Midnight can't be gone. Not now. Not before me.

I swipe at my tears, annoyed I can't stop them. "Where is she?"

"I buried her in the cow-dog graveyard."

"In the middle of the night? Without me?"

He shrugs, eyeballs me like I'm making no sense. "I figured you'd want it that way. You can remember her the way she was."

The way she was. In a flash, I'm back there again, screaming at the tractor, my mother crushed beneath it. When her fingers twitched, I pushed and pulled and grunted until I saw stars. Then I collapsed in a futile heap in the grass and reached for her hand. I can still feel it now. The warmth of her fingers.

Dad clears his throat. "Chet helped me dig the hole, and Wyatt said he'd make a stone for her. Like he did for Bert."

"What really happened?"

"Whaddya mean?" he stammers.

All these years, I let him hide out, let him avoid reality. I never pushed him. Certainly not this hard. But if not now, when? Knowing I'll be dead in two weeks gives me unexpected courage.

"What *really* happened to Midnight, Dad?"

"Oh, honey. It was old age. It happens to us all."

I hate that he underestimates me. That he thinks I'm just a dumb kid. But most of all, I hate that he actually believes he's protecting me when all along I've been on my own. It's far too late for that now. "I don't believe you."

The blow barely registers on his face. He simply nods. Which only intensifies my indignation.

"You never go to the garden, Dad. You're afraid of it. You don't want to face what happened there. You want to pretend that—"

He smacks his hand against my door so hard a hairline crack appears. "Enough."

IT'S nearly dawn when I sneak out of the house with my dad's heavy-duty flashlight and make my way around the back of the house. I can't explain it, but I have to see it for myself. I fight through the thick grass and into the tangle of tomato plants that overtook my mother's tidy garden. Sure enough, I spot a few of my father's boot prints in the soil leading to a rotted planter where my mother's marker—*ONIONS*—protrudes like a small gravestone.

I move closer and direct the beam of light to follow a trail of ants marching along the spongy wood. A tuft of Midnight's black fur clings to the splintered edge. Slowly, carefully, I reach out a finger to touch it, and my heart leaps into my throat.

It's wet.

I look at my hand in the flashlight's glow. I'm not twelve anymore. My mother's been gone for six birthdays. But somehow, here I am, back in her garden with blood on my fingers.

In a panic, I drop the flashlight. It cracks against the planter, leaving me in darkness. Disoriented, I stumble backward. My foot catches an object in the weeds, and I land hard on my butt. I sit there, stunned and sore, and wait for my eyes to adjust.

As the object takes shape, I can hardly believe it. The front wheel of Blair's fancy blue dirt bike twists in on itself, damaged from a crash and unrideable. I stare at it for a while, wondering when she left it here and why. Finally, I work up the courage to touch the wheel.

I hear myself wail. I sound like a wounded animal. Feel like one too. I don't know how long I lie there suffering. Scream-crying and balled up in the weeds.

"June! What are you doing out here?" My father appears in front of me, in the first light of morning, wild-eyed and barefoot. "You scared the bejesus out of me."

I hold out my hand to him, my fingers still red with blood from the tire. "Blair killed Midnight."

"I know. It was an accident."

I would rather he'd slapped me, punched me. In that moment, I wish for a father like Chet Landry. Because I want to hit back. "You already knew?"

He kneels in the grass and tries to comfort me, but I push his hand away. "She was upset, not paying attention, and she lost control. She hit Midnight and ran the front tire into the ash tree. Midnight limped off, and we found her out here. She didn't make it."

I bury my head in my hands. I can't stand to look at him. "Why was Midnight outside in the first place? I thought we agreed to keep her in the house. She's too old and frail to be out there on her own."

Was, I think. Because she's gone now. Forever.

"That's my fault. I wasn't paying attention, and she must've snuck out."

I rise, my blood boiling. "You never pay attention to anything but your stupid work!"

"June, please—"

"Why didn't you just tell me the truth?"

"Blair begged me not to. She said you already hate her." He makes it sound like an accusation. Like I'm the one in the wrong. "That doesn't sound like you."

"I do hate her." A shot of pure rage sends me to my feet and running back toward the house. Away from him and the bicycle and Midnight's blood.

"You don't mean that," he calls after me.

I stop hard and whip around, yelling so loud my throat burns. "I do mean it. I hate her so much I hope she dies!"

CHAPTER THIRTY-EIGHT

NOW

"OPEN it," Macy urges, laser-focused on the envelope taped to the wall.

It's hard to explain how stunned I am. How eager. How terrified. My legs, heavy as sand bags, carry me toward it. I tug it free and open the flap.

Macy widens her eyes at me in anticipation. "Any day now."

"I can do this." I reach into the envelope and immediately change my mind. "Actually, I don't know if I can."

"You can." She gives me an encouraging nod. "*You have to.* What if he wrote about Blair? About what happened to her?"

I'm too ashamed to tell Macy that's exactly what I fear. My father writing about Blair. That his last note to me would be about her. But also, I fear the opposite too. That he won't mention her at all. As if none of it ever happened.

"What if he left a clue about the person who murdered him? We already know he was onto something." She lunges toward me, grabbing for the envelope.

It's the final push I need to take the leap.

At the top of the letter, I find the date: April 9, 2017. One week before he died, and two days after he left me the voicemail I ignored. Then, a page of his familiar handwriting. I glance up at Macy and start to read aloud before she demands it.

Dear Juniper,

If you're reading this letter, I'm somewhere smiling. Because it means you came home and bothered to find and read it. Mainly because Luke Perry is finally off your wall. I got tired of looking at his pretty face a long time ago.

Also, if you're reading this, I'm dead. Duh, as you used to say. How I got there might be up for debate. Wyatt says I'm paranoid, and hell, maybe he's right. Maybe the cancer crawled into my brain and ate the sense-making part... whatever's left of it these days. But then again, it sure feels like I've had a bullseye on my back, starting the day I said no to Toby McLean. Can you believe he wanted to repurpose my Livestock Gold formula for the damn football team? Cows ain't people, that's what I told him. So he went out and hired Dr. Jim to compound his own steroid concoction. But that didn't stop the two of them from trying to buy, cheat, or steal mine.

After McLean got caught fogging up his truck windows with a cheerleader, I thought it was finally over. Then, I hear about this kid in Adamsville. Chase Moseley. I knew they were behind it, him and Dr. Jim and God knows who else. New town, same old story. They only care about themselves. About getting rich and winning football games. So, yeah, I am paranoid. If they'd kill a rooster, why not a sick old man?

Getting old sure puts life in perspective. For one thing, I know I let you down when you needed me most. After Annette died, I holed up and pushed you away. I stopped paying attention to what mattered. Up until Wyatt spilled the beans, I had no idea the hell you went through in school, and I understand why you couldn't tell me. I was a lousy father and a shell of a man. I all but stopped living. Sure, I kept working. What else did I know how to do? Nose to the grindstone, hoping it would somehow change the unchangeable. Me, a man of science, bargaining with God. What a hoot. Now, when I look back on those years, I can hardly remember them. It's mostly a gray fog. But graduation night, I'll tell ya, that sure shook me awake. That poor girl pregnant and alone. I let her down too. Until Wyatt told me otherwise, years later, I believed she was carrying his child—she let me believe that—and the cops already had him under the gun. I couldn't risk losing him too.

Then, Chet died, and Wyatt did what he did and ended up in the big house. Still, I always thought that night started it all. A curse on you and me and all of Sweetbriar. But you know what? Our curse started long before graduation night. With me and my ego, my ambition. If I hadn't been so hellbent on Livestock Gold, on making it perfect no matter the cost, none of this would've happened. It's the reason I had that damn pentobarbital in the first place.

I think about that night all the time. It replays in my head, and I can't shut it off. I blame myself for all of it, and let me tell you, guilt sure is a son of a bitch. Maybe that's the cancer too, spooling all the bad stuff onto a lowlight reel that'll play when I ride off into the sunset. There are good things too... you and Annette. But the bad stuff, it clings. It kills me that you feel guilty too, so guilty you ran away from me. I wish I knew how to take that burden from you. A life consumed by guilt is no life at all. If it helps, I know what you did, and I love you anyway. And in case you still haven't gotten it through your thick skull, so does Wyatt.

Love,
Dad

P.S. Go alone to the place Midnight died. You'll find the last piece of your inheritance there. Many times, I wanted to burn it, but I never could bring myself to strike the match. Do with it as you will.

"I was right. He knew about Blair," I say, trying to accept it. "He knew." The letter comes in and out of focus, while my heart pounds hysterically in my chest.

Macy and I stare at each other, dumbfounded, until she says, "What are you waiting for? Go."

"You're not coming with me?"

She shakes her head. "Your dad said *go alone.* You should probably listen to his last words."

I know she's right. That she's so much wiser than me at her age, but somehow just as stupid. Still, it feels incredibly lonely to walk out the door and leave her behind.

The midday sun spotlights me as I hurry toward the garden, carrying the weight of my father's words in my pocket. *A life consumed by guilt is no life at all.* Wading through the weeds, I find the planter, the ONIONS marker lost long ago. I kneel beside its rotted frame, take a wild breath, and plunge my fingers into the warm soil. No different than I'd done three days ago in the school courtyard, searching for the bones of the past under the light of the moon.

My fingers brush against a solid object. I reach in with both hands and tug it free. Sweep the dirt from the plastic document cover. Inside, in bold typeface, it reads: LIVESTOCK GOLD CHEMICAL COMPOUND.

With Eugene Pickett's voice in my head, I open it and scan the page. I immediately recognize the distinctive four fused carbon rings of the steroid nucleus.

"Unbelievable," I say out loud to the ghost of my father. "You finally let me in your workshop." My tears come again, hot and relentless. I sit down in the grass, with his life's work on my lap, and surrender to the flood.

After crying myself out, I spot a red ant crawling on the toe of my sneaker, then up and along the rotted planter board. My stomach wrenches at the thought of that night, twenty years ago. Of Midnight's blood and fur. Of the lie my father told and why he told it. Of graduation night too. He wanted to protect *me.* I know that now.

I have to show his letter to the police.

A noise from the road startles me. Like a common criminal, I jump to my feet, ready to take cover behind an ash tree. Instead, my legs grow roots beneath me, and I can only watch as an unfamiliar car turns into the driveway, its tires kicking up dust. By the time I unearth myself, a new fear grips me—*Macy's alone in there!*—and I take off running, my frantic steps making quick work of the tall grass.

As I round the corner, I see it's worse than I thought. It's not Detective Voss come to cuff me up and interrogate me all the way from San Francisco.

It's Hugh Lockwood, Macy's stepdad.

CHAPTER THIRTY-NINE

MY thoughts take off without me, zipping recklessly through my brain like lawn chairs in a tornado. But I force myself to put one foot in front of the other until I'm face to face with Hugh and his lime-green rental car. If I had a choice, I'd take the lawn chair headed straight for my face.

Hands on his hips, Hugh looks me up and down. He's already sweating. "Well, well, well. I guess you didn't drop off the face of the earth after all."

"That's debatable. You're in Sweetbriar, Texas. There are more cows than people around here." I stare off at the pasture, trying to still my heart and steady my voice. "What are you doing here, Mr. Powell? How did you find this place?"

He snorts. "Did you forget who I am? I run a cellphone company, Dr. Pickett. Turns out you are one of our most loyal customers. Unlimited talk and text since 2007."

"So, you tracked me here? That's illegal, you know. I assume you didn't tell the cops about that." I pray he didn't. "You certainly came a long way to chew me out again. Wasn't having me thrown out of the hospital enough?"

"Don't play dumb with me. Where's Macy?"

"I have no idea. Why would she be here?"

Because the words she'd intended to be her last mentioned me and Sweetbriar.

"Because for some crazy reason she looks up to you even though your license isn't worth the paper it's printed on." Hugh storms toward the house with the conviction of a bowling ball speeding down the alley. "I'm going in," he announces over his shoulder. "And you can't stop me."

He flings open the door I didn't lock and barrels inside, stumbling over a box in the hallway. It doesn't slow him down. If anything, he moves faster, taking decisive, impatient steps. I follow him into the kitchen and out again. Living room, laundry room, and back. When he stomps toward my bedroom, I swear I stop breathing. In my head I rattle off the elements like I always do. My silent screaming meditation.

He drops to his knees to search beneath the bed. Flings the pillows onto the ground and glares at Luke Perry, still lying flat on the covers. Then, he stalks to the closet, and my vision blurs. Fainting would be a relief.

With a primal yawp, he hurls it open, and we stand there staring, both of us shocked.

"I told you she wasn't here."

Hugh shakes his finger at me. "If I find out you're lying to me, I will ruin whatever's left of your pathetic career. When I'm done with you, you'll be lucky if they let you counsel animals in the zoo. Understand?"

I walk toward the front door, relieved when he follows me. "I'm not the enemy here. We both want what's best for Macy. She did what she did for a reason. That should be our focus. Not tearing each other apart."

"She did what she did because she's sixteen. She's impulsive, reckless, and vulnerable to influence. To *your* influence, in particular. Aren't you the one who told me all about the juvenile brain?"

I cringe at my own words used against me. "You're right. She *is* vulnerable. To both of our influence. Macy looks up to you even if it doesn't seem that way. She wants you to be proud of her. She needs you to be her cheerleader right now."

Hugh's face softens as his eyes well. When he opens the car door, the vice around my lungs eases just a little. I see it then on the front seat. A Xeroxed copy of Macy's suicide note with Sweetbriar circled in red ink. Hugh follows my gaze, his anger reigniting like a lit match.

"I'm sorry, Hugh. I should never have told Macy about this place. I thought it would help her open up to me, but I—"

"Got it wrong? Yeah, I know. We all know. And my stepdaughter paid the price. Did you know she used my credit card to buy that poison on the dark web?" I can only grimace in response. "Just remember, Dr. Pickett, I found you here. I can find you anywhere."

I wait until Hugh's rental car glides onto the Farm to Market Road and out of sight. Fighting against every impulse, I walk slowly, calmly back into the house.

"Macy! He's gone. You can come out."

I run from room to room, calling and then screaming her name. But there's no answer.

Panicked, I grab my purse and stuff my dad's letter, his notes, and the Livestock Gold formula inside it, along with the scrap of fabric from the intruder. I can't afford for any of it to disappear. Then, I wrap the strap across my chest and secure it tightly.

I replay Wyatt's parting words to me. *Were you gonna poison me too?* I can only hope my dad got it right about Wyatt's feelings for me. Because right now, he's all I've got left.

I park next to Wyatt's truck in the drive, but he doesn't answer when I knock. I turn my fist and prepare to give the door an aggressive smack when I hear him out back.

"Alright, Caleb, hop up there on Bodacious. Let's run the six-inch drill."

I follow the sound of their voices behind the house and past the shed, where Wyatt stands at the center of the brand-new practice ring complete with the barrel my father engineered for him. The precise way it's tethered to the fencing with thick bungee cords makes it obvious Eugene Pickett had a hand in its design.

Caleb Dupree sits astride the barrel, holding tight to the rope around its middle. He reminds me of a young Wyatt. Black cowboy hat and a fearless determination in his eyes. The rest of him, all Duane. From his smart-ass grin to his sleeveless mesh practice jersey with the name Dupree printed on the back.

Wyatt spots me and holds up a finger, telling me to wait. Which is a bit like telling the real Bodacious to calm down and eat some hay. With Macy missing and my father's letter in my purse, reminding me of all the ways I failed him, I can barely stand still.

"Position one," Wyatt says, and Caleb shifts his weight back on the barrel. "Hold tight with your legs. Keep that free arm neutral." Wyatt places a hand on one of the bungee cords and gives it a firm tug, simulating the bull's kick. "Core tight. Drive your hips forward. Lift up on your rope."

Caleb follows Wyatt's lead. Bodacious the Barrel bucks, and he responds. It's a slow dance Caleb has mastered. His movements, small and precise.

"Game time," Wyatt yells. As he ratchets up the speed and yanks harder on the bungee cord, Caleb starts to falter. "Don't sit on your pockets!"

Caleb tries to hold on, squeezing the barrel with his legs. While he dangles precariously from one side, I spot the tear on the back of his jersey, and all hell breaks loose as I rush toward the ring.

"You broke into my house!"

Caleb spots me, and his eyes widen with surprise. Just then, Wyatt gives the cord another tug, and the boy flies off the barrel and lands with a thud in the dirt.

"What the hell?" He sits up slowly, then gets to his feet and brushes himself off. Ignoring me, he stomps toward Wyatt. "You almost killed me."

"You lost your focus."

He throws up his hands. "What do you expect with that crazy lady yelling at me? She yelled at Mom too."

"When you're up on that bull, *he's* the only one that matters. I don't care if you see Sheriff Faulk twerking naked in the stands, you've got a two-ton beast underneath you. You forget that, you die."

"Are you done with him?" I ask Wyatt, not taking my eyes from the ripped hole in the fabric that matches the one in my purse. The missing puzzle piece. "Because the crazy lady has something to say."

Neither of them protests, and Caleb smartly keeps his distance inside the ring. I consider their silence an invitation.

"Where were you last night?"

The boy looks to Wyatt for help.

Wyatt shrugs at him. "Well, *where were you?*"

"Cody and I helped Mom in the yard till it got dark. Then we played Madden in our room until Dad came home and told us to go to bed. I didn't go anywhere near your house."

"You absolutely did. You snagged that jersey on a nail on the porch when you were running away. I have the rest of it in my purse." I approach the ring and wave the swatch of fabric at him. "How do you explain this?"

Caleb kicks at the dirt with the toe of his boot. His neck reddens.

"Did you break into her house, Caleb?" Wyatt asks. "Remember, bull riders live by the cowboy code. We do what's right. We tell the truth."

Caleb groans. "It wasn't my idea. He paid me fifty bucks to—"

"Caleb Archibald Dupree, what did I tell you about coming over here without permission?"

As Jessica launches toward us like a perfectly coifed grenade, Caleb hauls himself out of the ring and tries to head her off before she makes impact.

"Relax, Mom."

"Relax? First I catch you out here playing cowboys with a convicted felon. Now you're shooting the breeze with a suspect in my best friend's murder. And I'm supposed to relax? After I told you to watch out for her? She can't be trusted."

"We were just ridin' the practice barrel," Caleb says.

I doubt Jessica hears him at all. Her icicle eyes pierce right through me, and I pray that wherever Macy is she's managed to stay out of sight.

"*I* can't be trusted? Your son just admitted that someone paid him fifty dollars to break into my house."

Without suspending her death stare, she barks at Caleb, "Get in the car. Now."

"I'm going to report him," I tell her, as he scurries away. "He'll have to answer to the police."

"Oh, Junebug. Did you forget who I'm married to?" She smiles at me the same way she did at seventeen, at fifteen, at thirteen. As if she's better than me in every way. "I *am* the police. Speaking of, some folks are saying they saw a teenage girl in your car when you wreaked havoc at the gym yesterday. That she might be the one they're looking for. The attempted murderer. For your sake, I hope that's just a vicious rumor."

After she leaves, Wyatt and I stand there looking stupidly at each other. I hate the way he leans against the fence glowering at me from beneath the brim of his Stetson. I hate that I had to come crawling back here again. I especially hate the way he won't just say something—*anything*—which leaves me no choice but to speak first.

"Well, that was… interesting." I can't tell him Macy's missing. Not yet. I have to work up the courage.

"Yeah. She doesn't really approve of the whole bull-riding thing."

"Clearly. I can't say I blame her for that. But has she always been so…"

"*Mean?*" Wyatt suggests. "I suppose it can't be easy living with Duane, and Blair *was* her best friend. These last few days have probably been pretty tough for her. Like Christi said at the reunion, she and Jessica have gotten close with the Lennoxes over the years."

"As far as I remember, Jessica was always trash-talking Jim in the girls' bathroom when Blair wasn't around."

"I guess she changed her mind. Jim and Lydia are the twins' godparents. In fact, Jim is the one who bought the four-wheeler for them last year. They spend a lot of time together."

"That explains a lot. Jim probably paid Caleb to break in to the house to look for my dad's formula."

Wyatt frowns at me, and I'm reminded he knows nothing about the letter. About Macy. About my unfortunate encounter with Hugh. "So, um… I'm not sure how to say this, but I might have lost Macy. Her crazy stepdad showed up at the house and barged in looking for her. He didn't find her, but neither could I. I don't suppose you've seen her around here."

"You lost… *what?*"

"It's no big deal." Meanwhile, every fiber of my being insists the exact opposite. "She's probably just hiding out somewhere. I left her alone for a few minutes and… you know how kids are. I'm sure she'll turn up."

Wyatt must know I'm teetering on the edge here, because he only says, "I'll help you look for her."

"There's one more thing. I found a letter from my dad, and I have to talk to the sheriff about it."

"What does it say?"

I sigh, uncertain how to answer. *That you love me. That he protected us both. That guilt weighed him down until the day he died.*

Finally, I decide on the right word. "Everything."

He nods as if that makes sense. As if any of this makes sense.

"Walk back to the house with me to look for Macy," I say. "I'll fill you in on the way."

CHAPTER FORTY

THE NIGHT BEFORE GRADUATION

I wait until it's half past midnight before I slip out of bed and listen for the sounds of my father's snoring. I pad to the kitchen and take the key. When I put on my sneakers, I can't even look Luke in the eyes.

"I have to do it," I tell him. "This is the only way."

I slink through the grass like a fox tailing a rabbit. Swift, but careful not to attract attention. I don't use the flashlight until I'm past the fence. I skirt Red Mountain and take a right at the cactus grove, surprised how quickly I reach the workshop. Ten minutes to cross a six-year divide, to enter my father's forbidden world.

Nothing happens when I breach the lock. No sirens, no explosions, no portals through time and space. I simply let myself inside, leaving the door slightly ajar. A quick sweep of the flashlight, and I find the shelf. I scan the alphabetized rows until I locate the two bottles of pentobarbital between the palladium and the perchloric acid. I pluck one pentobarbital from its spot and tuck it into the pocket of my sleep shorts. Then, I nudge over the other bottles to fill the empty space.

I should be satisfied and leave immediately, but an aching curiosity pulls me like a magnet toward my father's desk. I prop up my flashlight like a lamp and open the drawers, hungry for this part of him. The essential part. The part he hides from me. I flip through his files until I find the one marked *Blair Lennox.* I glare at the stiff manila folder as if it's Blair herself. But then a small gold box at the bottom of the drawer catches my eye. I recognize the embossed logo of Tiny Treasures, a kiosk in Houston's Galleria Mall. I take it out and slide off the lid. Inside, on a bed of white flocking, rests a diamond tennis bracelet.

"Whatcha you doin' out here?"

I cry out and duck behind the chair. I am so dead. But when I peek at the figure awash in the dim glow of the flashlight, I realize it's much worse than that.

Duane leans his hand on the side of the doorframe, taking up so much space I can hardly see the night sky behind him. There's nowhere to run. In his other hand, he strangles the neck of a beer bottle.

"Come out, come out, wherever you are..." His singsong voice echoes in the empty workshop as he steps inside. My whole body goes cold. "I can see you, ya know? Might as well get out here and knock one back with me, Junebug. For old times' sake."

A drunk Duane could be better or worse. It's too soon to tell. Either way, he's coming for me, so I stand up and reveal myself.

"What are *you* doing out here?" I try to sound brave.

"What's it look like, genius?" He takes a long swig from the bottle, and a wet laugh sputters out of him. He holds it out to me, but I wrinkle my nose, shake my head. "Oh, c'mon. Live a little. We graduate tomorrow. What are they gonna do? Suspend me?" He cuts me off before I can answer. "They wouldn't dare. This year, next time... I mean, next year, next time. Oh, whatever. I'm gonna be the startin' quarterback for the goddamned Dallas Cowboys. How 'bout that?"

I offer a meager smile and a nod.

But it's not enough. He inches closer. "I said, how 'bout that?"

With nowhere to go, I brace myself against the desk. "That's great, Duane."

"Yeah. I'm comin' for you, Troy Aikman. I ain't never settin' foot in this hole in the road again. Me and Jess, we're gonna be on that show *Lifestyles of the Rich and Famous.*" His put-on accent sounds more Steve Irwin than Robin Leach. "We're gonna have two houses… at least. And Jess wants a boat. One of those big ones…"

The bottle of pentobarbital weighs heavy as he drones on about his future. The one he's so certain has been promised. The future I hold in my pocket. Not for the first time, I wonder if I have the guts to go through with it.

"Hey, what's that?" Bug-eyed, he looks past me to the Tiny Treasures box on the desk.

"I—"

He invades my space. I can smell the beer on his breath. The sweat on his body.

His python arm reaches around me and takes hold of the box. "Fancy. Are those real diamonds?"

I shrug, genuinely confused, a part of me worrying that my father bought it for Blair.

Duane takes out the bracelet and loops it around his finger. "Ain't that sweet," he says, tapping the charm attached to it.

A gold J. Not for Blair then.

"J for Junebug," he says.

I roll my eyes. "J for jerk," I mutter, feeling better. But also sad. Maybe Dad will miss me more than I thought.

Grinning, Duane jumps back. The bracelet disappears in his fist. "J for… *Jessica.*"

"*What?*" It's the loudest I've spoken since he waltzed in here with his half-empty beer bottle and his cartoon muscles and massive ego. "What are you talking about?"

"You don't wear classy shit like this." He waves his hand down the length of me to illustrate his point. "This here belongs on the wrist of a lady. A fine lady. Like Jessica."

"Are you seriously stealing my bracelet?"

"No, I ain't no thief." He downs the rest of his beer and flings the bottle out the open door and into the pasture. Then, he backs away from me, dangling the bracelet and snickering. "You're givin' it to me, Junebug. 'Cause you don't want me to tell Daddy-o you were out here snoopin' around. Am I right?"

As he pockets my bracelet, his smug face sends me over the edge of now or never. It's my last chance to tell him exactly how I feel.

"You really are a horrible person, Duane. Jessica deserves better. How can you be so sure I won't tell her that her pretty little graduation gift is actually mine? That her boyfriend doesn't think she's worth a single dime."

Duane steps beyond the entryway and leans around the side of the building. I start to pull the door shut. But he spins around fast and blocks it with a smack of his palm. I flinch at the sight of the hunting rifle in his other hand.

Hoisting it to his shoulder, he sweeps the site across the room and points it at the periodic table on the wall, then at my father's desk, then at me. "You ever shot a wild hog, Junebug?"

Drunk Duane is so much worse. I shake my head and step out of his line of fire.

"I reckon it wouldn't be much different to shoot a person. Easier probably. Hogs have got some thick bones, lots of fat. Takes a lot of bullets to put a big one down."

"Are you threatening to shoot me?" Part of me wonders if it would be easier to let Duane end me right now. One shot would do it. It would end Duane too. He'd spend the rest of his life throwing footballs in a prison yard to a receiver with face tattoos and a nickname like Snake Eyes.

Duane shushes me with a finger over his lips. He points out into the darkness near Red Mountain. In the moonglow, a massive boar roots its snout into the ground, foraging.

"There he is," Duane whispers, as he hoists the gun. "I've been tracking that SOB for hours. He's mine now."

The boar moves with impressive determination, keeping its head down, focused. Meanwhile, Duane wobbles like a toddler taking his first steps. It's hardly a fair fight.

"How about a bet?" I whisper back. "If you shoot that hog, you can have my bracelet. If you miss, you have to give it back."

Duane grins, his teeth sharp and menacing in the moonlight. "Deal."

But he forgets to keep his voice down, and the hog takes off for the cactus grove at lightning speed. Duane aims and fires, cursing under his breath. The first shot goes wide to the right. The second, wide left. The third decapitates a large prickly pear cactus.

"Dammit." He fires a fourth and fifth time out of sheer frustration. The hog is long gone. Duane groans and collapses against the side of the workshop. "I nearly got him."

"So close." I fight off a giggle, then hold out my hand. "Alright, I won fair and square. Give me the bracelet back."

"Sure thing, Junebug." The hardness in Duane's eyes makes me think he isn't drunk at all. Especially when he takes the bracelet from his pocket and loops it around the gun barrel, spinning it like a hula hoop as he backs away. "You can have it."

I watch him saunter to his waiting ATV.

"Psych!" he calls, before he rides off into the night. I hear him cackling long after he disappears over Red Mountain.

CHAPTER FORTY-ONE

NOW

OUR search for Macy comes up empty, but Wyatt reassures me. How far could she go without a car? Before I take off for the Sweetbriar police station, I read him the entire letter minus one critical sentence. While he wrestles with his shock, I leave him with the Livestock Gold formulation. There's no way I trust Sheriff Faulk with that.

I step into the front office, armor on and prepared for battle. My purse strapped to my chest like a bandoleer.

Christi waves at me from the front desk, baring her teeth in a phony smile. I assume she's out for blood and return the gesture with fervor.

"Junebug, I'm so glad you stopped by the office. The funniest thing happened. Eric sent you an email about Aubrey like you asked, and it came back *undeliverable.*" She squinches at the word as it leaves her mouth. "Then Jessica said you'd been terminated for reckless disregard of student safety. I told her that you hadn't mentioned anything of the sort when we—"

"It's all true. Every sordid detail." I hurry her along with a wave of my hand. "Now, I need to speak with Sheriff Faulk right away."

She raises her brows at me. "He took a late lunch. I don't know when he'll be back."

"Are you sure? It's important."

Just then, the door to the back office opens, and the man himself appears. Her cheeks flushed, Christi reaches under her desk and produces a white Dairy Queen bag.

"Hunger Buster, extra pickles?" he asks.

She avoids my eyes and nods.

After securing the bag and taking a sip of his milkshake—"Extra-large chocolate," Christi confirms—the sheriff finally looks my way and points a finger-gun at me. "Well, if it ain't Juniper Pickett. You're just the gal I wanted to see. Got a few more questions for ya."

With the Houston PD in town to impress, he'll be fully committed to his cowboy-cop role, but he's my best and last hope.

"I need to talk to you too. I found something that..." With Christi pretending not to listen, I shut my mouth until he ushers me into the hallway. "I found a letter from my dad. Jim Lennox and Toby McLean tried to steal his cattle formula to juice up the football team back in the nineties. They were still at it just a few months ago. That kid, Chase Moseley from Adamsville, his mom can tell you how he changed. He was taking an unprescribed antidepressant from Main Street Pharmacy, probably to counter the side effects. I'm willing to bet Dr. Jim gave it to him."

Sheriff Faulk stops in front of the lone interview room. The sight of my last interrogation. "Careful there, Doc. Those are some mighty big accusations. I assume you have evidence."

I retrieve my dad's note from my purse and hold it out to him. He takes it and gives it a cursory glance, then returns it to me. "Other than this so-called letter, which could be written by anyone. Including you."

"Years ago, Toby McLean had notes from my dad's office. Blair stole them during her research assistantship, probably at Toby's request. This morning, Caleb Dupree admitted that someone paid him fifty bucks to break into my house. Dr. Jim is his godfather."

"Impressive detective work for a school psychologist. I mean, *ex* school psychologist. No offense, but around here, you're about as credible as a hungry crocodile. I heard you came in hot and heavy down at the gym."

"I only asked a few questions. If Coach McLean can't handle that, it says more about him than me." One look at the sheriff's steely gaze leaves no doubt that I have officially crashed and burned. Might as well go out in a blaze of glory. "Have you seen his new girlfriend? She can't be much older than eighteen, and she looks exactly like Blair. I believe he was the father of Blair's child, and I think you already know—"

"Sit." He points through the open door at the lonely seat, and I walk to the guillotine. "There's a way to go about things, Doc, and this ain't it. That young lady has a name. Melody Pearsall. And rest assured, she's of age. You should know by now that you can't go flingin' accusations without gettin' dirty yourself. Your daddy never could get that straight either."

I shake my head, wondering why I came here. Why I expected it to be any different. Same characters, same setting, same old story. "What is it that you want to ask me now? I already told you I'm not answering any more questions without a lawyer."

"Do you have one?"

"Not yet."

"How 'bout this? You listen. I talk. You don't have to answer any questions unless you change your mind."

I should say *no.* I should say *lawyer.* But I'm too curious to leave, so I say, "Fine."

He draws his cellphone like a weapon from the back pocket of his blue jeans and opens his photo gallery. The screen, a window to the past. The time capsule—a heavy-duty box Mrs. Kendall purchased at

Smith's Hardware—sits open on a large evidence table. Next to it, the letters and items we placed inside it form a haphazard pile.

"Speaking of *letters,* we opened the time capsule. We read your letter. We read seventy-two letters to be exact."

"Seventy-two?" I ask.

"That's right."

"But there were seventy-three students in our graduating class."

Twenty years falls away, and I'm back in my room reading the words I wrote.

Before graduation, we'll gather around the flagpole—all seventy-three of us—and watch Principal Finch fling the first shovel of dirt over the time capsule. We'll each get a turn. If only I could skip a step and climb in beside it. Lie there, cold and gray and lifeless. But I can't. Not yet.

"You're right," Sheriff Faulk says, and I frown at him, momentarily suspended between past and present. "It was in your letter. Seventy-three kiddos in the graduating class of 1997. We checked it against Sweetbriar High records to be sure, and Mrs. Kendall confirmed that every student submitted a letter."

I shift in the hard plastic chair, trying to find comfort. But there's none to be had. Not in this room with Sheriff Faulk holding all the cards. I can only imagine what he told Mrs. Kendall about me. What she'd already heard.

"You know what we did next? Dupree brought in his yearbook, and we checked 'em off one by one. Guess what?"

I don't guess. I barely look at him.

"One letter is missing. And how 'bout that? It's Blair's."

"I didn't steal it, if that's what you're getting at. I have no idea what Blair wrote in her letter. I certainly never opened the time capsule. I wanted to, for obvious reasons. That's why I came back here. But things didn't turn out that way."

A knock on the door comes as a merciful interruption. Until I spot the face in the window. Duane stands side by side with a female officer I don't recognize. She wears a Houston Police patch on her shoulder that works magic on Duane. He doesn't crack a joke or make a face or tell me what a loser I am. He stands up straight and acts like an actual grown-up. But when his lips part, I spot the too-white replacement for the upper incisor that he lost to the bank robber otherwise known as Wyatt Landry.

"Officer Tillman and I've finished up the metal-detector sweep in the courtyard," he says. "There's something she wants you to see. We found it in the gravesite."

The officer glances past Sheriff Faulk for an agonizing second, and I know she read my letter. That she recognizes me as the prime suspect. It's there in her eyes. What a horrible person I am.

I can only watch while she shows Sheriff Faulk the plastic evidence bag. She speaks too low to hear, and I'm too far away to see its contents. But when she passes the bag to the sheriff, my stomach drops.

He holds it beneath the harsh white light. It's undeniable, and yet I can't believe it. Dad was right. We are cursed.

"That's not mine." I look at Duane, but he pretends I don't exist. My throat closes up and my brain shuts down, leaving me defenseless.

With an incredulous scoff, the sheriff returns the evidence bag to Officer Tillman. She and Duane leave us and disappear inside another closed door.

"We're gonna test that for DNA, so you better get your story straight." He ushers me from the room. I keep my head down and follow the echo of his boots down the hallway. "I hate to say it, Doc, but the next time we cross paths I'm gonna put you in handcuffs."

Sheriff Faulk waits for me to catch up to him, then looms over me until I meet his cold eyes. "I had a talk with Detective Voss from San Francisco this morning. A little hoity-toity but a nice enough fella. Seems like you left quite an impression out there."

His mouth moves, but I can only see Hugh barreling through my dad's house like a runaway train intent on blaming me for everything.

I see Macy too, sitting on my office sofa and hugging the stuffed elephant from my Emotional Support Bin. *Did you ever think about suicide?* she'd asked me. I couldn't lie to her. *Once. With one of my dad's chemicals. It was called…*

The sheriff comes back into focus, still droning on. "But I told him: sonny, you've gotta wait your turn because she's the number-one suspect in my cold case. And you're gonna want to hear how she did it…"

A wave of nausea sloshes in my stomach. In my head, I only hear one word: *pentobarbital.*

I slap my hand over my mouth and run for the bathroom, nearly knocking Duane to the ground. I open the stall door and retch into the toilet until my throat burns. Exhausted and empty, I curl my legs beneath me on the hard tile floor and read the graffiti inked on the stall. I know I can't stay here forever. I have to face Sheriff Faulk and Duane and Christi. Officer Tillman too. It makes my head hurt to think of that evidence bag.

As I struggle to my feet, the blare of the fire alarm rips through the tomblike silence, and I clench the grab bar to steady myself. My breath quickens. Heart pounds. Sweat starts to slick my armpits.

I look up to the water-stained ceiling and say a silent prayer. To God. To my father. To Blair even. How much more can one person take? Overwhelmed, I sink onto the toilet and start with hydrogen. By the time, I reach 118 oganesson—which I memorized after its addition to the table last year—I decide I'm not going anywhere.

TEN minutes later, with the alarm still wailing, I emerge from the bathroom and wander out of the building, dazed and confused, like a creature stumbling up from the depths into a strange, new world. A small crew of police and office staff gathers on the sidewalk in front of the police station. Behind them, my car waits for me, ready to take me far from here. If I can just get to it.

"You alright?" Sheriff Faulk asks as I pass him.

I don't answer or slow down.

As I open the car door, Duane runs out of the station and points at me. "Hey, stop!"

Then, with at least twenty cop-eyes on me, he gleefully hammers the nail in my coffin. "She stole that evidence bag before we could log it in."

CHAPTER FORTY-TWO

DUANE runs toward me and slams me against my car, pinning me to the door until my lungs burn. When I wriggle to catch a breath, he secures my arms behind my back.

"Don't move. I need to pat you down." I start to protest, but he jams his elbow into my side, growling into my ear. "Keep your mouth shut or I'll end you and that little juvenile delinquent you're hidin' at your place."

"Okay, okay." I force my body to relax. I can't risk him going after Macy. She's already been through enough.

As Duane paws at me, Sheriff Faulk appears. He glowers at us both. "What's going on?"

Duane pauses his search, but I don't dare move. "The evidence bag is missing. We hadn't logged it in when the alarm went off. I left it right there on the table."

I rub my wrists, which reddened in his tight grip. My face too, feels hot. With the alarm cleared, they're all still standing here, staring at me.

"Well, I didn't take it. Why would I?" Of course, it's a stupid question. The stupidest. That night lingers like a ghost. Trigger-happy Duane and his shotgun. My tennis bracelet in his pocket. Who knew it would spend the last two decades buried beside Blair's cooling bones?

Duane shakes his head at me. "Don't be cute, June. You were the only one who didn't evacuate the station. And it has your initial on it."

I sneer at him, then turn to the sheriff. "Check the cameras. I can assure you it wasn't me who *stole* that bracelet." I take pleasure when Duane flinches at the word.

The sheriff snorts. "You're in Sweetbriar, Doc. Not the big city. We only have cameras on the outside of the building and half the time they don't work."

"Of course, which I obviously didn't know. But go ahead and search me, if it makes you feel better. Search my car too, if you want."

Sheriff Faulk nods at Duane. "Go on, then."

Duane resumes his humiliation tour. First stop, patting my pockets. Then, lifting the back of my shirt. Finally, he peers into the back seat. It's all for show, but he gives a worthy performance. The concern on his face so convincing, I start to suspect myself.

"She's clear for now," he mutters.

"Nothing to see here," the sheriff calls out, finally. "Head back inside. We've got work to do."

With his boss's back momentarily turned, Duane gives me another shove. "But come to think of it, she's sneaky. She probably stashed it somewhere. We should do a lap around the premises."

"You better do more than a lap." For once Sheriff Faulk aims his hawk eyes at someone other than me. "Why the hell did you let it out of your sight in the first place, Dupree? That's a rookie mistake."

"I wasn't thinking, sir. The fire alarm threw me off my game."

"Seriously? That's your excuse? Sounds about like the time you misplaced your damn patrol car." The sheriff spits onto the ground, his telltale sign of displeasure. "Don't make me put you back on probation, boy. Your daddy won't be happy, and neither will the missus."

Duane nods and scurries up the sidewalk. He stops at the door, long enough to fling a threatening glance over his shoulder. I pretend not to notice.

"And *you*..." Turns out, I also receive the hawk-eye treatment. "If I find out you tampered with my case, I will stop at nothin' to put you in a six-by-nine cell. Now, get the hell out of here before I find somethin' to arrest you for."

"Sheriff, I didn't kill Blair." When he doesn't yell at me or cuff me, I keep going. But I talk fast, in case he changes his mind. "Get Toby McClean's DNA. You'll see I'm right about her unborn baby. She knew about the steroid scheme. She was pregnant. He had more motive than anybody. Even me."

"You about done tellin' me how to do my job?"

I open the door to my little red sports car. I do not peel out. I do not speed. I keep it between the lines and under thirty-five until I reach the Wal-Mart parking lot. I pull into a spot at the edge, facing the two-lane road, and wait.

TWENTY minutes later, my patience pays off. Duane zips past in his police cruiser, heading beyond the city limits. From my position, I watch him make the left turn after the Sweetbriar Country Store. I wait for a count of ten. Then, I follow.

I turn off the main road and slow to a crawl when I spot the cruiser up ahead in the entrance to the tow lot. The gates part, and Duane drives inside. I park my car in the ditch, ready for a speedy getaway, and tail after him. I post up close to the fence, where I can make out the booth. But it's empty. From inside the lot comes the sound of grinding metal.

"Hey, Tom. How's it goin'? You about to close up shop for the day?" Duane manages to sound friendly despite the black hole where his heart should be. But I remember the way he and Eric called out *troll* every time Mr. Trolf appeared in the hallway, and how they once stole his cleaning cart and used it to push Freddie down the hill behind the school, where he'd ended upside down on the playground.

"What? Speak up, son! I can't hear ya over the crusher." Mr. Trolf's hound dog barks out a warning. "Pipe down, Scout. It's Officer Dupree. You remember him."

Of course Scout remembers the stink of pure meanness. At least he knows what we're up against.

When the grinding stops, Duane says, "I forgot it was car crushin' day. I shoulda brought the boys. They love that shit."

"Yep, you know the drill. Every Sunday afternoon, that ol' fella from up in Adamsville brings in his scrappers."

"You mean the chop-shop guy that pays you off with a bottle of Johnny Walker Blue to look the other way. *That guy?* Am I right?"

"Naw. Where'd ya hear that nonsense? I'm more of a Shiner Bock guy myself."

"How 'bout cash? Are you a cash guy?" Duane produces a wad of bills from the back pocket of his uniform.

I grab for my cellphone, annoyed I didn't think to record from the start. *What a total cave dweller*, Macy would say. One look at the screen, and my mind goes blank. Twelve missed calls from Wyatt in the last thirty minutes. Fumbling with the phone, I snap a few hurried photos through the mesh fence and run back to the car.

"What happened?" Already, I'm putting my V6 twin turbo to use the way I never could in the big city.

"Macy. That's what happened."

"Did you find her? Is she okay?"

His dry laugh gives me no comfort. I take the turn too fast and nearly mow down the Andersons' mailbox on the way out of town.

"Oh, yeah. I found her alright. She stole my damn truck right out from under me."

"She did what? *How?*'

"I was looking around for her out back when I heard the engine fire up."

Stunned, I take my foot off the gas and admit defeat. By Macy. By Duane. By life in general and its uncanny knack of yanking out the rug at the most inopportune time. "I don't get it. Why would she run away? Are you sure she wasn't…"

"Wasn't *what?*" Wyatt asks.

"I don't know… *kidnapped?* Her stepdad is a complete lunatic. And, well, I don't trust anyone around here. I saw Duane at the police station and he accused me of stealing this bracelet that he actually stole from me the night before graduation and—"

"She left a note for you. Well, for both of us, I guess." After a pause, he reads, *"I'm sorry for everything. I should've never dragged you and the cowboy into this. I'll try to make it right for both of us."*

A sharp pain pierces my side. I suck in a breath and press my hand to my ribs, certain I've been stabbed. But there's no blood, no wound. Just my heart pounding out of my chest.

"Breathe, June."

"I am breathing!" I yell. "You didn't call the cops, did you?"

Wyatt says nothing. I pass a farmhouse. An oil well. A herd of grazing cattle.

"Did you?"

"No, June. You'll be happy to know that I did not call the police to report a fugitive teenager who stole my vehicle and, oh, by the way, a hundred dollars out of my wallet. Because that would make absolutely no sense."

"Exactly."

Wyatt sighs like a man who knows the recklessness of the adolescent brain firsthand. After all, he did ride bulls for fun. "Just get back here so we can find her before she does something really stupid."

CHAPTER FORTY-THREE

THE MORNING OF GRADUATION

ON the last day of my life, I wake before the sunrise. To be honest, I didn't sleep. Not after the stunt Duane pulled. I kept thinking about his horrible cackle and the stolen bracelet and how perfect it would look on Jessica's dainty wrist. How my father would blame me for its disappearance. How he wouldn't be wrong. I lie there and stare at Luke with my chest burning until I finally fling off the covers and get dressed. It's that or implode like a supernova creating a vast hole in the galaxy.

I leave a note for Dad on the counter—*Took the truck to town, will be back soon!*—mainly so he doesn't freak out and call the cops. What do I care if he's furious, if he grounds me for the rest of my life? *Ha, ha, Dad.* Joke's on you.

Once I enter the city limits, Sweetbriar High exerts its gravitational pull, and the old pickup all but navigates itself to the courtyard. I park across the street and stare at the marquee.

CONGRATULATIONS, CLASS OF '97!
TIME-CAPSULE COMMEMORATION AND
GRADUATION CEREMONY
MAY 30 AT 6 P.M.
FRONT COURTYARD and FOOTBALL STADIUM

Two days ago, we submitted our letters to Mrs. Kendall in envelopes with our names printed on the front. After the letters are unearthed at the 2017 ceremony, they will be compiled into a memory book that we can purchase. *It'll be a small price to pay for these priceless memories*, Mrs. Kendall assured us.

She counted the letters herself, putting seventy-three check marks in her gradebook, before sealing them inside the box from Smith's Hardware with the other items my classmates had chosen. Jessica's blue-and-white pom-poms; a copy of the Sunday edition of the *Sweetbriar Gazette* and the May edition of *People* magazine; a grocery-store receipt and a shiny 1997 penny; a mixed tape with songs from George Strait, Spice Girls, Jewel, and 98 Degrees; a signed yearbook and a videotaped message from our elected class officers.

When Mrs. Kendall had called my name, I hesitated. My hands started to sweat, and I wondered whether I could do it. Whether I could even muster the courage to push the first domino. But then, Duane and Jessica giggled, and Blair muttered, "June bugs don't even live twenty years." That did it. I marched up the aisle and dropped my letter in the box. Mrs. Kendall smiled and thanked me, and I felt horribly guilty that she would probably be the first one to read it if I managed to do what I set out to.

"Hold up, Benny! That should do it!"

I jolt back to the courtyard, where Mr. Trolf directs a water hose at a parched grave-sized patch of earth in front of the flagpole. His one-man crew, Benny, salutes him before he hoists a shovel and starts to dig. Mr. Trolf shuts off the hose and joins him.

Digging a hole in Texas at the end of May takes time and sweat and STIX radio and apparently at least one Shiner Bock each before breakfast. When Mr. Trolf spots me watching, he grins and waves me over. Up close, I see they've made more progress than I thought. At least three feet worth.

"Today's the big day, huh?" He reaches out his hand to shake mine, oblivious to just how colossal today could be. "Your high-school graduation. I'll bet your daddy's real proud."

"Yes, sir." I smell the beer on his breath, but I don't mind. He's been kind to me and on your last day on the planet, not much else matters anymore.

"Seems like yesterday when I took that walk. Old man Herbert—he was principal back then—flipped my tassel. I was all set up with a scholarship to a voc tech in Houston. But then Marjorie got pregnant and we got hitched six months later. Turns out, I never left."

"Hell, at least you graduated, Trolf." Benny rests the shovel against his chest and laughs. "They booted me outta tenth grade. Said don't let the door hit ya where the good lord split ya. I spent two years in juvie up in Adamsville."

"That's what happens when you and Johnny Faulk get caught rustling cows. Did you really think his daddy was gonna bail your ass out too?"

Benny snorts. "Shoulda known better. Now here I am workin' like a dog and Johnny just got himself elected sheriff. Ain't that some shit."

"Sure is." Mr. Trolf drops his shovel in the dirt and reaches into a nearby cooler for the sweaty neck of his beer. He takes a long swig then winks at me. "You didn't see that."

"See what?"

We share a laugh at my joke. Then they pick up their shovels and get back to work while I peer into the hole and contemplate my future.

"What're you morons screwing up now?" Principal Finch rushes over from his office, gesturing wildly.

I can't look away from his pale chicken legs protruding from his golf shorts. Or his toes in those sandals, the dark wiry hair on them that matches his mustache.

"Oh, hello, Juniper. What I meant to say is: Gentlemen, I told you to dig to the right of the flagpole. Not the left. The gas line runs to the left."

Benny grimaces. "That's my fault. Coulda swore you said left. I guess I misheard ya."

Principal Finch throws up his hands again.

"So you want us to dig another hole?" Mr. Trolf shakes his head *yes* to stop Benny, but it doesn't even slow him down. "It's gettin' hot out here, and we only got a foot to go."

"Well, Benny, unless you want to blow the whole school to kingdom come…"

Mr. Trolf stabs his shovel into the freshly dug pile of dirt, then tosses it back into the hole it came from. "We'll get right on it, sir."

Principal Finch retreats into his air-conditioned office, his sandals smacking the pavement with displeasure.

After he disappears inside, I tell the men goodbye. Mr. Trolf pauses to wipe his forehead and to issue another congratulations. To assure me that my whole future lies ahead.

"Just remember that you wanna be the one tellin' 'em where to dig the holes and when and how big. Not the one diggin'."

"Ain't that the truth," Benny adds, flinging more dirt.

"And take it from me, kid," Mr. Trolf adds. "Get the hell out of Sweetbriar."

I drive home in a fog, ruminating about poor Tom Trolf and how tomorrow I'll be somewhere other than Sweetbriar and he'll still be stuck slaving his life away for jerks like Principal Finch. Maybe I should do him a favor and slip some pentobarbital in his beer bottle tonight. I'm sure he'll be around to clean up the mess after the party.

After the party. After.

I give my head a violent shake. Stop thinking, I tell myself. Don't think. *Do.*

But then I make the turn down Saw Mill Road and see my father standing in the doorway. Like he's waiting for me. The hamster wheel ratchets up again. What if he heard me sneak out last night? What if he found the bottle I stole?

"You okay, kiddo?" he asks as I walk up the porch steps.

I paste on a smile. "Why wouldn't I be?"

"Nice try, but I know you're still mad at me about…" I wait for him to say it for once. Just say it. "You know, the other night."

"It's fine, Dad. It was an accident. I know Blair's going through a stressful time right now, and she didn't mean to do it." The words come easy. They belong to him; I simply parrot them back.

"Exactly. I knew you would understand."

He holds open the door, and I follow him inside and into the kitchen, where an unopened package of Oreo cookies sits at the center of the table. I would rather it be anything else.

"For old times' sake?" he asks.

"Oreos for breakfast, Dad? It's nine o' clock in the morning." If I sit here. If I eat those Oreos. If I let myself start thinking, feeling, then I won't go through with it. I need to stay numb. Numb and vengeful. "I promised Wyatt I would help him with…"

Before I can invent a favor Wyatt never asked, my father's face darkens. He turns his back to me and directs his attention to the row of useless inventions on the counter. Anger tinkering.

"Now you're off to Berkeley, you need to leave Wyatt alone, June."

"What are you talking about? He's my friend. Why would I—"

"When a man makes a commitment to a woman, he needs to see it through. Even when it's difficult. I think you know you make it hard for Wyatt to do that."

"A commitment?" Genuinely lost, I stare at the Oreos for a clue. "A commitment to who?" But when I speak it out loud, I realize I already know. "Are you talking about Blair again? *God, Dad.* They're not together anymore, and it has nothing to do with me."

Dad stops tinkering, puts up his hands in surrender, and slowly turns to face me. Like I'm the one with the loaded gun. Maybe I am.

"I don't want to argue," he says. "Not on your graduation day. You're a big girl, and it's your life. I'm so proud of you. In fact, I got you a little something, but it's out at the shop. Do you want me to get it now?"

"No." It crushes him. But it's as necessary as turning down the Oreos. "Give it to me tonight. After the graduation party. When it's all over."

I spend the rest of the morning riding my bike to all my favorite places. Alongside the creek bed where Wyatt once caught a whopper of a catfish that he fried up for Midnight while his father slept one off on the green sofa. Through the pasture to the cactus grove where Bert dug up a flint arrowhead that sits on my dresser. Up on the hill past the cow-dog graveyard that has the best view of the farm from one fence line to the other.

At two o'clock, curiosity propels me down the gravel road farther than usual to the old Crenshaw place that now belongs to the Lennox family. Dr. Jim works at the pharmacy on Friday afternoons, and his wife plays bingo at the Baptist church, leaving Blair alone.

I lay my bike in the grass and wander up to the refurbished farmhouse. Music wafts from out back, and I follow the sound, inching alongside the rustic wood siding until I find Blair lying on a beach towel in the grass in her cat-eye sunglasses and black bikini, with *Teen* magazine splayed across her stomach. A boom box belts out Hanson's "MMMBop."

I clear my throat, but she doesn't stir, and I let myself imagine that she's dead. That she's already gulped down a cup of poisoned punch. Emboldened, my eyes drift to the house, to the back door she's left ajar.

As I creep toward it, I pass a frilly-curtained window and peer inside to the inner sanctum of Blair Lennox. To her canopy bed and the oversized stuffed dog I helped Wyatt pick out for her two Valentine's ago. Candid photos cover one wall, and I gawk at them, overcome with longing for her life. Her perfect life with her perfect smile and her perfect parents and her perfect friends. The way she fits in the crook of Wyatt's arm. Perfectly.

A dress hangs from the antique armoire next to her graduation gown. It's white and flowy with flutter sleeves and a designer label. I would look like a marshmallow in a dress like that. But on Blair's slim, tan body, it will be... *perfect.*

With Blair still napping in the sun, I slip into the house. It doesn't take me long to find the scissors in the knife block in the kitchen. To sneak into her room. To slice through her perfect graduation dress until it's nothing but tatters on the floor.

CHAPTER FORTY-FOUR

NOW

WYATT stands in the empty driveway, looking like a man who just got outsmarted by a teenager. He greets me with a defeated wave.

I roll down the window. "Get in."

Grumbling, he stuffs all six feet of himself and then some into the passenger seat. Cowboy hat and boots too. Then, he tosses his flip phone onto the floorboard in disgust. "Can I borrow your fancy phone please? My truck has an anti-theft tracker, but I can't open it on here. This damn thing is about as useless as lips on a chicken."

I pass him my phone and he takes one look at it and sighs. "A little help here."

A few profanities later, his truck's antitheft application opens on the screen.

"See that green dot." I expand the image on the map, already shaking my head in disbelief. A current of fear hums through me. Whatever happens to her, it's my fault.

"How long has she been there?" Wyatt asks.

"Looks like ten minutes. We better hurry." I punch the gas and leave the cottage in a cloud of dust. Once we hit the Farm to Market Road, I sneak a glance at him. "You can say it if you want. I won't hold it against you."

"I don't need to say it."

"Okay. Fine. Don't say it then."

Wyatt laughs. "Alright. *I told you so.*"

"Good. Now we've got that out of the way..." I talk as fast as I drive, filling him in on my hellish visit to the station. On Sheriff Faulk's indifference. On Blair's missing letter. On Duane's accusations and his shady stop at the impound lot.

"Are you sure it's the same bracelet?" Wyatt asks. "I mean, it has been a long time."

He's right about that. But some things you don't forget no matter how much you wish you could. "It's the same one. I remember everything about that day. *Everything.*"

That he doesn't question. "I do too."

I feel his hand rest on my leg. I don't dare look at it because I don't want him to take it back. When I blow past the city-limit sign seconds later, his cellphone rings from the floorboard, and he jerks his hand away.

"Is it Macy?"

Of course it's not. He shows me the surname on the screen, his face as shocked as mine. *Trolf.*

"Answer it!"

"Hello?"

I strain to hear the other side of the conversation, but it's only a faint murmur.

"Uh, Juniper Pickett? Yeah, I know how to reach her... I can... *Now?... Where?...* Alright, calm down. It's okay. I'll let her know." Wyatt hangs up and calmly sets the phone in his lap.

I want to shake him. "What did he say? Did he mention Duane?"

He takes a slow breath that reminds me of the past. Of his bull-riding days. The *I just drew the baddest bull in the lineup* kind of breath that always left me wringing my hands with worry from the stands before the chute flew open.

"Hang a left up here."

"But the CrossFit gym is that way. Is your truck on the move?" I slow down as we approach the stop sign by the Country Store. To the left is the road that leads to Sweetbriar. To the right, a no-man's-land that doesn't end until you reach the next town over.

"No. Truck's still there." He levels me with a hard look. "We need to go to the Roundup. Tom wants to talk to you."

"What about Macy? What if she confronts Coach Mac? What if they call the police? What if she gets hurt?" The what-ifs multiply too fast to keep up. Immobilized, I stamp my foot on the brake, uncertain which way to go and convinced that either is the wrong one.

"Tom says he has something you need to see. That the cops might be onto him. He sounds panicky. If we don't go now, he might change his mind. I promise I'll keep an eye on the green dot."

It takes everything in me to turn left. To leave Macy on her own. But I watch the store shrink behind me until it reduces to a flat line in my rearview.

We drive the next three miles in silence; the ghosts of the past riding between us. Blair. My father. Wyatt's. His left boot does the talking for him. It hasn't stopped tapping the floorboard since we got the call.

He points up ahead. "It's the gravel road past that mailbox."

I slow my speed and listen to the steady metronome of the blinker, but my heart races twice as fast. In eighteen years I'd seen most of what Sweetbriar had to offer—the good and the bad—but never the Roundup Saloon. It was as much a mystery as my father's workshop. I only knew that bad things happened there. Like the time Chet Landry whistled at Buddy Murphy's wife and got his neck sliced. My dad and I drove thirteen-year-old Wyatt to the hospital to see him, but he'd already checked out against medical advice and caught a ride back to the liquor store.

The car judders down the rutty path, and I turn on my headlamps to chase away the shadows of the impending sunset. On the other side of the road, I spot a set of muddy skid marks in the ditch.

"Probably had one too many," I joke, desperate to lighten the mood.

But Wyatt doesn't laugh. "Happened to me a few times. More than a few, if I'm being honest."

I swallow hard when I spot the sign. A hand-painted plank of wood nailed to a fence post that makes an announcement that sounds more like a warning.

Roundup Saloon
Hang a left at the old Baptist church
Sinners welcome!

"You sure you're okay to do this?"

Wyatt keeps his eyes fixed on the road. "Don't have much choice, do I?"

"I can let you out here. You can wait for me by the main road."

"Just keep driving."

I do, but I refuse to let it go. Especially once the dilapidated church comes into view with its peeling paint and crumbling front steps and an old pew grown up in the weeds. "Or in the car. You can wait for me right here. I'll leave it running."

"June. Stop."

"All I'm saying is I can hold my own. I'm not a kid anymore."

"No. *Stop!* You'll miss the place."

I slam on the brakes just in time to make a final right turn into the Roundup parking lot, which would be more accurately described as a cow pasture. In fact, behind the shack that masquerades as a saloon, a Jersey cow reaches her head under the barbed-wire fence to graze on a patch of Bermuda grass.

"So, this is it." I sound uncertain, but one glance at Wyatt and I know. He looks haunted. This must be the place. I pull in between a rusted-out Ford with a dented front end and a familiar cargo van.

"You've gotta be kidding me," I say when Wyatt points out the *H. Ross Perot for President* bumper sticker affixed to the back. "That's the same one he drove in 1997."

"I told ya, people change slow around here. Or not at all."

"Some people."

With a sad smile, Wyatt cracks the door and sets one boot on the dirt. Already, I hear Johnny Cash's baritone voice singing "Folsom Prison Blues." On the dusty front porch, Mr. Trolf's dog Scout waits patiently for his return. His tail thumps when he spots us, but he doesn't get up.

"You ready?" Wyatt asks.

"*Are you?* You really don't have to go in there. What's it been, fifteen years?"

"Fifteen years, twenty-five days, and roughly six hours, but who's counting?" He chuckles, but he can't hide his nerves. Not from me. "Listen, I always told myself I'd never set foot in this place again unless I had a damn good reason. Like it's the end of the world, and they've got the last can of beanie weenies. Or they finally convinced George Strait to play there on a Friday night. Or..." He steps out of the car and walks around to the driver's side. Opens the door and reaches for my hand. "Juniper Pickett needs me."

I roll my eyes, unable to fight off a smile, and let him pull me to my feet.

"And she needs my inside knowledge. Trolf always takes the back booth by the jukebox. A15 used to be his favorite song. C'mon."

Without hesitation, Wyatt flings open the door to his own rock bottom. It smells like cheap whiskey and cigarette smoke and sounds like bad karaoke. A sheet-sized Texas flag hangs behind the bar, flanked by two taxidermied deer heads and an unlucky bobcat. Wyatt nods at the grizzled bartender and the row of old men occupying the well-worn barstools. Then he meanders toward the back booth, where Mr. Trolf waits. A Cowboys hat pulled low to hide his face, he drums his fingers against a bottle of Shiner Bock.

As I slide in beside Wyatt, Mr. Trolf eyes the door.

"You sure nobody followed ya?" He leans in close, spitting out the words in one boozy breath. But if he's already drunk, I can't tell. He's wired so tight he's practically humming. "I swear, that numbnuts Dupree is smarter than he looks. He's been watchin' me. Can you believe he had the nerve to show up at the lot today?"

"What did he want?" I ask.

Mr. Trolf tears his gaze from the door, and it lands right on me. "Remember Friday morning when your car got towed? That's when it started. Dupree showed up right behind the tow man. He wanted to have a look-see in your car. He told me he caught you out at the school and that you dug up a body. Well, not just any body. But *you know who.*"

I stare at my hands folded on the wooden table. A stark contrast to that night. Digging through the dirt like an animal, desperate to cover my tracks. Or that *other* night so long ago now but clear in my mind. Clawing at Blair until she bled on my sweater.

Wyatt nudges my leg beneath the table, and I remember where I am. At the Roundup. With these hands—*mine*—that were once capable of murder. "Uh, you mean Blair Lennox."

"Of course I mean Blair Lennox. It's been goin' around about you for years, ever since you hightailed it out of here. That you mighta been the one who made her disappear, if you know what I'm sayin'." He glances at Wyatt. "You too, no offense."

Wyatt excuses him with a wave of his hand. "I've been told worse."

"Hell, for a while, old Johnny Faulk even had Benny and me on his radar on account of we were there that night to clean up after the party. It didn't help that Benny was three sheets to the wind, and I wasn't too far behind him. I could really throw 'em back in my younger days." Mr. Trolf takes a well-timed pull from his beer bottle.

"So, Duane went through my car at the impound lot?"

"I reckon he did. He paid me to look the other way. I figured, worst case, no harm no foul. Best case, I'm a hero. I catch a killer. Like *Murder, She Wrote* only an impound man."

Mr. Trolf is no Jessica Fletcher. Still, I glance over at Wyatt, hoping I didn't walk into a trap. "It wasn't me, Mr. Trolf. I swear."

He slaps the table with emphasis, then ducks down when the old-man crew at the bar swivel their heads in unison. They all seem to have the same leathery face, a topography chiseled by hot sun, hard labor, and too many Marlboros. "Hell, girl, I shoulda figured that from the get-go. You always were real nice to me. But now I know."

I wait for him to explain. Instead, with another furtive glance at the door, he reaches under the leather seat cushion and produces a familiar Sweetbriar PD evidence bag.

"Dupree gave me a fifty spot to let him toss this in the crusher. But you know what he's like. Always gotta be the center of attention. He reared back to throw it in Tom Brady-style, which got Scout all riled up. The dog grabbed a hold of his pants, and Dupree started runnin'. That's when I fished the bag out and took a gander."

With another quick check of the door, he slides the bag over to me. "It's some of your daddy's property in there. And… well… go on, take a look for yourself."

As I reach over, Mr. Trolf clutches my arm. "Wait! I almost forgot." He slips a pair of dirty work gloves out of his back pocket. "Better put these on before you go pokin' around. That's what Miss Fletcher would do."

With my hands concealed inside Mr. Trolf's oversized mitts, I set the bag aside and remove its contents. My stolen bracelet rests like a tarnished crown on top of Blair's file folder, the one that disappeared from the back seat of my car days ago. It's precious to me, that bracelet. Even with its stones dulled and its alloy setting discolored to a greenish black. Because my father bought it for me.

Underneath the folder, I find a yellowed envelope. It's just old paper—twenty years old to be precise—but it grabs me by the throat like a skeleton hand, long buried. Blair had penned her name on the front, the way Mrs. Kendall directed.

Next to me, Wyatt takes a quick breath. "I guess it's not missing anymore."

"Did you read this letter?" I ask Mr. Trolf.

With a sheepish shrug, he replies, "It was already open, and I'm a curious fella. Like Scout sniffin' every tree in the yard, I just had to know. It ain't every day you get a letter from a dead girl."

I slip the page from the envelope and carefully unfold it. I hear Blair's voice in my head as I read.

Dear Future Me,

It's 2017! Are there flying cars and robot servants yet? That would be so cool!

I hope you finally made the Kentucky Wildcats cheer team... after spending ONE semester (no more!!!) at that stupid community college... and that the agent Mom introduced you to in Dallas finally saw your potential as an actress. I hope you are in the Beverly Hills Hotel right now getting ready to walk the red carpet with your co-star/husband Brad Pitt and that you already have an Oscar on your mantel.

Who are you kidding?!?! None of that is ever going to happen now. Because you blew it. All over a middle-aged horndog. You aren't going to be a college cheerleader or an actress or Brad Pitt's wife. You're going to have stretch marks and undereye bags and get as fat as a house.

No one knows YET... except for Doc Pickett. Go figure that I would trust the town weirdo. But he swore he wouldn't tell. He thinks it's Wyatt's baby, and I let him believe it. Mom and Jim will have a total cow even though Jim is such a hypocrite. Mom was already knocked up with a kid... me... when she met him. And she wasn't even old enough to rent a car when they got hitched.

Toby won't want anything to do with me when I'm not young and cute and off limits. He's already been flirting with a freshman. Jessica and Christi will be the worst. They're so jealous of me they'll be happy to see me trapped in this Podunk town with a kid on my hip. Dumdum Duane thinks he's going to be making millions in the NFL and that Jessica won't have to work a day in her life. She wouldn't even be able to squeeze her big hips into a designer dress, and that's why I'm doing her a favor by exposing Duane as a cheater and a roid-head.

But he's not the only one. I know about everything! I've seen Jim with his big stacks of cash that he tells Mom are from his weekly poker games and Toby with his vials of "liquid vitamins" that he passes out like candy at practice. He even tried to get me to steal from Doc Pickett for him. They all think I'm just a dumb blonde. But like Dolly says—this dumb blonde ain't nobody's fool!!! Who knows who else might be involved? They're all going down!

So, what are my new goals for the future me? Well, have the cutest baby that Sweetbriar has ever laid eyes on... duh. Convince Wyatt to get back together and make him get an actual job (that doesn't involve cows) and become a sweet little family. I'll try to be grateful for what I still have... Remember, future me, it could always be worse. You could be Junebug married to Fat Freddie.

Love,
Past Me

I sit back in the booth, stunned. "At least we know it's authentic. It's undeniably her."

Mr. Trolf nods. "That gal always did have a mean streak. Guess it finally caught up to her. But she might still get the last laugh. It sure does seem like Dupree—"

Wyatt stands up, my cellphone in hand. "Truck's on the move. We should go."

I return the letter to the envelope and stuff it back into the evidence bag with the folder and the bracelet. Then, I slip off Mr. Trolf's gloves and linger in the booth, uncertain what to do next. I can't imagine leaving the bag here with him, but taking it seems risky too. I already look guilty enough.

"You keep it," Mr. Trolf says. "Dupree's already lookin' for a reason to haul me to the clink. I don't need a target on my back."

I feel the sudden urge to squeeze Mr. Trolf in a hug, but I simply say, "Thank you. I owe you a drink."

Wyatt snags the evidence bag, and I follow him out the door and to the car. Now that it's dark out, the rising moon bathes the lot in an eerie glow. He stands there for an impossibly long time, and I don't have to ask what's tormenting him or why he fled from the bar or who he's thinking of when he wipes a tear with the back of his hand and climbs into the passenger seat without a word.

"Where's she headed?" I ask as I back out of the lot onto the gravel road. I sneak a glance at the phone resting on his leg. The green dot creeps along at a steady pace.

"She's going back the way she came. On the Farm to Market Road. She's probably lost."

"Maybe she changed her mind. Or needs help. Or…" I zip my mouth shut. The more I talk, the more I panic. So I focus on my hands on the wheel. On what needs to be done to find Macy. The rest of it—the Jim–Toby–Duane conspiracy—will have to wait.

When I hit the highway, I hit the gas, chasing that green dot as if my life depends on it. In some ways, it does. I can't endure another mistake. Another crisis situation.

As we approach the turnoff for Saw Mill Road, Wyatt says, "We're getting close. Really close." He refreshes the screen. Then, again. A worried frown appears on his face.

"What is it?" I ask.

"The truck stopped moving."

"What do you mean?" As I lean over to catch a glimpse of the dot, a rabbit darts across the road. I slam on the brakes, straining the seat belt and sending my heart into my throat.

Now I see it ahead of us. The back end of Wyatt's truck, spotlighted by my headlamps. It's parked in the ditch.

I pull in behind it and fling open the door, yelling for Macy. No one answers. We circle the truck on foot. No sign of her.

Wyatt stops to examine the back driver's side wheel with his flashlight app. "Tire's flat and it looks…"

"It looks *what?*" I lean down to the small circle of light, illuminating the puncture hole in the rubber.

"Intentional."

CHAPTER FORTY-FIVE

GRADUATION

I measure my life in hours now. Less than five to go, surely. But first, I must endure this final public trial. An ordeal of epic proportions. I adjust my cap, fiddle with the tassel. Sit up tall and straight and ignore the sweat pooling behind my knees and under my hair, a product of the heat and my fraying nerves. Two rows in front of me, Blair adjusts Wyatt's collar, letting her fingers linger in his shaggy hair. Damned alphabetical order. To give myself strength, I touch the bottle in my pocket; I remember Blair's white dress, ruined.

Principal Finch taps the microphone. "Congratulations, Class of 1997. Tonight marks the culmination of twelve years of hard work, and…"

As he drones on about our bright and brilliant futures, I peer out at the crowd in search of my father in the bleachers. I find him in the front row, tugging at his Bulldog-blue tie. In a suit he hasn't worn since my mother died. The thought of that suit and that day and my mother's hand twitching in mine sends me into a silent spiral.

"I said, 'We will now hear from our valedictorian, Juniper Pickett.' Juniper, would you please come up to the stage?"

Sadie Piper elbows me in the ribs, and I jump to attention. The walk to the podium takes years. Every step slow and effortful, like moving through mud. Not to mention the whispers and the hoots and the baritone "Junebug!" that comes from the Clark–Dupree direction.

My breath sounds heavy in the microphone. When I speak those first few words—"Welcome, fellow graduates, parents, teachers… "—my voice echoes back to me and confuses my panicked brain. I fumble with my notes and nearly drop the index card.

Finally, I regain enough composure to read my speech. But with each bland line I recite, I hear my other words. The real ones I penned in my time-capsule letter. The letter that's buried in the ground now. Before we filed over to the stadium, Principal Finch flung the first ceremonial shovel of dirt over the time capsule. Then we each got a turn, before Mr. Trolf and Benny stepped in to finish the job.

"Thank you for the laughs, the smiles, and the memories," I tell my classmates.

There are things we would never put in our time capsule. Like all the awful names you've called me. All the times I felt left out, ignored, laughed at. The note Blair Lennox put in my locker that said UR BETR OFF DED. Things we can't forget. At least I can't. Maybe that's my problem. Too much remembering and not enough forgetting.

"The future is ours now," I tell the crowd.

There is no future me. By the time you read this, my body will be nothing but grave wax, and my spirit will be free to fly away, to leave this hole-in-the-road town forever.

"Make your mark on the world," I implore the class of 1997.

If you survive tonight.

I wait for the obligatory applause, then numbly exit the stage and return to my seat.

"Good job," Sadie whispers.

I merely nod and keep my eyes focused on the stage, where Principal Finch has begun to call our names to accept our diplomas and flip our tassels.

"Seriously, June, that was a really great speech. You're going to do awesome at Berkeley."

My anger sneaks up on me again. I want to yell at Sadie. To ask her why she never said those things when it mattered. Why she never stood up for me. Why she never tried to be my friend.

Instead, I paste on a smile. "Thanks, Sadie. Are you going to the party later?"

She nods. Her silly head bobbing like a cork.

"Good. I'll see you there."

CHAPTER FORTY-SIX

NOW

WHILE Wyatt shines the flashlight inside and around his stolen truck, I try to remain calm by pretending there's nothing to worry about.

"She probably went back to the house," I say. "That's what I'd do. It's a short walk."

"Alright." Wyatt sounds unconvinced.

Truthfully, so am I. But we head back to the car anyway. "Let's go check it out. We can always come back if we can't find her."

I force myself not to speed. If I give in to the panic now, there's no going back. I take the right turn down Saw Mill Road, the same way I did three days ago. Before I got caught digging up bones. Before Macy turned up. Before I realized my father didn't end his own life. The road hasn't changed. It's just as bumpy. Just as dangerous in the dark. The car hasn't either. It's still a sporty little tin can spitting out gravel. But me, I *have* changed. I can't say why exactly. Or when. Only that I'm not running away anymore.

Wyatt leans forward and squints into the dark. "Is that a patrol car? And who's driving that green monstrosity?"

The nearer we get to the house, the faster my heart beats. Because there *is* a patrol car parked in the drive, and that shade of lime green is all too familiar. From inside, the single sconce in the foyer glows. But the worst part is the padlock, which lies like a corpse on the porch, and the front door that stands ajar. A foreboding invitation.

"Something's not right." He echoes the voice in my head. The one that keeps telling me to freak out. That Macy's in trouble. Big trouble. "Wait here."

"What? No way." Here alone is the last place I want to be.

"Just do it, okay. Please."

I know how stubborn Wyatt can be. It's a losing battle. So I watch him get out of the car. When he disappears inside and pulls the door shut behind him, my watch reads 7:31 p.m.

I keep the ignition running and hum along to the static on the radio. Anything to distract myself. But my eyes stay fixed on the front of the house.

By 7:33, there's a nervous flutter in my stomach. Tiny wings of anxiety that won't be still. When a sharp crack of gunfire pierces the quiet, they swarm like bats in a cave, sending me into a full-blown panic.

I stuff the bag of stolen evidence under the floor mat and snap open the glove box, rifling through it for a makeshift weapon. But everything in it is useless to me now. Insurance card—*toss.* Kleenex—*toss.* The Ellington Academy ID badge that reminds me of all my catastrophic failures—*toss.* Inside the console, I find the pamphlet for the roadside assistance program I never signed up for. Because until last week, I tried to keep my world so small and so safe that I rarely left San Francisco. I toss that too and hurry to the trunk.

Next to the spare tire, I find what I'm looking for. A toddler-sized lug wrench will have to do.

Hoping for the element of surprise, I run around the side of the house and look through my bedroom window into the dark. At my

Luke Perry poster still lying flat on the bed. *What's happening, Luke?* A shadow flickers from the hallway and moves across the poster. I duck down, then peer up over the sill. Luke's eyes convey my dread.

Staying low, I scrabble toward the back of the house, where I spot the mystery ATV parked in my mother's garden. I try the knob for the laundry room. Of course, it's locked. But with a quick jab of the wrench, I break one of the small glass panels in the door. The shattering startles me like the shrill scream of an alarm bell. I wait for a response, another gunshot, but none comes. It feels as if I'm the last person on earth, standing in front of a door to nowhere.

Carefully, I reach inside and open it.

CHAPTER FORTY-SEVEN

AFTER GRADUATION

I go through all the motions. I do what's expected of me. I even sign a few yearbooks at the big table near the stage and let out a whoop when I throw my cap into the air. But when my dad finds me and hugs me and produces a disposable camera from his pocket, I fight the urge to run. To swig the pentobarbital right there and get it over with.

"No, Dad. You know I hate pictures."

He points over his shoulder at Duane and Eric cheesing for Mrs. Dupree's camera with their diplomas. "Juniper, it's your high-school-graduation day. I think you can make an exception."

"Fine. *One photo.*" As I slog over to the stage, I realize this photo will be my last. It will be the one my dad puts on his nightstand. The one he holds as he cries—if he cries at all. The one he'll remember me by. The least I can do is smile.

"There you go." He rewards my effort with a thumbs up. "Now that's my beautiful high-school graduate. Whaddya say we get a few more?"

I shake my head grimly. "You got your one. Don't push it."

He chuckles, and it shocks me how long it's been since I heard him laugh. "Alright, I'll see you tonight after the party. You're getting a ride with Wyatt, right?"

"Yep." My throat thickens.

I wait for him to remind me of Wyatt's *commitments,* but he only nods. "Okay. Don't forget, I've got something special for you at home."

My eyes flit across the field, searching out Duane and Jessica. The last I saw her, her wrist was bare. But what did it matter now? If I have it my way, she'll be buried in my bracelet.

"Have fun tonight, honey."

I watch him walk across the field toward the stadium exit. When he reaches the endzone, he hesitates, and I will him to keep moving. Do not turn around. But then, Blair calls out to him from the sideline, and he waits for her to strut over in her platform sandals. When they embrace, I spin away so fast I get lightheaded. Any hesitation drains from me, leaving only cold, cold blood.

It's time.

CHAPTER FORTY-EIGHT

NOW

I step over the broken glass and into the cave of the laundry room. It's dank and hot and suffocating, and I force myself to ignore the scrabble of claws inside the linen closet. Do not slow down. Keep moving. Keep breathing.

I avert my gaze from the matted fur in the snapped mouse trap by the washing machine. Eyes forward. Go. Go! But the smell follows me, clings to my nostrils. Reminds me that I'm not so different than that decaying mouse. That this house feels like a loaded trap, waiting to snap my spine when I least expect it.

Holding the wrench at the ready, I step out into the living room. With its maze of boxes, I can hardly make out the far side, but the single hall sconce casts a thin blade of light that cuts across the hardwood. I weave through the rows, placing each footstep with care while the silence ticks like a clock.

When I near the end of the boxes, I hold my breath and listen. A muffled cry comes from the kitchen. It grows louder. More frenzied.

As I inch closer, I see it. Red and wet and pooled in the hallway. Smell it too, the hot metal of violence. My brain takes off without me to graduation night. To Blair.

Frantic, I rush around the corner and lurch forward, landing with a thud that steals my breath and doubles my vision and sends the wrench flying into the hallway. Up on my knees, I scrabble toward it.

There. I come up with a fistful of air.

No, *there.*

No… I squeeze my eyes shut and wait for the floor to stop moving. *There.*

A tactical boot descends like a giant from above and stomps the wrench away. I cry out and lift my head to see Duane looming over me, still in his uniform. An officer of the law with my father's gun aimed at my head.

From behind me, a familiar voice says, "It's about time you got here, June. We can't start this party without you. You're the guest of honor."

Duane gestures with the gun for me to get up, to turn around. To face my reckoning. Twenty years overdue.

He kicks the wrench down the hallway toward the bedrooms and shoves me forward, into the nightmarish scene in front of me in the kitchen: Macy, Wyatt, and Hugh, gagged, their hands and feet bound with zip ties to the wooden dining chairs. Blood spills from a wound on Wyatt's shoulder, blooming like a carnation on his shirt, as he strains against his bindings. And Hugh's in worse shape. His head slumped. His chin resting on his chest with a trickle of red running from his nose onto his polo. I can't look away from it. Or from Dr. Jim, as unassuming as the first day I met him.

Duane pushes me again, but I dig in and throw an elbow behind me. It makes a satisfying thwack when it connects with his belly. He roars and tosses me into the dimly lit room. My legs threaten to collapse beneath me, but I manage to stay upright.

"Put her over here," Dr. Jim says. "In front of the stove. Where she can get a nice long last look at 'em."

I try to resist but Duane knows how to move me, and it's hard and cold and menacing when he presses my father's gun to the back of my head. Wyatt thrashes in the chair at the sight, while Dr. Jim circles him like a shark. But at least Wyatt's moving. Hugh still looks like a deflated blow-up doll.

"This one won't keep quiet since you hauled off and shot him."

"What the hell was I supposed to do? The bastard snuck up on me." Duane stalks toward Wyatt, nailing him with a punch to his wounded shoulder.

But Wyatt doesn't flinch. He survived Chet Landry and twelve years' worth of angry bulls. He can take pain by the truckload.

"Maybe listen to me next time, dummy. I told you to keep it manageable. Just the two of them. June and the girl. That we'd deal with Landry later. And now we've got Richie Rich along for the ride too."

"What was I supposed to do when the guy barged in the door hollerin' for his daughter? If you ask me, I saved your whole cockamamie plan. And June's here now. So stop complainin' and just get on with it."

Grim-faced, Dr. Jim reaches into his pocket and removes a small baggie with a syringe and a vial of liquid. He places it on the kitchen counter and shakes his head at me, tutting.

"I didn't kill Blair," I blurt out. "I won't tell anyone about the steroids. None of us will."

"Oh, June. You poor girl. Lost your mother at a young age. Father couldn't be bothered with the important duties of a parent. You were a ship without a moor, adrift in life. It's no wonder you fixated on Blair. She had everything you didn't. Beauty, popularity, a family who loved her, and endless possibilities. She would've been a star."

I pretend to look at him, but I see past him. To the black helmet resting on the counter. To the needle and the vial nearby. Beneath the brand name Vet-Aide, the label reads: Pentolanol. Though I don't recognize the name, I hear my father's voice in my head. *Use your noggin', June.* The *pento* is easy enough. Pento for pentobarbital, everyone's favorite barbiturate. *Ol* for an alcohol additive, possibly more than one.

"And you, what have you done with yourself? No husband, no children. No friends to speak of. Estranged from your father. You lost your job after you encouraged this troubled girl to poison her classmates and herself."

It doesn't matter that it's a lie. Everyone will believe it. Reluctantly, I glance at Macy. Her eyes meet mine. In them, I find raw terror. Terror and desperation. But determination too. I steel myself for her. Her life will not end this way. Not if I can help it.

"Then you ran home to Sweetbriar with a plan to conceal a brutal crime you committed years ago. The murder of my precious stepdaughter." After a dramatic pause, he goes on, eyes still dry. "You dug up Blair's body, only to learn that she was pregnant. You believed it was Wyatt's child. We all did. Your one true love had betrayed you. You tried to hide the evidence. You stole from the police. You burned down your dead father's workshop. But you failed miserably. Because everyone knew you were guilty. Even your own father. That's what killed him. The knowledge that he had a murderer for a daughter."

Dr. Jim's words sink into my soul like their own kind of poison. He's not right. But he's not entirely wrong. It's the in-between space where I've been living for so long. Not living. *Hiding.*

"You couldn't go on, and who would blame you? What more did you have to live for? So, you did what you set out to do all those years ago. A murder-suicide. Isn't that right? The very thing you wrote about in your letter for the time capsule. Duane showed me. *Bottoms up*, right?" He waves a hand in the direction of my apparent captives. "You ended their lives and then your own. We stumbled upon the scene and tried to render aid, but it was too late."

With his dark tale lingering like toxic smoke, Dr. Jim removes the vial from the baggie and uncaps the impossibly long needle. "Which one shall we do first?"

CHAPTER FORTY-NINE

AFTER GRADUATION

I stand outside the gym, listening to the sound of the Spice Girls and my overjoyed classmates. Moving closer to the door, I peer through the small window, zeroing in on my target in the dark corner. The punch bowl sits on a lunchroom table beneath the blue and gold streamers the student council strung from the ceiling.

"You going in?" Wyatt has traded in his cap and gown for his standard uniform. Boots, Wranglers, and his signature black cowboy hat. "Or are you just gonna stand out here doing recon for your secret spy mission?"

"What? What are you talking about?" My voice reaches the octave of *thou doth protest too much.* I need to pull it together.

But Wyatt just laughs. "Relax, James Bond. I'm only kidding."

He holds the door open for me, and I step across the threshold and into my final act. Here, in the air-conditioned gymnasium with a gaudy disco ball spinning overhead, and Wyatt gaping at me like he has something to say.

"You look different."

I roll my eyes at the obvious. For once, I put on a dress and wore shoes without laces. I even followed the tips in *YM* for a "shimmery kissable glow." Might as well go out on a high note.

"Good different. I mean, you look… beautiful."

Goosebumps ripple across my skin and I pull my mom's sweater tight to me. It still smells like her perfume. I sway a little as a new song blasts from the speakers. It's that Bryan Adams hit from the Robin Hood movie. *A make-out song*, that's what Jessica and Christi would call it, giggling in the bathroom.

"I'm a teensy bit drunk," Wyatt tells me, laughing at the way he expands the distance between his thumb and forefinger. Teensy might not be so teensy after all. "Do you wanna dance?"

I glance at the unmanned punch bowl—*stick to the plan, June*—but I meander back into Wyatt's hazy brown eyes. "Sure. But I'm not really that good at the two-step."

"You're in expert hands," he says, offering me one of his. "I'll show you."

He pulls me onto the gym floor, and the world falls away. The world where I don't fit in. The world where I pour this bottle of poison into the punch. The world where I die and take the unlucky ones out with me.

Wyatt pulls me closer to him. He radiates heat and the scent of cheap beer and even cheaper aftershave. Still, I inhale him and wonder if I'm already dead. If I'm in heaven.

He brings my hand to his chest to feel his heart racing beneath it. He leans his mouth against my ear and breathes out three unmistakable words—though they sound more like one. "Uhluvya."

I don't dare move or say anything back to him. Obviously, I misheard, and he'd really asked me if I'd noticed his new boots or knew where he could find a lava lamp for his off-campus apartment. He's drunk anyway. Doesn't count.

"June?" he whispers.

Finally, I gaze up at him, and there's no question. I didn't misunderstand him, and he's not *that* drunk. But then Blair glides into the gym with her tan legs for days in her absurdly short blue dress that violates at least three tenets of the dress code. Jessica, on one side, with my bracelet dangling from her arm. Christi, on the other. Behind them, Duane and Eric hoot and jostle each other like teenaged baboons.

Wyatt's arms fall to his sides. He steps away from me as if I'm contagious.

Blair takes one look at us, and the color leaves her face. It's the second time I've seen her absolutely terrified. For a single gratifying heartbeat, she's speechless. It doesn't last.

"What are you doing? Are you actually dancing with *her*? That is so gross."

I stand there, waiting for Wyatt to defend me. To tell her the truth. That he *loves* me. I heard him say it.

"Uh, no, we were just..."

The fact that I'm planning on dying tonight makes me bold. "So we *weren't* dancing?" I ask.

"I knew it." Blair marches toward me. "You were hanging all over him, and you destroyed my dress. When are you going to get it through your ugly little head that he's mine? We're going to be together. You won't even be in the same state."

I widen my eyes at church-mouse Wyatt. "I never knew you were such a coward. You two deserve each other just like I wrote in your yearbook." I flee toward the back exit.

Wyatt shouts and stumbles after me. "June, wait! I can't tell her the truth. She's not strong like you."

"I'm not strong!" I scream at him before I burst out the door and run like the devil himself is at my heels.

CHAPTER FIFTY

WYATT stops chasing me when I run down the hill and into the field behind the gym that leads to the elementary-school playground and the thick border of live oak trees beyond. The playground hasn't changed much in the last eight years. A concrete basketball court—the nets long rotted away—serves as the centerpiece for a slide, a swing set, and a rusted merry-go-round that creaks when I take a seat on it. As I catch my breath, my plan unravels like a pull in a dime-store sweater. Tug one end and the whole sleeve falls off.

I can't go back in there. I can't face Wyatt or Blair or anybody else. I certainly can't walk over to the punch bowl unbothered and pour in the contents of this bottle. But also, I can't go on. I don't want to wake up tomorrow to the same face in the mirror. The same miserable feeling inside. The thought of it—the never-endingness—weighs like a brick on my chest. Turns out my grand finale ends in a complete flop. The *wah-wah-wah* of a sad trombone. I couldn't even do this right. I am such a loser.

I jog my feet on the playground sand until the merry-go-round starts to spin faster and faster. I lie back and watch the stars turn and think about my mother gazing down on me. Round and round I go until the sky blurs. When the wheel finally slows to a stop, my head keeps spinning. I wait to regain my sea legs, then I sit up and reach into my pocket for the bottle of pentobarbital.

It's obvious to me now that my entire plan was a failure from the start. Doomed to end right here, right now. Because one small bottle diluted in a massive punch bowl would never be enough to hurt anyone. How would I know who drank the punch, anyway? With my luck, Duane would shove Eric into the table, and the entire bowl would spill onto the gym floor, or Blair and her crew would avoid the punch altogether in favor of their own fruity wine coolers, and leave it for the undeserving like Wyatt, Bonnie, and Freddie Figeroa.

Wyatt did me a favor exiling me out here, where I can't hurt anyone but myself. I need to put an end to this.

I uncap the bottle and inhale the faint chemical smell. I close my eyes and recite the entire periodic table. Twice. Then, with nothing left to do, I lift it to my lips.

"What is that?"

My eyes fly open to find Blair in front of me, her hand grabbing—just missing—my arm, as I pull it out of her reach.

"Nothing. Leave me alone." I jump up and back away from her. My feet wide, I balance at the center of the merry-go-round.

"I'm not stupid, June. That's your dad's poison. The one he gives the crazy cows when it's time to take them out to the pit."

"*And your point is?*" I wait for her to agree with me. To tell me I am a stupid cow.

"Are you actually going to drink it? God, you are so mental." She glances back toward the gym.

I can hear the faraway music and the laughter, but it's another world. Here, in this one, it's only me and her and this bottle.

"Maybe I am. Why do you care?"

"I really don't. But your dad does. And I like him. He can't help it that he ended up with you as a daughter."

"He'd probably prefer you." I picture them in a warm embrace on the sidelines, him telling her how much promise she has. I can still hear him defending her. Even after she stole from him. After she killed Midnight. After she made me not want to be me anymore. "Actually, I know he would."

"I don't think so." Blair reaches into her small gold purse and produces my tennis bracelet. "He bought this for you, right? He showed it to me a few days ago. Asked if I thought you'd like it. It's engraved to you. Not me."

Engraved? I frown at her. "How did *you* get it?"

"I know Duane stole it. He's an idiot. I made Jess give it back or else."

"Or else what?"

"Don't worry about it. All you need to know is that I've got major dirt on her and Duane. She's a backstabbing snake anyway. Honestly, I kind of hate her." She dangles the bracelet over the merry-go-round, luring me out like a stray animal. "*See.* I can be sweet."

A laugh slips out of me at her ridiculous contradictions. But I stay put. I hate that she's here interrupting me. I hate that she did something nice. That she made me laugh. I hate that I'm such a coward. Again, I raise the bottle to my mouth. Collision course. Do not pass go. Just freaking do it.

A small drop touches my tongue. It tastes bitter, but not terrible.

Without warning, Blair drops her purse and springs onto the merry-go-round. Grabbing one of the bars for momentum, she launches herself at me. We land with a brutal thud on the warm metal. Stunned by the impact, I survey the damage. Me, still in one piece with Blair groaning beside me. The bottle, miraculously still in my grasp. The bracelet, in Blair's. A cut on her hand oozes red.

I sit up and prepare to down the bottle in one gulp.

"Give it here!" Blair claws at me.

I claw right back, but she's better at it. One of her nails scratches an angry line down my arm. It starts to bleed.

I rear back and slap her, mildly horrified at the way my blood flicks onto her dress. "You hate me anyway. Just let me do it."

"You're so selfish. You don't even know how good you have it."

Her accusation startles me, enrages me. As staggering as a dodge ball to the face. I forget myself. Where I am. Who I am. Why I am. My body moves without me, deftly, swiftly. I grab a fistful of her hair, and she goes down hard, her head hanging off the wheel.

She scrambles up to rip the flower button from my mother's sweater, leaving her bloody fingerprint behind. The wheel judders forward. I lose my balance. In slow motion, the bottle fumbles through my fingers, hurtling through space like a meteor hellbent on destruction.

"It's in my eyes!" Blair yells, clutching her face. She drops the bracelet into the dirt. "It burns!"

"It's okay." I have no idea if that's true, but I say it anyway. Because I need her to shut up. But she's breathing fast, and I'm breathing fast, and my heart won't slow down long enough for me to have a single rational thought.

She rolls onto her stomach and slides off the merry-go-round into the sand, taking the bottle down with her. Like a baby deer, she struggles to her feet. "I can barely see."

Get help from an adult. An actual adult. Not me, who's eighteen but completely clueless in life. That's what I should do. But a twisted part of me likes that she needs me. That she's suffering.

"There's a water fountain by the basketball court," I say. "Go splash your eyes, and I'll get Mrs. Kendall."

A shadowy figure appears outside the back exit door of the gym. When I recognize the silhouette as my father's, I curse under my breath. *What is he doing here?*

"Please don't tell my dad," I hiss at Blair.

But I feel relieved. He'll know what to do, even if I can't face him. Staying low to the ground, I run into the trees and hide.

CHAPTER FIFTY-ONE

NOW

DUANE jams the gun into the side of my head, then grabs a fistful of my hair and forces me to look at Macy, then Hugh, then Wyatt. "You heard him. *Who's first?*"

"I'll go first, only me. It's not them you're after," I say.

"That ain't how this works, Junebug. You don't make the rules around here," says Dr. Jim.

"It's not me that you want either, Jim. I didn't kill Blair and, deep down, I think you already know that."

Dr. Jim plunges the needle into the vial and draws out a full dose of the clear liquid. When he returns the vial to the counter, I quickly scan the ingredients of the formulation, hoping my hunch about the ol in pentolanol proves true. Pentobarbital sodium, phenytoin sodium, ethyl alcohol, propylene glycol, and benzyl alcohol. That's a lot of alcohol. More than even Chet Landry could handle. And it's within my reach.

"We'll do the girl first."

"Duane killed her!" I shout. "Duane killed Blair."

Next to me, Duane puffs up, hackles raised. "What the hell are you talking about, Junebug? They found the fen… pen… pento—whatever—in her system. In her bones. It was still in there all these years later. You did that."

I shake my head. "The dose of pentobarbital wasn't fatal. That's not what killed her. But that's not news to you, Duane. You were there. You know how she died."

The way Dr. Jim cuts his eyes at Duane keeps me going. I'm onto something. Even if I'm one trigger-happy finger away from meeting my end.

"Think about it. Blair knew Duane was on steroids. She was going to expose him. He couldn't let her crash his dream. All he ever wanted was to play football in the NFL. He wanted to be rich and famous, and so did Jessica. He even stole the bracelet my father bought for me—it had a J on it—and gave it to her. Blair took it back from her on graduation night. She humiliated Duane in front of everyone. And you remember his roid rage. I know you do. The steroids you gave him made him crazy. He couldn't control himself. Ask him."

Duane performs as expected. "Ask *me*? Ask *me*! You're the crazy one."

"Ask him about the night he found me digging in the courtyard. Why was he there before me? He already knew where the body was because he buried her there twenty years ago. He knew that time was running out. That he better move her or—"

"I was just out there lettin' off some steam after me and Jess got into it about her spendin' too much money again. How the hell would I know where Blair was buried?"

"Ask him about the evidence he threw into the crusher at the tow lot. Ask him about Blair's letter. He stole it out of the time capsule because it incriminated him, and he thought he destroyed it. But I have it in the car. I'll show it to you. I'll show you everything he never wanted you to see."

"That's not why I… I… she's batshit crazy. She's a loser! Always has been!" Duane points the barrel of the gun at my face. I don't look away. Not from it or from him. It's taken me twenty years to realize that the best way to beat a bully is to look him in the eyes.

"*You* stole Blair's letter? You said she did it." Jim shakes his arm at me. "What else have you been hiding?"

"C'mon, Jim. You can guess why I stole it. It named all of us. Me, you, Coach Mac. My kid did your dirty work. Why don't you tell her about that? About the damn rooster he strung up and the useless folder he stole out of her car to calm your paranoia. Like some chicken-scratch code was gonna give us away. Hell, while you're at it, tell her about how I stuck my neck out for you and changed that goddamned first-responder report. All for a measly thousand bucks. Tell her how her daddy really died. A two-by-four to the back of the head and that shit forced down his throat. Tell her how you set his workshop on fire and locked her in there to burn."

Dr. Jim rushes forward, aiming himself like a cannonball at Duane's gut. The moment he makes impact, Wyatt jerks himself wildly, toppling his chair to the floor. In the chaos, I grab the vial and flick the knob on the gas stove to ignite a small flame. I smash the vial on the burner and duck the explosion. As the fire erupts, Duane and Dr. Jim tumble to the ground, grappling for the gun. The poison-filled needle vanishes in the scuffle.

I run to Wyatt first, desperately clawing at the zip ties. No use. Then to Hugh and Macy. As the heat from the blue flames intensifies, I grab the back of Macy's chair and pull her toward the front door. If I can just get her outside.

"Don't you dare move," Duane tells me, emerging from the kitchen with the gun. "I'll finish this myself."

But a pounding on the door interrupts him.

"Sheriff's Office, show yourself!"

I reach for the handle.

Duane raises the gun and pulls the trigger.

CHAPTER FIFTY-TWO

AFTER GRADUATION

MY head feels all mixed up—I can't even name element 75—as my father traverses the field of grass. He stops briefly in front of the merry-go-round and stoops to retrieve the bracelet Blair dropped. *Rhenium!* my brain finally shouts at me. Meanwhile, Blair runs water from the fountain on her face and hand, then sits on the tall concrete edge of the basketball court, crying softly.

"Blair, did you steal the bracelet I bought for June?"

She wipes her eyes again and looks straight ahead. I wait for her to tell him what a horrible person I am, but she just sniffles.

"No, of course not. I was trying to—"

"Jessica Carrington told me you did. I came here looking for June after some things turned up missing in the shop, including that bracelet. I was worried about her. She hasn't been herself since that accident with Midnight. Then I ran into Jessica in the parking lot.

She said you confessed to her. That you broke in and took it from my workshop. I found it right there on the ground."

"Why would I take June's bracelet? It has a J on it. It's engraved to her." She stands up and staggers toward him, still swiping at her eyes. "Anyway, I need help. June and I got into an argument, and I spilled something in my—"

"The pentobarbital!" My father spots the bottle on the wheel and rushes over to it.

"Yes," Blair says.

"You stole that too?"

"I mean *no.* I didn't steal anything."

"Blair, be honest with me. The bottle is empty. This is a dangerous chemical, and you know that. I trusted you, even after I caught you snooping through my notes."

"June stole it. I don't know why. She was trying to hurt herself, I think. I tried to stop her, and it got in my eyes."

"Did you harm June? Did you hurt my girl?" There's a sharpness to his voice. An unfamiliar hard edge. "Where is she?"

It's my moment then. My chance to step out of the shadows and reveal myself. To say that Blair's telling the truth. That it's all my fault. Well, most of it.

"*Where is she?*" My father lunges at Blair and grabs her by the shoulders.

"I don't know!" She whips out of his grasp and backpedals toward the court. Still unsteady on her feet, she loses her balance. Her arms flail wildly, and she trips over her stupidly high platform sandals and goes down hard, cracking her head against the raised concrete edge of the court. Beneath her splay of blonde hair, a sickening darkness spreads onto the concrete.

My father flinches at the sound of my gasp. When he gazes into the trees, I stop breathing, certain I've been caught. Then, he shakes his head as if he wants to unsee it all, and I sink to the ground.

In the leaves, a June bug buzzes and takes flight. A heartbeat later, so do I.

I go the long way around to the school parking lot. Over the ditch behind the tree line and down Park Street. I take my time, waiting for the lights and sirens, but the night remains impossibly quiet. Too quiet.

I push it all into the smallest corner of my mind. The dark, cobwebbed one where I keep the memory of my mother's accident.

I find Wyatt by his truck, throwing back beers with Duane and Eric.

"I want to leave," I tell him. "Now."

Duane lets out a low whistle. "Sounds like your *other* woman needs you, man. Better keep her satisfied now that you blew it with Blair."

The need to escape beats like a second heart inside me. It's so loud I barely register any of them.

Wyatt downs the rest of his beer as he unlocks the door. I know he's drunk, but I climb inside anyway. He smells like his father. Looks like him too, wobbly and red-eyed. I say a pathetic prayer that we crash into a tree on the way home. That I die instantly.

He looks at me way too long. I feel his eyes on me, saying what he's not, and I know that if I start talking, I might not stop. I might tell him everything.

"Wyatt," I say to the windshield. "Don't speak to me. Ever again."

"Noted."

CHAPTER FIFTY-THREE

NOW

SADIE wraps a Mylar blanket around my shoulders once again. "We really should stop meeting like this."

I flinch at the slam of a patrol-car door. Because it sounds like a gunshot. Like the one Sheriff Faulk fired that dropped Duane to his knees. He collapsed in front of me, still holding my father's gun in his trembling hand. A single bullet meant for me lodged in the wall.

"Are you alright?" Macy asks me from beneath the shroud of her own blanket.

"Are *you*?"

She nods, then clarifies with a snort. "Sort of."

"Same."

"I can't believe Hugh showed up here again. He burst in and even tried to fight that crooked cop. I didn't know he had it in him."

"Love for a daughter will do that to a dad."

She doesn't roll her eyes, which I take as a massive win for Hugh. "Do you think he'll be okay? Mom will never forgive me if…"

I pat her on the shoulder. "Sadie said he took a couple of hard hits to the head, but you saw him in the ambulance. He was threatening to sue the county for their slow response time, so I think he's good."

We sit side by side, staring out into the pitch-black. Neither of us stating the obvious. The small, alcohol-fueled fire that destroyed the kitchen. The wailing ambulance that took Wyatt away with a bullet wound to the shoulder. The coroner's van that came for Duane and for Dr. Jim, who Sheriff Faulk discovered on the kitchen floor with the needle of poison protruding from his arm.

Sheriff Faulk saunters down the driveway toward us. I wait for him to tell me I'm under arrest. That he thinks I fabricated the evidence in the bag. That I'm a liar. A liar and a murderer. But he only tips his hat at Macy.

"This young lady may have a future in law enforcement."

"Oh, really?" I cast a quizzical glance in her direction.

She shrugs. "It's not a big deal. I told Coach Mac that my brother was desperate to make the varsity football team in Adamsville. That he needed something to make him bigger, stronger, and more of a meathead. He told me he could hook me up."

"And she recorded the whole thing on *his* cellphone. Texted it to the Houston PD tip line. Now that's resourceful."

"On his own cellphone?"

"I just smiled at the guy and offered to show him some of my photos on Instagram and to put my deets into his contacts. It was kind of a no-brainer. Like taking candy from a baby. A perverted baby."

I'm surprised to find I can still laugh. Even if it comes out clunky and sad.

"Safe to say, they were pretty interested since they got the presumptive DNA results back this morning on Blair's unborn child. They've gotta confirm with further testing, but it's looking like you were right, Doc. He was the daddy."

Sheriff Faulk clears his throat then, and I prepare for the worst.

"You know, Jim wasn't all the way gone when we got to him. He managed to say a few words. Three to be exact."

I wait. This is it. This is when the past catches up to me. Runs me right over like a train barreling down the tracks.

"*Dupree murdered Blair.* That's what he said, plain as day. With that, and the evidence you found, it seems like you're off the hook. Of course, we have to tie up some loose ends. Talk to old man Trolf, etcetera, etcetera." He sounds disappointed.

"I didn't kill her," I say again, mainly to hear the words out loud. To know the truth of them. The truth and the fiction.

"But we both know you ain't that innocent."

I wonder then about Blair's letter. About what the sheriff knew and when. About all the times he looked the other way and how he still managed to be the last one standing. The cattle rustler with a badge.

My lips curl in a sly smile. "Neither are you."

HOURS later, I sit alone in my car outside Adamsville Hospital, waiting for Wyatt to wake up from surgery. Macy didn't want to leave her stepdad alone. *For the nurses' sanity*, she'd told me, and I didn't call her bluff. Since her sleuthing efforts at the CrossFit gym, Sheriff Faulk had agreed to keep quiet about Macy being in Sweetbriar until Hugh was well enough for discharge. Still, he'd stationed Officer Sitkowski outside the room to supervise her, which seemed prudent.

When my cellphone rings from an all-too-familiar number, I don't let myself chicken out this time.

"This is Detective Voss. I've been trying to reach you."

"I know." I breathe in and let it go. "I'm finally ready to talk."

CHAPTER FIFTY-FOUR

THE NIGHT OF GRADUATION

I lie in bed, not sleeping, but listening for the other shoe to drop. Surely the police will be here soon to collect me, to ask me what the hell I was thinking tonight. To examine my mother's sweater and the spot of Blair's blood on the missing buttonhole. I pick up the receiver and dial the Adamsville Hospital, but hang up when a kind voice answers. *Is Blair Lennox a patient there?* I say out loud, with no one on the line to hear me. *Is she okay?*

As long as my father doesn't come home, I can pretend I don't know the answer. But he returns to the house around midnight. Numbly, I watch him through my window while he walks into the pasture and disappears. When he comes back, he's carrying a shovel and a gray wool blanket he kept in the workshop for the times he slept there.

The truck door opens and closes again, and he drives away into the night that seems to go on forever.

I wait up for him until my eyes get too heavy to open. The next time they do, it's morning, and yesterday seems like a bad dream. One of those broken nightmares with pieces that linger. But the angry scratch on my arm leaves no doubt. It happened.

I slip out from beneath the covers and peek through the curtains into the sunshine. The brightness shocks me, and I shrink away. But not before I spot his truck in the driveway, same as ever.

At the old Crenshaw place down the road, the Lennoxes will be waking up soon.

To open the door takes all the courage I can muster. I've never felt so alone or so afraid or so ashamed. My father stands in the kitchen, staring off into space. He has the look of a man who's been up all night doing the devil's work.

"Dad?" That word. So small but so heavy.

Our eyes meet.

"I made breakfast," he says.

EPILOGUE

ONE YEAR LATER

MACY clears her throat into the microphone and scans the small crowd assembled in the cafeteria. When she finds me, her eyes brighten, and I lift my hand in an inconspicuous wave. Even in the juvenile-hall-issued purple graduation gown and khakis, she manages to look sophisticated. It's been a month since our last visit. Since she told me she'd been awarded valedictorian of the 2019 San Francisco Juvenile Hall of Justice graduating class, which apparently had brought tears of joy to her parents' eyes. I spot Hugh off to the side of the stage, snapping photos in a *My Daughter's a Graduate* T-shirt. It's amazing what miracles a brush with death can do.

What's next? I'd asked Macy, though I already suspected the answer. The idea had come to her almost immediately after she pled guilty to a lesser charge of seven counts of poisoning and the judge issued her sentence: eight years in the care and custody of the juvenile court.

I can finish my degree in Criminal Justice here. If I stay on track, the judge will seal my juvenile record, and I'll be able to apply to the SFPD when I get out.

So, Officer Powell then?

Hopefully, Detective one day. SVU Unit. Taking down bad guys one creep at a time. She twinkled with mischief. *That or fashion designer.*

Devin, too, had faced his day in court. With Macy set to testify against him, he accepted a plea deal for multiple charges of unlawful sex with a minor and was shipped off to San Quentin to find out what happens to men like him in the big house. As for me, Macy's sworn statements had cleared me of any wrongdoing in the Ellington matter. Which I took as a small gift from the universe. My own mulligan.

Before beginning her valedictory address, Macy catches my eye again. I follow her gaze to the left side of the room. It doesn't take long for me to zero in on the black Stetson two rows in front of me or for the butterflies to awaken in my stomach after a year-long hibernation. *It's your call,* he'd told me in the hospital room while doped up on pain meds and leftover adrenaline. *If you want me, you know exactly where to find me.*

A call I hadn't made, not because I didn't *want* him. But because I did. Too much. Because first I wanted to be the right person, with my demons exorcised for good. The kind of person who could tell the whole truth without flinching. When I finally dialed his number two weeks and eleven months of therapy later, he hadn't answered, and I told myself it was for the best. That there were entire songs about *not* falling in love with a cowboy for a reason. But looking at that hat, those broad shoulders, the reasons escape me now.

"Welcome, classmates, family, and friends. Today, we gather to celebrate our graduation from high school, but also our first steps into society as young women. Through my studies, I have learned so much about the world and the people in it. But real life has taught me other invaluable lessons. Lessons I couldn't learn from a book."

A raucous cheer goes up from the seven graduates seated to her right.

"Today, I will share a few of those lessons with you. First, parents… bless their hearts. They try so hard." That gets a laugh from the crowd. "They really do. But we don't always give them credit for their efforts.

In fact, some of us—*not me, of course*—forget that parents are people too, with their own struggles, doing the best they can."

My chest aches at the truth in her words. At the thought of my dad doing the best he could to protect me. He took my side that night with Blair. No matter how wrong it made him. He left me with his life's work—the formula for Livestock Gold—which I promptly donated to the National Livestock Producers Association in his honor. I touch the tennis bracelet on my wrist, the one my dad had bought for me and then buried in Blair's grave, along with the bottle of pentobarbital and that flower button, to shield me from suspicion. Sheriff Faulk mailed it to me months ago with a simple note: *Case closed.*

I'd ripped into the package then puzzled for a moment at the engraving: 53 71 23 92.

Iodine, lutetium, vanadium, uranium.

I Lu V U.

"You've probably heard that you shouldn't judge a book by its cover. I've learned that even the most beautiful, most popular, most athletic books in the library have a few pages missing, some writing in the margins, or a broken spine." She gives a sad smile, and so do I. "Don't assume that someone who seems to have it all together isn't struggling.

"But the most important lesson I've learned is this: it helps to have a friend. Even if it's just one." She takes a dramatic pause, just the way we'd practiced. "Inspired by two of my friends who are here today, our class has decided to commemorate our graduation with a time capsule. Earlier this week, we wrote letters to our future selves, describing our hopes and dreams. In twenty years, we'll meet back here at the juvenile hall and dig it up together to relish in just how far we've come. Congratulations, fellow graduates, and yeehaw!"

AFTER the director awards the diplomas and the girls flip their tassels, Macy descends the stage to the waiting arms of her parents, and my cheeks hurt from smiling.

"Howdy, stranger."

I spot the boots first, then the black hat. He tips it at me.

"Hi," I say stupidly. "I guess you can take the cowboy out of Texas, but you can't take Texas out of the cowboy."

"Something like that."

"I wasn't sure if you'd be here." That seems the wrong thing to say, because Wyatt's shoulders slump. Me putting my foot in my mouth again. "I mean, I hoped you would be. Because you never did tell me why you hate Wave World. And I have some things.I want to tell you too."

His laugh warms me, quiets my nerves.

"To be honest," he says, "I didn't know if you wanted me to come. And that plane ride was worse than eight seconds on Bodacious. I'm not sure I belong here in the big city."

"I still feel like that. Every single day." Especially with my new job in crisis intervention at an inner-city public high school in Oakland. It didn't get much farther from Sweetbriar than that. "So, what changed your mind?" I ask him.

"Actually, Macy. She mailed me a flyer." He reaches into his pocket, unfolds a well-worn piece of paper, and holds it out to me. "Did you know there's a junior rodeo here? At a place called the Cow Palace? *The Cow Palace!* It doesn't get any more country than that. Figured I'd scope it out for Caleb. He's almost as good as I was, and it gives him something to stay focused on with his dad gone. A couple weeks ago, he took second in the Texas High School Rodeo Association Finals."

I listen intently to his nervous chatter as if I didn't already know. As if I haven't bookmarked Wyatt's new training website, Black Hat Bull Riding. I'd also heard from Bonnie that Jessica had moved on quickly past the speedbump of Duane's death and was already engaged to the widowed owner of Sweetbriar Community Bank.

"Is that the only reason you came?" I ask Wyatt. "For the Cow Palace?"

He looks down at me shyly. "I knew I'd left you hanging. About Wave World, I mean. It'd be cruel to let you go the rest of your life with any unanswered question like that, and—"

Macy runs up and puts her arms around both of us. "C'mon, you two, we're going to bury the time capsule."

Wyatt and I exchange a glance. It only lasts a second, but the ancient history between us unfurls like a scroll. I'm ten years old, stitching the gash on his forehead. Fifteen, in the stands watching his eight-second ride. Eighteen in his arms, beneath a disco ball. Thirty-nine, standing in front of him, still hopeful after all this time.

"Actually..." Wyatt takes my hand, and Macy grins. "We never officially opened ours." He reaches into his pocket and retrieves an envelope with his name printed on the front in boyish scrawl. "It's for you."

Dear Future Wyatt,

It's hard for me to imagine what your life will look like in twenty years, but I sure as hell hope you make the PBR so you can get away from here. Otherwise, you're doomed to be a drunk just like him, and that's a bull you can't ride. It won't matter how hard you try to stay on. It'll buck you off and stomp your head and leave you as dead as Lane Frost. I guarantee it. You've gotta get outta here, man. I hope you grow some damn balls and walk away. But first, you need to tell Juniper Pickett that you're crazy in love with her. Just spit it out already. If you can't do that, you're screwed. Good luck, loser. You're gonna need it.

Kick up some dust,
—J. C.

ACKNOWLEDGEMENTS

LIKE Juniper Pickett, I grew up in a small town in Texas, where everybody knows your name and your secrets… well, most of them. So much of who I am was born in my very own Sweetbriar—my resilience, patience, capacity for hard work, and faith in the goodness in others. My creativity too. Because in a small town, you make your own entertainment. I am forever grateful for the community that raised me. But after I ventured out into the great big world, I quickly realized that not everyone flourishes in a small town. For those who don't fit the mold, it can be suffocating. Stagnating. Intolerant of difference. It's those experiences I hoped to capture in *Long Buried.*

From start to finish, *Long Buried* took eighteen months to complete. Perhaps I should've titled it Long Writing. During that time, I took a nine-month hiatus to care for my ailing father (the ultimate cowboy), who relocated from Texas to California to spend the last few years of his life near me. This book is dedicated to him. He was everything that's good about a small town. A cowboy through and through, he lived his life in the service of others, and he wore his pride for me wherever he went, as boldly as his cowboy hat. Though my mom passed away many years ago, she gifted me her love for writing, and I know they're both cheering me on even though I can't see them.

I owe a tremendous debt of gratitude to you, my avid readers, for joining me on another adventure. Hearing that my words have impacted you is a little bit of magic, and knowing my stories have a special place in your heart makes it all worthwhile. A special thanks to Ellery's Entourage, whose members go above and beyond in supporting my work!

I am fortunate to have a fabulous team of family, friends, and colleagues who have always been there to support and encourage me on this journey, and I've assembled an all-star team—Lauren Finger, Liz Hatherell, Mallory Rock, and Giovanni Auriemma—to take the book from a lowly Word document to a formatted, edited, fantastically covered masterpiece.

To Gar, my special someone and partner in crime, thank you for patching all my plot holes without complaint, for cheering me on when I need it most, and for championing my dreams as much (and sometimes more) than I do. From the moment we had our first spirited argument about a plot (circa 2014), my books became just as much yours as they are mine. I wouldn't want to argue about plot points with anyone else, and I couldn't do any of this without you.

Lastly, I have always drawn inspiration for my writing from my day job as a forensic psychologist. We all have a space inside us that we keep hidden from the world, a space we protect at all costs. So many people have allowed me a glimpse inside theirs—dark deeds, memories best unrecalled, pain that cracks from the inside out—without expectation of anything in return. I couldn't have written a single word without them.

ALSO BY ELLERY KANE

LONG *Buried* is the sixth installment in the Doctors of Darkness series of psychological thrillers by forensic psychologist and author, Ellery Kane. If you want to be the first to know when new books are released, sign up for Ellery's newsletter at ellerykane.com.

If you enjoyed *Long Buried*, look for these other great reads from Ellery Kane.

Doctors of Darkness Series

Daddy Darkest
The Hanging Tree
The First Cut
Shadows Among Us
Lucky Girl (A Dose of Darkness Novella)

Rockwell and Decker Series

Watch Her Vanish
Her Perfect Bones
One Child Alive

Standalone Thrillers

The House Sitter
The Wrong Family
My Missing Daughter
The Good Wife

Legacy Series

Legacy
Prophecy
Revelation

www.ingramcontent.com/pod-product-compliance
Lightning Source LLC
LaVergne TN
LVHW050925080826
845145LV00001B/215

* 9 7 8 1 7 3 3 6 7 0 1 8 0 *